SOMETHING Eternal

JOEL T. MCGRATH

A POST HILL PRESS BOOK
ISBN: 978-1-68261-471-6
ISBN (eBook): 978-1-68261-472-3

Cover art by Christian Bentulan

Post Hill Press
New York • Nashville
posthillpress.com

Published in the United States of America

With love and faith, Jessie made this dream possible.

Free will is an illusion.
Destiny is a lie.
The truth is *something* in-between.

Chapter One

Sweating heavily, Vincent threw the blankets off his bed. The room was dark, yet emitted sunny splices of midday heat. Beams of light shot through his blackout curtains. The temperature in the tiny, empty room rose with each passing minute. His eyes shifted back and forth beneath closed lids. He was dreaming, but not just dreaming—something eternal was guiding his dreams, feeding him purposeful, random memories of recent days.

Random words and pictures of his brother Jak, his girlfriend Noemi, and his master Malum, sped through his mind in echoes along with his own confused thoughts and feelings. Most of all, he dreamt about that terrible night not long ago in the New York City subway station. His bitter memories and sweet dreams merged, returning nightmares upon his unconscious soul.

Vincent dreamt about the golden wheat fields. He was hand in hand with Noemi. She smiled with a sort of playful lust. He grabbed her hips and kissed her inviting lips like a man who wanted something more. He held her by the waist, but she disappeared from his hands. Droplets of cold rain descended from a sea of dark clouds. An ominous sky choked out the last remnants of the sun's glimmering rays, and thunder rolled in on him.

Vincent was suddenly in a foggy haze by himself. Words and pictures floated around on all sides, but none stayed very long.

"I love you more than anything, Noemi."

"Have you ever wanted something so badly, but no matter what, you couldn't have it?"

"I'm the one that loved you like no one else ever could."

"Vincent, help me!"

Suddenly, Vincent found himself in a black room and then in an abandoned subway station. The dream broke from memory for a moment, and whispers cluttered, fading low and loud in a never-ending circle.

"Noemi's filling your head with lies."

"She loves me. I bet that just kills you, doesn't it, bro?"

"Stop being an arrogant little prick."

"Don't forget, little brother, I win. I always win!"

"Stop calling me little brother!"

"You are a lost soul in a lost world."

"I'm not obsessed. The Shroud, the knights, they're all lying to us."

"You're selfish."

"Don't go back. Malum will kill you!"

"I'm sick of your empty promises."

"Malum's too powerful."

"I'm risking my life to be with you."

"I certainly don't need a man to save me, never mind a boy."

"What other stuff are you hiding from me?"

"You've changed. Jak never treated me like this."

"Well, I'm sorry I'm not him!"

"I bet you really did kill Jak."

Vincent's heart raced. He tossed and turned. His arms and legs kicked and punched the empty bed. He kept dreaming. Some things were clear while others remained jumbled

Out of their proper place and time, random memories mixed with images and insights not previously known by Vincent. It was dark, and then broken lights hummed and blinked on and off inside a deserted subway station. Vincent knew the script, yet was powerless to effect change. He knew what was coming, but he could not stop himself or warn Jak. He was trapped in a memory so real, it was haunting the conscious portion of his unconscious mind.

Vincent, sitting, held his skateboard and looked straight ahead. "Are you still mad about us?"

Jak, in a trench coat and sunglasses, at first, refused to answer. He clenched his teeth and glared sideways at his younger brother, yet took a deep breath as he put his hand on Vincent's shoulder. "It is true. I loved her once, as she loved me. However, Noemi's heart grew cold with deceit. Her treachery became daggers to my soul. This thing she offers you, it is a lie."

Memories of angry, emotional banter ensued. Vincent's dreams turned ever more distressing. He felt an upsurge of hate and rage while he slept. Pictures flashed and words shot back and forth between the brothers.

"You're mad because we're together now, and that's eating you up. I can feel it." Vincent reacted to benign comments with hasty perceptions.

Jak struggled to remain calm. "You don't actually think you mean anything to Noemi, do you? I was always her first choice you know. She had a crush on you, little brother, but she loved me."

"That's a lie!"

"No, Vincent. The Shroud's evil deceits have twisted your mind. But you are not beyond redemption. You need to be noble and have faith as you were taught by the knighthood."

"The humans aren't like us. Lord Malum says they are beneath us. We're perfect. They're not."

"These words are not your own. They are the ramblings of a mad man who would rather see everything burn than have peace. You must see reason, little brother."

"Poor, poor, Jak. You'll never change. You always think you're right about everything."

"Vincent, your emotions are being manipulated. I feel another immortal's presence."

"You're delusional. It's all lies, lies, and more lies."

"It is not. I swear to you."

"It is. And you have a funny way of apologizing."

"I cannot ask for forgiveness if you will not tell me why I should ask for it."

"Noemi said you'd say things like that. I didn't believe her. How stupid could I be for trusting you?"

The dream became clearer, almost coherent. Vincent wrestled with his sheet as he thrashed about. Yet no matter how much he convulsed, he kept sleeping.

Inside the subway station, Vincent clenched his jaw and flung his skateboard at Jak. He then summoned a pair of translucent red katana swords from nothing.

Jak twisted his body, avoiding the skateboard. "Do not do this. Withdraw your strikers!" he yelled.

Vincent braced for battle. His face devoid of emotion, he wrapped his fingers tightly around the swords he summoned. "You are no longer my brother. You are now my enemy." Vincent thrust the glowing strikers toward his brother's stomach.

Jak somersaulted backward. "I will not fight you like this!"

"Why? Is it too real? It's one thing to play gallant knight in the confines of the temple, but it's another thing to fight for your life. Now summon your striker or I'll put you down like a dog." Vincent waved his pair of translucent red, blazing strikers through the air. The heat from the blades swirled waves of trailing light as they moved.

Jak opened his palms, displaying no weapon. "I will not fight you. Why do you resent me so?"

"Get over yourself. You will fight, or you will die." Vincent paused. "Wait. I remember. The code. What was it? Oh, yeah, how did it go?"

Jak extended his hand toward his brother. "Don't!"

Vincent smirked. "Until the last enemy..."

"Has been brought to nothing." Jak hung his head, as he was obligated to finish the rest. "Why did you say that? I have no choice now."

"One thing I know about the knights, they keep with tradition. Even when it kills them."

Tzzzztt. Vincent's blades hissed with electric energy.

Jak looked down, closed his eyes, and waited.

Vincent charged with a battle cry and raised strikers.

Jak summoned his translucent blue sword just as Vincent chopped his katana blades down toward his neck.

Vincent huffed. His blade radiated sparks against Jak's sword.

Jak gritted his teeth. His biceps strained from the pressure of two swords against his one. "We are family." Jak grimaced.

"Stop pretending that you care!" Vincent shouted. "You don't know anything about me!"

Jak grunted. "You have a choice." Vincent's strength pushed him to the ground. "We all have a choice. No matter what others might have us believe."

"I...I want to..." Vincent felt an emotional tug, and in his heart, there arose a conflict.

Jak's arms started to weaken from fatigue. "Good, now remove your strikers so we can talk."

At that moment, Vincent also sensed a presence urging him onward. "Lord Malum will..."

"Do not fear Malum, for he is no lord. His only true power lies in the illusion of fear," Jak said. "Come now, release your grip," he urged his brother, "and let us talk of a reunion like in times gone past."

"I don't want to talk anymore! You always get your way, and I'm sick of it!" Vincent pressed his strikers harder.

Jak soared backward. "That is enough! I am not indulging you any longer. You are nothing more than an ill-tempered child. I will drag you home if I have to." Jak charged toward his younger brother with a determined, focused stride.

Vincent braced.

The blades of the brothers clashed together in violent fury, causing an onslaught of blue and red sparks. The mystic currents sizzled and hissed with each violent blow of the swords. A transcendent clash between two immortals began in a mortal world that was ill-prepared for what was secretly unleashed upon it.

Vincent was relentless. He kicked and swung his blades repeatedly.

Jak fended off Vincent's overcharged, explosive attacks. He coiled his entire body through the air, landing with a knee to his younger brother's stomach.

Vincent fell on the ground. He cradled his abdomen. He spread his fingers and reached out to the side. He moved his hand toward his brother, causing a trashcan to fly toward Jak, who promptly sliced the solid metal container in two.

"Is that the best you can do, little brother? Because I have to say, I am not impressed." Jak casually walked toward Vincent who remained sitting on the grimy subway floor. "Why do you not remember all of the good times that we had growing up together? All of this just for a girl..."

Vincent interrupted. "She's not just a girl to me. Maybe Noemi was just some girl to you, but not to me. And for the record, you had way more good times than I did." Vincent hid his tears. "Maybe this will impress you!" Lying on his back, he reached into the air, straining his entire body until his skin reddened and quivered. With invisible power, Vincent pulled the broken subway lights and some of the ceiling down on top of Jak. The concrete piled over him with dust and debris several feet high.

Shrak-ak-ak-a. Screeech. Shrak-ak-ak-a. Screeech. The faint sounds of a distant train broke the eerie silence.

Vincent, shocked by his own powers, withdrew his blades and rushed toward the pile of debris. "Jak, Jak, are you all right? I'm sorry. I didn't mean to hurt you." The fear in his voice resembled that of a younger brother rather than a mighty equal. He frantically dug through the mess.

A bloody hand reached up and grabbed his arm. Jak emerged from the pile of dust, fragments of ceiling, and shattered glass that covered him. Miniscule drops of crimson red flowed along his sleeve, down his pinky finger, and dripped off his hand as globules of deep rose blush on the ground. Jak seized his brother by the arm, easily lifting him off his feet. Without hesitation, he abruptly threw Vincent across the subway floor.

The momentum carried Vincent until he skidded off the safe confines of the platform and plummeted onto the tracks.

Jak looked down at his trench coat and dismissively flapped it off. Clouds of chalky, powdery dust consumed him. He coughed and hacked from the concentrated residue that engulfed his senses. "If you will not stop this petty rivalry, I will." Jak, so preoccupied, failed to see how Vincent had fallen onto the tracks and into the path of the oncoming train. "I see the Shroud has taught you a couple of new tricks. But they are simply that, tricks. You are no more a match for me now than before, little brother." He coughed and kept dusting his clothes off.

Shrak-ak-ak-a. Shrak-ak-ak-a.

As the train neared, the sound captured Jak's attention. He looked up and saw his brother slumped over on the tracks.

Vincent was semi-conscious. "Aeeee. Agggh." He rolled and moaned.

"Vincent, wake up! Come on, little brother! Get off the tracks!"

The lights of the train filled the dark tunnel ahead.

Vincent groaned. He blinked through a set of blurry eyes. He sluggishly shook his head, but stared idly at the train. Finally recognizing the imminent danger, he staggered to his feet. Yet, he remained between the tracks as the train barreled toward him.

Jak ran to the edge of the platform. "You are injured. Give me your hand!" Jak got down on his hands and knees. "Whatever you do, do not touch the third rail or you will get electrocuted!"

Vincent slowly reached for his brother's hand as Jak extended it toward him. He squinted at Jak's hand and then withdrew his. He looked behind at the third rail and up at the oncoming train. His eyes remained fixed on the train's glaring light. "No, Jak. I can't let you win again. I've worked too hard for this. I won't let you have Noemi. Unlike you and the other immortals, I'm not afraid to die." He briefly paused. "That's why I'll win this time."

"Stop it! Just stop it!" Jak shouted, pounding his fist against the concrete platform. "This has gone on long enough! If you want to win so badly, then fine, you win!" His arm nervously shook as he reached his hand out again.

"I can't win like that. Not like that." His face lost all emotion. "No, today, I'm taking what's mine."

Vincent reached over and gripped the third rail, causing the train to jump its tracks and slam the subway wall. The ground quaked. The lights blacked out in the station. Then they flashed on and off before bursting like sparklers. The lights popped one after another in grand fashion.

Slowly, and with a painful wince, Vincent screamed as he pushed his free hand toward Jak. Seven hundred and fifty volts of electricity exploded from Vincent's hand, and he directed a thick, electrified current at his brother.

Jak summoned his striker and deflected the massive surge. The electricity parted, blasting the sides of the walls behind him.

KA-BOOOMMM! A deafening pop thundered through the station and resonated up to the streets above, shattering windows and tripping car alarms as sound waves pulsed throughout the city.

Vincent released another wave of voltage. It pushed Jak beyond his physical limit, forcing him backward from the platform's ledge. Beneath Jak's feet, the cement floor buckled and the ceramic tiles burst like a series of spastic dominos until he was pinned against the far wall at the back end of the station.

"Ha! Do you like that?" Vincent laughed devilishly. "You never respected me! But after today, you'll never win again!" He pushed even more lightning bolts toward Jak. "You'll have to go home and tell them that you were beaten by your little brother. Everyone will see that you're not so perfect after all."

Jak's blue striker crystallized from the intense heat of the electric bolts. "Aaaahh!" he screamed. He tried to deflect the powerful torrents.

"You are nothing!" Vincent yelled.

Jak wheezed with the last of his strength. His words strained from the bottom of his diaphragm to the tip of his tongue. "It is a shame. Your first victory will be our last moment as brothers." His face tightened. His brows merged. Moisture soaked his forehead. His knuckles whitened around his striker. His muscles locked up. "You need to know two things." Jak paused to catch his breath. "I love you. I always have...Aaaahh!" A chilling scream bellowed forth before he could finish.

Vincent's anger softened once he had won. He tried to release the rail and stop the flow of electricity, but something from beyond held his hand on the track. He vigorously struggled to let go, but it seemed an invisible force kept his hand there against his will.

Jak's power met its limits. His striker could no longer take the electrical assault. It exploded into fragments of tiny blue shards. The lightning bolts devoured him.

Everything went dark as Vincent collapsed.

A strange, uneasy silence fell.

Face down, Vincent clumsily groped his way through the pitch-black tunnel. With a remorseful tone, he called out to his brother. "Jak, I'm sorry." He began to stutter. "I was just...I don't know...I was being stupid and mad about dumb stuff. I've never felt that kind of anger before. I didn't know what I was doing. I swear. I'm really, really sorry. ANSWER ME!"

Chapter Two

Vincent's nightmare shifted locations. He was given insight on things he had not seen with his own eyes. In a strange, third-party view, Vincent watched Malum give orders.

"Noemi's heart is disloyal to the Shroud. She loves the traitor, Vincent."

Dominic, Malum's new first-in-command, added, "I'll make Vincent watch as I slowly kill her. I want his last thoughts to be of how powerless he was to protect Noemi from me. After I'm done with her, he'll beg me to end his wasted life."

Malum shouted, "You're not even half the warrior she is. You could have learned a few things from her. Noemi's life is in my hands, to do with as I please. Perhaps, in time, if she fails to satisfy me, you may do what you'd like with her. But until such time, you shall not lay even a finger upon her!"

"Aaah!" Startled, Vincent woke up. Drenched in sweat, he sat upright in bed. His heart raced. He placed his hand over his head. "God, Jak, what did I do?" He sobbed violently before stumbling to his feet. Throwing back the blackout curtains, he dried his tears on them. He shielded his eyes from the midday sun, and inhaled a cleansing breath. He rubbed the dark circles under his eyes. Vincent looked out upon the city of Los Angeles. He leaned his head on the sliding glass door and slapped his open palm against it. "Noemi, hold on."

Vincent washed and dressed in a flash. He got on his motorcycle and sped through the city, weaving in and out of traffic. He raced north, following the rocky coastline.

The overcast sky threw shadows, so that the bright became dark and the dark turned gloomy. Gray clouds draped over the roaring ocean tide, making the steep cliffs high above the water's edge appear bleak and forlorn. A foreboding wind blasted in manic spurts. The long, slender stalks on the grassy ledge bent and bowed to the wind's command. In the distance, a strong gust rustled the leaves among the murky forest. Sea squalls drove angry whitecaps toward the coast, bashing waves against rocks beneath the cliffs. From high above on the grassy ledge, the ocean seemed black and unending.

Barroomm. Barroomm. The black motorcycle wildly sped up the twisting road that scaled the ledge overlooking the ocean.

Vincent wore a black helmet, a black leather jacket, black jeans, and even black shoes. With nary another vehicle on the road, he jetted the bike across traffic lanes and came to a screeching halt, leaving long tire marks on the pavement. He stopped at the entrance to a dirt path. Vincent revved the engine and then bolted up the trail. He rode with hastened desperation, jumping over dead tree branches and ducking under limbs. Though the bike looked out of control at times, the motorcycle gradually slowed with a controlled purpose as Vincent approached the top of the cliffs. Near the end of the woods and just before the open grassy ledge, he steered off the tiny dirt path.

Vincent twisted the key and shut down the engine. With his helmet and complete riding gear still on, he cautiously began walking toward the top of the cliffs.

A single crow flew overhead in a circle. *Caw! Caw!*

Vincent wandered over to the sharp drop-off and peered down to where the land ended and the seemingly never-ending ocean began. He turned toward the dark forest, waiting and watching from the grassy ledge. He looked at nothing else other than the distant outer rim of the shadowy woods.

As anticipated, a scruffy, middle-aged man appeared from out of the dense forest. With a leisurely gait, he walked without hesitation toward the biker in black. The disheveled man pulled back his sackcloth hood from his robe. He strolled to the edge of the cliff. "Vincent, you can take off that ridiculous disguise. I sensed you long before you ever arrived here on that loud contraption of yours."

Far below the grassy ledge, the tides crashed against large rocks at the bottom of sixty-foot high sandstone cliffs.

Vincent removed his helmet and carelessly tossed it to the ground. The back of his heels neared the edge of the slippery grass. He quickly peeked over his shoulder at the thrashing waves below the cliff's vertical drop. "Malum, no more games. Where's Noemi?"

Malum snapped his fingers and a large group of young immortals emerged out of the woods. Young men and women stood shoulder to shoulder in a perfect line far behind him. There were dozens of young warriors, all blankly staring at Vincent.

The line parted for one immortal female who shoved a blindfolded Noemi out of the forest and toward the open grassy area. Noemi stumbled and fell, scraping her elbow on a small rock. It lacerated her skin and a single, elongated drop of blood ran down her forearm. Noemi's female abductor callously jerked on the white rope tightly bound around her biceps. The captor lifted Noemi onto her feet. Though she was limping, she forced Noemi to walk onward. Her captor aggressively pushed Noemi in the back. With Noemi's arms securely tied, the female captor harshly pushed her again toward Malum. She kicked the back of her knee, causing Noemi to instantly drop to the ground. The female immortal ripped the blindfold from Noemi's eyes. She then backhanded her across the face. Noemi's head and neck jolted to the opposite side.

With balled fists, Vincent lunged forward.

Malum wagged his finger. "Not yet!" he scolded.

Vincent's heart pounded. With arms curled upward, his fists still balled, he yelled at Noemi's captor, "Vanessa, we all grew up together! What's wrong with you?"

"Never trifle with a woman's affection." She rolled her eyes and dismissively flipped her hand at him. "Whatever. I'm over you, loser."

Malum clutched Vanessa's shoulder. "Thank you. You may go back and join the others now."

Vanessa spat on the ground near Noemi. "Traitor!" She narrowed her eyes and crinkled her nose before she looked high and away. Vanessa flipped her long, frosted blonde tips in the air before walking back toward the line of warriors.

Malum turned to address his young followers who were standing at the edge of the forest. He raised both of his arms and shouted, "Behold, the traitor, and her lover, the murderer!" He pointed condemningly at Vincent. "He has graced us with his charming presence!" Malum snorted a facetious laugh.

Frozen with indecision, Vincent stood there helplessly. "You know that's not true, Malum." His expression mixed with concern and fear. He tilted his head and half smiled at some of his former friends. They glared at him with nothing but hateful contempt. Vanessa shot a personal glare.

"I know nothing of the sort." Malum smiled. "They can't hear us unless we shout, you see." He pointed his thumb backward. "The ocean drowns out everything here. Maybe even the two of you in the end." He chuckled. "That's why I chose this location." Malum gestured toward the edge of the cliff and then back at his warriors far behind him. "Vincent," he smirked, "I have to ask you, what's with the whole black décor?" Malum held his chin in his hand. He twirled his index finger at him. "A little drab and pretentious, don't you think?"

Vincent remained deadpan. "What, haven't you heard? Good guys wear black these days." He crossed his arms.

"Oh, give me a break!" Malum threw his hands up in the air. He glanced down at Noemi, who was battered and bound. He yelled out to his followers. "I want you to learn what true weakness is!" He turned toward Vincent. "Noemi has chosen your love and death rather than power and a life with us." Malum stuck out his hand with a thumb up sign before quickly flipping it to a thumb down. "Are you happy now? Does your vanity know no limits?"

Vincent gazed achingly toward his eternal love. His heart wished to free her. She appeared bruised with a troubled response. She struggle to move along the cold, wet grass. The right corner of her lip was busted, and dried blood caked down her arm. Most of her beautiful long hair had been hacked off, and one of her legs appeared injured. His heart thumped, his breaths became heavy, and he held numbness in place of anxiety. "Are you okay?" Vincent meekly asked. "What've they done to you?"

"I'm okay." Noemi could sense that he was scared for her safety, but she knew Vincent's fear would not help either of them in this situation.

Malum rolled his one real eye. "Yes, yes, I'll let you both walk away as long as you never interfere with the Shroud again."

"I don't believe you." Vincent tapered his eyes and slowly shook his head. "Send Noemi over to me."

Closing the gap between them, Malum crossed his arms and stood toe to toe with Vincent.

"Fine. You leave us alone, we leave you alone." Malum jabbed his finger into Vincent's chest. Malum smiled. He turned around and walked close to his followers, speaking to them loudly as he did.

Vincent locked a gaze with his beloved Noemi. Her stunning brown eyes had become dull and weary. Vincent felt the sheer essence of his living soul wrenched from his body. He knew Malum well. He knew he never intended for them to walk away together, nor would he ever set Noemi free. Realizing this could be the last time he saw her, Vincent grew determined to fight what he could not win. He would make one last stand against Malum and the Shroud, waging his own personal war until his final breath left his body.

"Can you get free?" Vincent quietly asked Noemi.

Noemi struggled to loosen the rope around her arms. She could barely hold back the tears she so desperately wanted to hide. "No...I...I don't think so." She tried to be brave, but she knew this was the winter of their springtime love. "Don't worry. I'm all right." She smiled for him, but tears ran down her cheeks. "Just focus on what you have to do."

Vincent motioned for her to look directly into his ice-blue eyes. "Together we can do this, but only together." He took a deep breath and then exhaled. "I know I haven't given you much reason to trust me, but we'll make it out of here." He stared intently into Noemi's wondrous brown eyes. "I swear."

She looked down at the ground and shivered. "No, no we won't. Don't you get it? I believe in you, but not in us anymore. We were doomed from the start." She briefly glanced at Malum. "Love can only survive so much misery." She squeezed her eyes tight and refused to look at Vincent. "Just go away. Get out of here while you still can." Her tears stung her face.

"Why are you saying this?" Vincent knew they only had a few precious moments left to talk. "I won't allow our love to be crushed. I'm not going to just go away." His jaw tightened. "We can beat anything together."

Malum began walking back toward them. "How inspiring, but then again, Vincent, you don't believe you, so why should she?" he snidely remarked.

Vincent took a cautious step toward Noemi. "Dammit, I believe!" All of his muscles braced for action. "It's not over! I won't let it be." He chopped his hand down and away. "We're so close." He gestured with his index finger and thumb, having just inches of space between them. "Don't give up on us now."

Malum tapped his foot on the ground and loudly grunted. He put his hands over his ears. "Oh, for goodness sake, will the two of you just shut up for a minute! I can't take your teen angst anymore!" He stroked his chin, and inquisitively looked them over. He tilted his head. "I wanted Jak to join the Shroud, not you, Vincent. But he was a disappointment. I'll give you credit though. At least you had the guts to kill your own brother, a fellow immortal and powerful knight."

"Don't talk about my brother!" Vincent shouted.

"Relax. He served his purpose." Malum quickly glanced over his right shoulder and off into the expanse. He stared at the tip of a castle spire high on a mountaintop. "You got the girl and I got the immortal war, of which you drew first blood. It's a two-for-one special, shoppers." He chortled.

Vincent gestured toward all of Malum's followers along the edge of the woods. "It's just too bad they don't know you like I do." Vincent peered over at his love and then back at Malum. "You were there that night in the subway station weren't you? Jak couldn't be turned or manipulated, so you used me to kill my own brother instead."

"Oh, bravo." Malum sluggishly applauded with an unimpressed frown. "Wow, there's no fooling you, is there?" He sneered. "Well, here's something that I knew right away. You always wanted to be Jak, and you coveted what he had so badly," he looked down at Noemi, "your heart already killed him. You want someone to blame. Then blame her!" Malum shouted, pointing at Noemi. "Why didn't you release the track when he begged you to stop?"

Indignant, Vincent shot back, "I wanted to let go of the track. I tried to stop, but something held me there. I'm gonna make you..."

"Hmpf." Malum cut him off. "Choose your next words carefully, youngling. Remember, it is my will alone that allows you to breathe." Malum noticed Vincent eyeing the castle spire in the distance. "What are you looking at?"

"Nothing," he quickly replied.

"Forget it! They won't help you." With eyes darting at Vincent, Malum motioned back in the direction of the castle. "You're a rogue. You have no place now." He lowered his chin with a menacing glance. "You're not Shroud or even a real knight. You're just a punk kid. A vigilante with a chip on his shoulder...A wannabe hero." Malum casually plucked some lint from his sleeve. "Besides, they never really help anyone. At least the Shroud takes action."

Undaunted, Vincent turned his attention along with a few tender words toward Noemi. "I'm so sorry for everything." His ice-blue eyes fell downward and filled with damp regret. "I've loved you for so long. I buried how I felt 'cause you were with Jak."

"No, stop!" Noemi called out to him as she slumped over on the ground. "Save yourself. You'll learn to love another. Please, I'm begging you!" She pressed her forehead against the wet grass and sobbed.

"Never."

Noemi slowly tilted her head up. "I didn't mean it when I said I should've married Jak. You need to understand that I never loved him like you." Her eyes mirrored shame when she looked up at Vincent.

Malum loudly belched. "Up here, buddy, I'm talking to you." He put his hand over his stomach. "For crying out loud, you're giving me indigestion! Noemi, if Jak really loved you, he'd have joined the Shroud. You both could have had the benefits of power without surrendering your personal freedom to the knights' traditions." He waved his arm sideways through the air. "Cut to the chase and stop your blubbering. That joker didn't love you, but this sap over here does." He shrugged. "You want to hop on the back of his motorcycle and live happily ever after?" He gritted his cracked yellow teeth and stomped the ground. "Well, it's not happening! Say goodbye and prepare for a long, cold journey into everlasting death!"

"Wait!" Vincent put his hand up at Malum. "Just loosen her arms and let me hold her once more."

Malum rubbed the deep scar that ran from the top of his left eyebrow to the bottom of his cheek. "Yeah, I don't think so. But I will do this." He lifted his hand in the air and sent a wave of invisible ripples toward Vincent, knocking him down and pushing him backward.

Vincent dug his fingernails into the ground. He slid toward the edge of the cliff. He grabbed handfuls of long grass. He stopped himself from plunging off into the crashing ocean waves. His shoulders hung over the ledge. He quickly peered down at the rocks rising past the breakers.

"Drat! What do you know, I missed." Malum brooded. He tucked his elbows back, bent his bony fingers, and charged another shot.

Vincent leapt to his feet, raised both hands, and blocked Malum's next surge. His eyes shut briefly with a strained press. With his chin tight, his calves flexed forward, his bodyweight wobbled sideways and backward. He grimaced, yet never took his eyes off Noemi. His power and control faded. Bursts of hot and cold tingled throughout his skin. "Aaah!" he yelled. Gathering the last of his strength, Vincent returned the surge upon Malum. The pulse wave flung the dark lord head over feet tumbling to the ground.

At the forest perimeter, some of Malum's young warriors squinted and gawked, their mouths agape, while others shook their heads.

"Argh!" Malum looked over at them, and then glared at Vincent. He wrinkled the folds of skin on the bridge of his nose and arched his brows downward. He gnashed his teeth. He hastily stood from his flat position, shaking the grass off his hooded robe.

Malum screamed, "So this is how it's going to be, eh? I never should've wasted my time teaching you the finer things of the dark arts and sciences!" Malum summoned two translucent black, serrated strikers. He charged toward Vincent. His blades smoldered a ghostly trail of smoke in their wake. Malum jumped, swiping his swords down.

Vincent, his chin up, his chest raised from a confident breath, summoned his red striker, easily fending off the attack.

The weapons clashed together violently and repelled both of them apart. Sparks scattered and hissed. Malum charged again, swinging his strikers. Vincent quickly dropped to his knees and sliced Malum's chin. The blow tore a deep gash. A second, bloody mouth it seemed. Stunned, Malum withdrew a striker and pressed the skin on his chin together. Blood squirted through his fingers and onto the green grass. He stared at Vincent in disbelief and retreated a few steps.

"How..." Malum's pupils dilated.

"Oh, I'm about to do much worse." Vincent stood tall, waving Malum onward. "Like my brother Jak, I am a knight."

Malum dabbed the back of his hand across the gaping slit on his chin. He licked his blood and spat the rest to the ground. "Wipe that silly grin off your face!" he shouted. "You've changed nothing by wounding me. That was a lucky shot," he yelled as blood trickled down his neck. "No matter what happens today, I've already written your ending."

"I'm not afraid to die, are you?" Vincent replied in a low, serious tone.

In an instant, the sky opened, the clouds parted, and a single ray of sun glistened. The beam radiated on top of Vincent, illuminating him and nothing else. Noemi squinted, for she beheld the sudden glow of a golden spirit.

Malum glanced back at his followers. They gawked at Vincent, whispering amongst themselves. Everyone except for Vanessa. She crossed her arms and turned her head away.

"What are you all looking at?" Malum flapped his arms. "These are but a few tricks he performs. They are nothing more than smoke and mirrors. Now see true power!" He thumped his chest with his hand.

Vincent snickered. "I don't know, Mal, I think you're losing your audience."

"Enough!" With both hands, Malum raised his striker over his head. He thrust down the serrated blade, driving it into the earth with a mighty stab. The ground rumbled. A rapidly moving fissure carved its way across the grassy ledge. The jagged rift split the ground between Vincent's legs, weakening his footing, thus toppling him onto his side.

Malum crouched down. He launched, propelling his lean frame twenty feet into the air. He lifted his blade high, aiming it at Vincent. With eyes red from broken blood vessels, Malum clamped his cracked yellow teeth. His sackcloth robe fanned as he sailed with his fiery sword on target.

From a defenseless position, Vincent quickly swiped his katana striker across his body, deflecting Malum's blade. *Clang!* Red and black sparks flew as the swords collided.

Malum stood over him. Vincent jabbed his blade. Malum blocked the attack, pushing the edge of Vincent's striker back toward his own throat. Their two weapons were locked together. Malum exerted his strength against Vincent's neck. Vincent's hand trembled. His own blade inched closer to his throat. The sword grazed his skin. A line of blood dripped down the side of Vincent's neck. A single, cold drop tickled, seeping behind his ear.

Noemi fought to loosen her bonds. She couldn't bear the sight of Malum beheading her Vincent. "Hold on, I'm almost free!" she desperately shouted.

Malum peeked over at Noemi. She thrashed like a fish on dry land, while struggling to release her arms. In that brief instant, Malum was distracted. Before he could even turn his head back around, Vincent seized the moment. He drew up his knees and launched his legs, kicking Malum in the middle of his chest. Vincent sprung to his feet as Malum jetted high and far through the air.

"Boo-ya!" Vincent exclaimed. "How'd you like that?" He raised a fist.

Thud! Malum smacked the ground. His striker dissolved. "Wait just a minute!" He rolled over onto his hands and knees. He slowly stood up and staggered around, nearly falling again. He blinked sluggishly. He rattled his head from side to side. "Fight fair!" he slurred and wobbled.

Vincent, self-satisfied, grinned. "Oh, it'll be fair." He withdrew his blade. He dropped to the ground and did pushups. He jumped to his feet and punched the air, bouncing around like a boxer. "Booo-yaaa!"

Malum snarled. "I'm ready, you blasphemous twit." His sword rematerialized. He clutched it between his bony knuckles.

Vincent made an obscene gesture, pointing his fiery red blade at Malum. "Bring it."

"Your conceit will be your undoing." Malum adjusted his robe with one hand while tightly grasping his striker with the other.

Noemi yelled, "Vincent!" She grimaced while attempting to free one of her arms. "He's too powerful. RUNNN!"

Malum casually walked over. "Ya know, I've been thinking." He gave Noemi a passing glance, slightly nodding his head at her while keeping a watchful gaze upon Vincent. "What good is immortality if it can't be controlled?" He tapped his finger to his brow. "Think about it."

Vincent tilted his head to the side, and paused. "You're crazy"

Malum grinned from ear-to-ear. "My dear boy, I've spent thousands of years on Earth. There is so much that I could still teach you."

"I just want her." Vincent pointed his striker at Noemi.

"You can have each other, but...you can also have money, power, fame, you can have it all." Malum held a puzzled stare, before raising an eyebrow and tapping his cheek with his index finger. "Well?"

Vincent remained on guard. "What, you're bargaining with me?"

"If you act now, the first immortal will grant you your heart's desire, if...you help him first." Malum's form eased, his stance relaxed.

"Help him with what?"

Malum's left glass eye glinted a cryptic reflection. "The halflings, David and his sister, Danielle James." He curled a single edge of his lip upturned. "Their father hid more than just his two hybrid children from us. He concealed the fact that he was the last heir to the eternal throne. The first immortal wants them... well, one of them anyway."

Vincent's eyes shifted down and toward Noemi. He shook his head. "No! I will no longer serve the Shroud," he roared.

Malum leered. "The knights protect the halflings from afar, but soon, their ancient ways will be gone, and they shall never rise again. When that happens, don't forget you had a chance." He gestured toward a bound Noemi.

Vincent smacked his lips together. He took in a slow, reflective breath before exhaling. He peered back up at the distant castle spire. He thought about Jak. He thought about Noemi. He thought about Malum. His jaw tightened and his nostrils flared. "The knights will..."

Malum refused to let him finish. "They'll what? Stop the Shroud? Save you? Save her? Right all the wrongs in the world?" He hooted. "Not here and not this time, and they know it. They're dying just like everyone else in this realm. But you and Noemi don't have to die today," he hissed his words through clamped, yellow, cracked teeth.

Vincent lowered his blade. "Okay. What do you want?"

With a smug look, Malum replied, "See, I knew you still craved dark truths."

"Stop speaking in riddles and TELL ME!" Vincent screamed so even the woods echoed his frustrated voice.

"Let's keep it real, shall we?"

"What's your point?"

Malum let his striker slowly vanish from his hand. "My point is, you and Noemi can get on that ridiculous contraption of yours and just ride away, but only if I allow it."

"Please, Vincent, stop!" Noemi cried out. "Whatever he asks, trust me, I'm not worth it! You're better than him. He's a liar!"

"It'll be all right." Vincent lowered his hand at her and withdrew his blade.

Malum excitedly tented his fingers. "Now we're getting somewhere." He paused and let out a sigh. "I want you to make your way back into the knights' castle and crush them before the immortal war begins." He scowled at Noemi and pouted. "Destroy the last flicker fruit tree in the middle of the castle gardens."

"What? Why?"

"Because I said so," Malum seethed.

Vincent fidgeted. He paced back and forth. "Even if I agreed, how the heck am I supposed to get into the castle? In case you hadn't noticed, I'm not exactly welcome there anymore."

Malum smiled a devious grin. "You will earn redemption with powerful signs. They will have no choice but to reinstate you."

"Okay." Vincent gazed at Noemi. She wistfully glanced back. "I should have listened to you all along."

"Good, then it's settled," Malum gleefully replied.

"No, I was talking to her." Vincent motioned a nod at Noemi. "She was right. No. The answer's no. We're leaving now."

Malum creased his forehead and snorted. "You rude, ungrateful brats! How dare you talk to me in such a manner!" He materialized a striker. *Bbvvv.*

Vincent summoned his blade. It sizzled hot and red. With an intense stare, he walked toward Malum. "You killed my brother Jak. You hurt Noemi. And for that, I'm gonna slice you open." He directed his fiery red blade at him.

"Yesss," Malum hissed. "You forgot the part where I helped your powers grow until you roasted Jak," Malum sharply replied. "You're not innocent. You're not an unwilling victim in all of this." He sneered while raising his misty, black sword. "Your hands are red with fault, bucko."

Vincent never broke stride. "Piss off."

"Oh, what could have been." Malum stuck his lower lip out at Noemi, before addressing Vincent. "Well then, I guess this is adieu."

"Yeah, for your head! Until the last enemy..." Vincent picked up his stride.

"Has been brought to nothing!" Malum boomed.

The two immortals rammed each other as the sun fell beneath gray clouds on the somber horizon. Muted glints of pastel faintly lit the seascape. Thick, salty fog darkened the ocean until it covered the land and sea alike.

With strikers drawn, Vincent and Malum charged again toward each other for what both knew would be the final time. Their eyes focused, faces drawn, muscles constricted. Time appeared to slow for a moment, and then sped up when their blades clashed one to the other. *Whoosh! Clank! Clang!*

Chapter Three

The briny air hinted with traces of smoke, radiating an eerie spectral glow through the foggy haze. As the two immortal adversaries slammed against one another, flaring sparks rained down upon the ground, scattering among a rising vapor. The barrage of clashing swords produced a fierce metallic chorus that rang out over the cliffs. When their strikers collided with flesh, crimson drops smeared the long, slender stalks of grass like careless red brushstrokes on nature's masterpiece.

All the spectators, the young immortals following Malum, and even Noemi, knew Vincent could not prevail against the dark lord. This was less fight than lesson. Yet during battle, a strange occurrence happened. Vincent became stronger. Something eternal and mystic coursed through his body. His skin rippled with tiny bumps. His hairs stood on end. He evaded every one of Malum's swipes. Vincent soon realized not only was he good, on this particular day, he was finally good enough.

With each blow and jab of his sword, the battle turned in Vincent's favor. Malum felt a growing swell of fear and doubt. Death did not vex him, but his sovereignty gradually slipped from his grasp. He worried his followers viewed him as not an unbeatable deity, yet as somehow less than immortal, less than invincible.

Malum backed away, quickly scooping up a handful of dirt. He threw it at Vincent's face.

Suddenly blinded, Vincent tried to wipe the grit and sand from out of his blurry, watery eyes.

Malum smiled as he calmly approached. His sword cocked back over the side of his head.

Noemi called out, "Vincent! He's coming at you from the right!" She yelled, "Duck!"

Malum swung his translucent black striker at Vincent's head. Sensing the motion of his swing, Vincent bent his body backward. The blade missed by inches. Vincent felt heat as it zipped by his cheek. The blade sliced a portion of leather from his jacket, yet he remained intact.

His vision still blurred and teary, Vincent wiped away the stinging grains of dirt. "Throwing sand in my eyes, really? That's pretty cheap, even for you."

"Despite what anyone says, they'll do whatever it takes to survive." Malum circled Vincent like a shark.

Vincent closed his eyes and held his blade steady. Multiple Malums appeared to pace around him. "No, you're wrong. Not everyone will do that. Jak proved that. I fought Jak because I was jealous of him, but he loved me until his last breath."

Malum growled. "How poignant." He furrowed his brows. "He, like you, was weak."

Malum upturned the corners of his lips. He spun from Vincent to Noemi. He abruptly extended his arm out at her. She gulped. She shot an aching gaze at Vincent, and then shut her eyes. Malum hurled a surge of power. A pulse wave slammed the ground in front of her. The ground quaked. Dirt and grass exploded into the air.

"Aaah!" she screamed.

Noemi flew backward. Her body tottered along the ocean cliffs. Sharp rocks amid the crashing tide waited far below. The earth crumbled beneath her as solid ground loosened.

Malum nibbled on his lower lip. "My aim's off today." He raised his hand again.

"NOOO!" Vincent frantically shrieked. He rushed in quick strides toward Malum, tackling him.

Vincent avoided rage since he killed Jak. But Noemi's life literally hung in the balance. His ire was now unleashed for the world to see. Hand to hand, he wrestled Malum. They rolled on the ground. They grappled and clawed at each other as they tussled. Vincent knocked his forehead against Malum's face, breaking his nose in the process. Blood gushed down into Malum's mouth, staining his teeth pink.

"Bwahahah!" Malum smiled with a sort of demonic, wet laugh.

Off near the tree line, Vanessa whispered and wrung her hands, "Kill him. Kill him." She eagerly observed.

"That's good. Show me your anger!" Malum strained to free himself from Vincent's grip. "You're a killer, that's all you'll ever be, so let her go, and come back to your master. Come back to me!"

His countenance flush, Vincent's heart pounded. His temper festered. His thoughts turned dark. Sweat dripped from his brow onto Malum's face. He put Malum in a stranglehold. Pressing firmly against his windpipe, he started choking him. Vincent glanced up at his former friends. The immortal warriors seemed thrilled by his uncontrolled hate. His heart felt weak. His stomach ached. He relaxed his grip on Malum's neck while looking over at Noemi. She stretched out toward him with her free arm. She gingerly stood and balanced herself on the uneven ground at the edge of the cliff.

Her words were muffled by the hungry, incoming ocean tide. "Vincent, don't do it! You're not a killer..." Noemi shouted. She took a step and tripped. A large chunk of earth rumbled, and a massive boulder dislodged underneath her feet.

For the first time, Vincent believed he could overcome his past. He released Malum. He hopped to his feet, extended back toward Noemi while yelling, "Don't move!"

"Well, wannabe, what's it gonna be?" Malum rubbed the red circle around his neck. He leisurely hoisted himself. Copious amounts of blood ran from his nose and chin. "You can kill me, or you can save the girl, but you can't do both." Malum leaned his head back. He submissively spread his arms out to the sides and waited. "I know you want to take my head, so be a man, and do it!"

"No!" Vanessa balled her fists and smacked her thighs from the tree line of the forest.

Malum put a hand up, motioning for her to stay put. "There, there, he doesn't have the stones..." His heart raced by what he saw next. "Or maybe he does."

Vincent summoned his fiery red blade. He licked his lips and lifted the sword high overhead.

In the background, Noemi yelped. "I'm falling..." She fell to the ground and the ground fell away from the earth. She grasped at anything, but only ripped away pieces of grass and specks of dirt as she plummeted downward upon the thrashing ocean waters.

Vincent withdrew his sword and raced to the cliff's edge. "Next time, old man."

"Ha! There won't be a next time, you fool!" Malum pointed his index finger. "I knew you'd wuss out for a girl."

Vincent bounded headfirst over the cliff. He dove after her. Down the steep drop, he leapt toward the fierce currents and jagged rocks below. He molded his body in the shape of a bullet, propelling himself in order to catch Noemi. She flailed, one arm still bound, it restricted her movements. Noemi's locks flapped in the wind. *Swoosh.* The air rushed. Vincent closed the gap between them. Her eyes widened and his narrowed. He extended his hand and grabbed ahold of her wrist, but she slipped from his grasp.

"I'm sorry you died for me," she cried out.

"NO!" Vincent yelled. He seized her hand, clutching it in his.

Fffffffffffff. They embraced and fell as one. The air swiftly rushed past them.

Malum pried loose a boulder with his sword and sent it hurling toward them. Noemi looked up and saw the large rock barreling over top their heads. Tons of compact stone pursued them.

The two lovers looked deeply into the other's eyes. Noemi's startled brown gaze held the reflection of Vincent with an ever rising boulder behind him. Vincent's ice-blue eyes soaked up Noemi's beauty, and uncovered the watery deep, amidst jagged rocks below them.

"I'm scared!" Noemi closed her eyes.

He pulled her close. He held her firmly and whispered in her ear. "Don't be, I'll..."

SPLOOSH! KERPLUNK!

Together the two hit the turbulent waters. The waves swept over the rocks. The large boulder smashed onto the breakers seconds later, erupting the tide with a volcanic spray of seawater before it sank over top them.

Malum peered inquisitively over the edge of the cliff, and soon, one by one, his young followers joined with expressions of wonder and wait. The churning waters settled. From above, all eyes examined the rolling waves for signs of life. However, there were no broken bodies on the rocks, nor floating remains in the water.

Fizz. Frothy bubbles foamed where the two lovers had fallen into the sea, along with the boulder. An odd and sudden serenity quieted the angry ocean and driving winds. *Arrrh, rhrrr, ahrrr.* A chorus of seagulls cried as they flew over the fizzy breakers. The sun dipped beneath the gray clouds, parting ocean from sky once more.

Malum broke the hush. "Now THAT was impressive!" he shouted. "It was dumb, but impressive." He shook his head and grinned. "It's not the choice I would've made."

Vanessa scanned the watery deep intently. "Where're the bodies?"

Malum wiped blood from off his nose and chin onto his sackcloth sleeve. "It doesn't matter. The traitors are dead. I can no longer sense them." He stared down over the steep cliff. "Besides, no one could've survived that fall, mortal or immortal alike."

"What about the castle?" Vanessa fluffed her long, frosted blonde tips, and stuck her hands out, spreading her fingers. "I chipped a nail!" She pouted.

"Yes, well, your nail aside, now we'll need more resources to invade the castle." Malum ran his index finger down the scar above his glass eye, from the top of his left eyebrow to the bottom of his cheekbone. "I suppose we'll need a larger army to topple those walls." He held his elbow and tapped his fingers to his cheekbone. "Now where am I going to find a mindless, unending army these days?" He shifted his eye heavenward. "Ah, yes, I know. In the catacombs under the city streets of Paris, that's where I'll find my horde. Come, we have work to do."

Malum dismissed his young followers and they obediently marched back into the forest. They vanished into the dense woods. Malum glanced over his shoulder one last time toward the sea. The sun vanished below the skyline. Its final rays beamed across the seascape. The gray enflamed as dusk fell, casting deep scarlet hues upon the water. Softly and slowly, fragments of light faded until the landscape sheathed in darkness, and Malum continued into the murky glen.

Chapter Four

It was late, in the early, dark hours before the approaching dawn. The once lively crowd had lulled. Most of the partygoers had left the club on the lower east side of Paris for the night. Others had fallen asleep wherever they could rest their weary heads.

The band played a song, a last call for the night, as workers swept the floors, preparing to close for the coming day. The trumpeter blew loud notes with quick, lively action, his cheeks ballooning red, his fingers nimbly pressing the valves, purposely waking the sleeping heads, rousing them to go home.

Of the handful of patrons remaining, one young man in particular had left his napping girlfriend inside before he staggered out into the cool, dark street to clear his dizzy head. With a few deep breaths of briskly chilled air, the young man gradually stirred from his woozy nap. He looked up at the dark sky. What was sunny and warm when he last recalled, was now black and unusually cool for this time of year.

He watched his breath crystallize upward, mixing with the air, forming clouds of fleeting vapor and misty frost. He robotically glanced behind his shoulder as the club powered down the lights out in front on the street where he stood. The bulbs, too bright to stare at, in chorus dimmed until their electric spirit drained out. Yet still, the music blared throughout the club, filtering onto the mostly abandoned, and ever now, darker city lane.

A worker closed the front side windows to the club, muffling the loud trumpeter's horn. No longer feeling the warmth from inside, the young man huddled his shoulders, flipped the collar of his jacket up against his neck. He covered his skin from the cold, along with a black and red scorpion tattoo, which stretched under his earlobe down five inches.

He vigorously rubbed his hands together, blowing, sucking in, and puffing breaths into them. He peeked in through the windows, between the chipped paint, through the frosty panes at his girlfriend. The back of her head remained unmoved on the tabletop, so he turned and wildly shivered. He turned away as the cool air chilled his bones.

Across from the club, past the broad, dark empty road, in the shadows of a long narrow street between buildings, the young man saw a pile of trash move without cause.

He peeked through the club's window at his girlfriend, before crossing the street to investigate. He neared the rustling trash pile and slunk cautiously. He paused stiffly whenever the pile frantically shook. Curiosity inched him onward. Balancing tiptoed, he stretched to catch a glimpse over the shifting heap of rubbish.

Layered bags concealed what was beyond. He quietly shuffled his feet closer. The murky night, along with the shadows cast by the alley, made it nearly impossible to see. Yet behind the bags of trash, something lurked in the hidden, dark recesses.

An ominous, pungent rot infected his nostrils. He gagged and became uneasily weak. Covering his nose, he looked back at the club. It was now farther away than he realized.

Closer he quietly shuffled his feet. The murky night, along with the shadows cast by the alley, made it nearly impossible to see, but something slouched and recessed in the dark corner on the other side of the garbage bags.

As he considered retreating, a mass of clouds parted and showered down beams of moonlight. Scattered lines of ghostly rays lit the alley. The haunted glint illuminated a sight so foul, he suddenly braced. Grim fear halted his breath.

A grotesque, clumsy, diseased-looking creature feasted on rancid waste with its back facing the young man. Spiny, finned vertebrae protruded from the beast's back. Grayish green, waxy secretion covered its glossy skin, giving the beast an oily appearance. Its joints had branched, bony growths with fluid-filled sacks. The creature was totally bare, except for a single, tattered loincloth.

When the moonlight parted the darkness, a thin sliver gleamed, slanting a pale bar across the beast's eyes. They were large, black, reflective saucers, dead as coal, and devoid of emotion. The young man saw his perfect reflection in the creature's dark, lifeless globes as its eyes dilated into a black horror. The unworldly beast held a stare at the young man, each sizing up the other. The young man's eyes widened as the creature's black orbs narrowed. One was prey, the other was a predator, and for a brief moment, each knew what the other one was thinking.

The creature growled and snorted warm puffs, which drifted upward into smoky clouds of wrath. And with a low pitch, its body angled, it sprung backward into a bestial, pouncing position. The young man panted heavily, refusing to blink or look away. Time slowed. Each subtle movement amplified a hundredfold in the tense alleyway standoff. When the beastly creature growled again, the young man leaned away in nervous expectation.

He stumbled.

His feet tangled, but he remained upright, never taking his eyes off the beast. Rather, he collected his calm. And like a runner, on the eve of mark, he prepared all of his muscles to take flight. However, when the monster spoke words to him, he recoiled backward, straight-legged, his body jerked off the ground, and his color blanched, draining him until only the hue of terror remained. Insensible will spun him around. But pure adrenaline propelled his rush toward the club.

The boisterous music continued loudly. He could hear the music and see people through the windows, sweeping, stacking chairs, and playing instruments. Most of all, he saw his girlfriend. She was still asleep. Her head flat on the table. Her face turned away from him.

At first, he could only hear his heartbeat. It raced fearfully. Without reason, his breaths labored. Then a menacing voice from behind called out. He resisted the urge to look back. He kept both eyes fixed on the club. He had to make it back to her. He had no choice, nor doubt he would make the short distance from the alley to the club, because only a few good strides and a street separated them.

"Where do you think you're going?" The creature soared like a puma with speed and power well beyond that of any human, but spoke like a person.

The young man ran from the alley.

His heart thumped rapidly, it seemed ready to explode. He felt the beast's snout huffing moist, foul breath down the back of his neck. Still, a fleeting smile crossed the young man's face. He had made it out of the alley and into the street. The creature, right behind, pinged from one building wall to another until it bounded down on top of the young man's back. It tackled him to the ground.

"Aaah!" the young man screamed out. The band played a long, last note louder to wake the few remaining patrons before the club's close. "Help me!" he said, face down, and on his stomach. He reached toward the club where his girlfriend stirred from her slumber. She stretched and yawned, pulling her head from off the table. She looked from side to side and around the club for her boyfriend, but she did not see him, so she sat and waited.

The creature stood on top of his back with heaviness. With four feet, it trampled on top of him. The beast constricted his breaths, and made simple movements impossible. Nevertheless, the young man slowly propped one elbow up and then awkwardly he braced the other. He struggled, crawling toward the club on his belly. Puzzled, the beast simply hopped off and dragged him by the ankle back toward the dark alley. The young man screamed. He flailed his legs, and frantically clawed at the cold street, grinding his fingernails against the abrasive ground.

The beast let forth a disgruntled growl. It raised a hand up and rapidly plunged icy hooks into the young man's soft flesh. The beast tamed the young man. It sank penetrating claws deep into the muscle fibers around his spine. The young man rang out a shrill cry, followed by a chilling shriek. From his back, a gush of red fluid oozed. With the last of his strength, the young man ripped his leg from the beast's hand and freed himself. He shouted toward the club. His voice hoarse, it strained from yelling. His vocal cords filled with his own blood. He needed someone to see him. He crawled on his belly. He hoped to be seen. His body was already broken, but now he had lost his spirit, too.

The creature ground its jaw full of sharp fangs back and forth. It seethed at the young man's resilience. The beast aggressively thrust another hand of razor-tipped, black talons into the young man's back. This time, with a more violent, cruel push, it twisted its claws.

The young man convulsed, his body jerking uncontrollably.

A snap echoed from his spinal column.

The young man's head and limbs flopped down.

His body lay broken and shattered. His skin took on a blanched paleness, but his eyes remained open, blankly staring not at, but through the club. The beast pulled him by the leg back into the alley, leaving a wide trail of bright, freshly smeared blood. Like a forgotten memory, both the young man and the beast disappeared into the night. His girlfriend crossed her arms and huffed. She waited and looked around from her seat. And the trumpeter's cheeks eased as the last note tempered into sweet silence.

Chapter Five

Later the next day, and just blocks away from the beastly attack near the club, Emma Rose was browsing some of the finest boutiques Paris, France, had to offer. She clamped her teeth, grinding them, while glaring at her mother.

A few months prior, Emma adored every thought about her first trip to Paris, telling her envious friends in Viola, Kansas, all of the wonderful things she was going to do while there. Now, here she was. This was the vacation city of her dreams, yet the same could not be said about her unwanted travel companion. Maybe some daughters enjoyed going on vacation with their mothers, but not Emma.

This, after all, was the city of lights. Love abounded, and beautiful couples made romantic gestures to each other on almost every street corner, or so Emma had seen on television. However, she...she felt like her mother's handbag from last season, clutched too tightly, worn out, and filled to the brim with needless things.

This was supposed to be *her* trip of a lifetime, not her mother's. Instead, she felt like her mother's clone. This was her coming of age experience, but it had turned into her mother's second go around as a teen instead. Emma was tired of her mother dragging her around the city. She felt smothered, never free, it seemed, to do what she wanted to do. And after two weeks of doing nothing, except what her mother wanted to do, it was time to return home in the morning from her frustrating vacation. So, with every look, Emma glared, with every word, she groaned, and with each thought, she dreaded with obsession the string of lies she'd have to tell her friends about her amazing trip to Paris.

Emma's mother hooked her arm inside of her own, attempting to lock them like chains. Her mother sipped her latte, hauling Emma down past the boutiques. "Oh, here, I want to take a picture." Her mother pulled out her phone, leaned up against Emma, and snapped a picture of them. Emma squinted and frowned. Her mother attempted to smile. "Oh, will you look at that."

"What?" Emma asked. She pouted. "I'm sure it's like a postcard or something," she said, glancing up and down the old Parisian street. Quaint park benches, manicured trees, and classic, seventeenth-century merchant shops filled the avenue. "I mean...we are in Paris," her voice carried notable irritation.

"Huh?" Her mother's attention diverted. "Oh, no, would you look at that!"

Emma pawed at the camera to see. "It looks great." She raised one eyebrow over the other.

"No, it doesn't. My chin looks terrible. My face is puffy." She felt around her cheeks. "And my nose looks fat. My cheeks...I had all of this work done and... uh, well, these cameras take the worst pictures. It's like going to the DMV." Her mother tossed her camera phone back into her purse.

With a squint of disgust, Emma reclaimed her arm. She frowned and mumbled under her breath, while the two window-shopped the latest trends of the season.

Emma looked up at her mother, and then at a reflection of herself. Emma was sick of everyone back home saying her mother used to look exactly like she does at her age now.

Her mother attempted to smile again. Emma sighed, shaking her head, staring, but not into the tiny boutique window on the bustling, overcrowded side street. She stared at her mother and herself in the window, swearing privately she would never turn into the woman standing next to her.

Emma pulled a piece of gum from her pocket. She methodically unwrapped the folded squares of paper. She then popped the gum in her mouth and watched all the beautiful people zip past them. She chewed the gum loudly, blowing bubbles, while wishing she could just stay there in that city forever, yet with mother not included.

Emma popped the gum repeatedly. She chewed and chomped, at first slowly, but then faster as her mother prattled on about the dismal details of her own disappointed life. She only stopped talking to occasionally glance at Emma for approval about the dress that she herself admired in the window. Her mother frowned, quickly whipping her phone out every few seconds, while scanning the street from side to side. Emma lazily blew large, pink bubblegum bubbles, popping them over again.

"Spit it out now!"

"Spit what out?"

"The gum, missy," her mother quickly searched for a napkin from her overcrowded purse. "It's unladylike."

Emma tightened her lips and rolled her eyes. "Um, whatever." She knew all too well about the first unspoken rule between mothers and daughters—mothers resent their daughters belonging to a certain age, and daughters hate their mothers for trying to live their teens all over again. Nevertheless, this remained unspoken, so she reached into her mouth and smeared the gum on the white napkin her mother held in front of her. "Happy now?" She crinkled her nose, protruded her lower lip, and tapered her eyes until they were resentful slits.

Her mother anxiously held an attempted smile. "Honey, you don't want these fine people thinking that you're uncouth."

"Why? It's not like I'm ever going to see them again anyway." Emma waited a moment. She crossed her arms, darting her resentful slits toward her mother. "Who are you trying to impress? I've seen you do lots worse..."

Her mother cut into Emma's sentence, diverting the conversation to more pleasant things. "I refuse to argue with you," she said, then abruptly changing tones, her mother tapped her raised chin with her index finger, before eagerly continuing, "Now what about that dress? Isn't it so rad? I think it would look cool on you. I'm getting you that dress." She pulled Emma by the hand and dragged her into the boutique. "You're going to try on that dress. I want to see how it fits."

After an eternity in the dressing room, Emma stomped out, wearing the dress, along with a smug grimace and furrowed brows.

"Okay, twirl around. I love it!" Her mother gave a short-handed, quiet clap. "I bet all of your friends back home will be jealous when they see," her mother said, smiling enviously, that is, until she noticed Emma had not even tried to put on the matching high heels, but rather, was still in her plaid socks and brightly colored, permanent marker patched sneakers.

Emma halfheartedly twirled. She bobbed her head from side to side. She kicked out her feet and hummed a tune. "La-tee-da. La-tee-da." She made every effort to rile her mother while in the boutique. "There, I'm done." She tossed her hands in the air. "This is totally stupid."

People looked. The shopkeeper tightened his once cheery expression into annoyance.

Emma's mother drew her legs together and placed her purse on her lap, with a tense smile and unnaturally straight posture, she uneasily caught eyes with the shopkeeper. Her smile froze and faded. She gently raised her finger in protest as if she were at a PTA meeting, but Emma kept loudly ranting about all things she currently hated.

"I don't want this dress!" Emma stomped. "Besides, my friends don't care about the junk you care about. They don't!" She pointed straight at her mother. "I'm in Paris and they're not." Emma told anyone listening before she trudged toward the dressing room, wishing to change back into her comfortable jeans and shirt, while her rant continued from behind the curtain's veil. "My friends don't care about some crappy dress, please!" She slid the fine dress to the floor, not even hanging it. Emma carelessly emerged, forcefully pushing back the curtain, its metal rings scratching against the steel rod above the changing booth.

Emma stormed past her mother and out of the boutique.

Her mother remained rigid, her thighs clenched together in her seat, while white knuckling her purse. Looking down at the floor, her mother departed as well. She cleared her throat. "Ahem." She gave a weary smile.

The shopkeeper picked the dress from off the floor, hanging it back in the window before shooting a disapproving frown at mother and daughter.

Unlike Emma, her mother pretended. They stood outside the boutique. This time her mother crossed her arms, and the two remained uncomfortably silent.

Emma stood in the street and stared at the recently hung dress for a moment. It was a nice dress. It felt good, but it looked like something her mother wanted her to wear. The gray clouds gathered above and behind her. She readied to move on, yet in that moment, she looked upon her own drab, shapeless reflection in the paned glass. She hated her own appearance. Her lackluster brown hair plainly tied back in a straight, dull ponytail. Her face, though not ugly, was lacking any type of distinguishing attractive features. She straightened the wrinkles from her shirt. Emma lamented as she watched, through the reflection of the boutique window, many curvy, voluptuous women elegantly walk up and down the street behind her. Even her mother had cosmetically enhanced her appearance. Her skin was so tight, her mother had ruined her ability to smile, at least for a time, yet she inflated her own self-worth, but in the process, carelessly damaged Emma's.

With her hands pressed tightly on her hips, her mother replied, "Well, what's gotten into you?"

"Chillax, will ya." Emma sighed, avoiding eye contact. Her tone turned a mixture of downhearted and cross. "I wanted to come to Paris more than anything, but I didn't want to hang with you the entire time."

Her mother batted her eyes, with plowed brows of furrowed ire, but then she upturned a single eyebrow. "Oh, I know what this is all about."

"Yeah, right." Emma indignantly hinted surprise. "Wait, what...you do?"

"Why of course I do." Her mother dug through her oversized suitcase disguised as a purse. "Here," she handed Emma a granola bar. "You're just cranky because your blood sugar is low again."

"It is not!" Emma faced her mother. The skin along the bridge of her nose crumpled, nearly touching her sharply creased eyebrows. She slammed her hands on her own hips. Her mother extended the granola bar toward her, but Emma released a hand, slapping the wrapped treat to the ground. "Ugh, you just don't get it, do you?" she yelled. Her arms flung up and around into the air. "No, you, you're my problem. I want my space!" She overlapped her arms, spinning, she turned away from her mother. "You're always the problem," she mumbled.

Her mother, cheeks flushed, had finally ceased speaking, while Emma enjoyed a brief moment of silence, before slowly turning back toward the shop window just to smirk at her mother's reflection. Yet the enjoyment wore thin, for the harder Emma tried, the more she thought about tomorrow, about leaving, and that's when she noticed the gorgeous boy in the window.

Chapter Six

Emma tilted her head. He stared back on through. She tried to figure where he was without turning to look. He wasn't in the store, but was across the street behind her. Emma, having just turned fourteen, believed that he looked to be around her age, if not a few years older. He brazenly eyed her up and down as he leaned against a small tree. He flirted brashly with her through the window's reflection.

He wasn't like any of the boys she knew back home. He seemed confident and mature. And from what she could tell, his skin was perfect. There wasn't even a pimple in sight.

He was tall and lean. His jet-black hair was short, except for the shaggy, side-swept locks nearly covering his eyebrows. He was a clean, purposely jumbled mess to most adults, yet many girls walking past found him pleasing to the eye. His clothing flashed style, appearing new yet purposely faded, but vintage, with a revolutionary theme. He casually ignored the random stares by the crowd of finely dressed, older observers. They gawked at his fresh-from-bed look, but with a couldn't-care-less expression, he defiantly stared back, making them uncomfortable as they passed by.

With a posh attitude, he rubbed his side-swept locks quickly up and down. He teemed with self-confidence, indignantly dismissing all who walked by him with a charming candor. He took a last puff of his self-rolled cigarette, passionately blowing rings of leisurely expanding smoke into the air. He boldly dropped the cigarette's remaining end, crushing it under his foot, littering the clean ground, while a trashcan sat mere feet in front of him.

Their eyes met and locked through the reflection in the glass. Each read the other's glance. He lacked emotion, but Emma found that alluring. She looked around for another girl, but it was just her he was admiring, so she smiled.

For most of the day, a thick overcast clouded the skyline, cutting off the top of the Eiffel Tower with a pocket of hazy, chilled air. And though there had been many sunny days since she had arrived in Paris, this was the first time Emma's cheeks flamed a reddish tint.

"Are you even listening to me?" her mother scolded, annoyed and oblivious. She wagged her index finger back and forth.

"Huh? What?"

"I knew it. The whole time I was talking, you've been ignoring me."

"Um." Emma abandoned her sentence. She felt unsteady. Her mood wavered. She felt good. In that moment, nothing else really mattered. She lent her full attention to the hot boy with the piercing look. "Nah...no," she briefly stuttered. "I wasn't ignoring you. Go on, the granola bar...right?" She trailed off near the end.

"Oh, forget it!" Her mother shook her head, clamped her jaw, and began texting on her phone. "You think that I'm such a terrible mother, don't you?" Her fingers typed fast. Her attention equally diverted. "Tell me. What other fourteen-year-old girl from Viola, Kansas, gets to go to Paris on a whim?"

"Whatever, Mom." Emma darted her eyes toward her mother and let loose her tongue. "You wanted this trip more than I did. Just because this is what you wanted when you were fourteen, doesn't mean it's what I want now." She smirked, pressing a known nerve ending. "But your poor little mommy couldn't afford to take you to Paris." She curled a tight smile with a self-satisfied expression, enjoying her pithy remark.

Her mother stuck her nose high and away. She huffed loudly out her nostrils, making a slight whistling sound. She pulled out her phone and madly texted. "Yeah, well, I could have brought Jody instead of you. She REALLY wanted to come you know."

"HA!" Emma laughed. "Jody, your four-hundred-pound BFF from your old high school?" Emma covered her mouth and chuckled, glancing up at her mother, hoping to elicit a response. "Yeah, right." No reply immediately came, as her mother continued texting, so Emma kept talking. "You would've had to book half the plane to accommodate her fat ass, and you didn't get enough money from Dad in the divorce to pay for that." She stopped laughing. Agitated, she glared directly at her mother. "Though I'm sure you'll try to get more out of Dad once we get home. Hey! Listen to me!" She stomped her foot. Her arms straightened with elbows locked by her side. Her wrists bent outward as her fingers curved inward. Her whole body quaked with rage. "Who are you talking to?" she demanded. "I know it isn't me, 'cause I'm right here, you witch."

"Stop it!" Her mother's face turned several hues of pinkish red, though not a wrinkle could be found amongst the Botox. "And you watch your mouth!" Then she calmed. Putting her phone away, she noticed people both inside the shop and on the street glancing, and some gawking, but all with eyes of judgmental displeasure. "Listen, you're right. Why don't we spend some time apart on our last day here?" Easing her tense shoulders down and relaxing her back, she held her rebuke, feigning a sweet smile instead, partly for her daughter, but mostly for the couple sitting at a street-side table nearby. "You're stressing me out." She continued. "You can only go up and down this street where the shops are." She moved her index fingers back and forth from the top of the street to the end far past them. "And be back at the hotel before dark," she tapped the clock on her phone, "so that leaves you about...three hours to do whatever you want." She smiled faintly, stroking Emma's hair as she did.

"Whatever." Emma yanked her head from her mother's reach. "The real reason you didn't bring Jody is because she can't afford all of your plastic upgrades." With falling eyes and folded arms, she refocused her restless gaze on the reflection of the fascinating boy behind her across the street. He gave her a wary glance. He seemed to pose simply for effect, leaning against the public tree, appearing to claim it as his own.

Her mother snapped her fingers, turned her head opposite her daughter, held her arm straight, and raised her palm up to Emma's face. "Oh, no you didn't. Talk to the hand."

Emma unfolded her arms and twiddled her thumbs. She looked away, arousing intense dislike with a set of rolling eyes up and away. "Yeah, okay, Mom."

Her mother lowered her arm on a whim, and pulled out a mirror from her purse instead. She affixed her eyes with a favoring glance of herself. Applying lipstick, she angled her cheeks from side to side for a better view. She centered the mirror, touching features on her face that she enjoyed, almost overlooking everything around her for a brief moment. "Why can't you just grow up?" she said, approving her own image.

Emma drew a long breath. "I was just about to say the same thing to you."

Her mother, now conscious of her surroundings again, stiff-necked, straight-backed, her feet regimented side by side on the ground, darted a quick look toward the table where people had been sitting, but had since left. Her eyes narrowed. She clicked shut the mirror, slipping it away. "You think I'm a terrible mother or something, don't you?" Her glazing eyes shunned Emma's gaze.

Emma, her chin touching her chest, gave a distrustful glance up at her mother, and begrudgingly said, "No, I just think..."

Her mother rapidly interrupted, hearing only the part she wished.

"Good, then it's settled. We both agree. I'm not a terrible mother." She had a self-satisfied smile.

Emma mumbled lowly, "I was going to say, I just think you're selfish."

If her mother had heard the last mumble, she did not show it. "I'm going out to a club with some friends tonight, and you," she pointed her long fingernail, "had better be in before I leave to go out."

"What? You're letting me actually do my own thing for once?"

"Don't be smart." Her mother said in a commanding tone. "But, yes. And remember, I know how you think, so you can't get one over on me." Yet the entire time, she failed to notice Emma's budding, captured attention between mutual gazes with an older boy just feet behind them.

Chapter Seven

Impulsive, piercing looks were exchanged at high rates between Emma and the older boy in the window's reflection. The fact that they shared this in front of her mother made it harder for them to look away. After a while, he became a mysterious thing. Even when he hunched forward to stretch, it was beautifully significant.

They seemed to have an unspoken language of their own. Everything he did appeared to designate and signify a meaning to Emma. Each met the other with wondering eyes, more powerful than forces of reason and logic. He appeared bold, striding, and confident. Emma, on the other hand, bowed her head and folded her hands, but by degrees, the stress lines on her forehead eased in chorus with his subtle gestures of interest.

"Now here's some extra money." Her mother unknowingly interrupted the moment, shoving crumpled pieces of currency in Emma's half-open hands. "Ugh! I hate carrying cash." She opened her arms for a hug. "Are we friends again?"

Emma drew back while counting the money. "Oh, yeah," she facetiously said, looking only at the crinkly paper as she unfolded the bills. "Best friends forever, Mom." Emma squeezed the money tightly in her hand. "You're so stinking cheap! Dad would have given me more, ya know." She scowled a devious grin.

"I'm not cheap!" She rubbed the top of Emma's head. "I've always tried to be your best friend," she then rummaged through her purse, "but this isn't little ol' Viola, Kansas, it's a very big, foreign city, and a young girl can get in lots of trouble before she knows it, especially if people know she has money." Her mother looked from side to side before attempting a frown. She then reached deeper into her purse, pulling out and handing Emma some more crinkled bills.

Emma scrambled to grab fistfuls of cash. She fanned the money toward her mother. "Yeah, yeah, Mom, whatever. Stop telling me what to do, I'm fourteen, okay. I know what I'm doing." She extended her lower lip and then stiffened her mouth with an offended glare.

"No, I'm being serious." Her mother's voice deepened. "There was this thing on the local news last night. A couple of city workers found the body of this twenty-year-old girl dead in the sewers under Paris." Her mother kept fishing through her purse.

"So, that stuff happens everywhere these days," Emma casually replied. "That's just how the world is. It doesn't mean it's going to happen to me."

"Yeah, but the weird thing was, the city workers said they'd just been down there the day before."

"Again, so, what's your point?"

"Well...here's the creepy part. Everything she was wearing looked fresh and new, but her face and body was all like shriveled up as if she had been rotting there for months." Her mother, eyes glued downward, pushed lipsticks, foundations, and eyeliners to the side of her purse, finally reaching its bottom. "Great, I'm out of money!" her mother exclaimed, with a showy display of irritation she stomped the ground. "Now I have to go back to the room for more money." Frustrated by distraction, she began mumbling to herself, still digging, fishing, and moving things about in her purse. She then turned and walked toward the end of the small street and back up to the larger main road. She glanced briefly over her shoulder at Emma, attempting a smile through her Botox-tightened skin. Her lips held straight, making an uncomfortably odd smile. "Remember, be back at the hotel by six o'clock, okay, honey?"

"Um," Emma muttered and groaned.

"I said...okay!"

"Sure!" Emma said aloud. She mumbled the rest. "I guess, whatever, as long as you don't tell me that stupid, creepy story about the girl in the sewer ever again." Frowning, she closed her eyes and shuddered, and then glared down the street at her mother. "For god's sake, leave," she whispered under her breath.

"Good," her mother shouted, looking back for approval as she walked away.

Emma huffed. "Hello, you can go now." She waved the back of her hand with a sweeping motion and a belittling smirk.

Seeing only what she wanted, her mother turned back around and sped toward Emma. "How about a quick hug?" She opened her arms wide.

"Uh, yeah, no thank you. People are like, watching." Emma quickly glanced only at the hot boy. They caught eyes for the first time without the safety of a reflection between them. With her mother's back facing him, he blew Emma a kiss, and her cheeks warmed an instant pale pink.

Emma wrestled her mother's grabby, locked upper limbs, warding off her outstretched arms once again. She raised her hands in clenched frustration, slapping her mother's hands down and away with a hard chopping motion. She finally turned her back completely on her mother. "Can you just go?" Emma abruptly said. She took a defiant stance. She pretended to look in the boutique window where the dress she tried on for her mother hung unworn once again.

"Okay." Her mother swung her head back, taking melancholy strides in the direction she had come. She finally walked up the street, around the last corner shop, and then out of view.

Emma relaxed with a deep purging sigh, blowing out a loud puff. She focused on the window and the dress, but only for the reflection it offered, yet the hot boy gazing back had vanished.

"God, I hate that selfish friggin' cow," she slurred angrily to herself, "but at least she's gone. I hate..."

A strong male voice with a slight French accent interrupted. "I hate that dress, too. That's what you were going to say, right?"

Emma swung to one side and then to the other. He was right there. They were face to face. She gulped and bit down on her lower lip. "Oh, totally, yeah." She bobbed her head in agreement, flipping and blowing her long, brown, stringy hair off her face.

"Your mother's right. A fourteen-year-old girl can get into a lot of trouble in Paris." He leaned over as he whispered the rest. His warm lips neared the outer portion of her ear. "But it's awfully fun." He pulled back and grinned with a deviant sort of charm.

She got her first glance at his ink. One was a tattoo of a black and red scorpion, behind his ear, on the back of his neck. "I...um, I gotta go...I mean, I should be somewhere else." Her stomach felt unsettled. She was attracted and repulsed at the same time.

"What? Don't you like the way I look?" He opened his arms, pulling up his long sleeves. His arms were inked on both sides up and down to his elbows and beyond. He glanced from side to side at his own black velvet sports coat and white t-shirt with the French flag colorfully plastered across his chest with a single, messy dyed design.

Looking down and away, she beamed with flaming cheeks. "No, I mean, yeah, you look totally fine." Emma tucked long, stringy, brown strands of hair behind her ear. "I can't believe I just said that, what I meant was..."

He interrupted by quickly kissing her lips. She slapped his face and then he backed from his bold advance. She turned, looking at the dress in the window, pretending as if nothing had happened at all, and so did he. Stunned by his daring move, she remained motionless for a moment, and the two stood side by side looking at the dress in the window together.

"I didn't take you for the shy type." His cool did not waver, and his poise persisted. "Well, now that we got that out of the way, my name's Killian," he said with little emotion.

Emma wanted to be outraged by this scoundrel, but his kiss had left her feebly craving another one from him. With a faint blush, she unconsciously mimicked his stance. Not able to hold her feelings in, she broke her silence. "Whoa, have you ever heard of boundaries?" she ranted, yet instinctual feelings darted a swift, inquiring look his way.

"It's your last night in Paris, no?" He got close and played with her stringy hair. "This is the city of lights and of love." With his lips near her cheek, he said, "Your hair is as fine as silk." He whispered the next words in her ear. "I can show you some things that aren't on any tour guide map. Things that your friends back home won't believe...things, I dare say...you'll never see again."

She tried to be mad at him, but he was thrilling, attractive, and had a certain allure with a magical hold.

"Oh, what the hell," Emma said, leaning in for another pass.

They passionately kissed along the crowded street, and Killian became even more desirable to the eye.

"I've always wanted to taste France." She ran her tongue over her own lips. "I think I like it...a lot. I've French kissed before, but I've never actually French kissed a French boy while actually being in France. Now that's something to write home about," she confidently stated, smirking, her eyes lighting toward his with thoughts of delight.

Killian reserved his cool, only floating a single eyebrow in return.

The rest of that day, Emma and Killian toured museums and gardens as they ate, drank, and breathed in the best that Paris had to offer on her mother's five-hundred-dollar budget. He led her by the hand, occasionally twirling her toward him on a whim, dipping her in public, while they danced all over the city streets. She laughed, giggled, played, and devoured attention as she never had before. Killian wildly kissed her neck and caused mischief wherever they went, and she loved it. On several occasions, guards chased them out of galleries and shops for exposing amorous episodes.

Emma had never felt so free from her brittleness. She hated her life back in Kansas, and she wanted to stay here with Killian forever. Emma adored him. She felt a natural attraction, and a longing to be near him always. However, Killian's words did not match his gestures, and he remained affectedly nonchalant about her.

There was something about Killian. There was something more than just his attractive features that both freed and corrupted Emma. Though she could not explain, nor understand, she felt as if they had known each other for much longer than a few hours. He helped her abolish all doubt, and side by side, they captured Paris. The ambiance of the city lights were now their lights. The lovers embracing on every poster became portraits of them in her eyes.

The hours sped by like grains of dwindling sand in a bottom-heavy hourglass. Before long, as Emma had promised her mother, it was time to leave his company and go back to the hotel. With simultaneous confliction, her hand slowly slid apart from his, but their eyes remained affixed, long after they had stopped touching hands.

The two of them hopped the next trolley. Once packed aboard the full and swaying ride, their passion dimmed. Cramped between strangers, Emma and Killian turned away from each other.

Instead, they each silently grieved the beautiful city as tall lampposts blinked one after the other, announcing night's fall. Emma watched while clinging to the trolley safety bar. Her heart now like sandpaper, Emma wiped a stray saline drop from her cheek as the sky broke open rays of heavenly splendor near dusk.

The gloomy mist atop the Eiffel Tower dissipated and a sudden warm torrent of light covered the sides of their faces. Two faces now half-dark, half-bright, half-sweet, half-sad, stared into the other. Meanwhile, the whole city transformed from gray into a glimmering, crystalline gold. A southerly breeze kicked up, invading the streets with rushing air. The swift gusts drove clouds in retreat. The sky opened for the first time that day, and stars clustered a brilliant show at twilight. A new moon left nothing to drown the stellar parade gifted above, ending Emma's perfect day. Her heart all but eclipsed the breaking dawn of artificial sparkle, which Paris now buzzed. Lampposts shimmered white dots off the long river beside them, and combated the growing darkness taking siege over the city.

People filtered off at each stop. Among the now less than half filled trolley, Emma broke the silence, turning toward Killian at the day's last light.

"You showed me more in the last few hours than I've seen in my entire life." Emma's bottom lip quivered. "I don't wanna leave." She rested her head on his shoulder and watched the lights twinkle and dance off the river, occasionally glancing up for a non-verbal response. "What are you thinking?" She tried to read his emotions, but she mistook stoic for distant when he simply put his arm around her waist.

Killian said nothing. He was icy, without a trace of emotion washing over his surface. His carefree, cheerful manner was gone, replaced by a group of rigid, unconscious body movements. And as the trolley approached her stop, he still said nothing, but panted, moving air forth with labored compression.

Emma gently pulled a tiny yellow flower from her hair, and thread it through Killian's empty jacket buttonhole. With a brief downward peek, Killian tightened his lower lip. Emma prattled on about her life back home, sighing deep from her belly whenever her mother entered the story. As they neared the glitzy hotel, the trolley brakes made a low, hard grind and slowed to a stop at their regal front gates.

Killian was staying on the trolley, having no intention of talking or looking at Emma again. "This is your stop," he said, his voice chilly, his expression frozen.

Emma shook her head. Her two hands wrapped around his limp arm. "You gave me a really nice day, the best ever." With eyes asquint, her voice spun frustration. "Why are you being like this?" She dropped his arm.

Killian flashed a radiant look, but forced a smile all the same. It was his first smile since they got on the trolley. "I'm a cad you know." The driver rang the stop bell. Killian held onto the trolley's bar with one hand, and with his free arm, he pulled her chest to chest and cheek to cheek. "You probably shouldn't stay, but don't leave."

"What? I have to."

"Maybe, but then again, maybe not."

"Don't do this."

"Do what?"

"Make me leave sad and lonely." Emma hung her head with falling eyes and a sigh.

"You've bewitched me." Killian's eyes gleamed.

"I can't..."

"Fine, go then." Killian withdrew his offer. "Your mother's waiting."

Emma leaned back against the trolley's inner side panel. She raised one eyebrow, while lowering the other. "I don't understand you," she said with a befuddled headshake.

"What's to understand?" He playfully teased. "You're afraid for this to end. You're afraid for us to end." Killian deviously half grinned.

"This?" Emma aimed her forefinger and thumb back and forth. "What is this anyway?"

"Whatever you want it to be."

The trolley driver yelled. "Okay kids, wrap it up. It's getting late and I have to get this thing back to the station."

They were unfazed, neither detaching their affixed eyes from one another. Killian reached for her hand, caressing it with his soft pads. Emma faintly blushed.

"Ya know...until today, I was always available, but unwanted," Emma plainly said.

Killian held a brief, intimate silence. "I'm a poet, and poets always want the best." The back of his hand caressed her cheek.

"You said you were a cad." Emma smiled, closing her eyes and leaning into his touch. "What's a cad anyway?"

Killian held the back of her head against his shoulder. His eyes peered off in contemplation. "I'm both a poet and a cad." He brushed his hand down her neck. "A cad is a man who wants to write the finest poetry you can take back to America and always remember him by."

Emma hesitated. "I can't."

"Listen, after your mom goes out for the night, come back, and see me one last time. I still have places to show you." He gently refused her no with a devilish smile.

"I don't know..."

"Trust me, if not for my wonderful poetry, then you need to see the catacombs under the city streets of Paris before you leave."

The driver leaned over the back of his seat. "Don't make me come back there."

Still they ignored him.

"What's in the catacombs?" Emma peeled away, glanced down, and then back up at him. "Wait, wasn't some girl just found dead in some place like that?"

"No." Killian scoffed. "Don't believe everything you hear." He raised her hand to his mouth, gently kissing it as he caressed her fingertips. "I have something amazing to show you, and I promise that once you see it, you'll never be the same again."

Emma sighed. She grieved their parting, and even the relaxed luxury of the ritziest hotel in the city felt uncomfortable somehow.

The trolley driver grew hot with anger. Emma looked up at the third floor window of the hotel. It was her room. She saw the silhouette of her mother peering down at her from behind the drapes. She quickly hooked her elbow around Killian's neck, pulling his collar down, revealing his black and red scorpion ink, opening her mouth, crashing lips, and enfolding her tongue around his. She glared defiantly up at the silhouette. Unlocking from Killian, Emma jumped off the swaying trolley.

Killian stayed aboard the trolley as it started rolling again, past the glitzy, majestic hotel. He sulked at their bitter departure, yet smiled at the sweet-tasting, tawdry laced kiss Emma planted across his tender skin. His eyes a daze, two fingertips slowly rubbed while his tongue extended for a lick over his own lips. Emma's grape-flavored balm now smeared tastily, with an aroma of fresh bounty on and all over him. He watched her as she carelessly pranced and trotted away from him and toward the hotel's main lobby.

Just short of the hotel's doors, Emma stopped, turned, and cupped a hand at the corner of her mouth, shouting, "I'll be there!"

Killian twirled one foot and one arm off the trolley, nearly falling off. He held a single hand on the bar as it drove away, while yelling back, "Meet me at the dress shop, *ma chère*." He rode the side of the trolley as if he were windsurfing a rising tide of emotions. He waved with all smiles and Emma watched him until she could no longer see the trolley among all of the other traffic intermingled along the busy street.

Chapter Eight

Later that evening, Emma lay with the top half of her back off the bed. With her head and shoulders upside down, her hair hung over the blanket's edge. She anxiously flipped through the television channels in rapid succession. Her mother had been in the bathroom for what seemed like hours, fiddling with her hair, dress, earrings, and makeup.

While curling the ends of her long, straight locks, her mother stuck her head out the bathroom door. "Honey, could you turn that down for a minute, I can't hear myself think."

"What!?" Emma shouted, increasing the volume instead.

"I said...could you turn down the T.V.?" her mother yelled this time.

Emma ignored her mother, but she herself was keenly aware of the time. Her eyes were glued to her phone. Emma stared at the clock on her phone and the wall, and with each tick, angst and tension matured unbearably.

Time appeared to both race by and stand still. Emma compulsively chewed on her thumbnail in expectation of seeing Killian again, spitting the tiny slivers onto the floor. Her heart aflutter, she could not get him out of her mind. She obsessed over his beautiful façade and fluid, uncomplicated movements. She knew he was different from any other boy she had ever met before, and yet, she did not know exactly why she felt the way she did. But, she also did not care why she did not know, for all it seemed she ever wanted now was him. Emma just knew she had to see him again, and soon, or else she would explode.

Emma rolled her eyes toward the direction of the bathroom where her mother readied. "God," she groaned, in quiet frustration, "what the hell is taking you so long?"

The bathroom fan whirled, rattling an inconsistent hum from above. Her mother raised her voice, calling out. "Honey, could you come in here and help me zip up this stupid dress?"

Irritated, Emma sat up, looked at the clock, and then tossed the television remote to the floor. She sighed longingly, and waited for her mother to call again, this time dragging herself, feet shuffling, forward into the bathroom.

Emma clenched her teeth and quickly grabbed the silver zipper, tugging it forcefully upward on her mother's short, overly formfitting, tight red dress. The zipper was stuck. Biting her tongue, she tussled with the zipper, pinching her fingers with white knuckled grip.

"Geesh, Mom...put on a few pounds since we've been here?" Her eyes stable, they focused on the silver zipper, tussling to pull it up. "You better lay off on the truffles if you ever want to get in this dress again." Emma huffed, smirking behind her mother's back.

"Stop it! Don't be rude. You stop those horrible comments right this instant!" Her mother wiggled her body forward. "And be careful with the zipper or you'll break it." She reached blindly behind, awkwardly trying to grab the zipper away from her daughter. "You don't talk to your friends like that and you shouldn't talk to me like that either. Besides, I work out five days a week. I'll just work out more when I get back home."

"Whatever...or maybe you can just get Dad to buy you some more liposuction."

"Stop it! Stop it! Stop it!" Her mother slammed her pink hairbrush on the sink, cracking the brush in half.

Emma knew her night with Killian was only possible if her mother went out, and at this rate, it was almost a total wash. Emma instantly changed her tone. For her mother to go out, she had to feel good, and Emma wanted her mother to feel just good enough to leave.

"Say," Emma asked with a slightly interested nature. "Where are you going tonight anyway?"

"Oh, stop being patronizing!" Her mother snorted angrily.

Emma said with a sincere tone, "No, I really want to know."

"Really?"

"Yeah, you're my mom and my best friend, and I want to make sure that you're safe, too."

The two shared a laugh and a hug. "I'm going to this really nice restaurant with a friend," her mother said with a relaxed ease.

"What friend?" Emma put her hand over her mouth, her eyes open wide. "You didn't tell me about any new friends." Emma pretended to giggle, while pulling straight the coarse top fabric of her mother's short, tight red dress. The zipper loosened, releasing its way, and sliding with one relaxed tug up to the top. "OMG, you've got a date, don't you?"

"Maybe." Her mother smiled, pulling at the bottom of the red dress, smoothing the lines and bumps on the fabric, after which, she pushed up, with both hands, under her bosoms, until she looked precisely how she imagined.

Emma stood beside her, putting her arm around her shoulder. "You look beautiful. Say, whatever happened to 'don't trust men,' you know, after you and Dad split?"

"This is different." She twisted away from her daughter's arm. "You're going to wrinkle my dress and mess up my hair." She fluffed her hair upward as she continued to talk. "I'm just going out to have some fun. Ralyo makes me feel young again." Her eyes swelled with the mention of his name.

Emma tilted her head down and pretended to vomit. "You're making me sick. Will you just go already?" The corners of her lips quirked upward, but the rest of her face did not smile.

Still, her mother saw only what she wanted as she contoured the final touches of color to her cheeks. She hummed a song while applying eyeliner, after, standing back a step, gazing at her own lovely image in the mirror. "Just because I'm a divorced single mom, doesn't mean I can't have some fun."

Emma knew her mother's self-absorbed sureness was intact again, and that was a good thing, so she went back to her bed, and started flipping through the television channels and just waited. She counted the seconds as they loudly ticked by. She synced the clock on the wall to her phone. Time drove her mad, so she impulsively threw her phone across the room. Emma then scrambled to find her phone. Her stress level rose until she dug it out from under the dresser, after which, she put her phone in her back pocket.

Her mother unexpectedly walked out of the bathroom, threading her earring as she passed Emma's room. Her mother stopped, looked in on Emma, and narrowed her eyes, giving a quick look in at her daughter, but soon continued walking toward the closet to choose an evening coat.

"So, who were you talking to down at the trolley?" her mother asked from the other room.

"No one, and besides, ever heard of privacy?"

"Nothing's private between friends."

"Stop being so controlling!" Emma shouted. "Ugh!"

"I'm your friend," her mother meekly replied. "I'm not trying to control you."

"Dad never sneaks up on me and asks me a bunch of stupid questions."

Her mother, now with jacket on, silently waited by the hallway door and pondered if she should even go out at all. Something did not feel right. But still, she brushed aside her doubts, fishing for her own phone, looking at the passing time along with a flurry of recent texts. Shaking her head, her mother looked back toward Emma's room. She arched her lips downward at the corners, shaping a frown. She then grabbed a handbag that matched her red dress. "I'm going to trust you...I'm going to trust that you'll keep your promise and not leave this building once I'm gone." Her mother tilted her head up in the direction of her daughter, yet no answer came. Rather, just silence enveloped the room. "Are you alive in there?"

"Yesss...I heard you!" Emma growled. "Now go, I just want some time to myself, that's all," she said as she nervously watched the clock. Mumbling the rest to herself, she continued, "Just leave you fat, ugly cow."

Her mother smiled, stretched her neck around the corner, and blew a kiss at her daughter. "Don't wait up. Oh, and feel free to order whatever you want from room service for supper." She then strolled from the room entirely, her six-inch heels clicking on a piece of metal floor panel leading out into the hotel hallway like a hammer smacking a nail. She hummed a song, the same song she hummed in the bathroom earlier, as she read a text from her phone and left the hotel room for the night.

Emma rolled off the bed and started rifling through her suitcase, which was tightly packed for tomorrow's trip back home. She tossed clothes here and there, to this side and that, and soon her wears heaped up a volcano of fabric, covering the entire floor. She picked up a low-cut shirt, scanning it from front to back, and then laid it on the bed, along with her favorite pair of hip-hugging jeans, rainbow-colored socks, and favorite sneakers.

She ran to the bathroom and tied her hair up, then down, once to the side, and then down again before she clipped it up on top of her head. She pulled her phone from her pocket and quickly checked the time, racing from one room to the next.

She dressed until she got to the front door, one piece at a time, and when she was out in the hallway, she put on her shoes and bolted from the room. From there, Emma ran down to the lobby, and out to the main road, waving her hand vigorously and flagging down a cab.

An anxious, uneasy knot formed in the pit of her stomach. Her imagination reconstructed every inch of Killian's gorgeous face, and over the last couple of hours, she had recreated every little part of him perfectly, making her trip more than surreal and rather agonizingly pleasurable.

She was finally on her way to see him again. She could not believe this was really happening, and she did not care if she ever saw her mother's face again, as long as her own eyes gazed upon Killian's embellished form once more.

Chapter Nine

The cab ride seemed endless, yet flew by in a blur. The amazing city was drab and boring now as she waited, sitting on the edge of the cab's back seat. Killian was all Emma fawned over the whole ride. She passively scanned faces in the dark city, yet only saw apparitions of him in those walking along the street.

Engrossed with the memory of his lips, eyes, nose, she dreamt of more, and in a stupor, Emma yelled out, grabbing the back of the cabdriver's seat. The driver slammed on the brakes. The car's suspension sprang forward with a hard jerk, and then back with screeching rubber tires to pavement. Emma vaulted forward. Upon rapid deceleration, her neck whipped and her wrists bent as she braced against the cabdriver's front seat. Emma rubbed the deep muscle sting around her collar, but she did not care about the pain, for she had almost missed her stop.

The frustrated driver scowled a glare from the rear-view mirror. Emma threw money at the driver, and jumped from the cab.

She walked halfway down a familiar street, but the flickering buzz of the lampposts, and the shadows they cast, made even the boutique window where she first met Killian appear strangely different somehow.

Emma was anxiously annoyed that she was there first. She felt lonely, and unsure. And even more so when Killian was nowhere to be found. She checked her phone. As far as she was concerned, she was still mostly on time, give or take fifteen minutes, but he was not there. She glanced up and down the empty side street, yet Killian was not present.

A while passed, and a few seconds poured into many minutes. Several busy couples walked the lanes past her, disappearing into a host of doors along an extended chain of shops, clubs, and restaurants. One entangled duo passionately strolled by, their hands held close, their arms wrapped around each other, their faces touching cheek to cheek. The tangled lovers hardly noticed another thing while walking from city lights into pocket shadows along the once eventful, but now solemn lane.

Evening had settled under a fallen black sky. Paris, once bustling and energetic, now slowed to a relaxed mood and leisurely pace. Of those around, chic, tight dresses, high heels, fragrant cologne, along with contoured hairgel, overwhelmed Emma's vision, hearing, and smell. All that was left of her five senses was to taste and touch and Emma craved the last of her unfulfilled senses badly. She liked it, and wished to do what they were all doing.

Where the city's merchants clamored with customers, restaurants, and clubs, now swarmed a tide of loud music. Exciting temptations abounded with pleasures not far up from where she stood, but where she stood quietly, the discreet air of melancholy surrounded her, if not without, then within.

The shops had all closed for the day. A distant streetlamp refracted light into the nearest shop booth, catching Emma's attention, and by chance, she saw the dress her mother wanted to buy her. It sparkled, but hung lifelessly on display through the uneven, square panels of the boutique window.

She pulled out her phone, frowning for a time, before peering to the left and right, but Killian was neither up nor down the deserted lane. Emma sighed of fleeting sadness while looking at the dress, then shrugged her shoulders, and clenched her jaw in a moment of rage. She paced back and forth, mumbling with heavy breath. Clarity revealed itself, so Emma ceased pacing and ambled over to the window with the dress, pouting, she put her nose and forehead to the cold glass, staring up into the window from a set of fallen eyes.

"I guess it's not totally ugly," she quietly confirmed to herself. She placed her fingertips on the outward condensation of the store window. With her index finger, she outlined the dress's bell-shaped form in her accidental vapors along the glass. The night settled in and cooled her warm breath, slightly chilling her skin. With a shiver, Emma left smudged fingerprints, turning dense mist into solid drops of water sent trickling down the glass boutique window. She closed her eyes and leaned her head sideways against the window, scratching her fingernails to the glass up and down over again.

Emma sniffled, and then blew a long, warm puff on the cold glass, drawing two vertical parallel lines, and an upside-down arch. After, she encircled the two lines and arch until a sad face appeared in the moisture she created for herself. She puffed until she clouded her view of the dress her mother loved on the other side of the boutique window.

A pair of strong hands wrapped themselves around her waist from behind as an unseen kiss approached her blindside. She turned around. To her outrage, fear, and surprise, it was not Killian at all. Rather, it was an old, heavily intoxicated man instead.

"Eww, get away from me." She pushed him back with both arms.

The drunkard puckered his lips, and grabbed ahold, reaching out to hug her, he pulled her close to him. "Come here and kiss me, my sweet." His kerosene-smelling, dry, cracked lips were just inches away from hers.

Chapter Ten

"No!" Emma screamed, turning her head, she stretched her neck far from his smelly face. She swung her hands, flailing them for freedom.

Powerful hands reached up and held her forearms in the air. Emma's eyes fastened shut, she was now defenseless, and so she fretted. She fearfully peeked at morbid, unwanted things to come. However, there came a surprising view instead.

"Emma. Emma! It's okay. I took care of him." Killian pointed to the drunken man, now slumped over, unconscious, his back facing them, lying sideways on the street. "I'm here now, and you're safe."

Shaken, her whole body trembling, Emma pulled away for a moment. "Well...where the hell were you!?"

"I'm sorry I'm late, do you forgive me?" Killian hooked his index finger under her chin, gently raising her face until their eyes met.

She quickly wiped a stray tear from her cheek. "I guess...I was on time, ya know." She rushed into his safe arms, hugging his chest. "Don't let it happen again." Emma propped her head on Killian's broad shoulder. "He tried to kill me."

"I doubt it," Killian replied. "There's a lot of drunk, old fools around here at night, but they're pretty harmless." He half smirked.

Protruding her lower lip outward, Emma sulked. "Well...he didn't seem so harmless to me."

They both looked down at the drunken man, now limply flopped over on the ground. He lay with an arm stretched above his head as if holding a pillow, while resting motionless on his left side. Darkness and position covered his face as they stepped over and walked past him up the street. Emma grabbed Killian's arm tightly, refusing to look at the man as they walked over him. She firmly held her fingers locked intertwined with his.

"What did you do to make him stop?"

"Not much," Killian casually replied.

"You must have done something."

"I grabbed him and he must have just passed out on the street back there."

"Okay, well where did you come from?"

"What do you mean?"

"I mean one second you were nowhere in sight and the next second you were like there."

"I was there, you just didn't see me."

"What...like I'm supposed to believe that?"

Killian's respirations became forced and deep, and his face cast a stony expression.

Emma figured he felt bad enough, especially after what had happened. She pulled him close, slowly kissing him with prolonged, intense signs of affection, forgetting all remaining questions with daubed, hot pink marks across his lips, but this time, he tasted differently when her mouth parted his. She pressed her fingers to her own lips, gliding them over the sensitive skin. Killian took a relaxed breath and then kissed the top of her forehead, putting his arm around her shoulder as they walked up the street. He peered back at the drunken man who remained motionless on the ground. The drunken man's face had recessed in on itself. His eyes were withered, his mouth agape, and his skin was parched, wrinkled, and deformed, with a yellowish gray hue. The drunkard's cheekbones, skull, and jaw bulged. All life had been sucked out. This left the drunken man with only the outline of skin covering bones. Even the joints in his wrist and fingers were held together by mere threads of gummy, thin flesh.

Killian whipped his head back around, curled his lip upward, and with a brief admiring smile, said, "We're going to have a lot of fun tonight." He kissed Emma on the cheek.

Hesitant, Emma kissed him on the lips again, but this time he tasted right, so they walked and kissed, closely wandering a lover's path down the dimly lit section of the street, leaving the drunken man far behind.

They walked for blocks.

"How far is the club?" Emma's feet began to hurt.

"Club?" Killian chuckled.

"Um...yeah. You didn't think that I wore this outfit for nothing, did you? Plus, I'm hungry."

"I'm taking you somewhere much better than any club, but don't worry, you'll get a bite there." He held back a smirk.

They traveled between dark alleyways, where shades of hazy light cast spectral images of familiar and benign daytime objects into sinister appearing items. The distant streetlights, which befriended them, now stretched out with dark, ethereal shadows, appearing to grab whenever the wind howled. The air moved, pushing her from behind, like a hand of ill fate urging her onward. A gust would stir, clattering leaves and paper rustled with a menacing, yet submissive tap around and past her feet.

Killian led Emma past boisterous nightclubs, where the music poured into the street and many voices mingled in laughter and loud talk as one inaudible noise. She planted her feet to have a quick look inside, but hand in hand, he pulled her onward.

The bright, colorful lights of the city were now on full display, but also far behind them. Rumbling engines of automobiles on the main road became faint hums only heard among a few moments of select and complete silence.

Tall, old French buildings lined like bars on graphs of different heights in rows ahead of them. Through many dark neighborhoods they skulked, while muted lights from random rooms high above faded into black one by one.

This was the Paris that Emma wanted to see, yet not at night. With little said, Killian curiously rushed her to parts unknown. He held her hand, tighter when she pulled back in hesitation. He only stopped to urge her with an annoyed wave toward the direction ahead. Dark streets and alleyways filtered into silent lanes where the ugliness lived. Replacing glitz and glamour, shattered windows, broken concrete steps, and the odor of rotting waste drifted in the breeze.

Emma ripped her hand from his. "I'm not taking another step unless you tell me where we're going."

"It's just up there." Killian pointed.

"No!" She thumbed from the direction they came. "I want to go to that club back there. That's where I want to go!" She glared without a blink.

Killian tilted his head. "I have something amazing to show you," he softly said. He then gently held her hands together, wrapping them close between their chests. "Then I promise to take you anywhere you'd like." His words and face appeared truthful.

The gloomy light sketched an outline cutting off half of Killian's lovely face. Emma caressed his soft, warm skin. She ran the back of her hand from the top of his thick hairline, down to his strong cheekbone, and under his pointed chin, all the way to his solid, raised pectorals. She kissed the tip of his finely chiseled aquiline nostrils, and then the fleshy ridges of his forgiving lips. The two rubbed tongues over each other in a rapid series of want and desire. Emma opened her eyes for a moment and looked deeply into Killian's soul. She suddenly pulled away, after seeing black fill the white of his eyes. For a second, he seemed dead to her, void of the living spark she had come to know.

Her eyes widened. Slanting her chin down, she kept watching him from behind furrowed brows. She shifted her eyes from side to side for a possible escape.

He walked toward her with open arms and a look of bewilderment. "What's wrong, my love?"

"Stay away from me."

"Why? What happened?"

"I saw your eyes..." Emma pushed him away. "Who are you? What kind of stuff are you on?"

"I'm not on anything. It's me, you know, Killian." He threw his head back and laughed exuberantly. "The night plays tricks on you. Here, have another look."

"No! Stay back!"

Killian inched closer as she reversed her steps. He stopped. His arms stretched wide, his palms toward her, his fingers spread apart. Emma released her shoulders, extended her neck, and squinted with a cautious peek into his eyes. She looked again as he blinked several times for her comfort. His eyes looked normal again, and she relaxed. Emma let forth a brief sigh, a puff of air, sucking in the next breath slowly, while her body settled its rigid tension.

Emma clamped her eyes, nodding while shaking her head once, then twice. "I guess you must think I'm crazy or something."

"Nah."

"You mean after I just totally spazzed..." Emma's voice ended in a high pitch. "You still wanna be with me?"

"Of course."

Her head askew toward Killian and with brows raised, Emma timidly asked, "Really?" Her eyes moistened at the inner corners. Emma dabbed at them, hunching her dampened face midway to meet her own consoling hand.

Killian impulsively pulled her body close to his. "As I said, the city lights, they play tricks on the eyes." He gently caressed the side of her face, tilting her frown back up toward his smile. Killian calmly kissed her chin, cheek, and then tenderly her mouth. "Are you ready to go now?" Emma stared willingly into his eyes, letting go of herself, and he hurried them onward to their endpoint with the skill of a calculated planner.

She glanced over at one of the packed clubs named Spectacular-Spectacular, which nightly erupted with people. Emma paused, trying to get a better peek into the club. She was mesmerized. The big red sign, which topped the doorway, had elegant, giant letters, each ten feet tall, reading Spectacular-Spectacular in spectacular flashing neon.

In a momentary preview, Emma saw inside the main door of the club. Showy laser lights blasted forth, moving and changing colors from red to blue and then green before back to red again. Confetti showered from above onto the dancing crowd. Elbow to elbow they partied. The music was fast, weighted with heavy bass, and it shook the building all the way out the door until it rumbled under Emma's feet. Then Killian, with Emma reluctantly in tow, marched toward the opposite side of the spectacular club, and down a tiny, dark alleyway. This was familiar ground for him. He looked up at the sky, and said, "We haven't much time." Emma tossed an odd squint at him, so Killian reformed his words. "You know, before I have to get you back to the hotel, so let's hurry up, we're almost there." He took her by the wrist and roughly hauled her along.

Chapter Eleven

After many blocks of neglected buildings packed tightly between curbs, and tiny, empty lots where houses once stood, Emma and Killian reached an unkempt, old city park.

For some time, they had been the only people either of them had seen. The packed clubs and restaurants, the hectic nightlife, and loud chattering voices, were absent among the deathly silence of crumbling cement, and rusted man-made metal structures.

Buildings in this particular neighborhood had been vacated and boarded up. With unwanted furniture and trash thrown about, the area invited every sort of illicit and devious activity.

The old city park was an overgrown garden full of long grass, nearly shoulder high. Broken benches and overturned birdbaths sat like gravestones upon the discarded heap of earth. Wilted flowerbeds languished upon thirsty soil. Splendid fountains had dried, leaving only stained, cracked, empty basins. Exposed to wind and cold, heat and sun, the park lacked care and routine pruning to sustain a certain level of vibrant, green beauty. Forgotten in the deepest, darkest corner of Paris, the park had become a blemish upon the city.

Once the pride and hope of a past generation, the city park sat withering in decay as an urban misfit of time and a shell of its former glory. The ill-kept garden overlaid its metal-gated confines, spilling over onto the street with dead vines and pointy, yellow grass spikes. Shaded by small trees, shrubs, and vines, even in death, life sprouted, as wild new growth wrapped around the rusted iron gates, while reclaiming the desolate park. Branches abounded like sharp daggers. Twigs and brambles littered the ground, snapping as Emma and Killian hiked without a word through the tall reeds. The soft lawn had become parched grassy stalks that crunched with each step. Drifting winds curved waves of tall grass up under itself, making a sinister rustling crackle, like lungs struggling to breathe one last breath.

With a secret fear, Emma followed Killian through the dark, lifeless garden. She crept along as he bounded forward.

Once near the back of the park, Killian easily lifted a long, flat, frayed piece of plywood board from off what seemed to be an arid wishing well. The well's top bricks were broken into various chunks and pieces, and sloppy orange paint sprayed the words 'Keep Out' written in runny lines along the plywood board.

Killian ignored the words and uncovered a large, circular pit with a rusted metal ladder.

The ladder descended deep into the ground below them. Killian eagerly signaled for Emma to join him. She was immobile, reluctantly leaning only her neck over, gawking at the deep pit before stepping back and glancing at the dreary and ominous park that surrounded her.

"No!" Emma tightly crossed her arms. "There's no way I'm going down there." She shook her head.

"Come on." Killian held his grin, while enjoying the muddled, decomposing park. "You've come all this way to see the most amazing thing, and it's as close as the bottom of this well." He reached for her hand.

"Ew, yuck." Emma did not give her hand, but instead, turned her nose high and away. "Why would I want to climb down there? Besides, my mom warned me about some girl who was found dead in the sewer the other day."

"Adults lie all the time." Killian narrowed his eyes and frowned. "That's just what they do. I've heard the same old story to keep me from going down into the catacombs my whole life." With forceful intent, he locked eyes with her. "I haven't lied to you, and I won't let anything bad happen either...I promise."

Emma begrudgingly sighed. "Why, what's down there?" She loosened her stance and her arms fell reluctantly to her sides. "Why? What's the catacombs anyway?" She stretched her neck out over the deep, black pit once more.

"Come." He waved her near. "It's better to find out for yourself."

Emma extended herself forward, with another fleeting glimpse behind at the dreary park. She stepped carefully toward the old brick well. As if he had done this many times before, Killian easily hopped over and down the dark well. He held the rusted metal ladder and flipped on a flashlight for her above. Her thighs leaned against the outer shell of the cold brick, and with a degree of uncertainty, she flattened one hand and tapped her fingers to her chin, removing them and grabbing ahold of Killian's offered arm.

She straddled the wall for a moment, one leg hung over, as her other hand firmly gripped the rusted ladder rungs, before she slowly lowered herself into the timeworn, dark well.

Emma ran her hand along, touching the chipped plaster between the loose bricks of the large, round well. She cast a fearful glance while descending into the seemingly endless void.

Stacked and compressed by time, many of the bricks were chipped into slivered blocks, the mortar long since weakened under its own weight. The grout, now thinly crushed between slabs, was in a constant state of decline, while the bricks uneasily rested one by one on top of each other, threatening to cave at a moment's notice.

Killian swung to the side of the rusted metal ladder, and allowed Emma to go down in front of him. He then followed closely behind her. He held the flashlight for Emma, it shined along the wall where the bolted, rusted ladder melded to brick. As they started the climb downward, with a single arm, Killian lugged the hefty piece of frayed plywood over top the well, thus hiding the entrance to the catacombs from the outside world once more.

The air, once pleasant and temperate in the city above, became moist, cool, and stagnant as they climbed lower. As they descended into the pit, Emma's anxiety quietly rose. Dew coated all surfaces, making the bent, warped, and broken metal rungs like bars of slippery, cold ice.

Emma's foot skated off the ladder, and in an instant, she screamed out. "Aaah!" She felt the sensation of falling, with an awful plummet into the deep unknown.

"I've got you." Killian, with great speed, reached out for her. With one arm, he grasped her upper limb, pulling her back onto the ladder.

"Oh, my god, I thought I was going to die." Her heart skipped and beat swiftly. Her respirations increased. She now labored to catch her breath in panic among the smothering, stagnant air.

"I told you, everything will be all right." He was calm, too calm, given the circumstances. With a serenely mechanical response, he stroked her hair as she huffed rapidly.

"Okay. I'm okay now." After a few moments had passed, Emma had regained her confidence, and the two continued slowly climbing the rest of the way down the dark well's black void together.

At the last rung, an immeasurable height of darkness obscured the bottom step from the end of the well. Emma strained her eyes for a landing spot. Killian held the flashlight, aiming it into the pit, but even the light was swallowed by immense darkness, and no view of solid ground did the void give away.

Emma asked Killian for the flashlight. He handed it down from above. The flashlight popped out of her hand when she reached up. Feeling her stomach jump, the sensation of another fall seized her body. So Emma gripped the rungs, wrapping her arms around the ladder and pulling her body close, allowing the flashlight to fall from her reach instead.

The flashlight sharply plunged down into the black void, clanking a few times as it hit the bottom of the well before its light darkened altogether.

The flashlight had become part of the void, a slave to gloomy despair, and Emma wanted to leave this place. She now only sought to go up and out of the well altogether.

"That's just great!" Emma shouted. "What the hell are we supposed to do now?"

"Jump," Killian casually replied.

"Jump!? Are you crazy?"

"Why not?" Killian calmly asked.

"Um hello, the flashlight just broke, what do you think it's going to do to my bones?" Emma tried pushing Killian's legs aside. "I'm getting out of here, so move!"

In a blurring instant, Killian swung like an acrobat to the other side of Emma and then plummeted from above her down into the void of the black pit.

"OH, MY GOD!" Emma yelled.

There were only specks of light from holes in the frayed plywood high above from which to see, but not nearly enough. Emma was not sure of what she had seen, but her eyes bulged after Killian dropped into and vanished at the bottom of the black void. Distressed, she called out, but she heard nothing except the bitter call of her own voice in echo, and then, awful silence.

Chapter Twelve

"Killian!" Emma shouted. "Are you okay? Where are you? Answer me!" she screamed the last.

Deflated, she rested her head on her wrists, her fingers now aching at the knuckles, and white from tightly gripping the rusted steel rungs.

She sniffled a few times and a tear dropped from her cheek to the bottom of the void. Then survival removed her sadness and fear. Emma regarded the climb back up as a daunting climb to escape what had become Killian's fate.

Cautiously, she reached one hand above for the next rung up, but suddenly, a light appeared, shining from below in the black pit of the void.

Delighted, her pitch sharpened. "Killian, you're alive!" She swung her head downward.

"But of course." He shined the light up at Emma.

"You jerk!" she indignantly said. "Why didn't you answer me?"

"I needed to find and fix the flashlight first. Now come on." He motioned the light back and forth from her to the ground. "See, it's not that high at all, so jump."

"Jump! We've been through this already! I'm NOT jumping!"

"Come on, you have nothing to worry about. Look, I'm fine." Killian quickly ran the flashlight up and down his own body.

"You were lucky. I'll probably break my leg or something," she mocked, while still high on the ladder above.

"You're overreacting. Just trust me."

"Just trust me." She mumbled to herself, "Like I haven't heard that before."

Killian pointed the flashlight up at Emma. "I can still hear you, ya know."

She looked down over her right shoulder and then over her left. She closed her eyes and took several deep, short huffs. "I can't do it. I'm going home..." Before Emma could finish her next word, the metal rung under her foot broke, and this time she fell backward, descending into the void. "NO!" A jarring, lasting scream bellowed forth. Emma grabbed at the air, up toward the last glimpse of fading light from the top of the well, as her body pitched downward. Gravity tossed her petite frame, twisting it, while she plunged uncontrollably in a reverse spiral, diving headfirst, tumbling her with malice toward the hard ground at great speed.

Emma braced for the impending agony. Her eyes widened. Her mouth gaped. She screamed again. A second lasted forever. Killian swooped in and extended his merciful arms, catching her before even a strand of hair hit the unforgiving ground where he firmly stood.

Stunned, she put her arms around his neck, and held him tightly as she forcefully kissed his beautiful face, each side over and over again. He gently placed her onto her feet. The ground proved soft, with a squishy muckiness rather than the hard rock she expected. Emma slid from side to side on the spongy ground. It was boggy thick, and she was unable to balance her legs.

Emma put her hands around his shoulders to stabilize herself. She merged lips with Killian, crashing supple, pink flesh together in bonded excitement with him. She unglued her lips from his. "Oh, my god, how did you save me?" Emma shook her head in disbelief.

Killian cracked an all-knowing grin. "I opened my arms and there you were." He took her by the hand. "Come, where we are going is just around the corner."

Killian shined the flashlight ahead. It dimly parted heavy waves of swimming black, immersive darkness. The light's beam, strong elsewhere, was overpowered by a vast haze of gloom in the tunnels around them. And of their senses, much valued sight turned helplessly blind upon them, until confusion grew. Even the tiny specks of light from the top of the well had vanished into nothing, and were absorbed by the unending darkness of the void that surrounded them. Yet still, they journeyed deeper into the damp, silent, and glum underground.

Killian led Emma by the hand. A faint light along with some whispered voices emerged from the tunnel up ahead.

"What is this place?" Emma asked.

Killian put his index finger to his lip. "Shh."

"Well...tell me something," Emma whispered.

Killian pulled her faster toward the light and sounds up ahead. "These are the catacombs, and here," they quickly turned a corner into an open room filled with candles, old chairs, and ancient carvings, "is a grotto."

"What's a...?" Emma trailed off. Her eyes instantly glanced over at the two strangers already sitting in the uncomfortably cozy room. Two teens handed a paper bag covered bottle back and forth to each other, and kept talking as if Emma and Killian were not there at all.

One of the strangers in the room, a young male, sat sprawled across a torn reclining chair with springs poking up this way and that outside its loose, worn fabric. He spoke English with a thick Parisian accent. "A grotto is just a party room for those belonging to a certain age group...an age group that no longer cares to dress up for the aristocracy of their exclusive clubs." He pointed at the ceiling. The young reclining man straightened to his feet from his torn chair, saluting Killian's shirt with the French flag slovenly dyed across his chest. "*Vive la France*!" He laughed afterward.

"What?" Emma squinted.

The young man now swayed as he stood from his sprawled sitting position and bowed, tipping his red beret while picking at the seams of his baggy trousers. "Where are my manners? I am Maurice." He then pointed to the young, attractive, pink-haired girl still sitting on the floor next to him. Her head was shaved on one side, but on the other side her hair was long and straight, covering her eyes. "And this is my associate, Sophie." Maurice dipped an open palm toward Sophie, but she just tightened her mouth with a passing, annoyed glance.

"I'm Emma." She flashed a short wristed wave. "And this is my..." Emma looked at Killian, not sure what they were to each other. "This is Killian." She awkwardly grinned.

With a set of hollow eyes, Killian glared at Maurice and Sophie from the entrance of the grotto. His usual charming nature turned unfriendly and withdrawn. He made Maurice fidget restlessly with a stare. Killian crossed his arms and scowled.

Emma put her arm around Killian. He shrugged it off. She looked up and over at the front of his face, but it was vacantly blank.

Sophie had an innocent cuteness about her. She wore thick, black eye shadow from the top of her brows to the top of her cheeks, yet a cunning glimmer of the streets focused pinpoint pupils, with a side of crazy behind her heavily shadowed eyes. Sophie pretended indifference to the new arrivals by tipping a bagged bottle up, and gulping a prolonged slurp, all while glancing a sideways peek of suspicion around the room.

Sophie's general tone and affect was one of boredom. Full-figured, she was upper endowed. Her ears were pierced up and down both lobes, and adorned full of beaded, glass pellets looped in a row of silver, from the back top of her ears, larger rings higher, descending into six or eight smaller hoops near the bottom of her lower earlobes.

"So, you are both fellow cataphiles like us?" Maurice tensely grinned and twirled his beret like a steering wheel. "No?" he asked.

Sophie answered for them. "No, they are just paupers like us."

With his chin protruded, Killian said nothing, so Emma answered Maurice. "What's a cataphile? And for god's sake, will someone tell me what a grotto is?" Her words vibrated off the jagged, rocky walls.

Sophie took another swill from the bagged bottle, and after, the scrunching paper bag rustled as she clanged the glass inside while scraping its bottom against the ground. She put her index finger to her lips. "Hush, or they'll hear you," she said the rest in French, "you stupid American girl." She hated Emma at first sight.

"Who'll hear me?" Emma only spoke English.

Sophie laughed scornfully. "The police." She wrapped her mouth over the bottle's stem. "They patrol some of the shallow tunnels trying to catch cataphiles like us."

Emma shrugged her shoulders. "So."

"So they'll throw you in jail if you're caught down here," Maurice said.

Sensing Emma's frustration, Killian answered. "This is a grotto." He pointed fingers on both hands to each side of the tiny, round room.

The grotto was a room carved in sharply arched folds from stratified rock. The room was filled wall to wall with lit candles. The floor was littered with bizarrely grotesque piles of relics and idols, along with a couple of stained, torn pieces of furniture against each wall.

Emma prattled forth, giggling for no reason as a sweet, relaxing, aromatic scent fanned in among the grotto's air.

Sophie leaned over and grabbed Maurice by the shirt. She climbed on the chair, and kissed him on the lips, her eyes drifted an inquiring look toward Killian and Emma. Sophie and Maurice shamelessly displayed their passions as if they were the only ones in the grotto.

Killian ushered Emma over toward the dirty, shredded fabric chair across the room from Maurice and Sophie. Killian sat, watching as a voyeur, rubbing his pronounced chin, but he was not deriving enjoyment. He was sizing things up with a curious regard of his own.

Emma, oblivious to his expression, bounced on his lap and began kissing him as briskly as Sophie was Maurice. Emma sat across Killian's lap, her thighs folded together and eyes closed as he teased her, while rubbing his soft lips across her indulgent creases. Still, Killian angled his head, and inspected Sophie and Maurice who enjoyed the company of observers.

Sophie nagged Maurice with playful banter, so Emma enticed Killian with gentle kisses and low talk of her own. Sophie meshed her fingers inside of Maurice's. Then, all at once, Killian broke lips, held Emma off by the shoulders, and pointed to an overused, dark blue backpack, which had flopped over on the ground after Maurice happened to kick the bag during his excitement.

"Hey, what's in there?" Killian leaned forward, nearly pushing Emma from his lap.

Maurice fixed his reddish brown dreadlocks, so they hung straight across his forehead again. His eyes gleamed, and he too flipped Sophie to the side, tossing her off the chair entirely as he reached for the backpack. "Here?" he asked with delight.

Emma wrinkled her nose and pouted, taking her new place on the hard armrest as Killian widened his legs, taking the entire seat for himself.

Sophie frowned, rolling her eyes at Maurice from the floor, locking lips only with the bagged bottle now. "Don't get him started." Sophie groaned as she wiped drink from her mouth. "Maurice may be good-natured, but he's a very stupid boy sometimes."

Emma, now interested, bent forward in their direction. "Why, what's in there?" She ignored Sophie.

Killian eagerly waited, hiding his fervor well. He watched as Maurice opened his backpack and pulled out several random items most cataphiles carried throughout the tunnels. He stacked water, batteries, food, and a flashlight from out of his backpack, while digging toward the bottom.

"I'm going to be the first cataphile to catch and kill a Dweller down here in the catacombs," Maurice gaily said, while burrowing through his carefully packed bag.

"Not this again." Sophie slapped her forehead with her palm, and then removed her button-down gray shirt, revealing a black sleeveless camisole, along with an inked left arm. She proudly revealed skin fully covered in pink, red, blue, and black tattoos from her shoulder to her elbow.

Her eyes asquint, Emma removed herself from the hard armrest and stood. "What's a Dweller?" She lightly shook her head from side to side.

"Um, uh." Maurice scratched his scalp rapidly, with a confused look. "Let me show you." He pulled a flask out first. "This is holy water." He placed the flask next to the outside of the bag. "And if that doesn't work, I've got this beauty." He pulled out and flaunted a handgun.

Emma gasped, jolting back. "Are you insane?"

"Relax, it's safe," Maurice retorted.

"Yeah, right!" Emma stiffened her back.

"Here," Maurice put it back in his bag. "Happy now? Anyway, I have this." He held an old videotape over his head. "This is proof that Dwellers really exist."

Sophie rolled her head back toward Maurice. "You only see what you want to see."

The two of them became rowdy, throwing their hands in the air, arguing violently in French, and then abruptly, they began necking and fondling each other all over. Emma put her hands on her hips, her eyes staring, her mouth gaping, but Killian remained detached as a mere calculating bystander.

"Hello! Can you two please stop the gross PDA?" Emma said. Then she pointed at Maurice. "And you, finish what you were saying," she demanded.

"Oh, yes." Maurice wiped black lipstick from his lips, pushing Sophie off to the side again. She landed on the ground with a grunt. Maurice kept talking. "How could I have gotten so distracted from such truly important matters?" He bobbed his head and tied his reddish brown, shoulder-length dreadlocks back with a white, industrial rubber band. "This is a grotto." He crossed his legs, and with palms upward, he flung his arms apart.

"Yeah, I know that," Emma flippantly answered.

"Okay...well, did you know that this limestone room has evolved over many years into a hangout for cataphiles just before they trek into the deepest parts of the endless tunnels ahead?"

"No," Emma simply answered.

"You see, when a cataphile makes it deeper than anyone else ever before, he..." Maurice caught a nasty, irritated glance from Sophie. He cleared his throat. "Or when she, in some cases, tags a deep section, it is a badge of honor, which is worthy of respect." Maurice shook a can of spray paint from his backpack. He rapidly mentioned the rest. "And then you take a picture or video and brag about it to the other cataphiles." He leered a self-satisfied look down at Sophie.

Maurice went on to tell how Sophie was not as interested in being a real cataphile, but that he was. He also explained how the Romans built the catacombs over fifteen hundred years ago, and how the tunnels cavern deep into the earth, so no one really knows how far the catacombs actually extend.

Maurice wiggled uncomfortably around in his tight, black gothic jeans and basic white t-shirt. He emphatically waved one of his skinny arms in the air, while holding the videotape with his other hand. His long neck swayed as he told of how a fellow cataphile had gone farther than any other cataphile, while traveling deep into the catacombs about two years ago.

Maurice went on to tell that this particular cataphile, like many others in recent times, had gone missing, never to be seen or heard from again. Maurice told how six months later, another cataphile found a recorder in the tunnels, with the videotape he was holding still inside the abandoned video recorder. The tape showed the original cataphile dropping the recorder, with only a sideways shot of the cataphile himself being dragged off into the dark catacombs by some creature.

Maurice's eyes bugged out. He flipped the videotape back and forth when telling of the monstrous hand with long, bony fingers, and sharp black nails that wrapped around the cataphile's face, while the cataphile himself kicked and screamed, trying to push the creature's hand off and away with both of his own. However, the cataphile was no match for the horrific, inhuman strength of the Dweller. Maurice finished by telling how shortly afterward, the recorder battery died, fading into slow black, but not before strange sounds of multiple people whispering, beating hearts, along with occasional bloodcurdling screams, filled the videotape's last audio portion before the tape went black.

"Is this for real?" Emma closed one eye and tilted her head.

Maurice opened his mouth, but Sophie blurted out, "He wishes." She narrowed her eyes. "Why don't you tell them how much of my hard-earned money they swindled out of you for that fake tape?"

"It's real, and I can prove it." Maurice again reached into his backpack. "See." With two hands, he struggled to pull a heavy, thick, large, ancient bound volume out of the bag with his lanky arms.

The story of the videotape did nothing for Killian, but he flinched, nearly climbing the back of his seat when he saw the book. "What's that?"

"That, my friend, is a borrowed piece of merchandise from the Notre Dame Cathedral, and it is not for sale." Maurice proudly unsnapped a pair of tarnished steel locks, popping them open with a key attached to a necklace inside his shirt. He gingerly opened the aged, leathery book. The four edged corners were damaged by time and use, with kinked up fringes. He ever so lightly turned the brittle pages, flipping them slowly, each one over onto the next withered, parched sheet.

"Ha!" Tipping the bagged bottle up for a sip, there came protest from Sophie. "You mean stolen. Besides...just because it's old, doesn't make it true. It's another piece of fantasy, trash fiction if you ask me."

"Shut up, Sophie. I wasn't asking YOU!" Maurice whipped his head toward her and roared. "Stop being so negative," he turned and yelled in her face. "Why do you always have to be so negative!" he shouted again.

Sophie and Maurice erupted at each other. Both screaming mere inches from the other's face.

Killian reached out as the two argued. "Can I see that?" he coolly asked.

Maurice pulled away from Sophie and drew the old book close, holding it cross arm against his chest. "No, no. For it's written in Latin, but I'll gladly read some of it to you."

"You dummy. You can't read Latin." Sophie laughed.

Chapter Thirteen

Emma sighed and groaned. This was not the night she imagined. She angled her head backward, shaking it in frustration.

"Shut up!" Maurice yelled, threatening Sophie with agitated tones, and bothered, menacing glares.

Emma sat on the dusty grotto floor, and watched dozens of burning candles lined in single file like quiet soldiers all around and along the walls of the room. The tiny flames shimmered, bouncing images of their shadows, sending them dancing back and forth as living objects of the grotto.

Wax trickled down into hardened droplets as the gleaming fire burned reddish orange at the top of the minuscule flames. Hints of bluish sparks fizzled inside the reddish orange blaze, which were swathed near the bottom of the candles' black, incandescent wicks. Altogether, the candles' beauty lit the room with a warm glow, an ignored splendor, leaving behind a coating of oblong waxy secretions on the ground and up the side walls.

Emma's attention drifted away in a dreamlike stupor. The grotto turned surreal, yet otherworldly with a mystic gleam.

One of the shadows dancing along the walls was not like the other three present that night. This shadow hid its demonic shape to the eyes, but told a starkly different truth to the candles, forming a body not like anyone in the room.

Maurice freed his recoiled grip, and delightfully held the medieval book on his lap.

Sophie swigged from the bottle, with the occasional glance of revulsion toward the others in the room.

Killian, intrigued, tempered his interest with a sly wisdom possessed only by those with the wrong kind of life experience.

Emma, immersed by the goings on, waited intently, leaning forward in expectation of the book's unveil.

However, all of them failed to notice an ominous tale written among their wicked and playfully dancing shadows on the living walls of the grotto.

"Well..." Emma briefly flipped her palms up and open. "What does it say?"

"Um, it says, uh." Maurice glossed his index finger under the words in an attempt to translate the Latin from the book.

Sophie let out a short, mocking laugh. "He doesn't know." She chugged another nip from the bagged bottle.

Maurice just glared at her. "It says," he cleared his throat, "these tunnels were built as a prison for those who shall forever dwell in Sheol."

"Dwell in Sheol?" Now sitting on the ground, Emma, mesmerized, inched closer toward Maurice. "What does that mean?"

"Stop being so bossy!" Sophie barked at Emma.

"Why don't you shut the hell up," Emma replied.

"Why don't you. You rich, little, ugly princess." Sophie drank again from the bottle. "Don't kiss a prince, or he might turn back into a toad." She glared at Emma, while smirking at her own retort.

"Why are you being such a jerk to me? I didn't do anything to you." Emma scowled back.

Maurice interrupted. "Now ladies..." He quickly looked up at a stone-faced Killian. "And gentlemen. Sheol means..."

"Ha! Sheol means..." Sophie cut into his reply, but Maurice, with a single hand, swooped down, knocking the bottle away from her mouth, flipping it into the air, and breaking the jug, spilling its liquid contents all over the ground. The glass bottle cracked and the bag saturated with its leaking fluid. The dry brown paper bag soaked up the sugary, fragrant beverage.

Acting as if nothing happened at all, Maurice continued. "Sheol means that I've read some of this book before."

"So." Killian grinned as Sophie slapped Maurice hard across the back of his head.

"You idiot! Why'd you break my drink?" Sophie growled. "That was mine! I bought it! I paid for it! Just like everything else you don't have!"

"Stop it!" Frustrated, Maurice shouted at her. "I'll get you another. Besides, don't you mean you stole it?"

Sophie attempted to smack him in the face this time, but Maurice caught her wrist in midair. Each glared heatedly at the other for a moment, but then the two began fondling and caressing passionately once more.

"Ahem!" Emma looked away. "I said, ahem!" She crossed her arms and frowned.

"Sorry. The French are a very passionate people, and..." Maurice did not finish his thought, but turned his head to the side and coughed. His eyes regulated a conversation with Sophie, revealing some nature of their relationship between subtle gazes, and then Maurice started talking about his primeval book again. "As far as I can tell, these Dwellers got their name from dwelling in the bowels of the earth, and this Sheol, is a grave, or perhaps a prison of some sort." Maurice put his face close to the open page. Narrowing his eyes, he ran his index finger along under a row of Latin words as he read parts in jumbled segments, skipping verses he did not know. "The book also mentions that immortal knights saved the world of man when civilization was still new. The knights struck down the Dwellers with the sword of truth, which flamed against the cruelness, pushing evil back into the land of eternal decay until they were no more."

"Oh, come on." Sophie held her elbows. She lobbed her eyes upward, and let out a greatly inflated sigh.

"Wow!" Emma ogled and gawked, drawing her knees up to her chest. "That's really cool, but what does it all mean?"

Maurice rapidly tapped his fingers to his lips. "I don't exactly know, but a couple friends of mine are working on translating the rest of the book." His eyes focused on nothing in particular, yet he seemed rather lost in thought.

"Are Dwellers demons?" Emma asked.

"No," Maurice replied.

"Zombies, vampires, ghosts?" Emma continued guessing.

"No." Maurice scratched his head. "Apparently they're some kind of other supernatural beings with great powers. And in this place," he said, pointing out the door of the grotto. "This place is the borderland." He blew dust from the spine of the book, which exposed gold sketching all over in circles, symbols, and lines. "Even though I haven't read the entire book...yet, I have looked at all of the cool pictures."

"Typical boy," Sophie said as she smirked. Her hands on her hips with elbows bent outward. "They only like books with lots of cool pictures in them." She flashed two fingers on each hand for quotation signs. "Ha!" She hooted a laugh.

Ignoring her, Maurice pinched a quarter of the old book's frail pages. "I'm only this far into reading it, but the next portion talks more about these immortal knights, the Dwellers, and even something called the Shroud." He squeezed his lips together and shrugged his shoulders. "I guess I'll find out more later." Maurice placed his hand vertically along the side of his face, blocking his view of Sophie, and said, "I'll tell you some things that even she doesn't know about." He thumbed toward Sophie with his other hand.

"I'm not deaf you idiot!" Sophie briefly closed her eyes and slanted her head, puffing a loud rush of air out her nostrils.

"Well...go on." Emma gestured to Maurice.

Killian deeply sighed from his belly. Distracted now, he scowled, while checking out the different mystic, superstitious-like, religious trinkets left throughout the years around the grotto.

"This evening's a wash." Sophie lamented. "I wish I at least had my drink to entertain me." Her eyes darted at all those in the grotto.

"Never mind her." Maurice flipped to different parts of the book. Emma scooted her bottom toward him. "Now it says here that these Dwellers are like apparitions, or phantoms, though not ghosts." He scanned several pages. "It also says Dwellers can take human form, using feelings and emotions to trick people." Maurice changed to a jolly tone. "You know, this book also has a nice collection of stories, poems, and songs, too."

"Huh?" Emma rubbed the goosebumps along the backs of her arms. "No, tell me the good stuff. I want to hear about the good stuff!"

"Okay," Maurice continued, "from what I've read, these Dwellers secrete a black, tar-like substance, I guess like a poisonous resin or something into their victim. Then they suck the juices, absorbing from inside out and then completely digest that which they hunt. They live a nocturnal existence, and shudder from the light as reviled fiends in a true form that is both male and female in one, or possibly neither. Dwellers are devoid of life, but beasts of prey. They are dead, damned, and unthinking creatures, lost in the season between summer and winter..."

Killian suddenly rose with an urgent desire to view the book. From a distance, he scowled with a covetous glare. "What is that, fourteenth century?"

"Actually, I think it's twelfth or thirteenth." Maurice looked at the binding. "Here, you guys want to see a picture of what a Dweller's supposed to look like?" His mood rose when his giddy excitement could no longer be contained.

"Sure!" Emma said, at first joyous, but after, she glanced oddly up at Killian. "Hey, why are you standing?"

"No reason." He gradually sat back in his chair, pretending disinterest. He casually spread his arms and legs, and then he closed up tensely, leaning forward toward the book.

Sophie rolled her eyes. "Ugh, don't encourage him, and please don't believe any of this stuff." She groaned. "Like I said, it's just bad fiction."

"For the last time, shut your mouth!" Maurice stuck his nose high in the air, glaring fiercely downward. His nostrils now flared, he expressed a quick, strong outburst in French toward Sophie, before calmly finishing the last part in English for Emma to hear. "All the stuff about the Dwellers is true. And like I said before, I'm going to prove all you doubters wrong." He quickly glanced at his companion, giving a loud yap of displeasure. He opened to a page near the middle of the book. With a care usually reserved for a mother holding her newborn child, Maurice gently separated the ancient, flimsy pages. He held his breath when a pair of thinly filmed pages gummed together. As if an adhesive bandage stuck to tender skin, he gingerly peeled them apart, wincing, biting his lower lip, and focusing on only the book as he freed one page from the other. A sigh accompanied cheerful eyes when he gazed upon the picture he was looking for. He took a deep breath and delicately flipped the book around so Emma and Killian could both see the picture, too. "Cool...no?" Maurice raised his right eyebrow and curled the right corner of his lip upward with pleasure and pride.

Emma inched back, grabbing ahold of Killian's arm. "Oh, my god, that thing, it's..." She searched for a word, a new word to define the visceral repulsion on her scrunched face.

Maurice nodded his head. "I know, right."

"What? What do you know?" Sophie dismissively turned her back away from him and faced the wall.

Killian acted with little interest. He rubbed his chin, stitching his brows together. "Seems like a joke to me."

Sophie turned to have another glance at the same picture she had seen many times before. Soon after, all the eyes in the grotto affixed to the large, colored picture of the Dweller in the medieval book.

For the first time, everyone stopped talking in an unspoken agreement of implied silence. The Dweller on the page of the medieval book seemed to come alive. Projecting off the flimsy, colored sheet, a fierce creature hunched over in a beastly side body profile, with its neck turned to face the reader. The image discharged an unreal, yet foreboding menace, appearing to hypnotically growl back at them from off the page of the medieval book taken from the Notre Dame Cathedral.

The monster had a diseased appearance. Its skin had a blotchy jaundiced, but a pale white anemic shine. It had pronounced, raised edges of spiny backbones. The skull appeared malformed and semi-oblong, with a bald, melon-like head, while only scarce, frizzy gray strands of messy hair grew from its bony scalp.

The Dweller had tiny, seashell-shaped ears, but a mouth full of protracted fangs, a set of large, saucer-like black eyes, and a vertical pair of slits for its blunt snout. It was lean, with a hostile, muscular sinewy frame up and down its torso, neck, shoulders, arms, and legs. Last of all, the picture painted a set of hands, each with five, large knuckled, thinly fingered, circularly rotated digits, perfectly designed for grasping prey with a most lethal hold. At the end of the fingers, the Dweller's sickle-shaped talons knifed forth. In scale, the creature's hooks appeared eight to ten inches long. The fierce, ripping blades seemed designed for slashing victims to pieces. Blackened as tar, the talons curved inward and tipped at the ends with razor points. The black tar, sickle-like talons were flawlessly sharp, ready to perforate, thus causing the entrails of its victim to spill out with a single blow.

"No!" Emma uttered a shout of disgust, and then snapped her fingers. "I know what that thing looks like. It looks like that little monster in the movie about the ring." Everyone looked strangely at her. "Come on, you guys know, the one where the little monster calls the ring its precious or something."

"Oh," Maurice said. He flipped the book back around, squinting, he held the book farther away, and then up closer. He tilted his head at the picture a second and third time. "I don't know. I guess maybe if you've never actually seen a Dweller before it would look like that other thing. But this book says Dwellers are angry, mean, and nasty killers, who eat, and multiply, and destroy everything they come across."

"Multiply?" Killian joined in.

"Yeah, I haven't read much about them multiplying yet, but apparently these Dwellers eat just about anything." Maurice read some more of the old script as he turned the book's pages with care. "Ah, here, the book says humans provide most of its diet." Holding the edge of the page with the tips of his index finger and thumb, he flipped back and forth from text to picture on the previous page about the Dweller. "Apparently it attaches its hand like a suction cup to the top of the victim's head and sucks everything out from the inside." Maurice moistened his index finger with his tongue. He slanted his neck downward and examined the Latin script closer. "Let's see now. Let's see now," he repeated to himself.

Sophie laughed. "Lost again?"

"No!" Maurice squinted at the words from the book. "Ah, here it is." He lightly placed a finger on the page. "And after that, the Dweller can temporarily take the shape of the one it consumed, and only then are Dwellers able to once again walk in the light for a single day."

"Once again?" Emma repeated with a curious expression.

Maurice began to read some more. "Yes..."

Killian interrupted. "I'm growing tired of this." He pretended to yawn, eyeing down at the floor with a musing, yet contrived disinterest. "Let's do what we came down here to do. Let's start exploring the tunnels." He quickly got up and pulled Emma by the hand, and said, "It's initiation time."

Chapter Fourteen

Maurice and Sophie shared a private thought in an instantaneous glance before they left the grotto. They each gave a half smile and Sophie winked once.

Maurice gingerly put his book at the bottom of his bag, wrapping it with a cloth, mitering each corner of the medieval volume with extra care. He then loaded all other contents, with as much as his arms could hold, filling the bag three quarters of the way high. He kept the one true tool every cataphile instantly needed, switching it on, flashing it as his only source of light in the dark tunnels ahead.

Sophie elbowed Maurice, who checked the batteries, flipping the button to the flashlight on and off several times.

Maurice, Sophie, Emma, and Killian all left the soft, ambient brilliance of a hundred candles, along with the relative comfort of the grotto far behind. Now a stifling darkness kindled their way. The tunnels seemed to beckon them with an eerie silence of freedom and foreboding.

Killian turned on his light and held Emma's hand, and the two left the grotto with haste.

Maurice looked over his flashlight as if for the first time. "Yep, these new batteries work just fine." He hurried to follow the rest of them.

Killian led Emma out of the grotto and down into the catacomb tunnels.

Emma drew slight resistance against Killian's tow. "Wait, what about those monster things?"

Killian stopped briefly and glared at her. "Oh, come on. Don't tell me you believe in crazy stories about make-believe monsters." He impatiently patronized. "What are you, a five-year-old?"

"No!" Emma pouted angrily. "Of course I didn't believe it. I just wanted to hear some more. It was a cool story." She tapered her eyes. "You can't just grab my hand and take me wherever you want. I'm nobody's thing. I'm not your property, ya know." She tightened her lips. "I'm my own thing." Emma protested, yet kept walking hand in hand with Killian without resistance.

"Listen, I'm sorry, but I don't trust those two," Killian quietly said.

Emma's eyes brightened. "What's not to trust? I mean, Sophie's a total witch, but the book Maurice has is like a thousand years old, and is like so cool."

"Nah...it was more like five to seven hundred years old," Killian replied with an undertone of arrogance. "Look, it doesn't matter how old the dumb book is, it's just a bunch of superstitious nonsense, and he...I mean they're up to something, but I'll play along for now."

With heavily arched brows, Emma puckered her lips into a soured face. "I want to go home."

"Okay." Killian sighed, sensing her fear. "Let's go then. But the closest exit to your hotel is up here." He pointed to the darkest end of the tunnels ahead. Killian felt Emma hesitate, so he leaned over and kissed her forehead. Looking over top of her, he whispered, "They're coming, but don't worry, I'm here, and I'll get you home...trust me, my sweet."

Sullen, Emma bowed her head. "Okay." Concerned, she asked, "Who's coming?"

"Don't worry, it's not Dwellers." Killian slyly grinned. He turned his attention to the dawdling Sophie and Maurice. "And here I thought you weren't coming with us."

"Four is safer than two. And after all, we are all fellow cataphiles," Maurice said with Sophie lumbering near his side. "We were just waiting for the right partners to tag the catacombs when back in the grotto." Maurice stiffened his lower lip. "Say, do you guys have an extra flashlight?" he asked with an air of pleased oddness.

"Yep." Killian pulled another, smaller light from out of his pocket.

The two couples ceased talking and turned, continuing up into the dark tunnels, toward the endless catacombs.

Killian hiked at a furious pace as if he knew exactly where he was and wanted to be. Emma, mostly blinded by the dark, only caught glimpses of light in the tunnels around her. The whirlwind, underground tour of Paris had her winded, leaving her without time to question or reason, but she trusted Killian.

Sophie and Maurice kept behind at an uneven pace, falling at a distance before catching up more than once. They subdued uneasy quarrels. Allusive glances between them exposed a shared, implicit nature.

The four of them set out to discover the secrets that the tunnels and the catacombs had to offer. Using two flashlights, they squeezed through some tightly cramped, narrow passageways. Crouching down from low ceilings, they folded their shoulders inward just to travel along, hardly able to extend their chest outward for even a deep breath at times.

Without notice, the cramped tunnels would open into a high archway. A large room, partly filled with brown, stagnant, murky water of uncertain depth would suddenly appear. Maurice carried his backpack over top him as he tread through the murky, waist-high water.

Killian, being slightly taller than Maurice, carried Emma on his back over the water's cool, thick grime, with only the tips of her shoes gliding across the wet surface.

Sophie glared at Emma from behind, and then puckered her mouth at the reeking, septic water Killian and Maurice waded through. She huffed loudly toward Maurice for carrying his backpack instead of her. Sophie stomped her foot, nearly slipping backward on the mud before she boldly followed the rest of them into the dirty, stagnant pool.

From the large room to the other side, the odor of raw sewage accompanied the ancient catacombs as each tunnel branched out into four different burrows at this point.

They emerged from the deep pool of backwater.

"Which one of those do we take?" Emma asked, looking into four dark passageways.

Killian let her down from his back shoulders, and pointed with certainty to one tunnel in particular. "This one," he confidently said.

"Are you sure?" Maurice asked. "How do you know?"

"I just do," Killian replied without hesitation, and moved ever forward like a person possessed.

The air became thick, with choking moisture, and from that, a weighted heaviness. It suffocated with every inhalation. Like a damp sweater, it pulled on the lungs, making crisp, clean air impossible for a useful breath.

The cool sogginess clung to them, leaving drops of condensation in a sticky film over their skin. Shorter respirations labored into oppressive gasps with every increasingly listless step. Winded, Maurice shut off his flashlight, saving the battery life, while only occasionally turning it on to shine behind him toward the direction of strange noises the catacombs made.

Sophie and Maurice chose to use the brightness from Killian's light to lead their way. Killian and Emma walked side by side when the tunnels allowed, and Killian led the way in front when the tunnels narrowed to single file.

Maurice stood directly behind Emma. Sophie held onto Maurice's shoulder, for she could see very little of the light this far back.

The single flashlight was nary enough to cast aside the darkness, which sought to submerge everything in repressive misery. The moisture cleaved around them in dense air, which tormented the spirit, and bathed the tunnels in evil, while dulling the senses in complete, yet quiet desperation.

Emma felt an unfamiliar crunching beneath her feet and, along with popping and snapping, the sounds reverberated off the walls as they crushed what seemed like fragile eggshells underfoot.

Emma was the only one of the four who did not know what she was stepping on, so she refused to move until someone flashed the light at the ground near her feet.

Killian pointed his light straight ahead, and never to the ground or the close side walls in the larger tunnel, where they now were traveling.

"I don't think you..." Killian paused.

Emma had had enough. "I'm tired of being down here. I thought you were taking me to one of those nice, spectacular clubs, and not down into the depths of hades." She quickly reached out and snatched the flashlight away from him.

Sophie and Maurice chuckled, each elbowing the other.

Emma accidentally flipped the light into her own eyes. Momentarily blinded, she clamped her eyes shut, slowly opening them for an adjustment from black to bright. Emma blinked, squeezing her eyes several times, all the while scowling from the giggles at her temporary loss of sight. Despite Emma's obvious discomfort, Maurice and Sophie openly engaged in fun at her mistake.

"SHUT UP!" Emma shouted at the two behind her.

"You stupid American." Sophie smirked. "You're just a spoiled little princess, aren't you?" She constantly harassed. "Your clothes are so nice and clean still, but you're so dumb that you don't even know how to work a flashlight. Ha!" She let out a single laugh, while crossing her arms, curling her closed lips, and arching her right brow.

The bottom of Emma's eyelids grew heavy with fresh tears. She sniffled a couple of times. Emma looked down at her new clothes, which were stained brown, black, gray, and waterlogged with dirt particles of sandy muck. Her palms and fingers now caked with sludge, she flipped them around and wiped her tears with the clean backsides of her hands.

Emma's voice cracked. "My clothes are dirty just like yours."

"Go ahead, cry, little princess pity party." Sophie balled her hands inward below the outer corners of her own eyes, moving them back and forth, while pretending to sniffle, cry, and wipe some tears of her own.

Killian and Maurice stood silently as Emma and Sophie argued. Neither of them interfered with their partners.

"You have a damn nerve," Emma shouted. "These clothes are worth more than everything in your closet, or maybe what you're wearing is the only thing you have." Emma snapped her fingers. "Jealous much?"

"Well...at least I'm pretty, and boys like me." Sophie turned her nose up and to the side.

"I've had it!" Emma dropped the flashlight and dove at Sophie's throat.

Chapter Fifteen

The two started fighting on the tunnel ground, rolling over the slimy, eggshell surface. Sophie took a handful of Emma's hair and pulled hard, causing her to scream. Emma grabbed a handful of Sophie's, short, pink locks, and then she smacked her across the face. They kicked and slapped as they rumbled and rolled all over the ground between the tunnel walls. Both yelled, grunted, and cursed at the other.

Maurice watched and smiled, occasionally skipping his feet out of their way. Maurice turned his light back on, pulled out his phone, and began filming the fight.

Frustrated, Killian cupped his hands on top his head. "Do something to control your girlfriend!" he shouted.

Maurice looked up and shrugged. "I haven't seen a good girl fight in quite some time. Come on...enjoy it while it lasts." He smirked. "Man, this is gonna go viral." Maurice angled his video for the best shots as he dodged the rolling combatants.

Killian stared at Maurice with deathly silence. "If you don't stop this, I will, and then I'll be coming after you next."

"You're no fun." Maurice gulped, pouted, and then jerked Sophie's arm, removing her from off Emma.

The two fighters, now held back, were pulled away while still swinging and grabbing at the other.

Sophie held strands of Emma's straggly, brown hair. Yet she sported several scratches across her cheek as payment from Emma.

Killian wrapped up Emma, and Maurice held Sophie back with a straight arm.

"Let go of me!" Emma struggled to gain freedom from Killian's strong grip. "I'm gonna kill her!"

"Now, Maurice," Sophie calmly commanded. "Do it now!" she demanded.

Maurice hesitated. "But we agreed, and it's not time yet."

"I said now!" Sophie shouted.

Maurice limply surrendered his straight arm from up at Sophie, now down by his side. He handed her his backpack. She reached into the bag, grabbing two hand-sized objects, after which, she flipped the pack over her shoulder. Sophie slowly raised a brighter flashlight and then unbent her other arm, pointing a gun squarely at Emma's head.

Emma twirled herself behind Killian, huddling her head in her hands, tucking it between her shoulders, while refusing to look. "Oh, my god! Please don't shoot me! It's not that big a deal, really!"

Killian seemed unfazed. "Be reasonable..."

"Shut up!" Sophie interrupted him. "Maurice, get their money and any valuables." She tightened her lips, raising a single corner slightly higher than the other. She clamped her teeth, elevated her rounded chin, and with a sneer, she glared down past her nose at Killian and Emma. A faint grin emerged, with a glint of smarmy enjoyment. "Hurry up, Maurice!" She pushed him toward Killian and Emma.

Maurice's voice trembled. "Um, okay." He held his own hands, wringing them off on his sweaty forehead.

Sophie swayed the gun back and forth. "Hands up!" She motioned the light sideways, implying that Killian step away from shielding Emma. She then waved the barrel of the gun twice into the air for their hands to go vertical, while Maurice hesitantly frisked the two for valuables. "Sometimes Maurice can be useful."

Emma could not believe this was happening. And it certainly was not the romantic night she had envisioned with Killian. Askew, Emma locked eyes with Killian. Her face packed full with distress, his, however, appeared detached from the current situation.

Killian acted bored and disinterested. The lavish attention he doted upon Emma was gone. Instead of attentive warmth, a new person emerged. A cold, emotionless, calculating, and brooding stranger appeared in his place instead. Killian was supremely focused on something else, something secret and within his control, yet he waited and watched Maurice and Sophie fumble through their dirty deed. Killian glanced down at Maurice while being searched and frisked by him. Killian snarled like a beast. When Maurice caught eyes with Killian, he plucked his hands from out of his pockets, backing away from his cold-blooded stare down.

"What!" Sophie snatched a few mushy dollars and Emma's phone from Maurice's grip. "Are you sure you even searched them?" She raised a distrustful eyebrow.

"Yes!" Maurice started to yell, but soon realized Sophie had the gun, along with an irritated pose, so he repeated more softly, "I mean, yes...my sweet." He sheepishly smiled.

Sophie knew how to handle a gun. She kept the gun aimed at Emma and Killian, even when her face was turned away from them.

Sophie, thinning her eyes, now glanced several times between Emma and Killian with a slight grin. "Despite Maurice's fantastic tales of Dwellers and tagging the catacombs, this is what being a cataphile is really all about." Her smile straightened. "It's not about superstitious nonsense." She glowered at Maurice. "It's not about adventure or fun, it's about taking back from those that take from us up there." Sophie nodded toward the ceiling. "Now give me your flashlight," she angrily demanded.

"Oh, come on." Killian slanted his head while frowning at Sophie. He stared in disbelief with a marked change in mood. "You've got all we have. At least leave us the light." He let his arms down, overlapping them in open defiance.

Emma anxiously shouted, "Please don't shoot!" Her arms still reluctantly raised, they floated in midair. "I don't wanna die. I don't wanna die," she repeated, puffing breaths rapidly.

"I said give it to me...NOW!" Sophie screamed at them. "And you can put your arms down, Emma, you're not under arrest. I'm just robbing you, you ugly dummy." Sophie aimed the gun at Killian. "Are you stupid and deaf? Give Maurice the flashlight, or I'll kill her."

Killian tossed the flashlight in the air to Maurice, who followed Sophie's lead by shining the blinding ray directly into their eyes. Killian used his hand to shield himself from the light, but Emma just squinted.

"Can I at least have my phone back?" Emma asked. "It's no good to you, and I can't get any service down in this hellhole anyway."

Sophie pulled out and inspected Emma's expensive-looking phone from the rest of what Maurice collected from them. "You mean this?" She held it, dangling it back and forth in front of Emma.

Her head dipped between her shoulders, Emma meekly replied, "Yes."

Sophie carelessly dropped Emma's phone to the ground and stomped on it repeatedly, flipping glass shards, micro-boards, computer chips, and torn wires all over the place, with some flying bits soaring into the air. "Oops, it slipped." Her cheeks drew up and in. Sophie's eyebrows folded down, nearly touching multiple crumpled waves of skin atop her nose. She contrived a frown, shrugged her shoulders, and then eased her facial muscles into a smug grin.

Emma somberly eyed the pieces of her broken phone. She held a tearful, irate glare with Sophie, before realizing the true nature of her dire situation. "Wait! I have more money," Emma pleaded. "Just take me back to my hotel room and I'll give you as much as you want."

"What do you take me for," Sophie uttered an insulted, noisy huff, "a fool?"

"How'll I get out of here without a flashlight?" Emma's hands tremored like never before. Her fingers shook hysterically, quaking up into her arms, and then out to the rest of her whole body.

"Maybe they'll help you find your way out." Sophie bumped Maurice on the arm. The two of them flashed their lights up and over toward the walls at the distant end of the tunnel ahead, as well as all over the ground below, and up the near walls just inches from Emma and Killian. "Go ahead...Have a look."

Emma, weary of turning on an aimed gun, swiftly glanced at her surroundings. However, Killian crossed his arms, refusing to turn, or look away. Rather, he stuck to his menacing, intense scowl as sketched lines, unnatural curves, and heated imperfections tainted his beautiful surface.

Sophie smugly beamed. "What, don't you want to see, Killian? Or do you already know what awaits?" she said with a slight chuckle.

Emma froze and gasped. "Wha...wha...what is this place?" she stuttered. "Are those...? Are those...?"

Chapter Sixteen

"Yes, you moron," Sophie snidely remarked. "THIS IS A TOMB!" she yelled. "And now, it's your tomb." Sophie aimed the gun at Emma. "Both of you are pointless, awkward bores, and you deserve each other."

Shocked, Emma unconsciously peered down. The cracking under her feet was now in clear view. The chipped fragments of what seemed like eggshells were human bones, mixed with pasty mud, and grimy water with slithering insects. Cockroaches and rat guts slathered underfoot, and the rank, foul odor of thousands of years in the endless catacombs rose up into Emma's prim nostrils. She choked and heaved. Death permeated Emma's new reality, shutting out any hope wherever she dared look.

Maurice and Sophie turned out the flashlights, allowing Emma and Killian to sample the immense darkness, along with a final taste of the last light either one of them would ever see.

After a few moments of forlorn acceptance of the pitch-black dark, the lights were turned back on. Maurice tossed Killian's flashlight in his backpack and clicked on his own, much-brighter light. He illuminated the tunnels ahead, and revealed a labyrinth of disturbing visions waiting for Emma and Killian in among the endless catacombs.

Emma, emboldened for unknown reasons even to herself, slowly turned her neck for a glimpse behind. "Oh, my god!" She slammed her lids shut, straining her neck, whipping it back around until her muscles stung with an aching lash. "No!" She frantically pleaded, "NO! NO! NO! Please don't do this to me!"

"You like this flashlight?" Maurice, admiring the silver casing, flipped it close to eye level. "Yeah...it's a quality piece all right. I snatched this baby off some other idiot last time we were down here." He glanced over toward Sophie. "Hey...what do you think happened to that guy? You think he ever made it outta here?"

A poker-faced Sophie did not respond.

Killian never looked back or around. He was not even tempted, it seemed. Instead, he remained determined, facing Sophie and Maurice with a poised rebellion.

Emma did not wish to look at her surroundings again. Yet everywhere, the horrible sight of skulls and bones, maggots, and vermin, overwhelmed her desire to look away, so she unwillingly raked it all in as a tormented bystander. "Oh, my god! This place really is a friggin' graveyard." Emma wailed. "You can't leave us down here like this! I wanna go home!" she cried out.

Sophie tightened her bottom lip. "You might want to drop and beg. It sometimes helps, but not often."

Folding her hands together near her lips, Emma briefly glanced at the ground. She snubbed it, refusing to drop to her knees and beseech submissively.

Ignoring Emma's plight, Maurice told a grand story about the human remains inside the catacombs. "These are the noble souls, who hundreds of years ago, fought and gave their lives in a forgotten war." He picked a skull out from the wall and held it next to his head. He shined his light through its hollow base section, allowing spectral beams to radiate from the eye sockets, while the eerie cranium illumined as red as icy blood in his hand.

Maurice took a moment to venerate the prized skull, gawking into its deep, hollow eye sockets before continuing his tale. "These gallant warriors pushed back the horde of beasts known as Dwellers into these catacombs. These soldiers were slaughtered by the millions." He gestured at the skulls, femurs, and rib cages stacked neatly, one on top of the other from floor to ceiling on both sides of the walls, and ahead as far as all of them could see. "They, along with the immortal knights, exterminated the Dwellers, banishing them to this underground realm, thus saving the world that we have come to know," he said, holding a pause, "or so the immortal knights thought." Maurice chortled sinisterly, "Bwa-ha-ha-haaa!"

Sophie cringed, and let out an agitated sigh. "You dunce! You blockhead! I told you to stop reading that ridiculous book. None of that is true!" Enraged, her voice moved loud and rapidly throughout the tunnels.

Terrified, Emma blurted out, "There must be like thousands of dead people's bones down here."

Maurice ignored Sophie and addressed only Emma. "That's where you're wrong! A thousand," he repeated as he held his stomach and laughed some more. "You don't listen very well. Try millions of skulls and bones, for these are the catacombs of the dead." He raised both his arms in symphony, instantly flipping his delight into a dull, solemn, Shakespearean frown. He tilted his head downward, eventually staring up at Emma, but her head had sunken low with a hunched posture.

Maurice slowly curled the edges of his lips upward with a grim bliss. "Hey, it's not that bad," he kindly said. "Maybe I can help you." He then belted a mean and sudden yell. "Look at me!" He clamped his teeth. When Emma faintly regarded him with a glimmer of faith, he flashed his bright light directly into her eyes. A harsh blindness stung her sight, yet darkened a rising callus upon her soul. Emma turned her head and winced. Maurice gleefully smiled with an oversized mouth of toothy amusement.

Emma shaded her eyes from the light. "Stop bullying me!" she barked at Maurice. She turned her face toward a passive Killian. "And why aren't you doing anything to stop this?"

Killian shrugged. "What's there to do?"

Pointing at Maurice and Sophie, Emma exclaimed, "He's a creep, she's a sadistic witch, but you're just a disappointment." A surge of disgust covered her face.

Killian tried to appease. "Emma, I..."

Emma planted her hands on her hips and turned away. "Don't even. I hate you! I wish we had never met." She half turned her body back toward his.

"Ah, a lovers' quarrel," Sophie interjected. "Thank you for all of your kind remarks toward me earlier, Emma, but this is where we take the crappy gifts you gave us and leave." Sophie flipped her hand backward, while turning the opposite direction. "So long, losers. Enjoy your time down here in hotel oblivion."

"No!" Emma hysterically squeezed her hands, recoiling into a wobbly shell of herself. The room spun. Her chest tightened. Her head felt light, and her arms and feet tingly. Yet before Sophie left, Emma threw one last distressful gaze in hopes of compassion. "Please...don't leave me down here like this. I beg you," Emma said with clutched and folded fingers.

"What about him?" Sophie mocked. "What about your boyfriend?"

"I don't care about him. I just want to see my ma..." Emma abandoned her sentence, ending short of saying "mom." "My...home and friends again," she finished.

Maurice liked the begging and chuckled. "Go ahead, get on your knees and put your face in the mud, and maybe, just maybe I'll think about helping you outta here."

Bent in on herself, Emma looked back and forth between Maurice and Sophie. "What?" She narrowed her eyes in disbelief.

"The Dwellers are coming," Maurice taunted. "I can hear them." He cupped his hand to his ear. "The catacombs are their home. Can't you hear them coming?" He smiled, shining the flashlight toward the endless, double-sided row of skulls and bones. "And remember, when you hear an unexpected scream, it's a warning that you're next." He pointed at Killian and Emma. "The Dwellers whisper to each other, and when the whispers turn into one voice, it means they're close, and a horrible end for you is near."

Emma closed her eyes and placed her hands over her ears. "No, stop it!" she yelled.

Killian silently lowered his head and glared up at Maurice. "Knock it off."

But Maurice garnered enjoyment from their fear, so he continued. "The screams foreshadow the end, but it's not a quick end, it's a slow, painful end." He rubbed his stomach. "They'll brutally tear you apart, limb from limb like a savory morsel. They eat your intestines while you're still alive. If you're lucky, the Dwellers will find you edible, and thus unworthy of being turned into one of them—doomed to live for an indefinite time between life and death, down here, rotting forever in the quagmire of darkness."

Sophie grumbled at her partner. Without warning, she hit him upside his head with the gun. Maurice winced, moaning from the sharp knock and pain that followed. He felt a cold sensation on his head. He instantly reached up where the gun hit. His eyes wide, his mouth gaping, his lower lip quivered. His hand quaked, and he nearly fainted at the blotchy sight of his own blood dabbed on his fingertips.

"Are you crazy?" Maurice shouted at Sophie.

"Stop it! Just stop it," Sophie snapped at Maurice with bored agitation. "Give her those." She tapped a small pocket on the side of the backpack.

Sophie and Maurice started loudly arguing in French, but Maurice halted when Sophie aimed the gun at him. With a frown, he begrudgingly reached into the small side pocket, tossing a used, worn-out matchbook toward Emma.

The matchbook spun like a square Frisbee, ricocheting off the tips of Emma's outstretched arms and fingers. She held a gasp as they fell upon the moist ground.

Emma got on her knees and ran her hands with outspread digits everywhere along the muddy debris until the matches were found. She stood up, and held them tightly. She eagerly opened the pack, reading the letters above its worn cover. A cute, green fairy winked from the matchbook cover at her. "Spectacular-Spectacular," Emma said to herself, briefly glancing down and then up again. "This was the club we passed on the way here tonight." After a moment, she opened the matchbook. "Hey! There's only five matches here!" Her forehead compressed layers of rippled skin.

"Yes, and I suggest you use them wisely," Sophie callously replied.

"But wait..." Emma extended a mucky hand.

"Like I said, that's all I can do." Sophie cut into her words.

Maurice, dazed, with rapidly blinking eyes, turned the opposite direction. He leaned on Sophie while holding his bloody head, and together the two walked down the tunnel from the direction they had come.

Sophie, without another word, trod backward, holding the gun on them, switching it between Emma and Killian, and once she was far enough away, she simply uttered, "I'm sorry." Sophie hinted honest regret. But she, along with Maurice, promptly turned, fading into the choking darkness until they had disappeared from view.

Chapter Seventeen

When Sophie left, so did all remnants of any light. A hopeless dark reigned over Emma and Killian, stifling all thought, crushing even the happiest of memories, and raiding the senses until misery finally had its long awaited company.

As an unlimited black plague of darkness engulfed her, Emma yelled one more time, "No...wait!"

Killian nudged her arm, putting his hand on her shoulder. "It'll be all right. We'll get out of here, and they'll get what they deserve."

The early stages of panic attacked, rushing in with burning sternal pain. "What?" Emma panted, while rubbing at her upper, middle chest. "You mean like stupid Karma, or something?" She yanked her shoulder away, claiming it back from Killian's comforting, rested hand.

"Yeah, I guess, kind of like Karma," Killian evenly replied.

Emma barked at him, "Don't be so dumb!" Her anxiety rose as her breaths shortened. "Karma doesn't exist!"

A dark so thick enclosed the tunnels like a noose around her neck. The black, unholy darkness choked and erased even Emma's own hands from her view. She waved them back and forth in front of her face, feeling only the movement of air, without any sight of her own limb. Now annoyed, frustrated, and fearful, her once pleasant tone inflected angry dirges upon Killian. Expressions the darkness had taken from her face, lent to her voice having a considerable uptick in anger and fear.

"Listen, I'm sorry," Killian said. "But we really should try to focus and find our way out of this hellhole as you like to say."

"Go away! I hate you!" Frightened anxiety surrounded and trapped Emma. She felt locked in a restricted, festering, waterlogged doom. "I hate you! I hate you! I hate you!" Her frame tensed as each breath constricted worse than the last. "And after I get out of here, I never want to see you ever again."

Killian stayed silent, he just took her hand and started walking along side. Emma pulled back her control, and began running her fingertips along the bumpy walls instead.

Killian could hear her fingernails gliding against the tunnel wall. "You shouldn't do that," he simply said.

"Why?" Emma kept her slow, steady stride, while her fingertips read the wall for directions. "It's not like you're any help," she snapped back.

"If you follow the walls to get out, you'll just end up in one of the many small antechamber rooms off the main path." Killian's somber gist resounded experience and truth. "You'll never get out, but instead, you'll just walk around in circles until you collapse."

"I'm doing this my way, and I don't need you!" Emma shouted.

Killian inflected willing reluctance. "All right."

After a few silent minutes of denial, Emma sighed a bothered, yet resigned puff of air. "Okay, I want to go that way then." She pointed ahead into the solid darkness, forgetting that she could not see her own hand. "We should follow those two...ugh!" She wanted to scream rather than utter Sophie and Maurice's names. Emma calmed herself with a deep inhalation before finishing. "And if we go back the way we came, I know we'll get out of here."

"No, Emma. They'll never find their way out." Killian gathered her arms and gently said, "Like I told you before. I know a way out back there, and it isn't far from your hotel." He tugged her in the opposite direction.

For the first time in a long while, she felt something like elation after Killian's last words. Even the frustrating thought of arguing with her mother back at the hotel room, appeared trivial by comparison to Emma's current situation. "Okay, but I still hate you, ya know." She held his hand tightly, and in the vast darkness, she cozied her arm intertwined next to his.

They walked through gloomy blackness so horribly immense, it stirred terror only imagined in nightmares and hallucinations.

Emma discovered an abundance of what lurks about the murderous portions of her unstable, fragile mind. Thoughts she never explored crept into her brain. Thoughts only the insane dare cross into reality, while treading carelessly amid the foul portions found between life and isolated horror.

They marched on endlessly, but in reality, it was no more than minutes strung together in bunches. Emma clung to Killian's shoulder, and rested her wary hand upon it. Her feelings toward him softened. She now worried about random objects jumping out and poking at her face while masked in the darkness.

Emma waved her other hand back and forth, straight-armed in front of her face, yet still, she was unable to view her own fingers. During one sweeping motion, she felt a tactile smooth, semi-rounded part of the wall. Lacking a full mental picture, she ran her fingers down the side of the flat, bumpy, yet raised item. It was smooth on top, with a semi-circular portion. Accompanied below the strange object, Emma felt two large, round inlets, which her fingers easily slipped inside the holes. The unusual object had a much smaller, third hole directly beneath the other two, except this one was shaped like a rigid triangle, with pointed edges replacing the smooth surface of the previous two larger holes above. She pulled her fingers out and ran them farther down the strangely formed surface that protruded from the wall. Underneath the three holes, Emma thought she found treasure, as a double row, top and bottom set of pearls fashioned an image in her mind. Some of the pearls were smooth, while others were chipped, broken, or missing altogether. Baffled, she let go of Killian and reached into her pocket for light. Emma struck one of the five matches Sophie gave her. With all the dampness surrounding the catacombs, the matches were soaked, and so she mumbled a silent prayer in hopes of sparking an extremely insignificant flame just this once.

Killian heard the repetitive scratching of flint with a rubbed grind. "Emma, wait..."

"No...I have to see what this is. I think it's some kind of jewelry..." She ripped the match, once, twice, three times against the book's rough, sandy paper strip.

The match hissed, flaring a tiny glow, at first brighter, yet then, like everything else, its light waned among the cloudy darkness of the tunnels.

Emma hastily stepped backward, almost dousing the newly flared match with her damp hair. She attempted to yelp, but Killian's hand quickly covered her mouth. She was touching one of the million skulls held by the wall in a twisted macabre, graphic work of deviant art.

The dark had become her friend for a while, and unseen, she had forgotten what unpleasant things had surrounded her the entire time. But unlike before, the skulls and bones, so neatly stacked on top of each other along the catacomb walls, hovered over her, and seemed to arch down from atop, bitterly choking out a piece of Emma's frail sanity.

The long since dead faces stared without eyes. The skulls smiled with yellowish, pearly, broken teeth. Bugs crawled from nasal cavity into eye socket and back again. She had focused so much on getting out of the tunnels, that Emma did not realize she had entered the main crypt of the catacombs.

This massive chamber was a tomb of defamed humanity, with skulls mounted alongside thousands of femurs. There were feet missing toes, hands without fingers, cracked rib cages, and millions of tiny vertebra bone fragments sprinkled throughout every inch along the kingdom of the very undearly departed.

Emma began randomly grabbing and soon pried Killian's hand from off her mouth. A nauseated, uncontrollable reflex from within the pit of her stomach washed over her face in ghastly harmony of instantaneous vomit. With a slow, disbelieving blink, Emma wiped her stomach's contents off her bottom lip.

Not long after, a prolonged gaze halted her words. Emma attempted a cleansing gulp, yet a lump crowded her middle throat, requiring numerous swallows before the bitter knob removed itself from her clogged gullet.

Cockroaches and snakes crawled in and out of human skulls. The vermin leisurely slithered and crawled through mouth, nose, and eyes of the stacked craniums. The hollow heads appeared cemented into the wall in infinite rows from top to bottom and back to front, as the only wall that seemed to exist in this place.

Emma accidentally crushed bugs and bones, which fused together underfoot. Though she had tried not to do so, the sheer numbers and enclosed space made it impossible to avoid the reviled wall of death.

Emma's favorite shoes were lathered in mud, guts, bone chips, and other unidentified parts and pieces from the many slimy, clumped, and grubby-looking things.

"Oh, gross!" Emma lifted a foot, sulking, while examining her shoe. "These are brand-new!" An irate tone resounded. "Do you know how much these cost!?"

Killian fumbled, "I, um..."

"Of course you wouldn't know!" Emma, her stomach now settled, frustrated, hoisted her arms upward. As the match faded, it lit a trail, and her face glowered with angry lines and shadows in wake of the tiny fire's waning light. "And this was your idea of a date..." The match seared down to her finger. "Ouch!" Emma yelled.

She shook her index finger and thumb, jamming the mud-covered digits into her mouth. Then, realizing where her hands had been, she quickly removed her fingers and hacked up spit on the ground several times. "That stupid match, it burned me!" Emma reached for another from the soggy book.

"No, save them." Killian put his hand across her forearms.

"What?" Emma nudged away and struck another match against his will. "Why? I thought you said we're almost out of here." She turned her frustration toward him.

Killian brought his hands toward his face, slowly curling fingers into a fist before he relaxed them back into five separate digits. "You are the most selfish, spoiled, inconsiderate brat I've ever met!"

Emma clenched her teeth. Warm blood rushed up until its heat burned from inside out her cheeks. "Why you..." A raised vocal sound charged.

Yet before Emma could finish her thought, Killian propped against, and gently touched the back of her hand, caressing her messy, angry lips. Mixed with anxiety and bother, fear and concern, the yearning attraction of this unexpected, passionate advance both stunned and excited her with a familiar tingle from head to toe.

If there was one thing Killian knew, it was how to kiss with a gentle stroke that buckled Emma's knees while snapping her will. He breached even the cold, angry, and seemingly impenetrable barriers within her, while easily piercing the layers of Emma's hardened shell. He engaged in soft conversation. His tender lips brushed up and down her cheeks, near her earlobes, and with persistent charm, Emma's doubt melted into confidence, which Killian spun to his favor.

Killian and Emma locked lips in a struggle of friction. Then he tenderly removed his lips from her. Goosebumps upturned tiny hairs, heightening waves of delightful senses throughout her body. Emma's hot-tempered blood now flowed into her lips, returning a speechless, giddy, slightly less-than-mature woman she'd portrayed just minutes earlier.

"You're a selfish, spoiled brat, but that's why I'm crazy about you," Killian said, maintaining an insistent, serious appearance.

She nearly collapsed under his enchanted pressure. Emma swayed back and forth as if whitecaps upon the high seas. His spellbound bewitchment lingered, and with half-closed eyes, she dabbed her tongue briefly to her top lip. "No," she faintly muttered, "I think you're just plain crazy." She threw another match on the ground and wrapped her arms around his waist.

In the midst of an adoring, intimate exchange, Killian and Emma intertwined, rapidly kissing while the precious light from the match crackled on the ground. The tiny fire shrunk until it flamed out among the hazy darkness, and soon, even the match, with a puff of wispy smoke, drowned in the thick, muddy dark tunnels like every other lost thing in the catacombs.

Chapter Eighteen

With the passing of time, minutes felt like hours in the swimming darkness of the catacombs.

Impenetrable blackness surrounded Emma and Killian, distorting time and space until they seemed as mere figments of the imagination.

Tiny sounds, usually indistinct, were magnified a thousandfold while in the tunnels.

It was dark, as dark as dark gets. The catacombs distorted all sense and direction. Drips of water clashed like brass symbols in a marching band. Multilegged critters scuttled around in the dark. Their creepy, crawly feet tapped in harmony one after the other, like a military battalion of soldiers in procession, trudging from every minuscule direction imaginable. Moreover, even Killian and Emma's breaths wheezed noisily with forced air, rushing in and out, resonating of labored respirations.

A shrieked cry broke open the hushed, dark noise. Emma jumped. Yet Killian remained constant. His lips charted a landing onto her soft skin. He honed in for another sweet kiss, all the while remaining unfazed, ignoring what he too had heard.

Emma instantly turned her head toward the scream, pushing at his chest with considerable resistance. Her head on a swivel, she whipped it back and forth. The shriek, the bloodcurdling cry, echoed, while traveling through her. The catacombs made it nearly impossible to know from which direction the scream came.

"Did you hear that?" Emma panted short and heavy. "It sounded like Sophie."

"Who cares," Killian dismissively said. "They robbed us and then left us down here to basically die." He closed his eyes, put his hands on the wall alongside her head, and leaned in for another grazing pass. "Besides, she probably just saw a rat or something."

It had happened quickly, and only once, so Emma doubted she had even heard what she thought she heard in the first place. Slowly, she trusted his casual explanation, letting down her guard. But before long, again, up from the tunnels, a shrill, jarring scream roared with ghastly desperation. Vocal cords strained, and bellowed forth a throaty, last sinking cry.

After the screams faded, words followed. Heavy words, fraught with panic boomed from all parts of the tunnels. "No! Maurice! No!" Then a patch of cold silence was followed by, "Someone please help us! PLEASE!" A female's voice rang shrill cries in the darkness. "Oh, my god! OH, MY GOD! NOOOOOOOOOOOOOOOOOO!"

This time, Emma did not doubt what her ears had heard, and so, without hesitation, pulled far away from Killian's calm, romantic hold. "That was Sophie." Emma pinpointed the sound, and walked back toward where the screams had appeared to come. She cringed while groping many weird, sharply pointed objects along the walls in the dark. Some were jagged, and pricked her searching fingertips. Others were slimy, while more than a few moved when she passed her hand over top for a grip.

The startling fright of both knowing the open graves all around her in the darkness, along with piercing screams and moving swarms, nearly cost Emma her balance. "Maurice is in trouble," Emma said, determined to find her way back toward the last set of high-pitched cries. "I hope he gets what he...they deserve."

Emma walked, not really sure of where she was going. She tripped on the uneven ground, stumbling forward. *Splosh.* She loudly splashed through many grimy puddles. Killian's footsteps became lighter as he more leisurely ensued. Emma, assuming the lead, hid her lost and disoriented state from him. She waved her hands frantically ahead of her moving position, but only empty, dark, and heavy air filled her path. Occasionally, she bumped into the walls and staggered over unknown items on the ground, yet still, she caught herself from tumbling the rest of the way down. With her rapid pace, the air clung with a familiar heaviness of choking humidity, dragging upon her lungs. But unlike the moldy smell from before, the air had a new odor. It was pungent, like the rotting of ten thousand years. However, a fresh but strong whiff of iron intermingled with a rancid stench. Together, the odor overwhelmed Emma's nostrils in a torrent of offensive waves, each one stronger and more vile than the last.

"Killian?" Emma searched backward for his hand, yet he did not answer, and she did not find a warm, soft hand to hold hers. "Killian?" she repeated urgently as she struck one of her three remaining matches.

The match flared with a brief hiss. Emma spun a full circle, but Killian had disappeared. She was now all alone.

For the first time, she felt the walls truly close in on her. Short, shallow panting recoiled her chest in and out until Emma felt woozy.

The screams she had followed disappeared. The silence was deafening, and in combination with the absolute dark, a recipe for crushed soul was served up with sides of dread and hopelessness, both dished out and splattered upon her emotional plate like mashed-up, slopped gruel.

Terror was so abundant that the simple act of swallowing knotted her throat. A single step became an impossible task. Her chest constricted. Her stomach twisted. And for the first time in Emma's life, she considered dying, yet not just dying, but dying down here in the dark, scary, and most of all, lonely tunnels among the remains of the already dead.

Her dry mouth parched, yet it overflowed regret from the tip of her tongue to the well of her soul. Though water resided in abundance down in the tunnels, Emma hated its bitter sound and sight, for it taunted her in ways she had never noted before.

Her empty belly grumbled, and for the first time, she felt deep pains of real hunger.

Emma worried that her mother would never know what happened to her. She feared becoming one of the forgotten people in the catacombs around her. Suddenly, Emma realized how a person could vanish without notice from the world, never to be seen or heard from again.

Hysterically, she stumbled through the tunnels. Her nice shoes were soaked, heavy as wooden clogs, while squishing out water with every step. Her eyes were sore and strained, and her senses dampened in agreement with her extreme, draining sorrow.

The prospect Emma wished for, of never seeing her mother again, now, as irony would have it, seemed a cruel joke. A recent turn of fate, coupled with her own distorted recollections, haunted her consciousness.

The insight of isolation in the absolute dark kept her mother constantly upon her distorted mind, and for some reason, that hated dress in the boutique from earlier in the day, flashed a searing image, which her fleeting thoughts would not allow a moment's peace.

Emma struggled to free a positive thought, but failed, and soon, her worries grew until fear expanded beyond what she could endure. Clarity took its place, a place she never knew existed, and now, finally, she saw the terror of an ugly thing she detested inside herself.

No longer walking with purpose, Emma slid her back up against and down the nearest wall. Dirty hands covered her face with resentful shame as she whimpered. Emma hooked her hands around her shins and pulled her knees in tight to her chest. She crowded into a misshapen ball. Her head weighed down like a brick between her legs. No longer did Emma resemble the woman she appeared above ground, but rather, she was now just a scared young girl, sitting all alone in a silent, dark sewer, noisily weeping with a paralyzed burden of uncontrollable doubt.

"Why is everyone so mean to me?" she mumbled to herself in a moment of her own uncertain clarity. "I'm sick of everyone. I hate them all!" she continued.

Emma, content to sit there and die, considered her escape from the murky tunnels and catacombs as a futile impossibility now.

Bleakness draped over her in waves of gloom, flooding all reason as it drowned her understanding, leaving only the unreasonable to take hold of her conscious mind.

A sound, hardly audible, scantly vibrated in her eardrums. Emma wiped a few tears and lifted her head. There was something new, and anything new had to be good.

Chapter Nineteen

Lub-dub, lub-dub, lub-dub. A faint beating sound, fashioned in rhythm like that of a heart, weakly thumped off in the distant air of the catacombs.

Everything in the black tunnels disoriented and confused Emma's senses. She stood. It took her a few minutes, but she willed her unmovable body up, preparing it to walk again, motivating her discouraged self to follow the sound of hope, while hoping she could find her way in the pitch darkness.

Surmising that Killian had seduced and then abandoned her for his own escape, or worse yet, was in on it with Sophie and Maurice, Emma discovered a new reason to live—the power of resentful anger and hate.

Emma figured they had had one last tormenting laugh at her expense by pranking those screams earlier, but since then, there had been silence, and nothing more.

At any rate, Emma surmised that Killian, Sophie, and Maurice were all long gone by this point, and probably having a good time in some nightclub above ground.

Begrudgingly, she walked toward the new, strange sound. The pulsing beat maintained a pattern, with consistent intervals between thumps, gradually becoming louder as she neared its source. Emma began to imagine that maybe this new sound could free her from the heaps of death in the catacombs, releasing her instead to where she belonged, up above, in the world of the living once again.

The thumping grew louder, crushing the silence. The previous faint noise now painfully drummed a beat inside her ears.

Emma was getting closer, if not by sight, then by sound. She reached down and struck a match to flint, two, three, four times before it hissed lit, but the tunnels, it seemed, were empty.

Nervous that the matches were overexposed to the soggy conditions, with quick anxiety, Emma shivered with unknown fright. She looked over her shoulder, yet neither a thing was in front nor behind, except for what had always been, skulls and bones up both walls from floor to ceiling, left and right, and front to back as far as she could see in along the catacombs.

Emma paused, her eyes wet and wide. She raised her shoulders up and down with disappointment, but the thumping beat loudly upon her exact location, almost as if it were beside her.

Emma talked to herself. "Where's that stupid sound coming from?"

From luck came a glancing side view at a hidden room to her left. A small room, an antechamber appeared, and then a hidden entrance recessed from the main part of the catacombs. *Dup-dup, dup-dup.* A heart beat and thumped from inside the antechamber open doorway.

Emma had never been closer to something other than dark silence. She was close, so close that the sound waves pulsated along the ground under her feet and up through her body, until the thuds chattered even her teeth.

Tossing the fading match to the ground, she lit a fresh one on first attempt.

Crouching, she cautiously neared the corner entrance of the room. With one eye, she peered around the bend. Emma's young face aged in an instant of terrible horror. Her pupils dilated and constricted, while targeting a hideous site, a site like no other she dared imagine. Her mind struggled to grasp what her eyes viewed. However, panic sent an automatic response, shocking her system with tremors up and down her spine as goosebumps raised tiny hairs all over her body. Her movements were arrested, and her breaths short and shallow. The once hopeful sound became a dreaded thumping noise, which pounded violently in her ears, and with each beat, the earsplitting clamor now directly threatened to end her own life as well.

Unable to blink, Emma watched and shivered.

In petrified silence, she observed the horrible event unfold. Maurice, felled on his knees, with eyes still open, stared off into nothingness. Though he appeared alive, he looked like someone already gone. Above him stood the monster in the picture from the old book that Maurice had shown Emma in the grotto earlier that evening.

The rhythmic, thumping beat came from the creature itself. Emma watched terrified as the Dweller, still unaware of her presence, attached one of its long bony hands atop Maurice's head.

The Dweller's long, ugly, emaciated fingers ran down Maurice's skull, nearly covering his face, while sharp claws hooked up underneath his chin, piercing into his skin as minuscule drops of fresh, bright red blood coated each tip of the Dweller's razor talons.

From the beast's palm, it sucked Maurice's body fluids out the top of his head. Maurice's skin, once a healthy texture and color, now turned a pale greenish white, the color preceding imminent vomit and death.

Ba-bum, ba-bum. With each throbbing, rhythmic pulse, fluid poured up to the Dweller from Maurice. His once full cheeks wasted away, sinking in on themselves. Emma watched quietly, sickened as Maurice's eyes rolled back and then deflated into his skull like withered balloons. Emma wanted to look away. She did several times, shutting her eyes tightly, yet she, unwilling to her own wish, mutely gawked at the beautiful disaster instead. She leaned around the wall's edge for a better look. Not believing her eyes, Emma discovered that, indeed, the thumping heartbeat, which reverberated throughout the catacombs, was the monster's hand attached to the top of Maurice's head.

Like a surgical instrument, its bony, skeletal hand covered Maurice's head like a bonnet, wrapping around his skull as if the two were one. Hundreds, possibly thousands of tiny, circular marble-like beads flowed up and beneath Maurice's skin, from his arms to his head, and then were seemingly digested into the creature's giant clawed, sickle-shaped hand. With each heartbeat, the circular beads under Maurice's skin moved, traveling upward, pausing between pulses. *Ba-bum, ba-bum.* The revolting, mechanical pulse thumped on and off, drumming an orchestra of death. But it was not Maurice's heart, for his had clearly stopped. Rather, as the Dweller feasted on its victim's life force, its own heart grew stronger with every pulse and thump before Emma's very eyes.

After a few minutes, the Dweller began to change in appearance. Shocked, Emma ogled, her hand covering her mouth as the creature's bony, emaciated frame, developed muscles, tendons, veins, arteries, cartilage, along with eyes, ears, and even sprouting hair as a nose grew, each part molding themselves over a rancid, decaying layer of the Dweller's body.

Soon, a fresh coat of skin rolled over the Dweller's rotting husk of an outer shell. The once horrible, aberrant beast, slowly morphed into something more human, but not just human, the Dweller started to look exactly like Maurice.

Unwell, Emma silently tiptoed backward. This was too much for her to view anymore.

Emma could no longer justify gawking at the strangely mesmerizing, wrecked, mangled mess that used to be Maurice. Afraid to turn her back on the creature, which continued to devour Maurice in the hidden, smaller, dark room, Emma quietly removed herself from the thumping beat and gory mess by walking backward. *Thud-thud.* Her own heart raced like a rabbit, pounding fast and hard from inside her chest. She held her breath while gasping for air, but the damp moisture of the catacombs hung as steel, woolly curtains, making any deeper breaths loud, uncomfortable, and impossible for her lungs to permit.

With eyes averted, she demanded her mind to wash away the lurid, nightmarish fright, which her eyes had unbelievably viewed. Yet a disfigured Maurice, combined with an otherworldly beast taking his form, burned into her corneas and branded itself upon her mind, haunting any peaceful space left, replacing it with an arcane fear, while wallowing her soul, splashing it red as blood and black as the air surrounding her in the catacombs.

Emma's core emotions clustered in panicked bunches of distraction, which formed a singular motivation, to flee from the horrid scene that now threatened to snatch her very soul.

Emma tipped on her toes, taking long, spread paces softly backward. She dropped the withering match.

Considering her distance from the antechamber was far enough to turn and run, she bolted from the gruesome sight. She blindly fled what remained of Maurice. Her heart skipped. Emma gasped rapid breaths of musty air, wheezing uncontrollably. Her fearful thoughts pushed her body beyond its limits as she fled the monstrous Dweller in the bleak, gloomy darkness of the catacombs.

Running, with her fingertips against the right side wall to balance herself, she had to stop after a short while, somewhat from panting, but mostly from stumbling over random objects in the deep darkness.

Unable to coordinate her movements, she clumsily tripped, finally leaning heavy headed across her forearm, and against the nearest wall while catching her breath.

The thumping sound of the hideous pulsating beat quieted as Emma straightened herself.

Cautiously she gathered her thoughts into a calm before pacing a controlled scuttle away from the Dweller through the pitch black tunnels.

Still trembling, but content that she eluded the unsightly beast back in the antechamber, Emma lit another match.

With the catacombs far behind, momentary relief lessened the gravity bearing down upon her shoulders. A tense empathy for the isolated darkness fondled her sanity. Emma smiled amid the solitary confines. Though being alone in the dark was something that had always frightened her, she now shared a peaceful blindness, a twisted sort of unclear symbiotic denial with her current, dubious surroundings. And while she still feared what she could not see, Emma hid under cloak of dark's unsettled refuge, for worse things crowded upon her mind, making irrational fears now seem ever more reasonable to her heightened senses.

Chapter Twenty

Emma lit another match. It hissed at first strike. For safety's sake, she turned and looked behind. Her own pulse jumped with each glance backward. One moment the tunnels were empty, the next moment, an apparition formed from darkness into a shadowy human figure.

It unexpectedly appeared just inches away, standing, yet pale as a corpse, and with unblinking eyes, it looked right through her. It was a familiar face, except befell with fossilized horror no human should ever imagine to see.

Emma attempted to scream, yet her voice failed. The familiar face put an index finger up to their lips, hushing Emma, briskly covering her mouth from any attempts to sound alarm.

Emma ripped the hand off her mouth. "Sophie...what happened to you?"

Sophie put a finger to her own lips. "Shh!" Her widened eyes darted left and then right.

Sophie's pink hair was tangled. Her fine, thin strands pasted together in a mix of encrusted clumps and, along with bloody, trickling lines from her crown, the red viscous fluid curved over and down past her pallid cheeks. A clotted scab broke free a bright weeping drainage from her hair to the ledge of her chin. The fresh wound bled swiftly down off her face, making a subtle plunk into one of the various muddy puddles on the ground. Her deadpan appearance had lost all hue. Few things but unthinkable fear or ultimate death changed features and drained living color so rapidly in a person.

Sophie's eyes had not blinked, but rather, they vacantly gazed off into a nothingness of the black void ahead. Yet Emma, after what she had seen and experienced earlier, was not only cautious of the real Sophie, but even more so of a vicious, demonic creature pretending to be Sophie.

"Please don't kill me!" Emma dropped to her knees, and prayed to the cold, hard ceiling above.

Sophie blankly wiped runny blood from off her cheek, smudging it against her drawn skin. She twisted her neck from side to side, looking over her shoulders down toward the catacombs and whispered, "Shh, it isn't safe here. We have to move!"

"So, you're not one of them?" Emma asked.

"You saw something?"

"Only out of the corner of my eye, so I ran."

"What do you mean, am I one of them?"

Emma simply replied, "No, nothing." She shook her head, while jetting out her lower lip. "I didn't mean anything by it."

Shock setting in, Sophie rambled her words as her body shivered nonstop. "That thing...that monster...it took Maurice. And I couldn't save him." Sophie's talk bounced from thought to random thought. "He was right. I should have listened. It grabbed me, but I got away." She hopped on her right leg, clearly favoring it over the other. "Oh, my god, Maurice was right. He was right about everything...I have to go back and save him."

Hobbling, Sophie nearly collapsed with a single step. She dragged her mangled, bloody right lower limb along, hauling it like a dead, wooden stump. Sophie turned on her flashlight. Emma tossed the match to the ground and stretched her arms toward Sophie for her much needed, one-legged relief. A hesitant sidelong glare melted away, and Sophie leaned on Emma's offered, stable shoulder.

Sophie groaned each letter of her words. "I...have...to...find...Maurice." She eased a bit for the remaining. "And then we have to get the hell out of here as fast as we can!"

Emma eyed Sophie's backpack. She knew it contained several things that could help her get out of the catacombs alive. Emma especially coveted the weapon brandished against her earlier, and wondered if it was still among the contents of the backpack now slung over Sophie's shoulder.

Emma smiled a quick, coy, and cheerful upturn with the corners of her lips. Emma kept her true feelings close and guarded. She would continue to support Sophie's extra weight on her shoulder until such time Emma felt only one of them could continue living.

Sophie winced. "Listen, I'm really sorry about what I did to you." Distressed agony bulged out between each word. "It was wrong." Shuffling her healthy foot, she skipped along while leaning extra weight upon Emma's shoulder.

Emma brushed Sophie's comments aside. "Oh...what? Don't worry about that. Be strong for Maurice." She snuck a peek into the backpack.

In tears, Sophie said, "No. I'm sorry. I'm really really sorry. I'll make it up to you. I promise. I don't know how, but I will."

"We don't have time for any of that stuff right now." Emma frowned, sighing at her failed attempt to look in the backpack. "Listen, do you still have the gun?" she bluntly said.

"Yes." Sophie patted the backpack. "That monster was so quick and strong, we didn't even have a chance to pull it out and use it. But I'll be ready next time."

Adding a hint of innocence to her tone, Emma volunteered, "Maybe if it wasn't in the bag, and I held it, we could kill that thing if it comes back."

Sophie protested, "No. I don't want to kill it. I want to find Maurice first." With her crooked foot bent and twisted back in an unnatural position, Sophie jerked her head upward and clamped her teeth together, stopping Emma from walking farther until the rushed agony of her leg's mangled spasm waned into a mild anguish. "Maybe that's..." She huffed loudly, nearly collapsing down and in, "a good idea. I'll get the gun out of the bag and hold it though," Sophie said.

"What about the flashlight?" Emma asked. "You can't hold both."

Sophie pulled her limp appendage for another short, painful skip, and paused for a deep breath. "Here." She handed the light to Emma. "By the way, where's your boyfriend?"

"Oh, Killian's not my boyfriend, he's just..." Emma hesitated, "some guy."

"So I guess you don't care what happens to him down here then?"

"No, not really," she coldly said. "He ditched me like a total loser, so no...I don't care about him at all."

"Well, I have to find Maurice. He's not just a guy to me." While balancing her weight, Sophie slipped from off Emma's shoulder and down onto her mangled, bloody leg. "GRR! ARGH!" Sophie quietly held her scream. She puffed her cheeks, filling them with misery's air, while panting vigorously in and out. With her eyes clamped and jaw clenched, she grabbed at her mutilated leg, falling hard to the ground this time. A pointed shinbone gouged through her skin with an unbearable sensation of torn tendons and muscle spasms. Only vast fright trumped her body's distress. With a muffled groan, and the fear of catacomb devils hearing her injured cry, she held back a scream at its height of escape.

Sophie thrashed about on the ground, dropping the gun to use both hands to brace her wounded leg. The weapon fell into the mud, just inches away from her fully occupied hands.

Emma stared unhelping at Sophie, but her flashlight drifted downward at the gun within her reach. Emma beamed the flashlight back at Sophie and then the gun. The two briefly eyed each other, and then soon after, each eyed the gun. A race ensued as Sophie and Emma scrambled to claim the weapon.

Emma, mobile and faster, snatched it from Sophie's slippery, muddy, blood-drenched fingertips.

Emma quickly stood, and while looking down the barrel of the gun, she swiftly pointed it, along with the flashlight at a passive Sophie, who bent over on three out of four limbs like a broken table. Sophie wobbled her balance, favoring her mangled, bloody stump. She defiantly narrowed her eyes into slits up through the beam of light, and willfully tightened her jaw at the unyielding shadow behind the gun's barrel.

Chapter Twenty-One

"HA!" Emma scornfully laughed. She flashed the light directly into Sophie's eyes as she wallowed helplessly on the ground. "Now I make the rules."

Injury exposed insult. Dried particles of encrusted dirt intermingled with purulent, bright red drainage. The mixture blotched over Sophie's pained look, yet even suffering could not hide her fury over the sudden reversal of fortunes between her and Emma.

"I thought we were past this?" Sophie angrily pleaded until her distress was palpable. "Maurice's life is in danger unless..."

"Unless what?" Emma scoffed. "Unless I help you find him." Her eyes wandered up and rolled right and left. "If you want my help, I think you'll..." Emma tapped her index finger to bottom chin. "You'll eat that dirt next to you first." She raised a single corner of her lip. "That is, if you really want my help?" She dangled the gun and shown the flashlight harshly into Sophie's eyes.

Sophie's pitch sharpened. "What?"

Emma held a stern, hard tone. "You heard me. Pick it up and eat." She now pointed the gun at her.

"No!" Sophie turned her head to the side.

In a little girl's voice, Emma distorted her words. "Then I guess you don't want my help after all." She quickly smiled, then frowned, and pouted.

With a throaty defeat, Sophie cupped her hand, scooping a pile of mud, holding it halfway between ground and mouth. She looked up at Emma with a mixture of disgusted dejection as she hesitantly raised the pile of gray muck to her puckered mouth. Eating it with her eyes fastened shut, she choked on the grit, while sandy lumps clogged her throat. Each tiny stone ground between her molars, leaving gritty bits in tiny crevices along her once sparkling teeth until she coughed uncontrollably. *Kash!.* Sophie hacked up chunks of thick gravelly mucous.

"There, I did what you asked." Sophie wiped her mouth with the back of her forearm, smearing the leftover mud across her once pretty face. "Will you take me to Maurice now?" She coughed with a raspy voice, and soon after, Sophie aspirated fluid secretions from her stomach and lungs upon the ground as she gasped for another rattly breath.

"Ha! He's already dead." Emma gave a short, self-satisfied grin. "But thanks for the show."

"That's not true!" Eyes bulging, Sophie slid forward.

"Oh, but it is," Emma cruelly replied. "I saw that creature, that thing...I saw it eating him from the inside out," she said with vicious pleasure.

"No, I don't believe you!" Sophie buried her face to the ground, smacking the mud several times with her fist. "I told you I was sorry, so please, take me to where he was. Maybe I can still save him!"

"Goodbye, Sophie." Emma ignored her tearful, frantic pleas. "I'm getting out of here now." She puffed. "Funny how life works out sometimes."

Grinning wide to each of her ears, Emma had all but turned to walk away when, *sussurrah, sussurrah*, the whispers of many voices from all around the catacombs and tunnels mumbled confusing gibberish. Multiple voices whispered at once, but not a single word was distinct.

Skrrreeek! Grating nails scraped along nearby walls and accompanied the loud, vulgar murmurs. Suddenly, the babbling whispers were joined by growls, clicks, clacks, and tapping of footsteps from every surface and unknown direction. Emma frantically turned every which way, flashing her light up and down, but the tunnels were empty, and would not give up their hidden, impending secrets to her.

"Don't leave me here like this! Not like this." Sophie used all of her strength, grabbing pieces of the adjacent wall, while pulling the top half of her body up off the ground as best she could onto her stiff, mangled, and bloodstained leg. "Oh, no! They're coming! Don't leave me!" Her body shaken, her eyes shifted. Sophie whipped her neck from side to side. "PLEASE!" she strained her voice to a hushed, fraught screech.

Emma cowered. Her head shrunk between her shoulders. Again, she looked behind and in front of her, now overcome by dizzying speed from each rapid turn. The whispers became louder by the second. Emma trembled as she backed away. Sophie pitched herself up and toward Emma. In a moment, each briefly glanced at the other. An unspoken doom repelled one, yet drew the other with a dreaded forethought of unwavering, fixed eyes.

"I'm sorry. I really am, but you'll only slow me down," Emma lowly muttered.

Sophie continued groaning on her rise to a stand. "No! Please!"

Shakiness in her voice, Emma crudely replied, "No!" She ever so slightly quivered her head from side to side as she gradually backed away. Yet with eyes connected, she inched her hand, reaching out toward Sophie for a kind of vain forgiveness.

Sophie, almost to her feet, winced with great pain and unsteady gait. "I can do this!" She slipped, and fell hard, hitting her face. Sophie quickly glanced up, locking eyes once again with Emma.

"Oh, no," Emma spoke to herself. She looked around at everywhere except at the only thing visible, a flailing and helpless Sophie.

Sophie thrashed, pulling herself up from the cool, muddy ground once more. Struggling, she rose with exertion, until tears overflowed and filled her bottom lids. Moaning through clamped teeth, she was at least half standing on her one good leg. Sophie was ready for that all-important first hop toward Emma. Not caring whether she liked it or not, Sophie was determined, with a streetwise resolve to find Maurice, and together, they could make it out of the catacombs alive.

Sophie smiled with a cleansing exhalation. She reached out for Emma's hand. Then a high-pitched screech interrupted Sophie's triumph, causing a skittish Emma to jump back and off the ground. Emma shined her flashlight on Sophie, who had insufferably fallen again onto the muddy, cool, hard ground.

On her stomach, Sophie rolled back and forth, attempting to hold her mangled leg as fresh blood streamed through her fingers from this newest trauma. She mashed her eyes downward, her nose creased upward, her cheeks tightened, and she bit her lips until her teeth broke her own skin. She grimaced, while moaning, yet still gazed up toward Emma with a desperately awful realization that these were her last moments of life.

Sophie, reluctant to let go of her injured appendage, reached up, but before she could utter a single word, she was abruptly snatched, dragged backward into the darkness of the catacombs.

An unknown force pulled Sophie away so quickly, that if not for the rearward stretching bloodstain, it appeared as if she had never existed at all. Emma, briefly paralyzed by extreme fright, spun the flashlight up in the direction, down the dark tunnels in which Sophie had been taken. However, only an empty tunnel, along with a smeared, bright red, vivid streak as long as the beam of light remained.

Emma's adrenalin jolted into overdrive. Her breaths sped shallow and sharp as beaded sweat enlarged from her forehead.

Emma swiftly turned, burning a path away from Sophie's bloody trail. She ran with a single thought and purpose, to avoid what grabbed Sophie at any cost.

At first, only Emma's heavy respirations were audible to her, yet the muted, loud whispers returned. They had quieted for a short time, but now reprised with a lurid chase upon her. She blocked her ears, still running away from the horrible undertones of death.

The whispers appeared closer and closer by the second. Emma, unable to think anymore, ran, but felt as if she were traveling in circles. Her beamed light bounced up and down from floor to ceiling inside the tunnels with each resilient, fast step. The muck, so thick, clung to her sneakers and collected inches of slowing tread. She slipped and fell, while the gun flew like a broken boomerang from her hand. Where her only weapon landed she knew not, but she knew she needed to get it back, and in a hurry.

While on her hands and knees, she scrambled through sand and watery dirt, shining her flashlight, while floundering about the ground wildly. She brushed the barrel and metal trigger just a short distance away during one hand sweep of the area. She crawled and reached out for the gun, pointing her light in its direction, but a filled pair of shoes accompanied the weapon. She had not felt them when she reached out for the gun at first, but dreadfully she recognized to whom the shoes belonged.

Chapter Twenty-Two

"Hello, Emma," a drone, chilly male voice said.

Emma swiftly grabbed the gun, stood, and aimed it at the person standing before her. "You're one of those things, aren't you?" she shouted.

"Hey, relax...besides, one of what things?" He raised his palms up, before pushing his arms back down to their sides. "It's just me, you know...Killian." He merrily dipped his head with a smile. "So you can put that gun down."

Though she had never held a gun before, she aimed the weapon straight at his chest. Emma's hands tensed and trembled around the handle and trigger. The gun nearly shook from her slippery fingers again. Along with a sigh, she flashed a glance of relief in his direction, followed by a sideward gaze of uncertainty. "Oh, yeah, well where the hell have you been this whole time?" Emma wished she could fall into his safe arms, but still, she kept her distance, and with scant trust, her eyes remained asquint on Killian.

He briefly peeked rearward. "I...um...I got lost."

"What!?" Emma rattled her flashlight. "Didn't you hear all that screaming... the whispers...the horrible beating heart sounds!?" Her pitch rose with traumatic gasps of anxiety. "And something just...Never mind." She quickly closed her eyes and shook her head at the mere thought of Maurice, Sophie, and the beast.

"Um...yeah, that's how I found my way back to you." Killian reached out but quickly pulled back his hand upon her low snarl. "Hey, are you all right?"

Emma calmed herself for a moment. She narrowed her eyes, looking him up and down. He did not have a scratch on him. He seemed like the same exact person she had joyfully toured Paris with earlier in the day. He was still clean, and from where she stood, just a few feet away, he still smelled great.

"Yes...I mean no!" Emma shut her quivering eyelids. She was tempted to catch a drop of sweat that dripped down her nose, but kept the gun pointed straight despite the consuming urge to relieve the tickle. "I'm not all right," she said weakly. "We've got to get outta here." With exhaled release, her knees buckled inward. "And why aren't you worried about all those screams?"

"It's okay." Killian slowly approached her. "People scream all the time down here. It's usually just kids playing games." He neared her and the gun she held.

"Listen, whatever this is, you can trust me." His palms faced her while hoisted back into the air.

With a forlorn glance, Emma gave a solaced shrug. She lowered her weapon with tears and overwhelming emotions of which she was not familiar. She leaned in tightly, hugging Killian.

Of all the weird sounds in the tunnels and catacombs that evening, a strange plopping down by her feet caught her attention most. Emma tilted her head, narrowing her eyes as she looked up at Killian. She instinctively waved her flashlight down, back, up, and over, before shining the light directly at Killian's face. Something was amiss. Emma felt unsettled because something was different. Something was absent. And despite wanting to trust him, something did not make sense.

A chill vaulted shivers down her spine. She instantly tore away from his embrace. "Oh, my god!" Emma struggled to get words out. "One of your...one of your...you're one of them! You're...what are you?" Emma raised her forearm and covered her mouth. Without blinking, she gawked. "Your ear, it just peeled away and fell off!" She shined her flashlight at the missing piece of his head, and then down where the ear had plopped onto the ground.

"No," Killian replied, still reaching toward her for a kiss. "Your eyes are playing tricks. You're just seeing things."

"Don't tell me that!" Emma shouted. "I'm looking right at a perfectly formed ear at your feet. And you happen to be missing one all of a sudden." She shone her light on the ear, which now appeared like a wax chip from off a figurine. The ear lay in a shallow pool of dirty water on the ground. Emma's face bleached with horror. "Your ear just fell off. Oh, my god! How does an ear just fall off!?"

Killian patted the sides of his head. "What'd you say?" He laughed. "I can't hear you." He sulked, flipping his hand at her. "That joke's wasted on you."

Emma quickly raised up a straight-arm, pointing the gun toward his chest again. "You got Killian just like you got Maurice and Sophie, but you're not getting me, you...you demon." She clamped her teeth. Her eyes had an uncanny focus as her lids drew tightly inward.

"I didn't get anyone. Besides, not just like me." Killian briefly paused. "Like we. Like we. Us you mean!" He corrected her. "We got Maurice, Sophie, and now...well...you, my dear."

Like a Potato Head doll, Killian pulled off his other ear. Emma's respirations increased threefold. Breaths were shallow. Her heart pumped rapidly. Again, she hated watching, yet again, she watched in horror, this time as he unhooked his nose before removing it like debris.

"I don't actually need these to hear." Killian displayed his human ear and nose in cupped hands before her. He then tossed them to the ground like unwanted garbage.

It seemed unreal to Emma as the tunnels appeared to spin around her. Killian continued. "This body you're looking at..." He grabbed chunks of skin, and pulled large sections from his face and hands. "I took it, you know. I took this form last night, well before I even met you up there when you were with your mother." At a steady pace, he removed bits, pieces, and chunks of his humanity while addressing his audience of one. Emma was unmovable with indecision, but kept the gun, shaking as it was, directed squarely at the deconstruction unveiling before her regretful and repulsed senses.

Killian casually talked. It became a one-sided conversation. He removed more and more parts of himself, occasionally cracking a lopsided, terrible smile here and there. He forgot it was skin at times. He forgot what skin meant, so Killian kept removing layers as if it were everyday clothing. "Hey. You ever heard that ol' saying, 'curiosity killed the cat?' Yeah, well like I was saying, there was some dumb, curious kid outside a nightclub last evening, so in essence, you could say I killed the cat and took its fur," he plainly said with a what-do-you-think type pout as he gestured from his shoulders down to his feet.

Shock gave way to denial. Emma settled on the meaningless, babbling forth a host of chaotic jargon. "Ew, so gross!" She wiped her lips, thrust out her tongue, while jetting her brows downward. "You're disgusting. I can't believe I kissed you!" She tried to find something clean to scrub her tongue against. Instead, she spit all contents of saliva out her mouth.

At first unsmiling, Killian let out an amused grin. "Yeah, well that's part of the curse. It's kind of like this reverse Cinderella thing." He scratched his head and clumps of hair fell out in large piles onto his shoulders, after which, tumbling down, and dusting the ground like balled weeds from the Great Western Plains. "If it makes you feel better. I was human...for a short while anyway."

Emma gulped. A dazed shock halted any rational thought. "How can you live like this, it's horrible, you're horrible." She puckered. Her intestines grumbling and unwell, she attempted to lurch the contents from her belly.

"Oh, I don't know," Killian casually replied. "It has its benefits. We have extra human speed and strength. Yeah, and did I mention that I've lived for over three hundred years now."

With each layer of humanity Killian shed, another piece of his repugnant true self emerged. Forgetting what he had previously looked like, he eyed a cockroach scuttling up beside his arm. He tried fighting the urge while in front of Emma, but impulsively, he quickly snatched the bug up, crushing its hard shell in his hand, then he shoved the bug's runny, yellowish green guts into his mouth. He munched on the insect with a loud chomping, before he noticed disgust mixed with revulsion altering colors across Emma's face, so he simply swallowed the rest. His neck ballooned with a protruding lump as the half-chewed bug made its way down. However, at a certain point, something inside his throat seemed to reach up and yank the bug down his stomach. Almost like a vacuum, it sucked downward before his neck returned to near normal size and shape.

Killian smiled, his teeth soiled yellowish green. He endeavored to lighten the situation by telling his made up, untimely joke. "And the French say they don't have any cockroaches in Paris. HA!"

Queasy, Emma began to hear the whispers creeping up on her from behind again. Afraid of Killian, she attempted to look over her shoulder, while keeping the person she thought she knew in the corner of her eye, and though her hand trembled, at times shaking violently, Emma kept the gun aimed always at Killian's chest or head. Troubled, her diverted attentions were unnerving.

Emma, now distracted by fear from every direction, turned aside and shone her light down through the dark tunnels, catching only skulls and bones in the distant catacombs. Her breaths uneven, they faded in and out, up and down, low and loud. With the thing she thought was Killian before her, she did not know where to focus her weapon. She waved the gun, targeting the barrel frantically around the tunnels, and then back squarely upon Killian.

"What's going on?" Emma's voice shook. "What are those whispers? What are you? How many are you?"

Killian blankly stared at her. The last of his humanity peeled away until only his eyes and lips remained.

Chapter Twenty-Three

Emma's arms shortened, gathering themselves closer without conscious thought. Her tightened muscles arrested movements, decreasing her space until she nearly dropped the flashlight. "What's going on?" She backed against the wall. "I can't breathe!" Her hands shook madly. She could not blink. Her eyes stung as they grew wider. "Oh, my god! OH, MY GOD!" she screamed.

With a swing of the flashlight, suddenly, Emma glimpsed many Dwellers silently closing in on her from the tunnels in the distant dark. The four walls appeared to close in, constricting Emma, pushing her downward. "This isn't happening," she mumbled repeatedly. Emma folded her hands over her ears, while closing her eyes. She shrank, sliding her back down the wall, pulling every limb in near her body. The mounting pressure and panic crumpled her into a contorted ball of fear and dread.

A ravenous swarm of hostile-looking creatures lumbered toward her with a single-minded goal. Some crawled spiderlike. Upside down on the high ceiling, their heads flipped completely around while eyeing her. Their necks twisted backward, growling, while their long, narrow, pointed tongues licked between their razor fangs.

Other Dwellers zigged rapidly as they zagged up and down the sides of walls, clinging to hard rock with relative ease. A few Dwellers crouched down and hunched over as they steadily paced the ground like a troop of soldiers, each carrying a hungry, determined guise.

The Dwellers coveted with menacing, hideous black eyes squarely set. In unison, they navigated toward the fresh meat. All of the lifeless, hideous black eyes, like doll's eyes, fixed squarely upon Emma. The swarm converged ever slowly in on top of her trembling place.

Emma struggled to gulp, but even in the moist tunnels, her mouth dried, and her throat knotted up. Her eyes shifted briskly about at the rotating threats hovering in, around, and almost on top of her. She looked for a way out, yet none could be had. She hoped to reason with them, but unlike her bright, sparkling eyes, theirs were filled with only blackness, death, and unreasonable fervor. Emma reflected uniqueness found deep within her soul, yet their black saucers mirrored an apathetic starvation, accompanied with nothing more than the image of what she had to offer them, a tiny bit of meat, from her skinny, little frame.

The whispers of gibberish became louder as the Dwellers approached. At first, the mixed jumble of murmured nonsense was just one of many other sounds displaced among the catacombs, but now they deafened her senses with angry tones, and with an increasingly rapid, nonstop succession. One in particular, repeated the last few words of every sentence, which was all Emma understood among the babbling nonsense.

The voices spoke different languages, yet soon, they fused as one, and as a solo hostile voice, they drove onward ever methodically.

The Dwellers advanced toward Emma with nary a shred of alarm or conscience. The garish whispers continued. Their bodies contorted in unnatural shapes as they crawled along, now close enough to reach out and touch her tender skin.

Emma shivered. Tiny hairs prickled up her arms. She wished to speak, yet fear had captured her tongue. However, it mattered not, for nothing gave pause to the Dwellers in their imminent pursuit of the impending wicked deed they prepared to unleash upon her, which they relished the thought of very greatly.

"A little thinner than I'd like, but she's better than eating more rats, more rats," one Dweller repeated the last words in a low, raspy tone.

Another Dweller vibrated eagerness. With jittery movements, its head rocked from side to side, while showing its whitish gray, semi-cracked fangs. "I like it when they run. It makes me feel like a hunter again." Its whole body twitched.

"I'm going to tear the flesh from her bones, and then crack them open and suck out the marrow," a different Dweller exclaimed in a deep, low resonance. It dragged its unusually long and thick, tar black, bladed talons, scraping them forcefully against the tunnel walls. This Dweller dug into solid stone with a jarring fingernail to chalkboard, eardrum-piercing screech. It snarled delightfully at Emma, chomping at the air several times in her direction.

Emma blocked her ears and screamed, "STOP IT! STOP IT!" Her voice yelped throughout the tunnels.

Killian, still standing without a word or movement, brusquely stepped in front of her, putting his hand up, signaling for the other Dwellers to halt their advance. "This one has potential. Let's turn her like us, and bolster our ranks instead of devouring her like the other two."

"No!" a Dweller called out. "You're selfish Killian. You ate the body you wear and left nothing for us, for us."

"Yes." Another shivered and shook uncontrollably. "You enjoyed life up there too much, while leaving us down here to rot in the cold, damp dark."

A long, thick talon pointed at Killian. "I think your heart resides above ground," a deep, low voice snarled. "No matter what, you are a Dweller, and you'll never be anything else."

Killian braced and stood his spot. He resolutely opened his arms wide with his fingers spread. His back faced Emma as his human parts continued to fall away. He shielded her from the other Dwellers' discontented grumbles, hisses, and groans.

Killian addressed certain Dwellers. "Think of all she could tell us of the modern world, Recur. We haven't turned anyone in hundreds of years. She could be a great asset."

"I'm too hungry, too hungry." Recur licked his fangs.

Killian turned toward another Dweller as they gradually closed in. "Slash, we can get other humans that come into the catacombs, but I want to keep this one."

"You're a fool, Killian." Slash dragged his oversized talons deeper into the wall. "You want every female we encounter."

"Not true!" Killian turned toward yet another. "Snare," Killian put his hand up, "don't even think about it." He backed his way closer toward Emma. He groped behind to assure her safety. He felt all over for her, but only stroked the empty space of air she had left for him instead.

"The hunt is on!" Snare barked. With a grin, he bolted off the tunnel wall and over top and past Killian.

"You fool, you fool," Recur said. "While you blabbered, she ran away, ran away."

"Not for long." Slash waved the other Dwellers onward down the dark tunnels after Emma.

Emma swung her arms back and forth. She huffed, panted, and gasped as the catacombs appeared to jump with her every stride. Winded with exhaustion, she wheezed for oxygen, but her lungs and feet were sore, tired, and heavy.

With a flashlight in one hand and a gun in the other, Emma sprinted down the tunnels. She continually looked over her shoulder as galloping hordes of Dwellers clopped and stomped, hunting in a pack, chasing toward her with colossal speed greater than any known predator on Earth.

The air was thick and musty. Emma started to cough. She sucked in a lungful of stagnant air, but labored from breath to breath, and as the Dwellers closed the gap, she wondered which of her breaths would be her last.

The Dwellers bounded down the tunnels with ease. With large strides and hurdles, using all four legs, they hunted as a singular unit, growling like wolves, they raced like cheetahs through the dark tunnels, each leapt over the other from wall to wall, and floor to ceiling in seamless movements.

Sweat flowed down Emma's face. She stopped looking back and held the flashlight straight ahead. She knew there had to be an opening to the outside, and a way to get up and out of the nightmarish catacombs.

Fretful moisture leaked into her eyes, stinging her sight. She wiped some from off her brow. Briefly dabbing her wrist to her forehead, she glanced at the shiny, metal object in her other hand. The forgotten object bolstered her confidence. Emma suddenly felt emboldened as if she still had a shot to get out of the catacomb tunnels alive.

Fleeing tensely for her life amid the traumatic darkness, Emma had forgotten about the object of empowerment. She had somehow forgotten about the gun she held white knuckled. Grinding her teeth, she readied to unleash its power on the Dwellers. Emma gripped the gun ever tighter. Without looking back, she felt time running out. Her heart pounded until it throbbed inside her brain. It was time to pull the trigger or die.

Up ahead, in the distant part of the catacombs, an ethereal light streamed into the tunnel from up above. An old, wooden ladder appeared vertical with the dim light. She ran even faster toward her way out.

Emma knew it was still too far, and that the beasts were gaining nearer her position. The Dwellers were almost on top of her, and she could feel the ground thump from behind. She stumbled, reaching toward the dimly lit exit leading out from the stench of the unholy, rotting pit of death currently surrounding her.

The light was so close she could hear noises from the streets above ground. A second wind lifted a heaviness from off her chest. Euphoric, Emma smiled, for she was finally free. Then, an unexpectedly sharp, cold ripping pain ruptured her hope. "ARGH! GOD!" she wailed from the deep, piercing sensation.

A set of sickle-shaped, penetrating claws dug into the top of her shoulder, tearing the fine cloth of her sleeve to pieces. In total reaction, Emma turned around. She squeezed the gun's trigger, shooting at the Dweller clinging onto her now gushing, wounded arm. *Ba-boom!* The gun popped, rattling dramatically. The bullet sent the creature hurling backward. The Dweller had released its grip, followed by a lifeless flop to the ground.

Emma's hand vibrated and stung as if she had stuck her finger in an electrical socket. The gun's echo rang out through the tunnels. Undaunted, more Dwellers pursued, so she blindly fired five more shots, clicking the trigger repeatedly without aim.

Before the Dwellers were only hungry, yet now their fangs, talons, and muscles showed fury. Their tiny slit nostrils swelled—the Dwellers jumped out from the black void of the catacombs—their arms and claws reached toward her, their mouths opened, their fangs sopping gooey drool. Emma yowled, firing one last shot as the beasts merged down upon her like a tidal wave.

Viip. The bullet hummed, ricocheting off the tunnel ceiling. *Voomp.* A massive cave-in erupted. A piled mound of rock and dirt now separated the Dwellers from Emma, and though stunned, she enjoyed a restful sigh, and an odd feeling of abrupt quiet, with an almost disturbing calm. She was now free to escape up the dim, dusty beam of light from the streets above.

Chapter Twenty-Four

A cloud of gritty particles coated her body and glazed the air. Emma coughed, hacking out the exhaled specks of airborne dust. The dirty air stabbed her lungs like that of a thousand tiny knives. Her eyes watered as she waved the thick, dusty particulates away from her face. She tripped and fell to the ground, losing both her flashlight and the gun. One was bright, its smoky light spread along the hazy cloud, but the other slid off somewhere far along the dark ground.

The once lifesaving weapon was lost. Emma plunged desperately to her hands and knees. She searched the muddy puddles, slapping the water, and blindly probing the ground in front of her, all the while, her flashlight faded in strength and brightness. At first, after the cave-in, there was only wonderful silence, but soon she heard the Dwellers burrowing from the other side of the walled hill of rocky dirt.

Emma hastily stood. She again waved the air in front of her face, and as the dust cleared, so did her senses. The gun no longer mattered. She stopped what she was doing and ran over toward the only thing that did matter—the dim light shining as a beacon from above. Her legs wary, her arm bloody and injured, she could not raise her shoulder. Emma sniveled. Any other time she would have already made it to the top and have been out of the tunnels, but as she eyed the wooden ladder, it turned into an impossible feat, it turned into her Everest. With a deep sigh, a gulp, and a vertical view of light from the safe world above, the ladder became a climb of doubt and fear nearly rivaling the Dwellers in fright.

Starting with one reluctant hand, Emma climbed the rickety, old ladder. Her injured shoulder fastened to her side, she forced her wounded arm to grab hold a rung. She refused to look anywhere except up, toward the light of salvation, even as the Dwellers broke through the massive, earthy divide piled between them.

With every step, the light from above ground got brighter, and the noise of cars and people soon carried her upward. She winced with every pull upon her wounded, bloodied shoulder.

The flashlight died, so she let it slip away to the bottom of the tunnel's black void. Her eyes needed time to adjust from the pervading darkness over the last few hours. Finally, Emma reached the top. There was a heavy, steel drainage guard between her and ultimate freedom from the catacombs.

The steel guard was solid, wet, and cold to the touch. Her thin fingers slipped through the metal slats with ease. She angled her face sideways, pressing her cheek close to the slats—trying to see some of the lights and people nearby. She caught a glimpse of her hotel, which appeared only about a block from where she stood at the top of the ladder. But from where she stood, it might as well have been a thousand miles away, as the heavy drainage guard blocked any hope of further advance.

Emma tried to lift the metal plate to the side, yet it did not budge. She desperately yelled, even screamed for help, yet no one heard her fraught cries of distress. The mining of burrowing Dwellers underneath her feet, at the bottom of the ladder, in the dark void below, opened a pit of despair inside Emma. Anguished feelings of melancholy fragmented panic to her very core. With each bang and scrape, she recoiled and flinched. The sound of Dwellers bursting through the mound of rock and dirt cost her a moment of balance. The whispers returned, with rushing streams of foul air shooting up past her, before filtering into the city's night air.

The Dwellers had broken free. They shook the ladder under cover of dark at the bottom of the tunnel's black void below. The Dwellers were not only coming after Emma...they were here. She braced the ladder tightly and looked down. Her injured arm let loose. Uncontrollably, she swung to one side of the ladder, almost falling, hanging on with a single arm and foot.

The creatures now surrounded the bottom of the ladder, kneading their talons in expectation of her dropping toward them. Her stomach, it felt, jumped into her throat. The creatures began climbing the ladder, and though stationary, the Dwellers spun around her as she flailed in and out, while dangling at the ladder's top half.

Emma steadied herself.

She grabbed the metal drainage guard, while holding her position.

Dread became anger. Emma was tired of being afraid, and she used all that fear for one angry push, a push strong enough to lift a solid, metal drainage guard nearly twice her body weight from off its loose fittings.

Emma's face reddened as the tendons in her neck strained into pronounced, corded lines. Her injured shoulder popped. She groaned deep and low from her diaphragm up to her throat. Her low, deep groan ended in a shrill cry when the drainage guard moved a mere impossible inch.

The drainage guard cracked open into chilled, yet free, nighttime city air of Paris.

It was a tight fit. She sized the gap. There was barely enough room between her body and the metal frame on each side.

She pushed the metal drain some more, sliding it a screech along metal to ground. Her whole body ached unbearably. The Dwellers nearly upon her, the ladder quaked. Emma slid through the constricted opening. Parts of her slight frame felt pinned. Her face mashed together, with a red so red, her skin turned almost purple. She felt a pressure in her blood until her head spiked an awful throbbing. "I can do this! I can do this!" she shouted to herself.

Slowly, her thin figure gravely wedged out of the catacombs, and up safely above ground. Emma leaned her head backward as far as it would go, holding her wounded and bloody arm in place of a sling. She enjoyed the noisy, crowded openness only the streets of Paris offered. Tears of distress were replaced with those of accomplished success.

She stood for a moment, her body swayed like a vessel at sea. She pulled her injured shoulder in against her chest, and lent her other hand straight armed, bending over, clutching one of her knees. Her stomach distended in and out rapidly, before her breaths calmed.

Emma straightened upward.

Elation filled her entire being, but her chest felt weak as if to faint. Emma took a step away from the drainage guard.

One Dweller boldly reached up, strongly gripping her ankle from between where she had wedged and slipped through to freedom.

Its firm clasp bound her leg, pulling Emma abruptly down and hard onto her stomach. Her chin smacked against the cold street. She twisted her body over. Her bottom side now dragged along the ground as she was towed back in the direction of the catacombs.

Emma used her other foot to kick the beast's hand off her ankle. She kicked, and kicked, biting her lower lip until her mouth bled. However, her best attempts were for naught. Her recent taste of freedom suddenly appeared fleeting. Against every part of her living will, she slowly drifted back toward the Dwellers in the underground boneyard.

Emma hysterically screamed over again, "HELP! HELP!" She rapidly kicked the creature's hand around her ankle, neither of which was to any avail.

"No one can hear you, hear you." Recur pulled her with ease, while grinning from just below the drainage guard. Its black, saucer eyes reflected the colorful, bright city lights directly behind her.

Emma scrambled frantically. She looked for another way to free herself. Her head whipped from side to side. Then she saw her only chance. She stopped kicking the Dweller's arm, and instead, kicked the hefty, metal plate where its long arm protruded out.

Again, she groaned heavily. She planted both palms as stops along the cold, wet street. Even her injured arm braced the weight it could.

She clamped her teeth, grinding them back and forth. Emma's whole body stiffened as she let out a single, garish shriek. It was every bit of strength, but with her other leg, she pushed the solid, drainage guard, until her knee ached, and the hefty, metal plate slid, clunking back over, down onto its fittings.

It slammed shut on top the Dweller's arm. A cracking of its bone, like a twig, smashed its upper wrist, trapping the Dweller's forearm, leaving it upright and leaning askew above ground.

Recur squealed a profane howl that carried throughout the alleyway, but it immediately released Emma's leg.

She jumped to her feet and sprinted from the drainage guard on a nonstop, direct course toward the visual shelter of her hotel.

Still shaking, but just yards away from her hotel, she slowed from a run to a hurried stride. Emma encountered groups of well-dressed people talking and laughing outside clubs and restaurants on the streets next to her.

Emma watched behind, looking back with a paranoid head flip every other second. Several people stared oddly. As she hurried by them, their gay chatter dulled in waves when she passed.

One young, elegantly dressed woman walked over to Emma. "Are you all right, miss? Do you need help?" The young woman gently placed her hand on Emma's back.

Emma slanted her shoulder up, down, and away, saying nothing to the woman, but giving her a wide-eyed, blank yet brief stare of dislike as she rushed by, fleeing from the elegant young woman's touch. She refused to look anyone else in the eye, as all eyes were scoping her. Emma saw fingers pointing, and heard people talking amongst themselves over her appearance and odd behavior. Yet for all she knew, they were one of those horrible, demonic creatures escaped from the catacombs, silently stalking her in human form.

Soon every person, no matter how nice they appeared, seemed like a potential Dweller to her. Emma ran until her heart felt weak as if it would explode. Her body could run no farther, but still, she pushed herself, and did not slow until she got back to the front gates of her hotel.

Once through the bright, main hotel lobby doors, Emma searched her pockets, but realized she had lost her room key. Her eyes shifting back and forth, she held her head high, tilting her chin upward as she calmly walked across the granite floors, while traipsing mud, along with a reeking stench of the sewers, through the glorious hotel lobby.

Emma stopped by the front desk for another key. She tapped the silver bell, ringing its chime. She clanged it once, and then several more times in quick, agitated succession. Emma smeared some grime across the gold stripe paint that lined the counter as she propped herself in an awkward, anxious sort of tension.

She breathlessly fidgeted, and without end, kept looking all around her. A shiver overcame Emma's hand. She could not stop the tremor, so she closed her hand into a balled fist. She tapped the silver bell again and again. The bell rang out with an unmistakable clanging of irritation, until another hand reached over and stopped its hollow vibrations.

The attendant, with hand on the bell, raised an eyebrow at Emma's sudden and unsettled appearance, to which even she was not fully aware, but began to guess by his repelled expression.

With his right eyebrow raised, the attendant cleared his throat, loosening his button collar, while tilting his head. "Um...how can I help you, miss?" he said unsurely.

"I, uh, lost my room key." Emma spoke quickly, too quickly. She nervously scratched her itchy scalp. Her fingernails dislodged pieces of sandy gunk from the catacombs.

The attendant just watched her. "Who are you? What's your name?" he asked in swift succession.

"Oh, hah, sorry. My first name is Emma, last name Rose. I'm in room 504 with my mom."

He typed into the computer keyboard. "Um...yes. I see." The front desk attendant short armed handing the room key to Emma. "Here you go. Will that be all, Miss Rose?" He cleared his throat again.

Emma rubbed her lips together. "Yeah...I mean no. I don't know. I just want to get up to my room." She awkwardly smiled.

"Miss..." The attendant clumsily volunteered. "Are you in...what I mean to say is, do you need any type of assistance?"

"No, I'm fine, really." Emma put her hand straight up in a stopping motion as she backed away from the desk. She lastly caught a glimpse of her own reflection in a glass sign to the side of the attendant. "Um...ah...I just had, ya know, a crazy night out is all." Emma feigned an uneasy giggle. "You know, what happens in Paris stays in Paris, and all that sort of stuff." The last words were muffled and rushed, as she blurted them without thought and while making her exit.

She had spent too much time in the lobby and thus hurried up to her room. The attendant, and a few others present, curiously watched until she was out of their sight.

Alone, she had rehearsed many excuses for her untidy appearance under her breath on the elevator ride up.

The elevator bell chimed.

Emma vacantly watched the flashing light inside the elevator. Then, she blinked several times, shook her head, and before the elevator fully closed on her, she sped out madly down the hallway.

Once up on her floor, she scuttled briskly to her room, all the while, continuing a lowly mumble as she walked down the hallway like a crazed person.

Despite everything that had happened that evening, Emma only worried about her mother, and the trouble she would find once she walked through the room's door.

She looked down at her sullied, ragged appearance. Her nice, new clothes were tattered and muddied. Her arms and legs were mixed with varying combinations of smeared blackish mud, scant drops of reddish blood, and large pieces of caked over, gray grime. Emma realized the awful truth. No made-up story could account for the real truth that evening, because truth was not even close to an option for her.

And so, Emma reached out and held the doorknob to her room. She inanely stared at the door in a sort of frozen indecision.

Chapter Twenty-Five

Emma gingerly turned the knob and slowly cracked open the door. She spoke before fully entering the room. "Mom?" her voice wavered. "Mom, I know this looks bad, but...Mom?" There came no answer. She rushed around the hotel room, looking for signs of her mother's return.

Back and forth, she roamed the room, before calmly stopping where she had started, the front door. "I can't believe it," she said aloud. "She's not back yet. But I don't remember leaving all these lights on."

Emma, stunned she had returned before her mother, dismissed all else and soon darted toward the bathroom. She was determined to clean and destroy all evidence of the catacombs. She was leaving for home in the morning, so everything would be okay now. Still, she rushed with a frantic haste many girls her age knew well, yet not for her insidious motives, which she reasoned a good cause to hide.

All evidence of her terrible night needed to be destroyed before her mother walked through the door at any given moment.

Finally, after a close look at her face in the bathroom mirror, Emma loathed her reflection. She frowned at her appearance, and had difficulty looking her own image in the eye.

Her mascara had filtered down in multiple, narrow lines on the outer sides of her cheeks.

She felt woozy.

Her skin had a pale tinge under encrusted layers of brown, gray, and black sludgy dirt. Her hair, being a tangled mess, was clumped full of sewage fragments. Her pants and shirt were soaked. Her clothes permanently discolored from the brown, muddy water in the tunnels. Her favorite shirt, which earlier was bright, clean, and intact, was now saturated dark red.

The fabric above her right shoulder had been ripped nearly off, yet was torn into frayed, unbroken strands. Grimacing, she gingerly peeled back the drying layer of cloth from her tender wound. She winced and clenched her teeth hard, while groaning. Tears flowed as the fabric, already adhered like a new part of her skin, loosened, opening her deeply macerated cuts, pulling both new and old skin off, leaving fibers of cloth imbedded deep inside her freshly bleeding, dirt filled wound.

Letting out a gasp, Emma jerked her head upward as she slowly pulled the cloth out of her deep gash.

The laceration on top her right shoulder, which had scabbed, now started to flow a stream, a river of bright red rushed half down her chest, while also pouring down her back. The blood gushed as she pulled quickly the last pieces of fabric from her skin, and with a final, uncontrollable scream, she cupped a hand over her mouth, now connecting affixed eyes with her sobbing reflection.

She once more moaned silently at the sting of her wretched appearance. Emma gripped the sink. She inspected her eight-inch skin tears, which arched over her shoulder from just above her collarbone to her scapula. What she believed to be a single injury, were in fact several equally long clawed wounds, and though the marks initially appeared deep, they seemed to only scrape the outermost cosmetic layers of her skin. And while her shoulder ached and burned, it seemed neither muscles, tendons, nor bone were damaged from the attack, yet curiously, pus began to foam around the site.

Emma dabbed a bit of toilet paper around the wound, while she poured rubbing alcohol over the site. She sucked in her stomach and held her breath. Her eyes slammed shut, squeezing even more tears out. Her teeth locked. Her cheeks tensed up and away from steady discomfort, to an instant, punishing sting.

Emma stripped all her clothes off and, along with a pile of mashed up bloody tissues, she threw all evidence of the catacombs into a large plastic bag, tying it firmly afterward.

She then ran, jumping into the shower, while yanking the curtain behind her. She turned the water as hot as her delicate skin could stand.

While in the shower, steam filled the room like a sauna. The water had a cathartic appeal. She slid down the edge of the bath with a thud. Her head arched forward and bounced as she started weeping. She huddled her knees close to her chest. With her arms around her legs, she pulled her body near and buried her head between her arms.

The hot shower invigorated her soul, helping her to forget the Dwellers. The warm droplets bounced off her skin like summer rain in the gardens back home.

She wiped her face, lathered up her hair, and stood, showering off the remaining muck.

The night flashed back upon her in spurts.

Emma watched the red, brown, and black rolling specks of dirt and coagulated blood form a thin, rolling canal. Down the middle of the tub, the night's particles fled toward the drain, along with most of her anxiety.

She stared without blinking at the stream of muddy bits and blood until it filtered down the drain.

Her eyes dazed half-open in sequence with timed puffs of thoughtful breath.

The hot, clean water and warm steam was the best thing Emma remembered feeling in some time. It felt so good that it felt entirely new to her. In a self-induced stupor, her eyes glimmered again, if only for a second. She then remembered that her mother could be back at any moment. Breaking the dead trance in her state of mixed grief, she finished her intimate shower before she wanted.

Refreshed, Emma skipped out of the tub. Now clean and almost dried, she brushed her hair. She stroked it blankly with both hands. The muscles used to smile sagged despite her best attempts to invent happiness.

Her eyes fell into a vacancy as she looked upon her troubled mirror image.

Emma grabbed two white, thin panty liners from off the sink, unrolled them, and placed the absorbent cushion over her wound, covering the gashes, while adhering the top sticky parts up under her nightgown. She tapped down the edges near her swollen, bleeding skin, wincing with every touch as she did. Shuddering, she patted over the clawed marks across her shoulder, firmly pressuring down on the pad in order to halt the reemerging, oozing blood from at the top.

Emma heard the doorknob jiggle. She flung her head in the direction of the room's entrance. Her hair, still wet in parts, whipped in chorus. She slapped at the wall, flipping out the bathroom light as she ran, diving head first for her bed.

Slipping between the covers, and while resting under their disguise, she suddenly realized what had been forgotten, a large, dirty bag of wet, soiled, bloody clothes in the bathroom.

Emma threw the covers off and bounced to her feet. She bolted toward the bathtub as the door to the hotel room opened. She steadily clutched the bag, and with one motion, she flung it under her bed, and hopped back in before wrapping the blankets over her face.

All of the lights in the hotel room were off.

Only the moon's soft, haunting glow illuminated pastel bands, which parted the darkness, yet cast evil shapes in the recessed shadows of the room.

The outside door creaked open when pushed. Emma peeped a single eye out from under her covers, while pretending to sleep. The bright hallway lights formed a silhouette in the doorway entrance before it slammed shut. Any hallway light, along with the silhouette, now melded seamlessly with all other dark amid the room.

Footsteps marched her way, slightly louder as they approached.

All sound briefly ceased.

Then, her bed's mattress sprung down as a weighted body sat next to Emma, ever so slightly rolling her toward the heavier figure now on the bed with her.

A soft, wonderfully familiar voice asked, "Honey, are you asleep?"

"Ma...Mom, is that really you?" Emma hesitated, her head still under the covers.

"Why of course it is, silly." Her mother chuckled. "Who else would it be?"

"Um...nobody, I guess." Emma unpeeled her blankets and sat up as her mother gently stroked her hair in the milky beams of moonlight. One hand covered by her coat, the other ran through Emma's hair. "I must have just had a nightmare, I guess."

"Why is your hair wet?" her mother's tone hearkened for more.

"Oh, um, well, I wanted to take my shower tonight before, ya know, we leave for home tomorrow." Emma's voice fizzled in and out. "I know how you always like to hog the bathroom in the morning." She forced the corners of her lips upward into a smile, accompanying them with a tiny, worried little laugh.

Her mother got up and twirled as if she were still at a party, while moving toward the bathroom. "I'm sorry I was so late." She had a giddy tone. "Ralyo took me out to this great restaurant. We danced the night away, and the time just flew by." Her mother talked as she walked away. "I tell you what." Her voice carried. "Since I was out late, and you stayed in like you were supposed to, you can buy anything you want before we leave tomorrow. In fact, why don't you wear your favorite shirt with all those different colors, and we'll go shopping one last time."

"Oh, um, well, that's cool. I don't really want anything. But it sounds like you had a great time tonight." Emma drew a long breath, for she knew that this was actually her mother. "Oh, and, Mom..."

"Yes, honey."

"I just wanted to say...I love you."

"I know you do."

"And I'm sorry for everything I put you through."

"It's okay."

"No, it's not..."

Her mother stopped her with a quick, yet dismissive reply. "You worry too much. Now don't tell me you don't get that from your father."

Her mother walked into the bathroom and out of sight as they continued to make small talk, mostly about her mother's night out.

Her mother dropped her coat and flipped on the bathroom light. She glanced wistfully at herself, tilting her neck, eyeing the mirror, and feeling her soft skin up and down. Her attention diverted, she then admired her long fingernails on her right hand, and gawked intently at her beautiful image. "Ralyo showed me something amazing after supper." Her enthusiasm faded monotone. "On second thought, why don't you get up and get dressed now. I have something to show you."

Emma sat up in bed. "What?" Her nose crinkled.

A small portion of the bathroom light framed a shadowy outline of her mother. While standing at the bathroom doorway, her mother propped herself left sided against the doorframe. Her left hand hid behind the bathroom wall. At first, her hand dangled, but then it ever so leisurely crept upward like a vine, slowly encasing around, while lightly tapping the bathroom light switch.

A sickle-shaped, black talon hooked over the top of the switch as a hanger would a hanging rod. With the light behind her, and still on, her mother glanced back at her arm. She watched as healthy, pink new skin grew, covering from elbow down, and filling in and around a once crushed forearm.

Unseen by Emma, her mother flexed the damaged hand as a thick layer of human flesh formed over a rotting coat of jaundiced tissue.

Her guard down, Emma smiled easily at her mother, yet despite the recent face tightening procedure, and unlike earlier in the day, this time, her mother could easily smile back.

Emma held a single breath. Her pulse jumped and pupils dilated.

Something was wrong.

Emma's face, now absent of all expression, stared at her mother's silhouette. A booming click by the flipping down of the bathroom light switch caused instant panic. Her heart thumped as darkness again found and entombed her soul. "Yawp!" Emma screamed, but a cold hand gripped her face, muffling all sound. Another beastly strong hand wrapped around her neck with sharp, piercing claws, grasping at her throat.

Just a faint whimper, tears, and a scant amount of warm, red fluid leaked from puncture marks around claws jammed into Emma's neck. Her body trembled, but the piercing talons held her neck in place. The sickled claws stabbed through her soft skin, pinching off her airway with a quick squeeze, followed by a detained, relaxed grip.

It was all clear now, but it did not matter anymore. Emma shivered. The wait of silence overwhelmed her paralyzed body. Wrapped firmly from mouth to neck, one hand had the warmth of her mother's, yet the other was evil, merciless, and cold.

The fight was over.

Emma sensed these hands were able to snap her in half as if a fragile twig. She was trapped more now than when in the catacombs.

There were things Emma desperately needed to say, yet her speech remained muzzled. She wanted to live, and had many things left to do in life, but instead, was only reminded of the grim, harsh, two-sided token left by the catacombs. "No one ever escapes, ever escapes," a raspy voice quietly hissed out her mother's mouth, "the Dwellersssssssssssss."

Chapter Twenty-Six

During a peaceful sunset, on a hillside in a mountainous region of Greece, the populous in a valley below scurried about daily life in the early evening hours of a busy city.

The high peaks around the valley protected, yet stole nature's beauty, shading the city from the last kindly hints of the day's sunlight, leaving just the mountaintops to enjoy their last splendor.

Twinkling stars birthed one by one in the sky, and from an eruption, they blinked in the heavens, while thousands of homes sprang artificial, stellar luminosities at dusk.

From present day ruins of a once great city—where long ago, a civilization worshiped many ancient gods faded into myth—sightseers now flocked with cameras, snapping pictures of a forgone empire turned tourist trap.

New and old collided.

An ancient world shrunk as a modern world grew. Where once mighty gods stood, mortals carelessly trampled along footpaths in rows with signs and guiderails.

A man, dressed in a solid white tunic, sat atop a near vertical set of stone slabs in front of a crumpling, ancient temple. The stone slabs—the makeshift steps leading upward to the temple—were well worn. Their edges smoothed, almost polished by time and traffic, with pieces of grass springing forth between the slabs' rocky and fractured cracks.

His white tunic, knee high in length, separated with a cloth mantle, was swathed wide over his left shoulder and thinly tied under his right arm. His plain, brown leather sandals hooked at his ankles. The man had a thick head of pepper hair, with wisps of salty specks intermingled atop his head, revealing a certain age to his wisdom. His strong, wiry, athletic frame was obvious, even in his sitting position. His nose was long and straight, with a slight slope at the end. His jaw strong, his eyes intense, he watched the sun slowly dip under the distant, modern-day city as he remembered a time when these same ruins teemed with other life.

Like a part of the ruins itself, the man was politely ignored by the vacationers. Though he appeared a historical actor, set there for the tourists' pleasure, he, like the ruins behind him, was a mere portrait out of its proper, chronological time.

His intense eyes jetted at the sightseers.

He examined them up and down as each person walked back to their tour buses.

Letting go a brief sigh, the man remembered how the modern, distant city before him, was just an unpopulated countryside field, filled with nothing more than quietly grazing sheep the last time he was here.

Leaning back, he supported his hands on a large slab of ancient, cut stone. He watched until the last of the crowds thinned out, while the imminent nature of sundown approached.

Many of the tourists walked right past him, but no one took note, or even glanced his way, for they were too busy looking at their phones and other electronic devices to take notice of him.

The man's fleeting smile dwindled, enjoying only for the moment while observing the people pass by, all of them remaining oblivious to his presence.

Creasing a simple, closed mouth grin, he sat forward, and placed his elbows on his knees, with his hands clasped under, supporting his chin. A great trouble then draped over his face. A trouble few in the nine-to-five world knew existed and fewer still could understand.

His brief delight had worn thin, replaced instead by gloomy frowns, short, nasally breaths, and dull eyes.

Appearing like a regal sculpture until all traffic left, soon he was the last person amid the ancient, lonely, and silent ruins. With all traces of his smile erased, in a sort of tranquil, astonished admiration, he turned his head from side to side, while reassessing his surroundings.

At the bottom stairs, far below his position, he scanned for any familiar face. He sheltered his eyes from the last, bright rays of the falling sun.

The minutes ticked away.

He tapped his foot, at first sporadically, but then without stop. Folding and unfolding his hands, he held them tightly, bowing his head, and curling his lips inward to nibble upon them.

Trouble vented with infrequent self-expressions. The man submerged his blank, worried glance, shaking off the physical signs whenever angst presented itself to him.

With a demeanor full of wisdom and strength, he succumbed to the weakness of trepidation, fret, and distress, combined with other mixed, disconcerting, all too human emotions. This would have been all right, that is, if he considered himself human, but he was no ordinary person.

Once more, he scanned the valley below, raised his head erect, and nodded with a deep breath, filling his lungs with self-assurance. He was reminded of his strength, of his immortality, and by his own estimation, he was far beyond such feeble, imperfect human emotions. Though he blocked the negative of humanity out, it still burdened his very spirit as spiraling thoughts of grief consumed him. He hid all of his disquieting concerns, and smiled again, when he saw a familiar face at the bottom of the distant steps beneath where he sat on high.

A younger, but mature maiden appeared from nowhere. The man in the tunic beamed an approving nod at her.

From the far right she appeared, not visible the moment before. Within moments of her arrival, another man looking to be about her age joined at the far left from where she stood.

The man to the left of her neither smiled nor frowned, and had little to show in the way of facial language. He had broad shoulders and a thin, well-kept beard along his jawbone. He appeared bold, striding, and carried himself with rigid poise.

The two now stood at the far ends of the bottom steps from each other. At the lowest row of a mountainous climb, the two recent arrivals briefly acknowledged one another, before ascending the near vertical steps toward the man in the white tunic at the top of the stone slabs.

The man across from the maiden also had a mature, but young thirty something appearance to his face. Neatly outfitted, he tugged the bottom seams on his ashen, short, open vest for a square fit. He looked at his clothes, checking his white, freshly pressed, button-down shirt. He then straightened one leg of his gray slacks, moving the pant hem from off his wingtip shoe. He gave the maiden a solemn look as they walked in unison to the top of the ancient ruins.

The maiden's long maxi dress was filled with floral patterns of colors. Purple gave the dress its dominant hue, along with earthy browns, greens, and blues. With long sleeves, the maxi dress ruffled in circled layers from just above her waist, wrapping both tightly to form, yet loosely down and around her firm body until it relaxed at her knees. And the dress, though long, fanned out, extending down to nothing but her beautiful bare feet, save for a gold charm, a trinket, dangling from her right ankle.

With shoulder-length, tied back, loosely curled locks of dark blonde, wavy hair, the maiden exuded a calm loveliness. She seemed more sculpted from the stone around her rather than born into a world of flesh. However, she was soft, and pleasant to the eyes, yet she, like the man at the other end of the steps, had an eager determination for being there, and not one like the leisured tourists browsing the ancient, Greek ruins.

The maiden rode a gracious stride.

Like music, she appeared to dance with each step. A fluid advance of rhythmic elegance, she was aglow and seemed light on her feet as if carried by only the wind.

The man at the far end of the maiden stood tall with an unyielding gait. His overall exterior made him also seem out of his proper, historical time, even though his modern attire attempted to hide such a thing from the world. He spouted a stern, or perhaps even a certain rugged quality. Compared to the maiden, he seemed uninteresting and dull. Prone to harsh expressions, he had the appearance of an austere person, full of pride and self-denial. A set of elusive eyes darted and fixed, and darted again. His short, brown hair was straight, thick, and parted down the middle of his scalp. His chin and cheeks were chiseled, with a threadlike, bearded growth from over his lips, down around his chin, and up in a thin line from his elongated jaw to his sideburns. Altogether, he had a chic look of business, without a mere hint of pleasure about him.

The two stood pat, midway up the near vertical steps, which they climbed with ease.

Closer now, they looked favorably at one another. It was a quick, but telling gaze, such as when people have been torn apart by immeasurable distance and time, never knowing if they would see each other again, and then when they do, no greater gift can be found.

Giving some signs of advancing years, they were surprisingly youthful, strong, fresh with vigor, and seemingly untouched by the ravages of time.

After the brief pause, the maiden turned. She beheld upward, toward the man in the white tunic, and began her mountainous hike once more. She, along with her fellow male traveler, ascended the steps at a gradual pace. Together they walked the vertical pitch effortlessly as the width of the steps narrowed to the very top. They merged both closer to each other, and also to the man in the tunic, sitting, waiting for them to arrive.

The man in the white tunic held his smile at them. His distress melted as they drew closer.

Joyful to see them, the man in the white tunic waved them onward openly to where he sat. From his sitting position, he reclined back once more, placing his arms straight behind like wooden poles. He planted his elbows on the hard stone slabs, each arm anchoring, holding his body in an uncomfortable-looking, rested position.

The travelers reached the top, and then halted. For a moment, they stood above the man in the white tunic, gazing at the other before casually taking a seat on opposite sides of him.

Now all three, without a word, looked out across the valley and over at the mountains as the sun set around the puffy, low-lying, pink, orange, and dark blue clouds.

The three briefly shone like golden idols in among the ruins. They appeared contented as the sun's passive slivers granted rays of hope upon an unsettled world below.

"It's good to see you again, Revekka, and you as well, Maximilian." The man in the white tunic dusted his hands and sat upright, breaking the silence first. He then placed an arm around them, hugging them inward. After releasing his affectionate hold, he opened his palm, while stretching out his hand with a slow sweeping gesture from north to south, he said, "Of earthly things, is a sunset from the Acropolis not the most beautiful thing of all?"

Chapter Twenty-Seven

The three quietly watched the burning orb slowly plummet from the sky. Revekka tilted her head toward the man in the white tunic. She grew wary of the silence. "Surely, Acuumyn, you did not come all of this way for a sunset?" she bluntly asked.

Maximilian turned toward the man in the white tunic, looking sideways at half of his face, he questioned, "It's bad, isn't it, Acuumyn?" A rough, frank manner broadcast his somber tone.

Acuumyn mildly replied, "Just enjoy the sunset." He patted them both on the knees.

The three sat there silently, watching the yellow-orange, warm circle sun brilliantly dissolve below the distant hills. Divine rays of the dominant star lasered through the puffy pastel clouds, evoking a red-violet backdrop—covering the modern city with a splendid radiance from horizon to marvelous horizon.

Revekka fastened her elbows to her knees, and rested her head on open palms, angling her view several times at the panorama. Not only was dusk her favorite time of day, but she also loved this particular vista as night fell upon the unsettled world.

Maximilian anxiously nibbled on his thumbnail, looking past the sunset and the valley. He secretly reviled all that he viewed while watching everything around him.

Acuumyn reclined again, inhaling a relaxed breath, quietly observing Revekka and Maximilian before sitting up once more.

Revekka leaned over and lowly spoke in Acuumyn's ear. "Though you appear at ease, you're more tense than I've ever seen."

"Quite so, Revekka," Acuumyn replied aloud. "As the Artifex is living, dynamic energy, it has gifted you with the power of an empath, and perception beyond that of any other immortal." He addressed both of them at this point. "Maximilian, the Artifex has given you the power of a knight, and though the Artifex grants many different gifts based on the abilities of that person, no gift is greater than another in this respect."

"My mission is not yet complete..." Maximilian let out a forced sigh. After, he hung his head briefly before glancing at the skyline, and then back up at Acuumyn.

Revekka interjected, "My mission is close to being finished. I need only transcribe my findings before approaching the council."

Acuumyn bent forward, covered his mouth, and repetitively rubbed the top and sides of his lips, for he grieved his next words immensely. "The knighthood is grateful for the missions you have performed over the last five thousand years, but they must now end."

Maximilian pulled his shoulders back and away from Acuumyn. His eyes restricted and fixed with a pinpoint stare. "What!? Why!?" His face tightened before he slowly cooled the muscles under his skin, and muttered, "Those damnable bureaucrats!"

"I understand." Revekka remained calm, her demeanor and position changing little with any good or bad news.

"I'm afraid the Doyen Council back home has discovered the covert nature of our missions among the mortals." Acuumyn gestured one hand toward the city as the evening tide washed over them, and night brushed away the day's sunny remnants. "They think us criminals. The knights' temple—the home of the Galinea—has been locked up, with only council member Corbrak holding the key." He then twice tapped his index finger to his own chest. "I myself am now a fugitive from justice. However, I could not turn myself over until I came to you first."

Revekka placed her hand on his shoulder. "Acuumyn, you must stay here with us instead of going back. The Shroud rules the council now, and if you return, they will..."

Acuumyn put his hand gently upon hers, thus saving the next terrible words from passing over her lips. "I know what they will do." He smiled and nodded with a wink.

"Yes!" Maximilian agreed with Revekka. "Come with us to the castle. There we can finish our case for humanity versus the Shroud. Surely others will see reason when we present our findings," he urgently said.

"That is not why I am here." Acuumyn solidly jetted his finger into the air, shaking his hand from side to side. "The people are why I am here." He exhaled sadly. "We are advocates for them." He pointed his finger toward the lit valley and then over toward the dark mountains and beyond. Noticeably emotional, tears canopied up under his bottom eyelids. "I am fond of the mortals. But evil is more prevalent now than ever before in their history."

Maximillian jumped to his feet, clenching his fist. "Then we should take the fight to what plagues this system!"

Acuumyn friskily tugged at Maximillian's elbow, prompting him to sit back down. "We try to refrain from interfering in the mortal's world." He hung his head for a moment of silence. "I have great sorrow and pity for the misguided Shroud, yet more so for blinded humankind, which follows the Shroud unwittingly."

Maximillian's mouth gaped. "Why would you!?" He thrust his open palms up, out from his chest, and away toward the city below.

"Because, while the knighthood is peaceable, the Shroud revels in warlike acts," Acuumyn said. "Knights are vigilant, with unselfish concern for others, but the Shroud practices corrupt things. Knights declare order, yet the Shroud spread exaggerated reports causing confusion."

Acuumyn compulsively wiped his hands together, unaware of the rubbing friction sound he produced. "Knights are masters of the arts," he stared off with distant focus. "Knights unselfishly use their power to balance the scales of justice. They make bare, uncover, and expose wickedness." He rose his head gracefully up toward the sky. "Knights signify, give meaning—they do good, and are kind. You..." he quickly flipped his head and neck from one side to the other, looking briefly at Maximillian and Revekka. "You are the greatest symbols of knighthood." He bowed his head with a stiff lower lip. "In a former time, these qualities abounded, but now...the Shroud is all that is left, and they justify twisted doctrine by abandoning what they once held true."

Acuumyn gnashed his teeth. "They have poisoned the air of this world. The system is a shattered illusion, and the Shroud thrives in misleading sick humankind. The Shroud causes rifts between nations and peoples of different colors and religions. Humanity feels the oppression, and while they lash out at each other in wars and strife, the oppression is not directed toward one race or another, but rather, the system itself, which the Shroud created, and in doing so, subjugates them all. Though the Shroud is not concerned with political matters, they subversively resist all governments, thus interfering unjustly with individual liberties. And why you may ask...all for their power and amusement." Acuumyn's breaths shortened and his knuckles curled, blanching white at the joints. "They are harmful to the welfare of all living things. The Shroud is a dry and barren group, devoid of value. They seek to dominate others by clouding over truth. They are disloyal at their core, whereas knights are obligated by duty to love. Hmmpf." Acuumyn grunted. "I am sorry for the rant."

"Hmm," Revekka interjected. "I have seen the Shroud perplex, bewilder, and baffle humans for thousands of years. The Shroud built this contrived system upon corruption, and the only way the system works is with the deception of freedom, though everyone is nothing more than just food to power the system itself."

"Bah!" Maximillian eagerly interrupted. "The knights are skilled craftsmen, perfectly capable of combating the Shroud," Maximillian added. "The knights were appointed stewards for this world until humanity was ready to see the control the Shroud had over them with their own eyes. Yet I fear we have reached the end, and so has the mortal realm." He bent his body forward, almost in half, as he leaned over and glanced down the near vertical, stone, block steps beneath his feet.

Acuumyn abruptly got up, and walked over to a large, ancient boulder wall in amongst the ruins, impatiently urging Revekka and Maximilian to follow him. "Come, see. For this is why I am here." He pressed three small stones in coded succession along the wall, and a large, several ton section of rock milled backward. It scraped and ground against the other stones as it slid sideways on its own power.

Acuumyn reached inside and pulled out two separate scrolls from the large wall. Both were coiled tightly, and each was tied with a cloth bow in the middle. The scrolls flared out wider with jagged edges at the farther ends away from the cloth bows. One scroll was beige and the other was transparent. Both scrolls were rolled securely in the middle, resembling an hourglass shape. And of the two tied cloth ribbons on each of the scrolls, one ribbon was blue, and the other green.

Acuumyn clasped the scrolls, arresting his movement before turning, after which, he simultaneously stretched his arm out and handed a scroll to Maximillian and the other to Revekka.

"What's this?" Maximilian asked, attempting to untie his scroll.

Acuumyn quickly put his fingers on Maximilian's hand. "No," he calmly said. "If the Shroud captures you or the scroll, not knowing what you have will be a benefit."

Maximilian looked at the scroll and then up at Acuumyn. "I refuse to take a mission I do not understand."

Acuumyn half frowned at him, but dipped his head. "Very well. Untie them then."

Maximillian rapidly pulled apart the blue ribbon. Revekka peeked over at Maximillian as she gently unwound her green ribbon. With the ribbons untied, both slowly unfurled the scrolls.

A look of puzzlement splashed across Maximillian's hard face. Revekka tilted the scroll from top to bottom, her head tilting one way and the scroll tilting opposite her head. Both extended their arms, locking elbows straight, peering from afar, and then pulling the parchment just inches from their noses.

Revekka frowned, her lips gyrating up, down, right, and left.

Maximillian huffed a sigh. "Huh?" He rubbed his thin beard, before dropping his hand, along with the scroll to his side.

Acuumyn folded his arms behind his back, and watched them, grinning as they tried to figure out what they were looking at.

Acuumyn waited a few more seconds. "Here." He motioned to give the scrolls back. He laid the two scrolls side by side on a waist-high, stone slab next to them. Maximillian and Revekka circled around the slab with Acuumyn. "Maximillian, your scroll appears to have nothing written on it at all. Why it is just a clear piece of parchment." Acuumyn raised an eyebrow. "And Revekka, your scroll is a tattered, beige rag, with blots of smudged ink scattered about. But together..." Acuumyn placed the transparent scroll over top the ink blotted, beige one. "They are magnificent."

Suddenly, the dull paper came alive. Like a living road map of the earth—complete with things that looked like streets, intersections, and potholes—the map flashed with blinking red arrows, black circles, along with blue and green lines from one landmass to another.

"What is it?" Maximillian's eyes shifted.

Revekka silently attempted to decipher the map on her own, exhaling when she could not. "What does it all mean?"

Acuumyn's face reflected the vibrant insignias on the active map. "This is the Sphere Atlas, and it is the ultimate instrument from our technological age." He paused for effect. "Well...next to the Golden Glass Orbs that is." He grinned.

The Sphere Atlas was elongated when unfurled, and nearly the length of the stone slab it lay upon, but Acuumyn pinched the ends of the scroll, two corners at a time, and like a computer screen, he shrank the paper to the size of a handheld tablet. He then handed it to Revekka, and she gazed wide eyed at the living map, she then gave it over to an impatient Maximillian.

Maximillian did not take his eyes off the beautifully colored, now hand sized object. "What am I looking at?" He cradled it with both hands, fingertips only, as if he were holding a small baby.

"That is a map of every portal on Earth. The black circles are dead zones where no travel is available. The red arrows are hot leap zones, with multiple connection points. And the green and blue lines are one-way and two-way travel points." Acuumyn nudged in close to Revekka and Maximillian, pointing at other less eye catching, but important parts of the map. He pointed near the bottom of the tablet. There's a list of what everything means down here, you just have to enlarge it." He touched the map with his index finger and thumb, flipping his fingers away from each other, and enlarging a single area of the map to readable form. "But this is just the basics of the Sphere Atlas." Acuumyn then took back the map. He laid it down on the stone slab and enlarged it to its original size. He then separated the two parts, thus returning each to its lifeless, abstract form, binding them with their ribbons again, before handing each half back over to Revekka and Maximillian.

"That was unreal!" Maximillian proclaimed.

"We're ready to secure these scrolls with our life," Revekka added.

"Good." Acuumyn became vigilant, anxiously glancing all around the ruins. "But you need to know why the Sphere Atlas is important, too."

"Go on then." Maximillian eagerly waved his fingers toward Acuumyn.

Chapter Twenty-Eight

Acuumyn puttered around the ruins, picking several stones of varying sizes from the ground. They rattled when he shook them in his hand like dice. He placed the small, loose rocks on the stone slab in front of them. "Say each of these rocks are portals, or as we know them to be, apertures."

Revekka leaned in, her arms crossed behind her back.

Maximillian, straight-armed, placed his fists on the edge of the stone slab, leaning over the diagram, examining it closely.

Acuumyn collected their attention, so he continued. "Apertures can be small, like this pebble over here." He pointed to one of the smaller rocks. "In fact, apertures can be as small as twenty feet or up to several miles wide." Acuumyn bent down and ripped some grass from the sprouting, stray bits between stones, still talking throughout. "One large aperture can have many different points of entry inside a single leap zone." After depositing a handful of grass on the stone slab, he piled a few thin, short sticks from the nearby ground as well. "And each entry leads to many different destinations around the earth." Acuumyn dropped the bent sticks in the middle of the flat, stone slab next to the shards of grass. He began arranging the rocks, grass, and sticks into a configuration. "Now an immortal can open an aperture without a map...but it's risky." He tapped his index finger to his chin. "For each aperture has a different feel or texture, so from memory, a familiar aperture will always take you to the same place, yet an unfamiliar aperture, one you've never traveled before, can send you places even an immortal may never return from."

Acuumyn positioned the blades of grass between the various shaped rocks on the flat slab. "Some apertures go back and forth. Like a two-way street." He then positioned the sticks in and around the rocks and grass. "Yet others travel only one way..." he looked up, narrowing his eyes. "Do you understand?" His head shifted between Maximillian and Revekka. They nodded agreement. "Apertures almost never go to the exact destination desired, but some do. The apertures that don't take you to your exact destination, may leave you with miles and miles of distance still needed to be covered, most likely by traditional methods of human travel."

Acuumyn wagged his index finger hard three times. "Apertures require a great amount of strength, power, and knowledge to operate." He flipped his palms toward the glittery, star-lit sky. He raised his hands shoulder high, and wiggled his fingertips randomly as if he were playing an upside-down piano. "The larger the object taken through an aperture..." the rocks on the stone slab began to levitate and float, defying gravity with the slightest movement of his fingers, "the more strength of control is needed, and therefore, the weaker the immortal becomes that opened the aperture."

Maximillian tilted his head. "Is it permanent?" He squinted one eye at an angled upward glance.

"What?" Acuumyn replied. The levitating rocks bumped into each other when he talked.

Revekka weighed in. "Is the weakness permanent after an immortal expends that large amount of power?"

Maximillian moved his chin down and then up again.

"No...it is only until regeneration occurs." Acuumyn scratched his cheek. "Some immortals may regenerate strength in minutes, some hours, and others, not for days."

Maximillian raised his hand. "I noticed that in this place, sleep is needed to regenerate from physical injuries. Maybe that's why my power is strongest after I've rested awhile."

Acuumyn puckered his lips in silent contemplation. "Perhaps." He then refocused his thought. "But did you know that every aperture leaves a tiny, open window for a few seconds after it closes?"

Revekka perked up.

Maximillian crossed his arms.

"It's true." Acuumyn began lifting the small rocks, blades of plucked grass, and sticks several inches off the motionless stone slab. The items moved in rhythm, harmoniously bending to his willed gestures. "And these windows are called echoes. In theory, if one could leap fast enough, they could follow the one who opened the aperture." Acuumyn crinkled two of his fingers back and forth on his right and left hands, causing a small rock to pin a blade of grass upon the stone slab. "However, this is dangerous, because one could be leaping into a trap, with no escape. Besides, apertures are always in a state of flux. An aperture can eject you in any one of a hundred other locations not even remotely close to the person that you were following in the first place. For instance, like in the middle of the ocean." He flashed a brief, closed mouth grin.

Revekka closed her eyes and massaged her forehead. "We already know that apertures are like highways, rivers, and subway lines. It's just a transit system."

"Yes, and like any transit system, it has perils." Acuumyn addressed her. "I see that you and Maximillian have done your fair share of leaping through apertures, but the Sphere Atlas opens important, new roads. Roads not just anyone can open. Not even powerful immortals are skilled enough to use the transit of apertures as they were intended to be used." He pointed to the scrolls in their hands. "New apertures are opening all of the time, and sometimes old apertures close altogether, and can no longer be accessed. The Sphere Atlas is a very sought after thing." He frowned, straining his eyes, while slanting his head. "It is a thing the Shroud will attempt to possess at any cost. For the Sphere Atlas is constantly updating the pipeline of apertures. This map shows where each aperture leads, which ones are still active, and what apertures are one-way versus two-way streams of travel."

Revekka looked down at her hand, which clasped around the scroll. She clutched it tighter, and said after looking back up at Acuumyn, "I'm ready."

Maximillian too, squeezed his half of the map tightly, raising the scroll in hand to eye level. "Let the Shroud try and take this from me."

With lips pulled in and closed, Acuumyn smiled. The corners of his mouth pleasantly extended up, and his cheeks outward. "Then I gather you accept your mission, dangerous as it may be?"

Maximillian and Revekka briefly looked at one another, and said loudly together, "Yes."

"Then I need each of you to take the farthest route from the other until you deliver this to Caaron at the castle..."

Revekka interrupted. "Have you not heard? Caaron is gravely injured from his encounter with the dark lord of the Shroud, Malum."

Acuumyn arched his neck until his chin bumped his chest. The rocks, grass, and sticks all fell lifelessly onto the stone slab. "I had not heard." His manner flattened. His head gradually rose as his sagging eyelids peered intently into Revekka's eyes. "And what of my son? What of Appollos?"

Revekka stared back. An eternal breath rushed up through her nostrils, releasing a swift lament. "I don't know."

"He's all right." Maximilian quickly blinked with a dipped nod. "Benoit has informed me that everyone else, including your son Appollos, is intact and doing well."

Acuumyn sighed relief in a moment of strength and hope. His eyes retained a glimmer. "All is not lost." He walked through the ruins, inviting his companions again to have a seat beside him on a large stone in among the magnificent Grecian relics. "Come. Tell me. What has your time here revealed to you?" He patted the large stone seat in front of him, ushering them to sit. "What have I missed?" Revekka and Maximillian warily sat, each at an angle, while facing Acuumyn as he spoke. "Humanity has not detected our presence in thousands of years. Yet we have been here since the beginning, and have fought to free their minds from the Shroud since the original rebellion," Acuumyn finished with a lament.

Revekka and Maximilian glanced an off-center look at each other with an inquisitive frustration. Each delayed, and silently wanted the other to tell first. Neither spoke, so Acuumyn urgently motioned his hands in repetitive waves, prompting one of them to speak up.

"Well?" Acuumyn asked. "What say you?"

"It's gotten bad over this last century," Maximilian said, reluctantly breaking his silence first. He frowned, looked away, and down toward the lights in the valley. He rolled his tongue inside his mouth. "I have become discouraged and frustrated during my time with humanity." He continued in a tangent. "As I already mentioned, the young knights who were trained to destroy the Shroud, have not only joined the dark lord Malum, but have become a powerful force of sinister warriors, loyal only to him throughout the world."

"I see," Acuumyn replied, while rubbing the side of his face. "Malum must have bigger plans than previously thought. This is even more reason the Sphere Atlas needs to reach the castle intact. The knights there can protect it."

Maximillian's eyes fell into sadness, before lifting them up at Acuumyn. "That is not all," he continued. "The former, young knights do many things against humanity without empathy. They have greatly influenced mortals on a subconscious level, spreading fear, doubt, paranoia, and hopelessness throughout the earth." His words charged ahead of him, and soon he became more provoked by the sound of his own voice. "Malum has appointed some of his new warriors as princes over many governments of the earth, in order to control the leaders and their blinded masses." Maximillian balled straight fingers into fists, and gasped a deep breath from his lower belly. "There are also rumors that Dwellers, once extinct, have risen...Why just yesterday, I had heard a mother and daughter had gone missing in Paris. I believe the Dwellers have been hiding in the catacombs all of these centuries. Maybe if I go now, I can save the missing people..."

Acuumyn quickly sliced his hand downward, interrupting Maximillian. "They are just rumors." He put his hand calmly back at his side. "The Dwellers... are all dead." His chest swelled and sank rapidly with increased speed. He loudly blew air out his nostrils during the change in conversation. "They never should have existed in the first place. Those...those things."

The skin between Maximillian's eyebrows bunched together. "But how do you know they're all dead?"

Acuumyn shouted the first half. "BECAUSE..." He gathered a moment of silence, uttering his next words intentionally short and low. "Ahem." He cleared his throat. "I ordered their complete eradication."

Maximillian sniffed. "No, that can't be. But that would mean..." His eyes slowly widened. "I see." He pinched his lips with his thumb and index finger.

Revekka gave a sorrowful glance at Maximilian, and squeezed shut her eyes. "This is not our way!" She then turned her head in Acuumyn's direction. "They were all human once. Those Dwellers who attacked the world, nearly destroying all life, yes, they deserved death, but certainly we could have found a cure for the others?" Revekka's voice mourned.

Acuumyn angled his face down toward his feet. "The only cure for a Dweller IS death," he grieved. "You're an empath, Revekka." He paused, raising creased lines on one side of his forehead. "How is it you have not become insane from the suffering you have experienced through humanity?" He shook his head deliberately.

The three took turns pondering each other in a sort of hushed, tense reflection.

Maximillian overlapped his arms and furled his thin, tightly clamped lips.

Revekka's bothered face softened, yet her eyes reflected solid optimism.

Acuumyn moved about restlessly, rocking back and forth, his shoulders flipped inward and slouched.

The cool night air set upon the warm stones of the ruins, pilfering their heat, and chilling them to the touch. The stars gathered with a showy display of spangled diamonds immersed from end to end in the black sky, as the universe watched, looking down from its sacred place.

Their eyes were fixed on the city below.

It was swarming with life.

It was packed.

It was bright, and filled with thousands of the socially isolated.

Some were good, some were bad, but all of them were misguided.

The valley seemed vast, but somehow sad with loneliness by comparison to the adjacent nearby mountains. Of all the things on Earth, only humans appeared grossly out of sorts with their surroundings.

Moving lights in the city below blinked along. Torrents drifted of food mixed with motor fumes, rushing up the mountain in pockets, displacing the peaceful, countryside air.

Horns beeped.

Music thumped.

A cluster of distant voices exploded, and multicolored lights filled the valley until the mountains turned dark. The stars recessed and dampened back from their natural brilliance.

Though Maximillian, Revekka, and Acuumyn appeared as immovable objects in a rapidly shifting environment, each knew change was coming, for both the mortal realm, and for the immortals like them.

The stoic Acuumyn covered his hands over his face and wept silently. Revekka put her hand on his back, while Maximillian leaned away, attempting to look up under Acuumyn's face through his hands.

Revekka filled the awkward moment with her testament of faith. "The halflings still live, and I believe in the prophecy. Where many of the young, immortal knights failed, the halflings will succeed."

"Bah! Is that it?" Maximilian hastily replied, shaking his head with a mocking, loud huff, and heavily crashing brows. "They don't have what it takes to destroy the Shroud. The immortal war is coming to Earth, and you place all of your hopes on two aimless, half-breed teenagers?" he scoffed.

Revekka's demeanor remained unchanged. She did not shrink back, but boldly defended her case. "I trust the prophecy. The halflings are not alone. There are others besides David and his sister Danielle James, and those others, are being trained inside the castle as we speak. They are also young, but ready and willing to fight the invisible evil that dominates this realm."

"Aw. Okay, so you have a few dozen human children, a handful of immortal knights, a few hundred mortal archers from the Bleary Guild, and a dying castle master in Caaron." Maximilian frowned distastefully. "You can't possibly expect them to defeat an entire realm that follows the Shroud, and then, defeat the Shroud!" He threw his arms above his head and limply flopped them down again. "Acuumyn, please talk some sense into her." He pointed his index finger hard and fast at Revekka.

Acuumyn removed his hands from his moist face and pressed his lips together, appearing to raise a smile for them. He gently lowered Maximillian's frustrated hands. He glanced back and forth between the two, and then said, "I admire you Revekka. You feel the best in everyone with your empathic nature. Yet, what Maximilian says is also true." He gave a single head bob and wiped his lips with his salty fingers. "The self-proclaimed, dark lord Malum is a dangerous sociopath. And he presently rules everything in this world. The former knights—his new, young shadow warriors search constantly to murder our friends, as well as us. These once good, young knights, now serve only Malum and themselves. They have abandoned the way of knighthood to indulge in selfish fantasies." Acuumyn's voice briefly cracked. "Ahem." He cleared his throat and started again. "Ah, but I do not believe in this all-knowing and powerful first immortal that Malum touts, yet, I do think the immortal war will rock the earth to its very foundation..." He hesitated. "Perhaps there is something even more ominous waiting for the last of the knights." He shivered as a cool breeze stirred. "I can feel the cold winds of disruption blowing toward us as we speak."

Chapter Twenty-Nine

With the sun now set behind the mountains, the ruins submerged in a host of oddly formed, misshaped shadows. A sliver of crescent moon hung behind them. The air became still and silent. The individual city lights glowed a single orange as thousands merged, yet each light, when looked upon closely, had a uniqueness of its own.

Maximillian got up and stood suddenly. "We have work to do. We have to train the halflings, as well as the children inside the castle to battle for their future. It's our only hope against the Shroud." He laughed madly into the night air. "Ha-ha!" Then he quieted. "I suppose it was all destined to end anyway. It was a failed endeavor. We might as well do with what we have."

Acuumyn hung his head toward the ground. He moved his toes up and down inside his sandals. "It was not a failed endeavor. I failed. I failed all of you."

"What!?" Revekka spun her neck in Acuumyn's direction.

"I failed," Acuumyn repeated. "I failed all of you. I failed this world. I failed all immortals. I failed my son. I..."

Maximillian reached down and grabbed his shoulder from his standing position. "Stop!" His heavy tone anchored a delayed pause into his question. "What are you saying?"

The air remained cool and calm as the leftover warmth vanished completely from the ground. Acuumyn stood up high, bending the top half of his body while bowing to his friends. "I must leave now. You have your new mission, so see that you get these scrolls to the castle," he said, pointing to each of their chests. "And remember. Keep yourselves far apart when you travel, for the Shroud must not gain possession of the Sphere Atlas."

"Aren't you going to answer me?" Maximillian tightened his jawbone.

Revekka remained quiet.

Acuumyn spoke, almost detached from his own words. "It is wrong to have secrets. It is wrong to keep secrets for any reason."

"But we must protect our way of life from the Shroud," Maximillian answered swiftly.

"The Shroud used our own fears against us." Acuumyn sighed. "Fears we denied having. That is why I will answer to the people. I will not justify our covert missions any longer. In fact, I will even tell them what I have done here tonight when I get back."

"What? Why?" Maximillian shouted. His countenance fell into confusion and anger.

"Because the truth demands not just part of the account, but the whole transgression as well." Acuumyn straightened his back muscles while standing tall.

Maximillian was speechless. "But, um, uh." He attempted several times to say something, but each time his thoughts, his logic, his understanding was inept and futile even to him.

Revekka appeared to accept, approving of what Acuumyn had said.

With one last sad glance, as a final homage to the pair, Acuumyn turned his back and summoned an opening between distant places. A colorful, swirling vortex appeared. The vortex was hidden from the world in among the Grecian ruins. It spilled out thick vapors and bolts of lightning, yet remained quiet as nightfall, save for a swoosh of rushing air.

Acuumyn readied himself a return to where all immortals originate.

"Wait!" Revekka grabbed his shoulder. "Before you go through the aperture, I just want to say..." Her eyes briefly shifted downward, then back up at him, as his anguish became hers. "You shouldn't think of yourself as a failure." She gently held, then slid her hand off his arm.

Acuumyn silently smiled, and turned back toward the vortex. Yet he looked once more at them from over his shoulder with a distraught glance. "I did fail. It is true, we are physically perfect, but I made a mistake. I thought we could fix this realm without the council's permission. A secret, no matter how much we are convinced it is right to keep, is wrong." His head plunged. "Many will needlessly pay for my pride. Both the people of this world and those in the eternal realm are paying for my arrogance. Please forgive me." He stared through blurred eyes glazed over with saline regret. "I was supposed to be the Acuumyn that brought true peace and security to Earth. The purpose of free will is an autonomous, self-governing existence, where all live independently in harmonious prosperity...but..." He abruptly stopped and closed his eyes, pressing out drops from them.

More words felt wrong.

Revekka again reached for his hand and cradled their hands together close to her chest. Her neck and head were downcast. Her long, flowing locks tumbled slowly forward from off her back shoulders, covering her face from the dispirit scrolled across her beautiful soul.

Maximilian, still flustered, felt renewed motivation by Revekka's faith, and advanced toward Acuumyn. "You must not lose hope now." He aggressively vibrated his belligerent fist.

The aperture swirled in the backdrop, commanding Acuumyn toward its unworldly gate. Revekka lifted her head, and let go of his hand with a cautious glimpse.

Acuumyn turned, facing both of them one last time. His eyes loosened doubt. His thoughts seemed decidedly shaped into something more tangible nearly uttered from out his half-open mouth.

"Yes," Revekka exclaimed joyously, waiting on encouragement. However, silence continued, so she exclaimed, "There is always hope. I feel it with all that I am inside...isn't there?"

Following her lead, Maximilian gripped his hand into a fist and a mighty weapon fashioned like a radiant, surging sword of pure energy appeared. It was bright green. *Rizzz.* The weapon droned, cycling upward from base to pointed tip, discharging electrical currents.

Like a lamp, the sword lit the surrounding ruins, tinting the dark gray, stone slabs with an eerie greenish, dull hue. "I will deliver this scroll with power and speed, and my striker," Maximilian beheld his droning, green sword, "will cut down any who get in my way." He held his portion of the Sphere Atlas over his head, and high into the air. "I will send archers to guard the halflings. And I swear to train and guard the chosen mortal children inside the castle from the Shroud, and from all other wickedness on Earth." His chest expanded. He clinched his teeth, and focused his eyes, tapering them with uncommon resolve. After, Maximillian kneeled on one knee and bent his head low to the ground before Acuumyn.

"You make me proud," Acuumyn rejoiced. "Benoit is not yet a powerful knight. He needs direction to assume mastery over the castle. If Benoit is to lead the few remaining immortals, like my son Appollos..." He opened his palm, extending his arm to the kneeling Maximillian. "You must challenge Benoit to become better, to become more. The knighthood will not fall, and the earth will be redeemed if you both can do this." Acuumyn perked up. "As the appointed spiritual leader of the knights, I could not be more pleased." His face swelled with happiness as he looked approvingly upon Maximilian before turning his attention toward Revekka. "And what of you?" he asked. "What gift can you offer the earth?"

"I have been gifted a vision by the Celestial Pyre," she meekly said.

Maximilian gasped. His pinpoint eyes widened. He then stood from off one knee and kneeled on both knees, bowing his neck forward, with his face bent near the ground.

Acuumyn rubbed his strong chin, tapering his eyes, darting them to the side, and then back again. He enfolded his hands behind his back, and remained standing, but humbly bowed at the waist to her as well. "The Celestial Pyre speaks to no one, or at least it has not in hundreds and hundreds of years."

"But it spoke to me," Revekka said with a sincere inflection.

Maximilian slowly lifted himself from off his knees, but kept quiet, withdrawing his powerful sword. He inquisitively eyed up and down between Revekka and Acuumyn.

A silent, tense moment passed, and then Acuumyn tapped the tip of his nose with his finger. "You have empathic abilities, so it stands to reason you are more sensitive to the Celestial Pyre. For the flame that burns day and night underneath the castle is the spiritual source of all life, and the reservoir of the Artifex–the active power that enables knights to summon strikers, move objects, bend wills, and hide from mortals in plain view." He inhaled a large breath, with thoughtful pause, deflating rapidly afterward. "And it has chosen you from everyone else. That alone is a sign, which gives meaning greater than what we can possibly know at this point. We may have a chance now." Acuumyn again rubbed his chin, while looking at her. He tilted his head from left to right. His eyes were staring, but absent with other considerations.

"It told me to..."

Acuumyn abruptly blocked his ears. She stopped talking, and he released his hands, relaxing them to his side. "Revekka...what the Celestial Pyre showed you, is for you and you alone."

Revekka's flowing, carefree manner turned blunt. "Then I must deliver two messages, one before I reach the castle, and the second while inside its walls."

"Agreed," Acuumyn simply said. "Which way does the Celestial Pyre send you?"

"To the southern hemisphere."

"Then, Maximilian, you need to travel the northernmost route until you reach the castle, so as I said before, the two of you never journey close to the other."

After that, Acuumyn had finished speaking to him, and the two had nothing left to say. The hush revealed an inaudible sound from bunches of unanswered questions, which were thought by each present, yet never voiced to satisfaction.

Acuumyn dismissed Maximilian with a simple flick of his wrist, and Maximillian ran toward the north, swift and sure, his feet propelling him through and out of the ruins.

Dust plumed and evaporated into wisps of falling specks where his feet flashed a new path. Within a matter of seconds, Maximillian disappeared among the distant lined, jagged mountainous region.

The dark mountains loomed like an apparition of tranquility around the bright city valley. They served as an unwise route for a mere mortal to travel during the night, but Maximillian was no mere mortal, and did not fear what recessed in the unknown crevasses of the steep, mountainous bluffs. Once he left the company of Revekka and Acuumyn, he did not look back. However, Acuumyn and Revekka remained standing in front of the swirling aperture, not knowing if either would see the other again.

A spirit of melancholy overcame Revekka, and even Acuumyn's stoic nature crumbled like the stone slabs in the ancient ruins, which once guarded a vibrant city, their mighty walls of protection, now smashed fragments of rock along the hilltop ground.

"I implore you, stay here, and help us in the coming immortal war," Revekka pleaded. "It will be the last war ever fought in the history of wars."

"I cannot."

"Why?" A befuddled hurt, crowded a portion of hope from off her face.

Acuumyn stood eye to eye with Revekka, holding his hands under hers, touching his fingertips to her palms. "I, even I am not above justice, no matter how I may personally feel toward my accusers' dubious accusations. The people back home would judge me evil, in league with the Shroud no less, if I did not return. That is why I must give myself over to them." He then rested his hands on her shoulders, took one last moment, and said, "I...am...guilty, just not of what I am being accused."

Revekka's mood drifted with misery. "Will we ever see you again?"

"I know not."

"What will they do to you?"

Acuumyn sealed his lips together, refusing to answer at first. "This...is dangerous information I give you now."

"Yes?"

"We share a single origin with humanity...with the mortals."

"What? No! No...that can't be possible." Revekka clutched the scroll, creased her lips, and wrinkled her nose.

"I cannot give specifics, but if I am correct, there will be a unification rather than destruction. But, if the Shroud..." Acuumyn cut his words short. He placed his hand over the scroll in her hand, pushing it toward her side until he finished. "Complete your first mission, then you must get this to the castle before the Shroud finds you." He again, with a turning of his head, this way and that, surveyed the ruins for movement. "I fear the Shroud is becoming stronger by the minute. They are looming in every part of this system, and the Shroud is fully capable of destroying us all."

Revekka looked briefly down at his hand, and then back up into his truth laden eyes. "There's more. What aren't you telling me?"

He reclaimed his hand from her shoulder, closed his eyes, and then slowly opened them. Acuumyn innately scanned the ruins to his side, with aloofness he peered off into the descending twilight. "The council, by which I mean Corbrak, has banned all travel by locking the temple shut, thus closing off the only aperture from our home realm to here." A resigned droplet sputtered down the outer side cheek of his stagnant, unaffected face. "Whatever happens to me, the price of true freedom is worth that sacrifice." With several short breaths, and a subtle grinding of teeth, Acuumyn crossed his arms with firm resolve. "Corrupt dictators, monarchs, and elected officials who rule their fellow humans with secret, malice intent, will no more be tolerated, for the time of the governments is over. The time of terror, the time of criminals, the time of oppression and fear, it will all end soon, and it will end with a knight's blade." He slammed his fist down on one of the stone slabs, cracking his knuckles against the hard, cold rock. He winced, shaking out his wrist a couple of times. He examined his hand, moving his fingers rapidly one at a time, forward and backward before placing it at his side again.

Revekka reached for him. "Are you okay?"

Acuumyn pulled his hand back behind his body, away from her sight. "It did not hurt. We are immortals after all." He glanced at the stone, arching the bottom middle of his lip upward, with his eyebrows curled down, and his nostrils flared between the two. "We are stronger than meager rocks."

Revekka glowered sidelong with a concerned frustration. "The Celestial Pyre's message, I must tell you...

Acuumyn closed his eyes and refused to hear. "No, Revekka. I do not want to know. But please, if you must tell something, tell my son..." his voice strained and cracked. "Tell Appollos...I will always love him."

"But, Acuumyn...this is a specific message for you."

"When you get to the castle, whatever that message is, give them that message for me."

"What if...?"

With her mouth still open, and forming the words, Acuumyn reached into a hidden pocket along the side of his tunic.

"Give them this." Acuumyn handed Revekka a round, bronze amulet. "And they must then listen to you as they would me."

Revekka gingerly reached her hand over top the amulet, and with a quick scan of Acuumyn's eyes, she took the round, coin-like object from him, peering at both sides, flipping it back and forth over again.

"What's this?" Revekka ran her fingertips along the amulet's ridged surface. "And what do these markings mean?"

Acuumyn stared at her beautiful face for a moment.

Revekka gazed at the amulet. Her eyes asquint, she was vexed by his silence.

Acuumyn looked over his shoulder at the swirling aperture. He then faced Revekka. "It means that you now speak for me in all things."

Revekka's eyes widened. "I can't...I won't...I'm not..." she stammered.

Acuumyn put his hand at mouth level, and forming it into a single index finger, he closed his lips, and pressed his index finger to them, afterward, removing his hand back to its place. "Yes," he modestly exclaimed. He sealed his mouth with a closed lip smile for a second. "May this amulet protect you from evil. And in my place, you will speak with words of gravity." He then abruptly turned from her. He walked into the colorful, swirling vortex, and disappeared into the aperture, after which, it boomed shut behind him, and the ruins became a dark, gloomy, and desolate group of relics once more.

Revekka stood motionless under the orange, crescent moon. Concealed by the night, in among the ancient Grecian ruins, she felt many conflicting emotions, but in the end, she dismissed them all. She chose to feel nothing except the scroll she had clutched in one hand, and the amulet in the other. She was too sad to cry, too angry to scream, yet the weight of responsibility tugged at her, pushing away the loneliness. Unlike Maximilian, she briefly scanned the bleak area one last time, before gradually trekking from the skeletal fragments and lifeless stone slabs of a former, mighty world power.

Revekka sensed that the Shroud was well aware of her mission by this point. The stakes were high.

She had given Acuumyn's words and meanings abundant thought. There were going to be immense losses. If human history had showed her one thing, it was that lives were shattered during times of revolution, and this would be an epic revolution for the hearts and minds of everyone on Earth. The Shroud's pervasive rule saturated the world. And like the air she breathed, the Shroud's poison enveloped every idea in human society. Nothing remained untouched by the Shroud's corruption, for they clouded motive and perception, especially that which seemed most noble.

She felt something close in on her.

To an immortal, the Shroud was like a cold wind from the north. Its agents were warriors of a lethal and supreme kind, having already dispatched to prevent her and Maximilian from reaching their destinations alive.

Yet still, she walked with a rhythmic grace that only unwavering faith granted. Revekka honestly discerned her own heart's intent, for she knew that reaching the castle was only an optimistic start. Nevertheless, an immortal war was nearly upon them, and based on the mood of civilization, a positive conclusion was very much in doubt.

Chapter Thirty

To the east, far from the ancient ruins in Greece, a warm gust of midsummer air sifted through boundless crops, dipping golden heads of wheat in fluid waves of gentle wind.

The near empty fields had a solemn majesty about them.

Out of seemingly nowhere, a handsome, strong young man with a gaunt beauty emerged from over one of the hills.

The meadows had a refreshing, pleasant odor. In the distant edges of the vast fields, thick brush and forest ruffled leaves in the wind.

He sauntered carelessly around the golden wheat fields along the lower Mediterranean countryside. His face slanted in strong, but lovely angles, like that of a cut gem. His cheeks chiseled and high, sloped down to a low, strong jawbone, and slightly cleft chin. Straight-faced, he ambled, while casually inspecting random heads of golden grain, picking a few, gathering several straws of wheat from open to closed hand at a time.

Round sunglasses, tinted black, with thin, golden rims hid the color of his eyes. His hair, straight and jet-black—not long ago had been much shorter, but now, like a revival, it liberally grew a dab past his ears, and merged with the beginnings of a full beard, concealing his ageless trait.

His attire, unflattering to the strongly toned body hidden behind woven fabric, clothed him in a pair of dismal, black-and-gray-striped wool pants, a plain white t-shirt, and solid black suspenders that elegantly swathed over his shoulders for fashion rather than need.

Beside him, a woman of untamed, classic beauty paced along his leisurely steps.

She seemed about his age, and together they were a stunning pair worthy of pictures in books and magazines, but neither wanted any attention, except for the jealous devotion mutely required from the other with every glance or subtle gaze.

The couple harmoniously strolled without concern through the fields. Hand in hand, they joined and leisurely strolled together.

Just like his, her hair was lush and black, yet despite her best attempts to cover up the past, it grew wildly uncontrolled. Rows of short, frayed ends unevenly sliced into her once flowing, long curls. Now, her hair bore a malicious frazzle, as if hacked off with garden sheers, thus robbing the patent shine of her rich feminine glory.

However, as most things go, it too had begun a restoration, revealing signs of lavish, extended strands of grandeur, budding once more as if new grasses in the spring.

She had a lovely face. One easily picked from out of a crowd. Attractive, she exposed a sparkling set of happy, unpretentious eyes. Her facial features appeared molded, smoothed over by fingers from a lump, into a superbly formed clay vessel, carefully molding her cheeks, nose, and lips from that of an artisan's pottery wheel. She was the face in a thousand that shone above the rest, with the kind of allure others desired to simply catch a fleeting glimpse.

His eyes naturally drew toward her.

They walked through the quiet, splendid countryside as lovers without a care.

The sun, the moon, the fields, and the tides, all of these were marvels, but to him, they were mere curiosities relative to her loveliness.

He pierced her soul with his musing glance.

She fluttered each time.

It was how every woman wished to be considered. With a simple look, he not only esteemed, but also eyed her girlish majesty with an admired passion. He looked upon her with the same wonder that a man does when he sees his bride dressed in white for the first time. In that moment, she felt loved as if she were the last, and only woman in the world, the only woman that mattered to him, and the only woman worthy of his undivided attention.

Her binary, easy movements made her clothes appear like a second skin. With a double layered, knee-length, pink cotton sundress, she rubbed the broderie trim between her fingertips to remember its feel on this day forever.

Thin spaghetti straps tied firmly up both right and left sides around the nape of her neck. She grabbed his hand, twirling in and away from his steady chest and arms. While he spun her, she giggled, exposing shining white rows of perfectly straight teeth, along with a sudden kiss upon his soft lips.

Into his arms, she fell in a moment of stillness. He dipped her backward, holding both her hand and her midriff in a long pause. The two peered deeply at every inch of the other's face. Her eyes scurried back and forth between his dark lenses, which hid a most revealing trait, yet reflected only her lone, sumptuous image.

He released her, and the two wandered along without a definite purpose or destination, but with contentment.

The sky was clear and blue, yet wispy beach clouds rode over the vista. The fields were dense, full of golden haze, waist-high and softly forgiving for a stroll or a stride.

The sun showered warmth upon their tender flesh. She brushed her hand along the tops of the wheat, smiling, gazing from side to side, and at him, while taking in all the pleasure she could on such a faultless day.

He plucked some more of the heavy headed wheat, briefly and casually inspecting it, beaming back at her, yet hiding his internal, unsettled disquiet.

Hand in hand, they continued up over the short hill. Their course had corrected to a singular endpoint. They lined a slow march toward the only shelter the fields provided for as far as one could see.

It was a humble abode on top of a small hill.

The cabin's metal roof covered a solid wooden, modest, but adequate structure as it proudly rested like a palace at the highest mountain peak. It did not boast. It gave only what was needed. Four walls and a couple of windows, but it had a shaded porch, facing west, which captured the solitary, magnificent day's end that their golden fields and vast panoramic skies offered almost every evening. The young couple stood still, her head rested on his shoulder, as they prized their exquisite kingdom, caressing each other with impassioned intent.

Soon, the embraced lovers entangled as one, hidden beneath the modest shade of their wood cabin.

He held her tightly by the waist and lifted her off the ground until she laughed, begging him for freedom. He abruptly let go, almost throwing her to the ground, but catching her gently, softly lowering her feet upon the trampled patches of grass.

She stumbled backward onto her bottom. Still laughing, she called out to him.

He recklessly threw off his sunglasses somewhere onto the field. He fixated on her. His smile left him, his eyes enlarged, and he sprinted over to where she was.

She reached out and pulled, towing his arm until his body fell down beside her on the cool grass, while lying in the shade of the rustic cabin.

On his side, next to her, he stroked a single lock of hair from off her cheek, placing it behind her ear, kissing her chin in one tender motion. "I...I um..." was all he could utter of the unutterable, which his eyes, linked with hers, had already imparted the rest for this flawless, captured moment.

She arched her back inward, her neck and chin out and up, putting her lips against his, whispering first, "I know...now kiss me, Vincent." Melding an all-consuming, tender, fleshy link, the two had never been closer to one. They were finally at peace with their choices, innocent choices gone terribly awry, but all the same, choices that had led them to the discovery of each other in this divinely tranquil place.

Vincent flashed a series of confident smirks, followed by a cocky grin. His smile, stunning, he had a gleaming quality, with the rare gift to comfort and assure her that all was well in the world.

A distress that once preoccupied her every thought, was now concealed by a promising freeness, which only her lovely mate had unlocked for both of them.

"Vincent..." She looked deep into his coldly beautiful blue eyes, and with the sun high and bright, he sheltered and cooled her from its pounding heat.

"Yes, Noemi?"

"Promise me that we'll be together forever." She cupped both hands on each side of his slanting, gauntly wondrous face.

Vincent curved his brows downward. "Always."

"And will you always love me?"

His neck sloped downward, stealing a quick taste from her cherry blossom lips. And with her sparkling teeth, she gently held his bottom lip for a moment before playfully letting go.

"I yearn for you, Noemi. Every time I see you, it's like seeing you for the first time." A single arm held Vincent's body off the ground, horizontal with hers, and his other hand he set across his heart. "I ache when you are not near. I almost lost you once, and that will never happen again."

Noemi batted her lashes, and turned her head away when Vincent swooped in for another kiss. She beamed, wiggling some, and then she impulsively flipped positions with him.

He was now on his back.

Her dainty wrists pressed hard against his strong hands.

"What's the matter?" Noemi briefly wedged the tip of her tongue between her lips. "Can't get up?" she teased.

Vincent thrust the tip of his tongue back out at her. While smirking, he raised his eyebrows, peeking up at each of his covered wrists.

Noemi, skilled at calculating his reactions in advance, giggled once. "Tee-hee." Her forefinger rubbed his palm.

She acquiesced her grip, sitting level on his stomach. Her body crouched. She bent a little bit forward. With a leg on either side, extending over, across his body, her hair draped toward him, all over his face.

Happy, possessive touching followed.

His fingers ran along the edges of her winding curves. His palms upward, she held out her trembling fingertips flat upon his warm, sturdy hands. He offered a demanding gaze. She was more elusive. Vincent abruptly stood with ease, and cradled Noemi's back, taking her with him on a dominant rise to his feet. Her legs remained wrapped around his waist. He pressed against her body. Noemi clutched the large muscles in the front of his upper arms. He looked at her figure. She had become very pleasing in form, shape, and in the midsummer sun, color as well. He slid his hand up her thighs, abdomen, and navel. She quivered.

"You excite my feelings." Vincent huffed, panting, speaking lowly as he rapidly kissed her neck. "You paint my world with the color of your passion."

Noemi closed her eyes and tilted her head back. "Go on," she said with intoxicated tone. She rubbed her hands through his hair excitedly. She loved his tasteful, sensitive beauty.

His lips locked onto her neck. "You quench all my desires," he softly said as she pitched her head back, tipping it for his access.

The two vigorously kissed, their tongues converging at the tips, their mouths wandering, and lips brushing soft, moist, warm skin, electrifying a tickled sort of static charge.

A faint aroma of pleasantly scented flowers hovered through the golden fields. The air was fresh and crisp, but patches of warmth gusted in westerly winds.

Zzzz. Bees buzzed, their wings hummed and vibrated from one purple wildflower to the next. *Chirr.* Crickets sharply peeped as they jumped and hopped sporadically throughout the field. *Chitter.* Sparrows plunged from the sky, scooping up bugs, before gliding up toward the clouds in an endless display, down, up, and over again. The sparrows tweeted songs to their mates, with harmonious, acoustic notes, and occasionally, entwining as one, circling up in midair with a lover's swoon.

The heavy arching grains bowed, and scant lavender arose in spurts, rushing past Vincent and Noemi.

The fields had opened themselves.

In the shade of the rustic cabin, the two curiously pondered the other's thoughts, holding hands, their faces sideways, their eyes inescapably met, their cheeks holding still against the cool grass. Their rapid breaths gradually slowed.

Wherever the sun's yellowish rays filtered through the white, bloated clouds, it spilt onto the ground, exposing miles of pristine meadows, hay bales, and rows of golden wheat. The fields laid out their bounty for them, baring their singular delight, while fulfilling every immediate earthly desire two lovers could share.

However, not all was right. An irritation crawled under Vincent's skin. His senses heightened. A disturbing tingle grabbed his attention, diverting it away from their amorous episode, replacing sweet with a dash of bitter.

He stood.

She stood with him.

They both looked in the same direction.

She grabbed his shoulders, hooking her arms up under his. Holding their chests close to one another, she pulled him nearer than he had been before. Her hairline stood at his chin. Noemi enjoyed the majestic vista, yet Vincent watched for something more ominous, something she did not feel, something he had not felt since they arrived in this wonderful place.

Chapter Thirty-One

"What is it, my dear? What do you see?" Noemi asked with hesitation.

Vincent scoured the fields for a sign, a presence, but all seemed calm. "Nothing, I guess it was just a group of birds over there." He pointed, yet his face belied another truth. He knew then that her abilities to sense things around her had grown weak when she neglected to feel what he had. "Here," Vincent said with a smile devoid of sincerity. "Why don't you go up to the cabin. I still have a few things to do down in the fields before I'm ready for supper."

"Well...all right..." She narrowed her eyes for a moment, yet surrendered her misgivings, and instead, she kissed him on the tip of his nose. She rested her head on his shoulder, then looked him in the eyes, and with playful banter said, "Now, now, don't be late." She laughed, giving him a last kiss on his cheek, and then they parted ways.

Noemi hopped, pranced, and strolled up toward the cabin, occasionally beaming over her shoulder at him. He clumsily waved to her, yet remained still and vigilant, watching for any moving threats from his spot.

His hawk-like eyes scanned the fields for trouble. Vincent smiled with his mouth only, his senses unmoved, he waved compulsively back as she did to him.

His ease now became irregular. He crossed his arms, and he twisted around several times, mumbling to himself for her to get in the cabin. Once she had reached the cabin, closing the door behind her, he hiked with purpose down the hill at a quickened, urgent pace.

Vincent anxiously marched toward a cracked, protruding, large chunk of timeworn foundation hid amongst the long grass and vines of thick greenery. The foundation was cluttered between the low brush, and fenced in by a brick wall at the bottom of the hill.

He had sensed someone else, and though he had not seen a person hiding behind the wall, he felt a person hiding there. He intended to find out just who dared stalk them.

His rapid stride brushed the arching grains of wheat in his direction, hastily crushing some underfoot. The wind shifted. A cool gust pushed down from behind.

His movements rustled the field, sending crickets jumping, birds flying, and bees buzzing all away from him. Alone, he stomped a new path through the meadow he had so carefully tread moments before with his eternal love hand in hand.

Puh-puh, puh-puh. His heart pounded and sweat formed at his brow as he approached the vine-ridden brick wall. He had a past he wished to forget. She had a past she never mentioned. Though their lives had diverged for a time, they shared a similar past, and a dangerous enemy.

This common enemy not only killed them, but also had the ability to know if he and Noemi had stayed dead.

The pit of his gut provoked nauseating flashes from recent dilemmas he hoped never to think of again, nor wished to trouble Noemi's fragile mind. He slowed as he approached the wall, and then rapidly stuck his neck out, viewing with eager queasiness both the wall and green overgrowth engulfing the wall.

From ten yards away, he stopped and considered the best vantage for his attack. He sensed an unmistakable tingle, an active vibration in his brain, which discharged throughout his body. He shook his hands, balling them up before releasing his fingers spread and straight. He rotated his wrist in circles, and his head from side shoulder to back, and squared it atop once more, while blinking an immersed vision toward the wall again.

He knew that like him, it was another immortal, and Vincent had come to hate all other immortals, except for Noemi, whom he loved for the new meaning that she gave to his life.

It had been a while since Vincent felt the sensation of another immortal.

It was foreign and magnified by comparison to the time he had spent not feeling anyone else except his love, Noemi. Now, more than ever, he was startled and uncertain.

Cautiously approaching the fragmented wall hidden inside clusters of bushy overgrowth, he briefly glanced up the hill at their home. It was dinnertime, and the chimney had begun fuming a tasteful aroma of Noemi's supper. He hesitated, thinking of her safety first. Ever since he lost her, he was determined to think of her first from then on, and he could not suffer her loss ever again. For if he had any doubts in his life, it was of only one thing, and that was if he could protect them from all the forces ready to tear their love apart.

Despite the risk, he continued down the hill. He was not going to just confront the unwanted guest, but also kill the intruder, and hide the body before it was time to eat supper.

His skills had eroded without practice and training. He promised her, he promised Noemi that that part of their lives was over. He knew how ill-prepared he was, and that scared him most of all. Up until now, he had dismissed his gifts and abilities, or so he thought. However, he worried, for if he lacked the conviction of skill to defend himself, how could he protect her. He glanced up the hill, wondering if he should flee to the cabin, get her, and run away from this place while he still had time. He needed to choose quickly, because two enemies approached, another immortal, and the time left to make the right decision.

In Vincent's nature, he was never one taken to flight when battle called. Vincent would rather bathe the golden fields red with blood than run away. He put one wobbly hand on the brick, gathered the deepest breath his lungs could hold, and then stepped out, facing both sides of the wall.

The air settled a disquieting calm. For a brief moment, Vincent could hear only Noemi's wind chimes on the cabin porch. He braced, crouched down, and turned inward, expecting his foe. He raised his arms and blocked his face from the attacking coo as a pair of doves flapped their wings, racing to escape his furious surprise.

Temporarily blinded by the fleeing birds, he tensely laughed. The birds had cleared out and flown away. Vincent's chest elevated and lowered calmly. His respirations slowed at the sight of nothing except the wall and the thick greenery.

The fields were empty.

They were as deserted as they had been all day. Puzzled, but still concerned, he scratched his head. He crossed his arms and stared at the backdrop ahead of him. His watch gradually lessened as Vincent dusted off his pants. He prepared to walk back up the long hill toward the cabin as nightfall rolled over the landscape with a familiar, peaceful glow.

"Hello, Vincent," from behind, a mild, yet foreign female voice said.

Chapter Thirty-Two

In one motion, Vincent jumped, turned, and summoned his sword of mystic energy. "Who are you?" He locked himself in place.

She calmly leaned over and picked a purple wildflower from the field, breathed its sweet fragrance, and closed her eyes before putting it in her hair. "I'm Revekka. I'm a friend, so you need not be afraid."

"I'm not afraid," Vincent scoffed. His translucent red blade droned as he cut the air. "You should be the one in fear." He held the weapon with both hands, cocking it backward over the side of his head. "This is where you scuttle back to Malum like the vermin you are."

"As you can see, I am unarmed." Revekka looked at him curiously. "And I'm certainly not an agent of Malum or the Shroud." She slipped her fingers together. She held her hands in front of her body.

His brows crumpled. "Yeah, right," Vincent mocked.

"Look, your power to control the Artifex has grown weak." Revekka pointed to his blade. The mighty weapon blinked and fizzled with all the flare of a defective electrical cord. "Even now, you could not protect yourself, or even her." She nodded her head up toward the cabin.

A woman's outline walked past the window from the other side of the curtains, while an appetizing scent bellowed from the pipe atop the cabin's roof.

"Leave her outta this," he commanded with a deep, threatening quality.

Vincent lowered his blade, keeping it between him and Revekka. He watched as his weapon, once trusty, phased in and out with a waning glow. His attention completely unfocused, to his dismay, the blade pulsed on and off several times before it dissolved into glassy splinters, and then into nothingness. The particles of his mighty weapon crumbled, dispersing along windy streams, briefly covering the field in glittery, sparkling dust, until the thousands of pieces from his sword had all melted from sight.

Revekka remained at a distance from Vincent. "You have lost your striker. It is a knight's strongest protection, and it has failed you."

"Are you gloating?" he attempted a witty remark.

"No, but knights are skilled craftsmen. They are masters of the arts."

Vincent exhaled and pouted. "What does this mean?"

"It means you need to listen to what I have to say, for I haven't long until I must go from here."

Vincent, stunned by the loss of something he took for granted, vacantly eyed Revekka. He fiddled with his hands, not knowing whether he should put them in his pockets or down by his side. "I thought I'd have my striker forever. Well...you've got my attention, so make it good," he narrowed his eyes, and insisted.

Revekka prodded, "Do you think I am still in league with Malum?"

He tightened his lips, gazed at the ground contemplatively and then back at her. "Maybe not, but then again, Malum uses many forms to gain an advantage."

"Hmph," she interjected mild contempt. "You have trust issues." Revekka let go of her hands, swinging them by her side. "I'm delivering an important message, and then I must go." Revekka was short on time. She wished to neither lead the Shroud to Vincent's location, nor alert him that they were following her.

"Message...what message?"

"Earlier, you correctly estimated that I, another immortal, was near. Your senses have not failed you. Never doubt your senses." The two shared an unspoken trust discovered in the other's eyes. "I know your mother, father, and I knew your older brother as well."

"What?" Vincent's face turned red. "No, that's not possible." He carried an air of boasting. "What do you think you know of me?"

"Well, I know that you talk too much about yourself." Revekka began tapping one finger off, counting her digits as items on a list. "You're impulsive, bold, daring, brazen, and insolent."

"Wow." Vincent frowned. "That was impressive. You have any more nice things to say?"

"Yes." Revekka deliberately sighed, slightly blinking as she did. "For an undisciplined knight, your skills are unsurpassed for a mostly self-taught person. And you're driven by shame and guilt over what happened to Jak, when you should not blame yourself harshly for your brother's death."

Vincent squeezed the bridge of his nose. He casually wiped a tear, pretending to sniff at the floating specks in the air. "This, uh..." He was overcome. "This happens sometime. You know...the pollen and stuff."

"I am not a knight. I am not a judge. I am an empath," Revekka explained. "I was sent to this realm long before you were ever born, and I have been here for the last five thousand years." She continued. "I have seen many horrible things, but also a few wonderful things as well. I have drifted through the world undetected, and never directly interfered, that is, until you were revealed to me. Never before had the source of all life contacted me." Her dancing eyes became steadfast. "Don't you get it, Vincent?" She uncharacteristically raised her voice. "It was your individual plight, your plight, Vincent, your misguided but redeemable plight."

"My plight?" His tears dried. Vincent chuckled and grinned. "Is this some kind of joke? 'Cause I have to say..." He placed his hand to his chest. "I'm not buying it." He tilted his head and smirked.

Without speaking, Revekka looked askance with a sidelong hint of disapproval. Her eyes widened, and she examined his soul with a sort of reflective sincerity he could not dispute. "Did you ever wonder how you survived Malum's brutal attack that day on the cliffs, high above the jagged, rocky coastline near the castle?"

His grin flattened. "How do you know about that?" His voice dropped.

"Because I was there."

"So you saved us?"

"No, the fire that breathes life into everything, which resides under the castle, saw fit to preserve both you and Noemi." She then waved her hand through the air. Revekka used her ability to recount a story in the breeze. The grass, wind, and leaves created an intense, but fleeting, silent moving image of past days for him to see. "I was there as a witness only."

Like a movie, Vincent watched Revekka wave the thin air, which played out that day again before his very eyes. Intently he observed, this time as a third party, everything that happened that terrible day on the ocean cliffs. He visually recounted his battle with Malum. He saw Noemi thrust off the high cliff by the dark lord. He watched as he jumped over after her, and the vision simply ceased, evaporating into ashy particles, as when things are burned to a cinder.

Chapter Thirty-Three

At first, Vincent went silent.

Then he bubbled forth. "What fire? What are you talking about?" Emotions stirred, flooding back simultaneous conflicting reactions, along with more questions and growing annoyance.

Revekka, as always, quickly listened, yet spoke with a calm, graceful aura. Her emotions were tried and true, composed under all circumstances. "Not many immortals know of the Celestial Pyre, and fewer are ever contacted directly by a vision, so consider yourselves special." She again quickly glanced up at the cabin.

Antsy, Vincent's palms moistened. His thumbs fidgeted in and out of his fingers before he placed his hands in his pockets. "No! I can't hear this." He pulled his hands out of his pockets and axed downward, slamming his eyes shut, then he gazed off to the side of her. "Let me get this straight. What you're saying is that there's this secret, what? This secret fire under the castle called the Celestial Pyre, which all life...I...I don't even know how to finish that sentence." He cupped one of his hands, rubbing his mouth from the bridge of his nose to his chin rapidly, and then up again. "And if it's true..." He shook a finger. "Why have I never heard about this before?" This both intrigued and provoked him.

"I detect doubt," Revekka said. "No matter, what's true is true."

"I'm sorry, but I've heard so many lies by Malum and the others that I..." He stopped and gave a frustrated look to the side. "You wouldn't understand." He placed his hand over his forehead. Without another word, he started to walk away, up toward the cabin.

His back now opposite her, she offered more answers. "The Celestial Pyre gave a vision of the events on the cliffs before they even happened to you and Noemi."

Vincent stopped, with his back still turned he said, "It's too much...Go on."

"Noemi and you, your hearts proved worthy, and so the Celestial Pyre gave me the ability to open an aperture just before you hit the water, and before that boulder Malum dislodged came crushing down upon the two of you."

He shrugged his shoulders. "So."

"So...what? What do you mean so?" Revekka was offended.

"So what does it all mean?" He cocked his head back at her from over his shoulder.

"I don't know."

Vincent brooded. "Great."

"But I do know that you...she...doesn't belong here. Immortals need a proper place to belong, and this isn't it."

Vincent groaned.

He looked straight ahead at the inviting cabin and started walking up the hill again. "I'm hungry. I'm going home now, and I never want to see you around here again."

Yet Revekka did not give up. "What's the first thing you remember after being plunged into the ocean by Malum?"

He stopped again. This time he turned around. "Noemi and I woke up on a beach not far from here, that's all I remember," he said with an utterly bothered aspect.

"As always, you can choose your path, Vincent, but if the Celestial Pyre did not have faith in the two of you, it would not have placed you gently on the seashore rather than dead at the bottom of the ocean." She quieted, letting him rub his chin, while contemplating her last words. "Remember, we may be immortal, but we're not indestructible."

"What did you just say?" Disbelief overlapped his face.

"You are gorgeous and brave, Vincent, I see why she loves you, but you're none too bright, are you?"

"Hey!" He arched his brows downward, stitching them together before releasing them apart.

Revekka restated herself. "I mean, you still have much to learn."

He pursed his lips in a frowning manner.

She smiled innocently.

"Listen, Vincent, what do you think Malum will do once he's destroyed the last of the knights?"

"It's not my problem anymore," with swift coldness he replied.

Revekka's hands hugged her hips. She gave him an unmistakable stare of baffled disappointment. "Your friends are not your problem?"

"They turned their backs on us when we needed them most, so why should I care now?" He shrugged.

"Because in your heart, you are still a knight, young gallant one!"

"I never completed my training." Vincent peered toward the sky. "Poor Jak was so fond of reminding me that I wasn't a real knight at all." Vincent examined his hands. "Hm. I guess I was just a kid playing games, wishing I had what it took to be a knight, to be a true Galinea, but I'm not. I don't..."

Revekka urgently reached out. "Even the knights can learn from the two of you, or otherwise, the Celestial Pyre would have revealed this vision to them, for they were nearer when the event happened, but I traveled from the other side of the world for you."

Vincent finally had pause. The words that usually rolled so easily off his tongue, stalled. His mind, so made up on all matters of life, now became open to another viewpoint. "It still doesn't matter. Even if I wanted to have faith in your words, my abilities are gone, as you can clearly see." He flipped his palms upside down, looking his hands over again.

She stretched an arm toward him, giving a closed mouth smile. "Nothing is ever gone. But they need to be strengthened. Remember, train to enhance your abilities, don't suppress them. From practice to reflex," Revekka repeated again, "from practice to reflex. And, Vincent, meditate and connect with the Celestial Pyre, and you will find where the road broadens once more. You will find your balance."

He began to nod in agreement, but then shook his head with a skeptical hostility. "What if I just ignore all of this and do nothing, like I've been doing all along?"

"That's your right, but we both know it's just a matter of time before Malum senses the two of you are still alive, and at that point, there will be no one left to help you stop him, and you will lose what you cherish, this time forever." Revekka's eyes saddened, not for her, but for his sake.

From up on the hill, at the cabin, Noemi opened a curtain and watched Vincent. She angled her head to see whom he was talking to, but the person remained veiled from the window's vantage point. The downward slope of the hillside curved outward, showing Vincent, but not Revekka. Vincent glanced up at the cabin windows, catching a glimpse of swaying curtains swinging closed.

His tone exasperated, he asked in partial defeat, "Why do you need me? Why don't you go recruit the mongrels, you know, that David kid and his sister, Danielle. Didn't they defeat Acerbus or something?"

"I'll be honest, as I have been." Her respirations nurtured deeply loud puffs of breath. "David James is an amplifier. Unknown to him, he needs others who are stronger than he is in order to summon his power. And Danielle, she thinks we have all gone away. She wants nothing to do with her heritage. She's interested only in earthly things."

"Well so am I!" Vincent crinkled his nose upward. "Can't I have a life, too?"

"Yes." Revekka rolled her tongue. "You can have a life, but even not making a decision has its consequences."

"All right, go on." Vincent sulked and shook his head from side to side.

"Have you ever wondered why all the hopes of a generation were placed on you and your young friends?"

Vincent remained expressionless. "No," he lied.

Revekka pleaded, "Malum is the god of this world. Every knight who has confronted him over the past hundred and fifty years has died, that is, until you. Sooner or later, someone will have to fight him and win, and I believe that is you...Vincent."

His lips parted. "What are you saying, that I'm what, stronger than Malum?" His eyes gaped.

"When the time is right, you will be."

"No...no, that was just a fluke." Vincent exhaled loudly. "I can't defeat Malum. He's too strong, too powerful. He'll kill her!" Vincent averted his eyes. "I mean...me."

"I know. And even with you, the battle may very well be lost, but we have to try." Revekka drew her upper body back a bit. "Though you lack the stature of a traditional hero, and while you might not be the knight we expected, it's clear—you *are* the knight we need! The knight we were waiting for all along. Yet we could not see it, but the Celestial Pyre read your heart, Vincent. It knew what we did not."

"I can't do it." He bent his neck forward, nodding it from side to side. "You've got the wrong person."

"Then become the right person," Revekka swiftly replied. "Become better. Judge your own worth accurately, and you'll see the truth."

"Speaking of truth..." He peeked up at the cabin. "What do I tell Noemi?"

"The truth, Vincent, always the truth."

Reluctant, he looked up at the cabin again. "But what if I..." Vincent turned back toward Revekka, but she had disappeared from view. He charted miles of open fields. Vincent placed his hand as a visor, blocking out the late afternoon sun. He looked in each and every direction, yet she was gone. He sighed, viewing the cabin from afar. He stood there pondering what he should do next.

Chapter Thirty-Four

Like the proverbial coin, every account has two sides. While some try to amend history on one side of the globe, strong opposition tears at the very fabric of reality, tugging and stretching at the foundations of all human institutions.

A system so sure of its checks and balances, has been weighed and dismissed by some, yet fiercely contested by others. Make no mistake, the world is not going to end, because it began its ending five thousand years ago. The present system is just a device, a bridge for the conscious mind, an illusion, a farce, a den of deception, a thinly veiled aberration of freedom and will, yet devoid of any true life, and thus, unfit for habitation.

The system does not involve any one particular race, religion, or government, but rather, a corrupted state of mind.

The system infects with disorder and confusion. It holds many down underfoot, yet raises up a ruling class of unqualified elite based on birth and currency. There is a delicate line between existing and living, between thriving and wasting time. The current system has been designed to cloud thought, to deflect scrutiny, and destroy individuality, replacing it instead with a form of mindless rebellion. For if one never knows who their true enemy is, the real fight can never be brought to them, and thus, never won.

That is why every human on Earth is controlled by the system. For it is here to subdue them. Petty riots, wars, social unrest, terrorism, patriotism, and cellphones, they are all devices used to cloud the senses by the architects of the system. Some of these tools have been used since the beginning of history and time.

The system is a dry gully, full of vanity and haughtiness, and above all else, the system will bring even those it exalts to eventual ruin.

The ones who put this system in place are greater than any human who has ever lived. They are greater in speed, strength, and intelligence. They are immortals, and they have experimented with many forms of human government throughout the centuries.

These powerful immortals perceive well beyond those of their human counterparts, yet while they secretly undermine humanity, other immortals push back against them and their cruel, false world.

Through immortal power, they are not always openly seen, and even when the average human sees them, they go unnoticed, appearing like everyone else in the world. Nonetheless, the pressure of their conflicts can be felt in waves by humankind, like contractions when a baby is due labor for its delivery, society feels invisible pangs of distress.

For there is a last war, an immortal war, its symptoms can now be felt more than ever from one end of the earth clear to the other. Immortals perfectly reflect on a past, which they have lived, a present undoubtedly controlled by them, and a future that has been planned since the birth of this alleged civilization.

In the wilderness, early streams of sunlight filter between leaves from a thickly covered forest. A large, green tent sits as the only livable structure in the clearing. Oversized rocks circle billowing ashes from a large fire the evening before. Half-cut logs in multiple rows project an empty audience for the smoldering, ashen residue. Millions of orange pine needles litter the forest floor, yet apart from that, no trace of human debris share even a footstep along the ground with the campsite.

At midday, the sun can only penetrate the dense covering of the tallest trees at their thinnest points. In patchy torrents of hazy light, the woods are disturbed in silence. The creatures of the glen have all left this place long ago. There are no crickets, birds, chipmunks, or squirrels. There are no sounds of buzzing bees or cooing doves frolicking even in the highest branches overhead. Altogether, it is a loudly quieted, uneasy, but untouched area, appearing incompletely unchanged as the forest was before the campsite arrived not long ago.

Yet this place is not devoid of life. For inside the flapping outer door to the tent, under its tarp cover, a series of subterranean tunnels, lined with burning wax candles on both sides of the excavated walls, light a network of crude, dimly lit passageways. Off the main burrow, a square room, with hundreds of candles on multilayered shelves built around and into the dirt walls, scorch back the darkness, sending gloom away for a time.

A middle-aged man stands by a table packed with beakers, flasks, stirring rods, test tubes, cylinders, and Bunsen burners. He carefully uses scoops to measure, tweezers to pluck samples, along with many other instruments and utensils of every kind, all of them neatly arranged on the surgical table from end to end and from back to front.

Some of the test tubes and flasks were half filled with different colored liquids. Some glowed, flickered, and fizzed with various shades of reds and blues, greens and yellows, purples and pinks, while others were murky black, thick as tar, with a sludgy and deathly appearance.

A large crow, with feathers dark as coal, watched, tilting its head with a pair of thinking, blue-gray eyes.

The crow sat on its wooden T-shaped perch, angling its head toward the man as he stirred some of the flasks, while others boiled under controlled flames. The man held one tube up near his face, and then another, comparing them side by side. He scowled and grunted at the concoctions before placing them back in their holders, frantically grabbing more to compare beside each other.

He wore a sackcloth-hooded robe, with the hood folded behind his head. His scalp, a shiny bed filled with sparse patches of straggly, whitish gray hair, which was thinly dispersed, appeared as a plain dirt field of weeded growth. He held the test tubes up for a closer look. Distracted by failure, he glanced at his fingers and then drifted toward the upper part of his hand. His wrinkled, scrawny hands had been fresher than a child's skin not long ago, but now were dried, aged, lined, weathered, and leathered, imperfectly maturing before his very eyes.

He placed one of the test tubes in its holder, and casually looked behind him. He touched his face, tracing the deep scar, routing a cavernous line from the top of his left eyebrow down to the lowest bulge of his cheekbone.

He had one good eye and one made of glass.

He moved his finger in and out of his deeply creased, old scar. He stopped just short from touching his left glass eye, briefly mourning its loss. For a moment, his clarity had vanished. Frozen by a memory of what used to be, he blinked several times before the crow on its perch cawed at him with a keen, shrill pitch. *Caw! Caw!* The crow bobbed its neck up and down. Rapidly, he began working at his table again, speeding up as if for show. *Gwuf, gwuf, gwuf, gwuf.* Pitter-patter footsteps pranced down the candle lit, dirt floor halls just outside his location.

His hands, full of knuckles, with bony rounded joints, reached for a glass ampule. His arm coolly slithered across the table, picking up one thing while putting down another. He continued his tests as if he expected no one at all. His long, pointed fingernails inched laterally, crosswise the tabletop, like spider legs, they tapped one vial in a predatory fashion, before quickly pouncing on another, snatching it tightly, and lifting it up toward his one good eye. Though his vision made him nearly blind, he had an uncanny awareness of observation.

He grew impatient.

He already knew a timid, young girl, with long, feathery, jet-black hair would peep around the corner of his room's entrance any moment.

She thought she went undetected. Peeking an eye up at his doings from the doorway, she was small in stature, thin, and famished, yet not for lack of food, but for her genetics. Her skin was brown, smooth as velvet, fresh and new. She wore a purple and black long-sleeved dress, with knee-high leggings, and heavy fur boots.

Each it seemed, waited on the other to reveal themselves. One grew anxious, and the other angry.

Chapter Thirty-Five

The man with the scarred face coughed. "Ahem! Come in, child. Don't be so insipid." His words rattled off his tongue with forked bother. "I'm sorry to be obtuse, but I'm very busy." He enjoyed using large words most others did not know.

The young girl cautiously entered the room. Her back clinging to the wall, she eyed the crow on its perch, which tilted its head sideways and eyed her back. "Uncle Malum?"

The crow hopped madly, now facing the young, timid girl. It opened its beak wide, harshly squawking at her in rapid succession. *Caw, caw!* It angrily watched her, flapping its wings and jumping up and down on its perch.

Her body snapped back toward the door, clutching the crook of the doorway as she cowered. The crow waddled with furious delight, almost smiling it seemed.

"Now, now, Alcazar." Malum picked a crumb from out of his pocket, walked over to the crow on its perch, and pet the bulbous part of the bird's head, while feeding him a snack. "Don't frighten Kimi. She's our friend." Alcazar gobbled up the crumbs, angling its neck upward as it swallowed them whole, then he hopped from the perch onto Malum's shoulder. "Alcazar can be so pedantic at times." He turned his attention to the young girl Kimi. "Now what is it you have to tell us?"

"Tell us?" Kimi stepped in closer and looked around the bright, softly lit room.

"Yes...Alcazar and I, of course." He mockingly chuckled.

"Uncle Malum, I'm bored."

"Well then, have you mastered your skills yet?" He turned from her and slyly walked back to his chemistry table.

Alcazar kept perch on his shoulder.

"Um, well, I...I'm getting close." Kimi smiled, swaying and moving about while standing, her feet planted as she leaned toward Malum.

He looked over into the crow's eyes and puckered at Kimi's reflection through them. "Alcazar is upset because you have not been able to even summon a blade with your mind. I think he's depressed." Malum turned around, giving her an odd, frightening smile. "I don't understand bored. How can you be bored when you have so much to learn still?" Malum flapped his arms up and then down, slapping them at his side. Alcazar wobbled, but remained perched on his shoulder.

"But I'm tired of training with Vanessa. I wanna do something different."

"Yes, uh huh, something different you say?" Malum whispered at the crow. He laughed, and said, "Good point."

"Thank you." Kimi smiled with reply.

"I wasn't talking to you," Malum said with a demeaned nature even a child like herself could understand. "I was talking to Alcazar. He has a clever humor, and some of the best, pithy sayings I've ever heard."

Looking sideways, she was in a stupor of puzzlement. Kimi huffed as Malum gave the crow another treat from his pocket. The crow, while still perched on his shoulder, lined its beak up with Kimi's face, and harshly squawked at her. *CAW!*

"Alcazar said that you weren't bored when I saved you from the slums of your village. In fact, you were so un-bored, I believe you were desperate to come here rather than stay with your family, or what was left of it anyway." He smiled, patted her on the head, and with his knuckled, withered hand he reached out and pinched her full cheeks. "You promised to do all that I asked after all. You have a duty to be loyal to the Shroud." Malum had a distinct way of insulting with kind tones.

"I know." Her entire body slouched. "But I haven't been outside of these tunnels in weeks."

Malum talked in riddles. In vague bits and pieces, he strung together unrelated ideas. He rarely came out and said what was on his mind, but he expected those with less intellect than his own to figure out what he was saying instead.

Full of smugness, his arrogant comments were backhanded even when they were meant to be complimentary. He did not attempt to hide who he was. He just disguised intentions whenever it suited his purpose. Still, tolerance for his own act became tedious now and again. However, when Malum had made up his mind, there was no going back. He had no remorse and no pity. His disgruntled face exposed much. He respected nothing, except his immortal life's work on the table, which he had been toiling at for a thousand years.

"Do you ever wonder what I've been doing in this room?" Malum uplifted his eyebrows, curling his middle lip upward, with the corners protruding down.

Kimi glanced around. Her opinion uneven, she asked hesitantly, "I guess, maybe you're making something?"

"Blah!" He grinned. "Very good, Kimi. I am making something." Malum laughed. "I've been trying to make something for the last thousand years."

Kimi looked bewildered, so Malum continued, if for nothing else, then just to hear himself speak.

"The flicker fruit gives immortals their strength. It once grew everywhere in my homeland, but now, only a few fruits remain."

"You have plenty over there." Kimi pointed to a bag covered in the corner.

"Hum, yes." He eyed the bag, and soon after, her, with an annoyed glare. "I'm afraid that's all that's left. I saved those from the evil knights in the castle not far from here. You see, they have the last tree. And do you want to know a secret?"

"Yes!" Her ears perked right up.

"The last flicker fruit tree grows right here on Earth. And if..." He pounded his fist in his hand, hanging his head afterward. "If they would just share, then all the people could benefit, but no!" He gritted and ground his cracked teeth. "The knights are greedy warmongers. Whenever something bad in the world happens, the knights are responsible."

Kimi's eyes, large and unblinking, fixed themselves to Malum. She was so engrossed, she had not heard Alcazar's angry squawks as he jumped back onto his perch, flapping his wings and madly pecking his beak at the wood under his own feet.

"This is why you brought me here, to help destroy the knights, isn't it?" Kimi asked, more surely.

"Why, yes." Malum indulged her. "The knights have said that it is a sin to dissect the components of the flicker fruit."

"Why?" Kimi narrowed her eyes.

"Because they are subject to their own inflexible rules," he said as gobs of saliva shot forth in fits of rage. "They believe the fruit is a gift...a gift, can you believe that!?" He pointed at the slumped over bag of flickering fruit in the corner. "But I know..." he reached over and picked out several different colored tubes of liquid, "each of these colors separately does something completely different from another color." He put down the test tubes and picked up a large flask, swirling its sparkling blue contents. "The trick is the preserving agent. I have yet to find one that doesn't break down the magnificent component inside the fruit's juice."

"Why not just drink the juice without a preservative then?" Kimi tried to help.

He put his index finger under his chin, tilting his head up, peering down his long nose while ridiculing. "Now why didn't I think of that?" Rolling his singular, real eye upward, he shook his head and scowled. "I'm an amalgamist."

"An imalga...?" Kimi struggled saying the word.

"No!" Malum frowned. "A-mal-ga-mist. It means I blend and mix things to make other things, better things."

"Oh," Kimi meekly replied.

Malum promptly tossed a hand toward the table full of liquids, test tubes, and flasks. "I'm attempting to find compounds that change the volatile, baser elements you see here in these different colored solutions. I have tried distillers, along with many other mixtures...but most of them have rendered the derivatives from the flicker fruit poisonous to all living things." He picked a round, glass cup from the edge of the table. He once again held it eye level. It was a cloudy, thick, almost neon green liquid. Malum swirled the fluid around, and then put the glass to his lips. Kimi folded her fingers into her palms, raising them to cover her mouth with a sharp gasp.

Malum gulped the green liquid down his gullet, his outer throat expanding and contracting with each swig. "Ah." He wiped his mouth with his sackcloth sleeve, and continued talking. "Besides, just minutes after the juice is drained from the fruit, the mixture's worthless, and apart from the fruit as a whole, it loses all effect..." Malum noticed Kimi's terrified appearance. "Say, what's wrong with you?" He aimed his good eye toward her.

"You just drank that poison!"

"Pish-tosh. Balderdash." He looked into the empty cup. "That was my favorite drink, Absinthe, or otherwise known as the Green Fairy. Mwahaha." He laughed, and then placed the empty glass back on the table. Malum tapped his cheek. "This reminds me, I'm running low. I need to get some more of that stuff."

"So that wasn't poison?"

"No, just a very delicious beverage, but on another note, I did have some success with a potion once." Malum grinned with the right corner of his mouth only. "Would you like to see the result of that success?"

"Yes." Kimi jumped, clapping her hands.

He methodically fixed his table, leveling every piece he touched until it was perfect again. "Kimi, do you know what the three worst things in the world are?"

"No."

His side profile away from her dimpled another grin. "Number three is not getting what you want in life. Number two is getting what you want in life..."

"And...?" Kimi asked innocently.

"And...I want you to think about those two for a while." Malum tried to smile from ear to ear, yet the nerves on the scarred side hampered that portion of his face. I'll tell you what number one is later."

Kimi pouted and crossed her arms. "But I wanna know right now!"

"You do then?"

"Yes, please tell me."

"Okay. What say we go on a trip first?" He turned toward her. "Go change your clothes and I'll be ready in a bit." His cold, bony hands ushered her out of the room, pointing her down the candlelit passageway.

Once Kimi left, Malum scowled. "She's a whiny little brat, isn't she, Alcazar? And we know what to do with whiny little brats around here." Alcazar jumped, hopping from one foot to the other, his head jerked back and forth. "Yes," Malum hissed, "we know exactly what to do with whiny little brats." Malum gave him another tasty treat, and Alcazar happily clicked and cawed several times.

Chapter Thirty-Six

Not long after, Kimi returned to the room, this time with her mentor, the older, teenaged Vanessa by her side.

Vanessa had an upscale, trendy prettiness. She was all about the glitz. Her hair was shoulder length and silky fresh, with frosted blonde tips. Every part of her was finely detailed, from the studded buckles on her black leather boots, to her long, French manicured fingernails. She adorned herself with the hottest, modern fashions of the season, from the shimmer of dangling earrings, to a metallic halter-top that tied around her slender neck.

Vanessa fluffed her locks, tugged her fitted jeans slightly up past her hips, and at the same time, she nonchalantly inspected the small diamond sword pendent at the end of her dainty chained necklace. She then adjusted the collar to her unbuttoned, denim shirt, rolling each sleeve up to the elbow. And if it looked as if she had just stepped out of the finest shops and salons along Sunset Boulevard, it was only because she just had.

Malum enjoyed the spectacle Vanessa displayed, scantily clad and skintight at times. For Vanessa's part, she knew about his roving eye, but did not care. She batted her lashes and nodded humbly. She was determined not to make the same mistakes her two predecessors, Dominic and Noemi, had made. So, she let him look all he wanted, but never would he be allowed to touch.

Vanessa stroked Kimi's feathery, jet-black hair. With her fingers remaining straight and spread apart, she cringed with each glide of her hand. Vanessa was careful not to touch the tips of her newly painted, French manicured fingernails on anything. Rather, she patted Kimi's head clumsily with her palm, and faintly opened her mouth in something intended to resemble a merry smile.

"So where are we going?" Kimi excitedly beamed.

Like a magician, Malum waved his hands through the air. "To an ancient place," he said. "You recently turned twelve, and this is my belated gift to you." Malum chuckled. "I'm taking you to a place of legend, one that time has completely forgotten about."

"Will I be back in time to do more training with Vanessa?" Kimi clapped her hands with glee, and then hugged the middle waist of her impassive mentor. "I think you're so beautiful." Wrapping both arms around Vanessa's inward curved midriff, Kimi gushed, "You look like my favorite doll back home, except her head fell off 'cause I brushed her beautiful, long blonde hair too much, but it looked just like yours." Kimi closed her eyes and held Vanessa tightly.

Vanessa quickly removed her hand from Kimi's head, inspecting her recently manicured nails. She raised the back of her hand to smack the young girl from behind. Kimi, unmindful, opened her eyes, looked back at Malum, and smiled delightfully.

Malum glared ahead at Vanessa, who grudgingly ceased. Instead, she placed her hand on Kimi's back, patting it and scowling as she did.

A sudden loving gesture emerged. Vanessa bent over, and curled her neck forward on Kimi's shoulder instead. "What Lord Malum has to show you is more important than our training, so don't worry, I'm sure you'll have the trip of a lifetime." She stood back and then tapped young Kimi gently on the tip of her nose, deviously grinning as Kimi openly smiled.

Malum suppressed a smirk, but he locked eyes with Vanessa, and in that moment, each shared self-satisfaction with the other. "Come along now," Malum said to Kimi. He opened a swirling vortex in the tunnel outside his laboratory. The wind gusted, blowing out some of the candles, while knocking down others along the burrowed corridors.

"I almost forgot something. Vanessa, I need you to be on the lookout for a female immortal that will travel near the castle any time now." Malum waved Kimi toward him. "Get to her before she enters the castle's boundaries. I've already sent word to Xander in Glasgow to be on the watch for a male immortal. They are both very dangerous, but possess something I greatly wish to have."

"Yes, my lord." She bowed her head. Vanessa crossed her right arm over her body, placing it atop her left shoulder. She concurrently extended her left elbow out, clustering her fingers together with an upward straight palm. She hailed a brief salute. "What is it you wish to possess from them?"

Malum issued a threatening, foreboding look. A stubborn quiet stifled his direct answer. "You'll be looking for one half of it in the form of a scroll. It's called the Sphere Atlas. There are two parts. Xander will obtain his scroll in Glasgow, but I need both parts. Do you understand?"

"Of course, but what does this Sphere Atlas do?" Vanessa fell prey to interest.

"That's not something you need to know." Malum tightened his lower lip. "You are an instrument of the Shroud, and curiosity can be a risky proposition."

Feeling scolded, Vanessa's eyes fell downward. "I understand, my lord."

"And, Vanessa..."

"Yes?"

"Don't let this female immortal say even a single word to you. Kill her and take the scroll before she has a chance to speak."

Vanessa signaled understanding and agreement through a nod. Though wonderment filled her, she dared not ask for another unoffered piece of information.

Malum led Kimi by the hand as they approached the swirling vortex. A low-lying mist poured from the entryway. "You remember this?"

Kimi motioned recall.

"It's an aperture," Malum said."

They walked briefly through a circular array of magnificent swirling colors. Kimi felt nauseous entering the opened aperture, yet she knew not why. She had traveled through apertures on several occasions, none had posed a problem before, but something felt odd, yet she soldiered on, ignoring her better judgment. Her tiny teeth smiled up at him, and she hid her aching doubt.

In an instant, the two stepped out of the old place and into a new one, but for Kimi, it seemed just like the place they had left, except darker, wetter, and with a certain unidentified foul odor, which promptly offended her senses.

Kimi reached down and pulled the collar of her shirt up over her nose and mouth. It helped a little, but not enough. The decaying smell saturated everything, and soon filtered through the fabric collar and invaded her nasal cavity. She breathed only through her mouth, but even the air tasted badly.

Once through the other side, the aperture closed behind them. Without any light, it was black, dark, and blinding.

Kimi raised her hand to her face, not able to see nary a digit wiggle in front of her. The air was damp and heavy, stale, with a musty ancient rot. Puddles of cool water mixed with slushy goo underfoot, making every step a slippery fall waiting to happen. Kimi reached for support. To one side, a stone wall with deep lines and elongated clawed marks ran parallel with the two of them, and on the other side it felt about the same.

Plip-plip-ploop-plip-plip-plip-ploop. The water dripped, pinging through the darkness.

Kimi stammered, "Wh-wh-where are we?"

"Why under the streets of Paris," Malum carelessly responded.

Kimi grabbed ahold of Malum's arm, holding it close. He took her from his side and placed her directly in front of him, grasping the tops of her shoulders, squeezing his fingers into them solidly. His fingers slithered up and down Kimi's shoulders, kneading pressure with each step forward.

Kimi looked back. "Shouldn't I be next to you?"

"No, no," Malum dismissively replied. "This helps me better guide you in this nasty darkness."

"But I don't wanna be in front, it's scary..." She heard a passing, beastly sound from the tunnels up ahead. "What was that?"

"Nothing. Probably just some rats. But don't worry, I'll protect you." In the blackness, he felt able to express the full nature of his non-verbal amusement with a full smile.

The two of them walked along, awash in widespread darkness, neither able to see a thing, but even without sight, Malum sensed many other things were closing in on them. He placed his right leg between Kimi's legs, tripping her.

He pushed her forward as she fell.

"Aaah!" she shouted. Her hands reached out to brace. *Fa-thud.* Down onto the hard, wet, muddy ground she tumbled.

"Oh, my dear girl, are you all right?" Malum held back a snicker.

"I think so." She pushed herself up off the ground. "What happened?" Her face heavy, covered in slimy muck, her knees soaked, and hands layered with abundant dirt.

"I guess you must have tripped." Malum's grin hid itself in the dark tunnels. "I tried to reach out and stop you from falling, but alas, I was unable."

"I can't see." Kimi waved her hand. She touched naught, except the openness of vast air. "Where are you?" Her voice boomed panic.

Malum remained silent for a moment. He waited for the eventuality. He became impatient, knowing they sensed he was not human, and so they feared approaching him, as they should have already attacked by now.

Chapter Thirty-Seven

The temptation of a free meal was too great for a starving clan. The bait was set.

Nonetheless, the creatures in the tunnels pondered if a single meal was worth the chance of being hooked by what they truly feared in the mortal realm, and thus they loitered in the darkness, just observing.

Borborygmus. One creature's stomach rumbled. What Malum had sensed all along, closed in, yet not on him.

Little did Kimi know, the creatures enclosed only around her in the unlimited, black void. She reached out and felt something inches away. It was an arm reaching out for her as well. Her fingers lathered with grimy sludge up to her forearms. Kimi's tactile awareness became mute. A hand lifted her up off the ground. Her fingers slipped, drifting downward toward the ends of the hand that helped her up.

Unexpectedly, she felt the sickle-shaped, razor-tipped edge of the helping hand. Kimi discovered it was not Malum's hand at all. Thinly bent, knuckled fingers accompanied the sickle clawed tips. "Ahh!" she yelled.

Kimi jumped back, slamming into a lean, slimy body. Without vision in the dark, she felt several bodies to the front, right, left, and behind her as well. Kimi even heard things snarling from the ceiling above. "Uncle Malum...help me!" her young voice shouted a throaty, fraught cry.

"You've disappointed Alcazar," Malum said with intended malice. "You have failed to make progress with your abilities, so you are no longer worthy of me—no longer worthy of the Shroud, and thus I release you from your obligation to serve our cause." One side of his mouth rose above the other. He chuckled. "Ha! And don't worry, my dear, Vanessa won't miss you. In fact, nobody liked you anyway." He crossed his arms and his expression turned blank.

Malum summoned his sword.

The blade glowed and steamed with a haunting translucent, grayish black tint. The sword burned and smoked with a hazy quality, yet without a true flame, it smoldered.

He held his blade down by his side, but it was more than enough light to expose all who were present in the tunnels.

"Aaaaaah!" Kimi yelled a prolonged scream. She beheld a cluster of ghastly, walking corpses surrounding her. She could see her own reflection in the dilated horror of their large, black eyes. A few briefly twisted their heads backward, looking at Malum. He moved an approving gesture. Instantly, the creatures turned their fangs for tearing, and sickle talons for ripping, into instruments of torture against Kimi. *Cling.* They opened their sickle claws. *Siss.* Each hissed, widening their mouths and spreading their razor-tipped claws as they focused in only on Kimi.

"What are you?" Kimi yelped. "Why are you doing this?" she implored.

With a singular amplified, raspy voice, they replied, "We are Dwellers, and you are a free lunch."

Kimi jumped to her feet. "I'm nobody's lunch." She glared past them, crinkling her nose at Malum in defiance. Her hands wobbly, she balled her fist, attempting to summon powerful weapons of pure metaphysical energy, like her teacher Vanessa had trained her to do.

The Dwellers shrunk backward, covering themselves and turning away.

Malum feigned disinterest. He placed an index finger against the side of his chin, hoping to see a strong reaction, but no weapon materialized.

"You've failed yourself." Malum yawned. "How pathetic."

Frustrated, Kimi opened and closed her fist repeatedly, wrinkling her brows downward. She clenched her tiny teeth, grinding them. The creatures recoiled each time. Some hid their faces in the crook of elbows, while others turned their backs, twisting away from her in protective defense.

The Dwellers knew this power well, being the only weapon that had ever struck them down to near extinction. The swords had earned their name as strikers, by nearly striking them from off the surface of the earth. Though they hated their half life, they still feared total death. They hated immortals. They despised the knights who killed their kind, felling them with strikers and power greater than what they themselves possessed. Yet, Kimi seemed an unlikely immortal.

"Nothing happened. Nothing happened," exclaimed one of the tunnel dwellers.

"Why would they," another Dweller shouted, pointing at Malum, "give us one of their own. It's a trick! The Shroud always tricks."

"Who cares! I'm starving." yet another Dweller replied.

"I agree. Better to die with a full belly than an empty one. Get her!" A Dweller signaled forward the others and howled.

"No! Please no!" Kimi squealed. She tried to break through them and run toward Malum, but a beast grabbed her leg and pulled her back toward the inner circle. "Help me!" She spread her fingers apart and reached up at Malum. "I'll be better. I promise."

"No, you won't." Malum turned his head, tilting his nose into the air. "You're simply not worth the time. It's just the nature of your devolving species." His bushy eyebrows inched up and down. "Humans lack purpose. You're defective." Malum wiped his baldish head. "Ha-ha-ha." He let go a hearty laugh. "All humans are primitive and worthless, and for that, I will allow these Dwellers to exterminate you and your kind with extreme prejudice." Malum drew a long, satisfying breath.

The Dwellers began tearing at Kimi's soft flesh with their piercing talons and fanged teeth. A group of them huddled, surrounding her in the dimly lit darkness. Kimi punched and kicked. The Dwellers stabbed here and there all over her legs, arms, and face. She screeched, bawled, and wailed with every piece of flesh they skinned from off her. She battled for her life, but as the Dwellers dug deeper into her soft tissue, feasting on clumps of bloody meat, her loud cries muffled, and soon disappeared altogether.

The Dwellers crushed Kimi as when a pillar is smashed into tiny pieces of gravel.

Red liquid branched out from the inner circle, drenching the Dwellers' feet. Several inches high, Kimi's blood sapped like copious, warm, vivid red bathwater from bloodstained wall to wall. The once living plasma, now dead, pooled with puddles of muddy water, mixing with dirt and filth, staining the black ground a brownish red.

Malum, for his part, stepped back as the gory mess trickled near his sandals. Malum hiked the coarse, woolen fabric from his robe away from the draining, reddish fluid. It was not that he minded gore, he just hated getting it on his garments.

Malum, with an unmoving affect, said, "Little boys are made of snips and snails, and puppy dog tails. Little girls are made of sugar and spice, and all things nice. Ha-ha-ha-ha-ha!" he shouted a gratifying laugh throughout the tunnels. "Now I know they're all made of the same things, just blood and guts, and lots of black stuff." Malum leered.

One beast turned. It slurped and slushed up a long piece of Kimi's intestine, and then wiped bright blood from its mouth, smearing the red across its lower face. "That was good. She put up a fight. It tastes better when they fight."

"She tasted different, tasted different," another Dweller added.

"We shouldn't have killed such a young girl." One Dweller slouched. "We broke the law."

"I'm sick of your laws, Killian." Another beast with long, thick sickle talons pointed a finger. "What? Should we all starve because the law is to only feast on those that are of the larger variety?" He shook his talon and snapped his jaws. "I say no more laws!" The Dweller raised its arm into the air.

"That is the Dwellers' only law, Slash." Killian straightened from his hunched position, and puffed his chest outward. "If we are to remember our..." He purposely stopped.

Slash challenged. "Say it! Say it! I dare you!"

But Killian would not say the word. Rather, he just shook his head, and remained quiet.

"That isn't my law. I have no laws. We Dwellers have no more laws, for we are no more human! Isn't that what you were going to say, Killian?" Slash folded his arms, smirked, and looked at the other Dwellers behind him. "I think everyone else agrees with me." Slash delivered a self-satisfied snort.

Chapter Thirty-Eight

Killian unexpectedly lunged at Slash in a quick, jerky motion. The two Dwellers clawed at each other with beastly, hooked scalpels protruding at length from the ends of their fingers.

Slash bit Killian's shoulder, its fangs clamping down. Profuse, black drainage spurt through the air and onto the wall. The black, oily fluid sluggishly rolled down the stone. The Dweller's dark, tarry blood soon reached the ground, mixing with and consuming Kimi's leftover red plasma. When the black tar mixed with the red blood, they bubbled and foamed upon meeting, and soon, the black coated all red in its wake, until the red was no more.

The other Dwellers withdrew from the fight, their eyes pasted to the action. They followed every move closely with sadistic enjoyment.

Killian stabbed Slash.

Slash ripped flesh from Killian.

A small Dweller near the back of the group appeared disinterested. It remained clustered in together with the pack, but in many ways stayed isolated from the others. It spoke to one Dweller standing beside it. "Where am I? What's going on?"

All the while, Malum was observing with a grin. One palm on top of the other, his blade directly in front, it slanted upside down as he gripped the pommel with both hands. The blade's translucent, eerie radiance lit the dim tunnel with ethereal shadows jetting upward, distorting faces and events. He tilted his chin in toward his chest and glared up at the Dwellers. Malum's good eye rolled forward toward the Dwellers, and with each distorted, murky shade of light, it gave him a fearful appearance, an evil spirit, it seemed. He stood there enjoying the carnage.

Malum slammed his blazing sword into the ground. "That's enough!" he shouted, his striker penetrating deep into the solid earth.

"Stop fighting! Stop fighting!" a lone Dweller repeated, telling the others to pull Killian and Slash apart. "He is our enemy, our enemy." The Dweller pointed.

Slash reluctantly disengaged from Killian and said, "Recur's right."

"Yeah, what's he doing down here?" Killian grimaced. He held his hand over his wounded shoulder, while trying to stop the flow of black blood from pouring out of his body. "We should be doing this to him."

"You have a real nerve, immortal. You're a fool to come down here." Slash bent his knees and opened his talons wide as he waved his fellow Dwellers in closer for backup.

Slowly the horde approached Malum.

Some crawled along the side walls, fanning out for an attack. Their heads twisting back and forth, their bulbous craniums pulsated with large purple veins. The Dwellers were all points, from jagged elbows and knees, to protruding, spiny vertebrae. Try as they might to hide any weakness, sunken ribs revealed another truth as structural organs grew abnormally large, while the visible underline of starvation endured through thin layers of glossy, yellowish gray covered membranous skin.

The Dwellers were without a definite form, being neither male nor female, and wearing only a loincloth. It provided little modesty, yet the basic portion of fabric reminded them to mourn something long forgotten, but nonetheless, forever lost—their humanity.

"He is evil!" the group of Dwellers murmured as one.

"What, me? I'm not evil. I'm an aristocrat." Malum put his left hand to the center of his chest. "Why I even brought you a gift...and this is how you repay me?" Malum calmly raised his translucent brimstone striker.

The Dwellers shuttered and hesitated, while some halted altogether. Slash kept moving steadily forward, and soon was ahead of the pack, a place no other Dweller wished to be at this point.

"Come on you cowards." Slash waved them forward. "It's only one immortal, and we are many. We are legion."

Malum chuckled. "You aren't many, you're only..." He quickly bobbed his finger in the air from right to left, counting the heads. "You're only twelve...well... twelve and a half if you count that tiny weird one back there." He held a hand over his mouth, snickered some more, and wiped a single jolly tear from his good eye.

"You dare mock us? Mock us!" Recur growled.

"No, but rather, I came to offer you all that your hearts, or for that matter, bellies desire," Malum said solemnly.

"All immortals are liars. We fend for ourselves, for ourselves."

"You devoured my peace offering, and yet you felt no difference when compared to other humans you have recently consumed?" Malum's voice lowered, steadily idle, his diaphragm pushed up against his vocal cords, discharging boxed thunder with each word. "Was her blood not invigorating?" He balled a fist near his face, shaking it at them. "Do you not feel its power?" Malum pointed his striker, illuminating the leftover blood spatter on the wall nearest him.

"Indeed," Slash said. "What was the origin of her power?"

"To answer that," Malum stared, "you'll have to come with me. And if you do, I'll show you an overly packed, fresh world." Malum smiled excitedly. "There's a world full of billions of distracted humans for you to do as you please. That is, if you'll do something for me first."

From his hunched over face, Slash glared up, his cold, black saucers rising with menace upon Malum. "I may not remember my first life. I've been so many people since then, but the one thing I never forget is a face. Your face."

Malum rubbed his lips together. "Do you remember anything else about my face?"

"Yes. You made us like this."

"A-ha." Relieved, Malum sighed. "Are you sure that's all you remember?"

"No...wait." Slash looked off to the side with uncertainty. "You promised us everlasting life for our faithful service, and then you gave us the drink, the black tar, the potion, and it turned us into...this." He motioned from his chest downward.

Malum interrupted. "I kept my promise, but it was those jealous knights who poisoned my perfect gift to you." He then reaffirmed himself. "Yes. Yes, it was the knights." Moving his hand from side to side, he recreated the events seamlessly for them. "I had stabilized the potion of life about eight hundred years ago in my apothecary..." He twirled his index finger, and then emphatically shook it. "That's when the knights must have tainted the additive and corrupted the batch, thus destroying the original formula. You had a reaction to the toxin before I even knew one of the knights had poisoned the brew."

"You lie." Slash growled.

The Dwellers, as a group, hunched forward, their protruding, spiny backbones lending to their gruesome shape. They inched slowly with aggressive strides toward the immortal intruder.

Two handed, Malum swung his blade up over his head. He then drove the striker into the ground, splitting floor and cracking side walls. The tunnels vibrated, and the Dwellers swayed. The creatures braced each other, grabbing ahold as others fell from off ceiling and walls, but the show of might stopped all Dwellers from their advance.

The Dwellers debated Malum's authority, yet dared not challenge his power.

Full of bravado, Slash grumbled and growled. "Why should the Dwellers do anything for you?"

"You need not do a thing for me, but trust the Shroud," Malum replied. A smile carried in his tone.

Slamming his long, thick talons into the wall, his ribcage expanded and recoiled from accelerated respirations. "TRUST THE SHROUD!" Slash repeated. This time the Dweller cared not if his fellow Dwellers joined him as he gradually neared Malum.

Slithering back a step, Malum curled one side of his lip upward, raising an eyebrow. "Don't be a fool," he snidely remarked. "Your extra human strength and super lifespan, whether accident or not, comes from the Shroud. You are no match for me, or any other immortal. I could kill you all where you stand, but I have come here to tell you the Shroud has every intention of fulfilling its original promise."

"How?" Killian trod ahead.

"The prize I brought you...the young girl," Malum raised his hand to his heart, looking to the ceiling, then down at the Dwellers for a reaction, "she possessed the power of an immortal in stable human form. Why even now you are more robust for consuming her than a thousand other humans at once."

"It's true. I feel stronger, feel stronger."

Slash bent his talons inward, flexing his underdeveloped biceps. "I, too, feel a power I have not felt before."

The Dwellers looked around at one another. Some moved their necks from side to side, others thrust shoulder joints up and down, and then they clustered together, whispering amongst themselves. The Dwellers broke huddle, and each bowed before Malum.

"I, Malum, am still your lord, and you are my children."

"What would you have of us?" Slash was the last to kneel.

"To make yourselves great in number again. And to do that...you will need to hunt the entire surface of the world above. No more will you be exiled to this demeaning life of only eating items found in the confines of these catacombs." Malum browsed from constricted side wall to side wall. "Rather, it is time to infest the world above, and exterminate the last of the knights, ergo, earning your revenge, along with your legacy. You will walk forever in the light of day once again. You will not be subject to wear the husk of another human just to walk for a short time in the sun. But in order to be kings and gods, you must first obey meeeeeeeee." Malum hissed until his breath tired.

Each Dweller stooped their neck, raising a single arm into the air, saying in a unified voice, "We pledge our allegiance."

Slash spoke up. "Tell us how to proceed, Lord Malum."

Malum stood tall over all of them. "Dwellers do three things very well. They kill to eat, they kill to briefly take the shape of a human, and they kill to create more Dwellers by reinfusing black tar blood back into the victim. I want you to do all three of those things for me. And in return, when the last knight is dead, I will give you the gift you all deserve."

Raising his hood over his head, covering the deeply lined scar on the left side of his face, he smirked, his heart thumped slowly with elation. The one part Malum did not want Slash to remember, had been forgotten by the Dweller completely it seemed, yet not by Malum.

Opening an aperture, a small circular fissure appeared and grew into a large, swirling vortex. It filled the darkness with blues and greens, along with hazy clouds emitting tiny flashes of lightning. The Dwellers shielded their eyes from the brightness. *Ppffsshh.* A loud whooshing air filled the tunnels, pushing back the stench of death as the wind howled through the hollow shafts.

Recur bred fear among the others. "But we cannot live in the light of day. It will kill us, it will kill us!"

"Your lord knows your limitations, and has already planned your nocturnal hunting grounds. Have faith lowly one." Malum withdrew his striker. Disbanding the sword, he flipped his palms up, facing the ceiling. He continued to raise his hands into the air. "I will open apertures each night from your new home. It will be as black and as dark as these tunnels. You will disperse into the corners of the earth at nightfall, and then you will bring me an army suitable enough to destroy the knights' castle. Immortal or not, they will all die!" Malum ushered them into the aperture. "GO!" He watched as they charged toward and then past him into the gateway vortex.

Each Dweller galloped on all fours like hyenas. They howled and snarled like baboons.

Killian tugged the hand of the smallest Dweller to follow the rest of them. However, this one appeared lost and despondent.

"My name is..." it said aloud to itself. Disoriented with intermittent confusion, the smallest Dweller kept repeating while standing still, "My name is..."

"You must come now," Killian said.

"My name is...Em...Em..." It tilted its head.

"What's wrong with that one?" Frowning, Malum raised a bushy eyebrow. "Is it defective? Does it need to be put down?"

Killian placed his hand up, motioning for Malum to stop. "This is just a new recruit. It takes a while for things to make sense to them."

The smallest Dweller was stuck on one thought. "My name is Em..."

"Yes, that's right." Killian briskly sighed. "Your name is M. The scrambled thoughts and the unsettled feelings will go away in time, trust me."

"How do you know?" Frantically changing beliefs about identity rushed around M's mind. Its eyes swelled. It began holding its breath.

"Breathe, M. Just take a breath," Killian urged.

"HAAAH!" M gasped loudly. "I used to know things, but I can't remember what I think I knew?" M became agitated, not wanting Killian to touch its skin.

Killian stepped back, giving M space. "When you take your first body, you'll feel better, I promise. And then the shakes will go away. The troubled thoughts leave, and soon you'll feel new again."

"But there are things I need to remember..."

"No, M. All of those things are gone now. You must let them go because they will be gone soon anyway." Killian lightly held M's hand.

Killian ushered M into the aperture. M, still blank and distant, followed the light, but Killian knew Emma would adapt to survive as they all had to at some point.

Something triggered a host of fleeting memories, which blended as one after a while. Killian now just felt like an *it* when he thought about his many lives, and so many times that he was a *he* or a *she*. The other Dwellers were just a *they, us,* or *we* now. It bothered Killian only when he thought about it, which was almost next to never, until now, for he was not sure if Killian was even *its* own real name.

Finally, Killian dismissed his own doubts. He and M were second to last entering the swirling aperture. Slash was the last Dweller left in the tunnels.

On all fours, Slash walked carefully up to Malum. With a bob and weave of the presently cloaked immortal's face, Slash sniffed Malum before the Dweller guardedly followed the others into the vortex.

Malum, with immovable fixation, watched as the last Dweller, Slash, entered the swirling aperture. He ran his index finger up and down the timeworn crease that gashed from the top of his left eyebrow to the bottom of his cheekbone, destroying his once good left eye in the process. No, Malum had not forgotten. He scowled. His breath hung hard and heavy. "Bwahaha!" He chortled emphatically, while considering the joys of retaliation. His dingy, cracked teeth gnashed crosswise. With narrowed eyes, his laughter abruptly halted. "Humph." Malum looked around. He was the only one left in the tunnels, so he sauntered through the aperture, grinning from ear to ear, whistling merriment as the doorway closed in on itself behind him.

Chapter Thirty-Nine

Three thirty in the afternoon, on a dreary, cloud-ridden day in the busy, downtown heart of Glasgow, Scotland, Maximillian cloaked himself in a long, black leather trench coat.

It had only been hours since his meeting with Revekka and Acuumyn in among the Greek ruins, but he preferred those warm, sunny skies in comparison to the cool drizzle that coated his face.

His collar up, Maximillian hid his face behind the black, pointed trench coat. He watched everything behind dark, tinted lenses, while marching through the middle of the bustling city street. *Spack-a-speck-speck.* The sprinkled drops of vapor fell in spurts from the ether. Hundreds, maybe a thousand people walked past, beside, and in front of him.

Upscale, new apartments lined along the right, while shops and office buildings cluttered the left-hand side of the street. The people were all about the town—working, shopping, laughing, eating, and living their everyday lives to the full.

With his hands firmly pocketed, Maximillian tucked his head low. His eye's darting, they carefully sifted the environment, before he roused ahead in a hurried pace. With a stern, joyless expression, he passed through with a quick apathy. Indifferent to the goings-on, the countless distractions afforded him a certain invisible quality.

A robust scent wafted fine food through the air. The chatter of voices mixed with car engines, while nearby rushing water filled in any gaps in clamor. Still, there was something out of place in the large, intimate city. Something wishing to remain hidden, but Maximillian was too powerful and wise of a knight to ignore when five thousand years tingled a warning to him.

In this world, Maximillian knew that there were immortals, and then there were experienced immortals. Despite varying strength and ability, not all immortals were equal, at least in the art of skill.

Bweee. Like radar, Maximillian sensed a tiny ping whenever another immortal was near. Though it was possible to go undetected with skillful stealth among a large group of humans, Maximillian's awareness could not be blocked by just any unskilled immortal. Calmly looking back, and from side to side, he briefly considered his options.

A fight was coming.

Nonetheless, there were so many people in the immediate area, detection of a single immortal left him at a disadvantage. It soon became clear that this other immortal knew what Maximillian did not, the target, and this time, being disguised as anyone in ordinary view, made matters worse.

To protect the people around him, and more importantly, to protect his portion of the Sphere Atlas from the Shroud, Maximillian sharply turned while in the middle of the crowd. Pushing and shoving people, he traveled with immense haste up a narrow, twisting side street. Watching behind him through the reflection of his own sunglasses, Maximillian tried to identify or flush out his pursuer. He sprinted, taking one rapid turn after another, but still no one seemed to follow.

Now racing through intersections and alleyways, the tingle of an immortal presence buzzed him like a shockwave.

Once through the busy downtown section, and past all the people, up ahead an abandoned Victorian Era structure emerged. With dusty brown bricks, two spired gothic towers, hundreds of windows, many of which were shattered and boarded up, it loomed as a large, unnerving, ghostly shell of a building in the adjacent skyline. A sinister assembly of run-down pieces, the massive structure whispered keep out well before Maximillian read the numerous city ordinance signs to avoid the area. Notwithstanding the warnings, it was the only haven from a menacing danger to come. A ten-foot chain-link fence enclosed the crumbling, fortress-like structure, but to Maximillian it was an inviting refuge.

To look upon the wasted remainders of this once elegant, if not ghastly vestige to the Victorian Era, inspired paranoia, shifts in mood, and a total collapse of goodwill toward men. Without so much as a pause, Maximillian climbed and flipped his way over the ten-foot fence. His forward stride heaved him beyond the high barrier with relative ease.

At the main entrance, carved into the gothic archway keystone, a symbol of judgment with condescending eyes and a hapless frown—perhaps an angelic or noble woman—looked down from overhead with angry sadness. Maximillian briefly glanced up at her.

He brushed aside dirt from the crusted stone engraving next to the door. It read, "Sanitarium." Reflecting on the insanity this closed asylum witnessed over the years, Maximillian hesitated at the entrance, yet against his better judgment, he marched inside anyway.

The light receded significantly once past the entry point. The illuminating currency was exchanged for ominous dark corners of a grand room, which appeared fit for a luxuriant hotel, but was now filled with flaking paint, tarnished moldings, and broken fixtures. The floors were littered with mixed soot and water-damaged chunks of wall and ceiling from a structure in vast decay.

Past the grand lobby, hundreds of hospital type rooms, many with their dingy, white doors still ajar, extended the length of Maximillian's view. *Kirrrik. Pooommfff.* The madness called out in creaks and pops of the building. The arcane permeated every inch of the structure, from wide spaces to recessed sections of rooms. *Woooeerrr.* Wind drifts wailed like banshees warning of approaching death. Maximillian felt an inconsolable wretchedness as he waited, watched, and uncovered his own extreme misery from this archaic, gothic hospital for the insane.

Chapter Forty

Crouching in one of the sheltered places, Maximillian heard only distant sounds of the nearby city. Police sirens waxed and waned, horns beeped, but all life seemed aloof and unreal from where he intently anticipated the worst.

Reality pulled him apart as he held his focus ever close. His forehead dripped sweat. The low sound of his breath caused him to wonder if he was already dead. His mind drifted. He tried to center his senses, but he felt them tumbling away. One mental mistake could be the end. Five thousand years of knowledge and life, could vanish in an instant. This was not the time to lose his head. He knew because he had seen it more times than he cared to recount. Friends, enemies, and perfect strangers, all with a mission, many with great will and ability to succeed, but each had failed, or been cut down in their prime, leaving the world's stage with a tragic, final act, and without so much a curtsy to the spectators centered round.

As the background noise faded, a brittle crunching of glass in the main entrance revealed a lanky teen with wavy hair covering his eyes. He was in a gray hoodie, skinny blue jeans, and a pair of retro black and white sneakers. With his long bangs, the gray hood masked his face. His shoulders sagged. His elbows wide and his hands sloppily dug into his pockets. The hoodie kicked some rubble at his feet, coolly as if he were playing football. He kicked a pebble into a rusty can, and raised his hands as if he scored the game winning goal of the World Cup. Unassuming, he looked neither like nor played the part of an immortal, but rather, just a local neighborhood teenager who was trespassing.

Maximillian easily snuck up on him from behind. "Who are you? What are you doing here?" He pointed an object squarely in the hoodie's back.

The hoodie raised his hands. "I...I know I'm not supposed to be in here, but a lot of my friends...you know..." his voice filled with indecision. The hoodie then asked, "What are you gonna do with me?"

Maximillian relaxed his breath. An uneasy pause heightened the distant sirens outside. "The hood, off with it, and slowly turn around."

A hand reached up and removed the hood, and he turned toward Maximillian.

Now facing each other, the hoodie appeared to be young looking, a teen in fact, and not likely the immortal that was following him. Maximillian, with a stick in hand, sensed a strong immortal presence still. Maximillian shifted a look between the teen's eyes, one at a time, and then in both. The teen appeared unfazed, or uninterested.

"You aren't the police," the teen said.

"No."

"Then I'm peacin' out, ya weirdo."

"Go on, it's dangerous in here. Read the signs next time." Maximillian flicked the back of his wrist, pointing toward the door ahead of them. "Get out of here before you get hurt, kid."

Maximillian lowered the stick, and the teen tossed his gray hood back over his long, wavy bangs, while walking past him toward the door.

The buzzing tingle swiftly roared.

Maximillian turned and summoned his emerald striker as a mystic, red blade, similar to his own, plummeted down upon him. *Swash!* The weapons locked with harsh fury. *Rizzz!* Electrical sparks flew, and with a firestorm, the blades' grinding sizzle crashed as one, repelling the two immortals away from each other. The teen in the hoodie drifted farther back than Maximillian.

The teenager in the gray hoodie hid beneath the partial cover of his bangs. His clamped teeth smashed together. He reloaded and drove his sonic blade toward Maximillian. *Whoosh.* With heightened reflexes, Maximillian, in one fluid motion, summoned a second emerald striker, driving the teen in the hoodie backward, sliding him across the floor. Still on their feet, the two stared, pacing at a distance from one another.

Maximillian and the teenager in the hoodie readjusted themselves for another go at the other. The element of surprise was no more. Now it was a battle until the pangs of death arrived upon one of them.

"Not half bad," Maximillian said. His strikers pointing toward the ground, the two stood about twenty feet apart. "But I wasn't born yesterday, kid."

The hoodie's nostrils flared. "The name's Xander, not kid." He waved his red blade, twirling it, generating a brief figure eight in midair. "Yeah, you like that? Huh. Do ya?" Xander winked.

"Wait, you're one of those punk kids who left the temple to join the Shroud." Maximillian snapped his fingers and then pointed. "That's why I didn't recognize you."

"You do a lot of talkin' for a geezer." Xander stretched his arm out and waved his fingers inward. "Listen, just give me the scroll, and I'll let you live," he said with authority.

"You're not getting the scroll, kid." Maximillian pulled his shoulders back, broadening them. "I will teach you a lesson though. Now say it!" His voice stern.

"Say, say what?" Xander shrugged.

"Listen, kid, it was pretty dirty for you to jump me from behind like you did. You know there are rules for an official contest between two immortals, so say it."

"Yadda, yadda, yadda." Xander hemmed, hawed, and sighed. "Until the last enemy..."

Maximillian finished the rest. "Has been brought to nothing."

The two paced back and forth, neither taking their eyes off the other. Xander dashed, cocking his red translucent blade to the side. Maximillian waited unmoving for his charge, and then smacked his emerald strikers against Xander's blade, slicing a downward motion. Xander slid, avoiding Maximillian's emerald swords. Xander flipped onto his side. He launched both feet in midair, with the tips of his toes toward the ceiling. Maximillian merely watched and waited for Xander to finish his versatile, acrobatic feat.

Xander landed and readied for a swipe at his enemy. Maximillian kicked him in the chest, sending Xander soaring through a wall.

With a noisy bang, a portion of the wall collapsed in on itself and Xander disappeared. All was quiet for several seconds, but then a tiny red glow, not unlike a laser pointer, burned intense heat from deep inside the wall's large, dark hole. *Shmm!* Xander burst forth with a primal roar, while cutting his way out from the chalky rubble. *Swash!* His blade eviscerated the cement blocks and steel girders in front of him.

The dust covered in a thick coating of fine powder. Xander's hood flipped back, he snarled. Maximillian grinned, while his black trench coat flapped behind like a cape.

Pointing at Xander's dusty exodus from the wall, Maximillian commented, "I think this look suits you better, kid."

Xander charged, dropping a dash upon his knees toward Maximillian. His vibrant, red striker cut the air in half with a mighty crack. *Flap!* Maximillian deflected his blow with only a single blade, jumping off the nearest wall, and then landing out of reach from Xander's sword once again.

Bunches of quick, lively action ensued as the two immortals sparred. They destroyed the inside of the asylum's main room.

Maximillian toyed with Xander.

Every time Xander charged with his blade, Maximillian moved about easily, swiping and deflecting his sword, jumping away from attacks, and mocking his attempts. Furious, Xander became unhinged.

Xander panted, holding his knees at times. "Stay still and fight me!"

"When a knight goes into battle, he can either be a scalpel or a hammer." Maximillian nodded. "It's a pity you abandoned the knights and the temple, you would have learned how to achieve both."

Unexpectedly, small rocks and pieces of the stucco began flying at Maximillian from behind. *Viip.* At first a single piece, then two, then many pelted him hard from all over the room.

"The knighthood never taught me this!" Xander stretched out a hand to objects in the room, flinging them at Maximillian.

"Ow!" Maximillian yelled. "What's going on?"

Maximillian was losing his focus. The barrage of rubble attacked him. One piece cut his cheek, causing blood to stream forth. The madness of the asylum appeared to come alive. A bad spirit wrapped over the place, sheltering hate, misery, and rage, the likes of which Maximillian had never felt in such a concentrated form before.

"I don't need your pathetic stories about scalpels and hammers, because I have the Shroud with all of its power at my disposal." Xander steadily approached with his striker.

Maximillian turned toward the flying rubble and cut the mounting debris into pieces as it flew at him. Yet still, so much soared around the air, it was impossible to block every airborne projectile from each angle.

Xander took his advantage. He rushed again, his sword raging for blood this time. Xander was close now, closer than he had ever been to taking an immortal's head.

Maximillian shielded his eyes, blinking from dusty particles in the air. His vision grew dim, watery, and blurred. He withdrew one of his strikers. Maximillian held his hand up, out, and spread his fingers apart. Coughing, he struck the air in front of Xander. *Voomp! Swoosh!* A wave of invisible energy pulsed, and like a brick wall, it smacked Xander in the chest, flinging him back into the air, gliding him across the floor sideways for several feet after his abrupt landing.

Woozy and shaken, Xander got up. His motor function displaced, he stumbled about the room. Xander soon lost his balance and fell backward, and all floating rubble plummeted to the ground. He had lost control of the barrage he was firing at Maximillian.

Xander quickly stood up again and staggered from right to left. His red striker broke into shards and vanished like an apparition. Xander clenched his fists and gnashed his teeth. Tears formed at the corners of his eyes. He was unable to summon another blade because his strength had left him.

"Give up, kid. It's over."

"Rah!" Xander shouted. He picked up a rock and ran toward Maximillian.

The knights lived by a strict code of ethics. These principals guided the knights so vigorously, that Xander counted on Maximillian lowering his striker, for he knew a true knight would never kill an unarmed person.

Maximillian, true to his beliefs, withdrew his blade and braced for impact. Xander hit Maximillian solidly. While absorbing the blow, Maximillian blocked a flurry of punches and kicks. His hands blocking, all of Xander's attacks were things Maximillian had seen many times before. He grabbed Xander's arm, slamming it against a wall, leaving a figured imprint along the sheetrock. Then Maximillian held Xander's limp body by the scruff and ran, smashing Xander through several hospital doors down the corridor before dropping him to the floor.

"I bet the Shroud didn't teach you that either." Maximillian overlapped his arms.

"Argh," Xander moaned.

Face down, Xander tried to get up, but fell and ceased moving. Maximillian kneeled close and picked up his wrist to check for a pulse. Seconds later, he dropped Xander's hand back to the floor.

Maximillian exhaled. "Remember, kid, immortals may be strong, but we're not invincible."

Chapter Forty-One

Black, blurry vision opened to a stinging slap across the face, and an upside-down view of the world. Xander's hands were tied behind his back, and his feet tied together from a rope attached to a beam high above near the ceiling of the asylum. The sounds were muffled, and the pictures fuzzy at first, but soon they all lined up again, except upside down.

"Hey, wakey-wakey." Maximillian leaned over in front of Xander. "Come on, kid, I don't have time to fool around."

"Where...where am I?" Xander wiggled violently to no avail. "Go ahead. Get it over with. Kill me."

"Kill you?" Maximillian straightened his back, slapping his hands against his own thighs, dismissing the dust. He walked around and behind Xander. He examined the rope tied to the floor that looped over the beam, binding Xander's feet. He plucked the rope with his index finger several times. The thick fibers, though shredded and worn, still vibrated when plucked, whirring with strength during the test. "The Shroud's done a number on your mind, kid." Maximillian scowled. "You're so full of hate, that you can't even see the light anymore."

Dazed, Xander asked, "So...you're not going to take my head?"

Maximillian tossed his hands into his trench coat. "No, but I am going to try and clear it."

Xander grimaced and wiggled once more for freedom. "I won't listen. Lies! All you have to say is lies."

"Why?" Maximillian cracked a rare grin with a slight laugh. "You don't even know what I'm going to say. Besides, it's not like you can block your ears."

"Yeah, well, let me down, and then we'll see who's smiling, you..."

Maximillian cut Xander off in mid-sentence. "You're immortal and I'm immortal. You're just a kid though. I've been here for five thousand years."

"Lord Malum was right."

"Right about what?"

"He told us the truth about the knights. He opened our eyes!" Xander shouted, huffing from his upside-down position. "You should look a lot older, but you don't, because you're behind the destruction of everything." In the same breath he continued. "And I know...I know the knights greedily keep immortality for themselves..."

"Geez." Maximillian pulled a silver roll of tape from inside his black trench coat. "Do you ever shut up?"

The blood pooled toward Xander's brain. He began to feel queasy and unwell. Maximillian tore off a large section of tape as his heavy shoes clunked around the creaky floor in frustration.

"And another thing..."

"No. No more talking." Maximillian slapped the piece of tape over Xander's mouth, yet still, muted sounds of agitation bubbled forth. "I may look young, but I've got mileage, kid. And in the Shroud's world, I've racked up a ton of miles lately."

Xander's upside-down eyebrows looked like smiles. The more he scrunched them down, the more they seemed to furl upward. "Waa waa." His angry discontentment muffled inaudible words.

Ignoring the muffled noises, Maximillian screeched a half-broken chair across the floor and sat down facing Xander. He rubbed his mouth and chin from side to side in a contemplative manor. He waited until Xander calmed. Maximillian watched him closely for signs of reasonable intelligence, then inhaled and exhaled deeply once, twice, and three times.

"Okay, I'm going to give it to you straight, kid." He looked away briefly with a half chuckle. "Heck, none of us are going to survive anyway."

Maximillian hated wasting words. He talked as little as needed. His worn-out temperament matched his tired eyes. Every word he uttered was for a purpose, unlike the nonstop chatter of the world. Communication was still a precious gift, and not something thrown away with thoughtless abandon for him. After a few minutes, Maximillian decided Xander had at least the right to know how Malum preyed upon the ignorant, especially upon his followers.

The circular room in the asylum, where Xander hung upside down, was much quieter than the room where they had fought. Not so much as a police car siren could be heard, but just rubbing of the rope to wooden beam high above, which ran from Xander's ankles, tied in a loop all the way at the back end, fastened to a metal pipe along the floor by a series of makeshift pulleys.

Maximillian knew Xander's mind, like almost all humans on Earth, he was blinded to light, corrupted by the Shroud, but he would still try to undo the damage, vast as it may be.

"You and the other young knights were beautiful babies when you were born. Perfect in every way," Maximillian said as Xander appeared confused.

"Your birth is a byproduct of your parents refusing to partake of the few flicker fruit that remained, and now, not even another child has been born since, for their power to conceive has dried up, much like the trees that bear the fruit."

Maximillian continued. "We have lost the source of immortality. We have lost our greatest weapon against the Shroud." He pointed at Xander. "You and the other young knights allowed the first temptation to be your last act against true free will toward all living things." He slid his chair closer. They were now a nose length apart. With a loud thunderous rising of his voice, his index finger high in the air, Maximillian shouted, "The Reckoning is here! Malum knows this, and that's why he means to start the immortal war, to stop the Reckoning."

Xander shook and flailed again, attempting to talk, yet nothing more than muffled grunts blurted out.

Maximillian took long breaths between statements, waiting for Xander to calm before he started again.

"Now I don't know fully what this does," Maximillian said as he pulled his share of the Sphere Atlas from his inner trench coat pocket. "But I'm sure Malum would only use it to destroy." He tucked the scroll back into his inner pocket as Xander's eyes grew large. "The Shroud takes great power from hate, violence, divisions, fear, and misery. The knights' power comes from the source of all life. We believe and hope the Reckoning will crush all power of one over the other. No more will one be greater than any other person, and this is what Malum fears the most, the loss of his power to control billions of minds. That is why he hastens the immortal war, and why I serve to set all life free from the Shroud's blinding ignorance and hatred in the Reckoning. Perhaps the immortal war and the Reckoning are one in the same...I guess we won't know until the final part of the end comes."

Xander began to wiggle again and his muffled, inaudible groans shouted. Maximillian got up and walked over to him, ripping the tape from his mouth.

"Ow, you jerk!" The skin around Xander's lips turned red. "That really, really hurt!"

"What say you? Do you see the light again?"

Xander spit. "Go ahead and kill me now! Anything would be better than listening to you blabber on with your propaganda..."

Maximillian, frowning, slapped the tape firmly back across Xander's mouth. "If I wanted to kill you, you'd have been dead." He sighed, rolling his eyes. "Other than becoming part of the Shroud, you haven't crossed any lines yet, but you'll have a choice to make some day, so I hope you make the right one."

Maximillian became suddenly concerned with time, eyeing about, and with rapid breaths, he talked at an increased pace.

Xander's face crinkled, crunching together, so that even upside down, he looked angered and resentful.

"You seem like a smart, but misguided kid," Maximillian said. "Malum's a bad guy, trust me on this one. Remember, you were a knight once." Maximillian extolled with a gentle, but serious mood. "Knights vow to be truthful, faithful, kind, good, and to endure in peace, with mild self-control, and one should never abuse their freewill, especially in the form of power, or abilities."

Xander slowed his violent, restless struggle for freedom. Dumbstruck, he seemed reflective, and with a newly owned clarity, which he had not collected since the two had met.

Maximillian began his next words with the demeanor of someone who had said all he could. He got up from the chair, talking as he did. "The Shroud is a thing devoted to evil. Though they claim good, they do not adhere to the faith." Maximillian adjusted his black trench coat, smoothing out any wrinkles. "Acquire your own mind on matters. Amend your conduct. Refrain from the strong desire for prestige and domination. Malum is an apostate and a renegade." Maximillian squatted, gently holding his large hands on both sides of Xander's face. "But you're a quick learner, with good, natural tendencies. I wish you peace, Xander. Hopefully we'll meet under better circumstances next time." Maximillian stood up and walked past him. "Just to let you know, there's a leap zone not far from here. I should be able to catch an aperture to California in a few minutes, and this part of the Sphere Atlas will be safe from Malum once inside the castle walls."

Tack, tap, tack, tap. Maximillian's footsteps faded from loud to quiet, from near to far. The round room promptly smothered with a deafening silence.

Drowsiness rushed in upon Xander, covering his head in warmth, his eyelids grew heavy, the room swung, and the only sound was of the hypnotically rubbing rope against the wooden beam above.

Pockets of light through holes in the ceiling provided a glimpse of stars and sun as time passed from day to night, night to day, and then night again. Sometimes it was cold, and he shivered. Sometimes it would deluge, and soak him. Xander, unprotected from the elements, found them both uncomfortable and stimulating.

Certain words swirled inside Xander's brain, recapping Maximillian's sincerity. Xander hallucinated in and out of consciousness. He began to wonder if he had dreamed the entire thing, or if it was somehow a test of loyalty to the Shroud. Yet still, in his heart, he felt something, he was not sure what he felt, but it was an unsettled agitation, a doubtful regret, a stain not easily shaken from off his soul.

Chapter Forty-Two

At the same time, along the southern route, a far-stretching meadow of green grass tussled in a salty breeze along high ocean cliffs. Seagulls flew as misty ocean waves boomed, crashing against the bluffs at high tide.

To the left of the cliffs, which Revekka had visited once before, a sea of cobalt beyond the tall overhangs melded with the azure sky in the distant expanse until the two, it seemed, merged as one.

To the right, a heavily wooded, remote area covered the earth's floor with browns and greens in intertwined shadows full of reeds, scaly leaves, bristly brambles, and enclosed by groups of smothering vines.

Revekka swayed gracefully as if carried by the wind. She ambled, strolling upon plush, low-growing grass that grew in long and short rows upon the cliffs to the left, while the gloomy, wooded glen sat to the right. Flower clusters dotted in patches, and Revekka inhaled their pleasant fragrance. Straight ahead, the imposing castle appeared sturdy and aloft.

The castle's pointed, highest tips rose above the tree tops, yet the fortress was still some distance away from her place, so Revekka enjoyed her casual advance.

Among the longer growing spurts, the grass drooped and swayed in symphony with the air. The wildflowers dazzled rich, charming hints under the carpeted pasture, each clinging to a delicate slice of existence the world offered, yet too few appreciated. Single rays of sun warmed, while hazy clouds of sea spray watered. A slight breeze brought forth pollinating winged bugs, which first collected and without command, dispersed with harmonious wisdom a bounty of good things throughout the lands.

The dark, primeval forest watched with its eyes upon Revekka. The undergrowth reached out in a despondent, edgy hunger. Twisted branches, fallen trees, moss, and thorns stained the forest floor russet from age and time. The woods trembled with an occasional swooshing gust, and tightly compact, it hid many secrets among its moist, jade flora. From the open grassy meadow, the woods looked clean and dense, but just inches into their border, the forest dumped twigs and dried leaves all over the ground in compost heaps of unkempt and unsightly mounds.

Revekka knew she was being observed as she slowly, and with calm grace, roamed the open field. "I know you're there. You can come out now." She invited softly.

Dead leaves crunched. *Krish, krush, krish, krush.* The ground rustled with footsteps from tree to tree inside the dense forest.

A beautiful girl appeared. She was a teen, with medium-length blonde hair and frosted tips. She wore a pair of hip-hugging jeans, a halter-top, a banded leather belt around her hourglass waist, and had French manicured fingernails. Unblinking, she stared at Revekka from the edge of the woods.

Sniffle. The girl rubbed underneath her nose. Tears began to flow from the outer corners of her eyes. She pointed a single French manicured nail at the tip of a bound scroll bulging over top of Revekka's crosswise, long strapped, shoulder bag. "If I don't bring that back to Malum, he'll kill me." She folded her hands together. "Please, you have to help me!"

"Come with me to the castle." Revekka casually looked at her bag, and then with a single finger, tucked the scroll back into her purse, pushing it down inside.

"No!" the girl frantically blurted. "He'll get me!"

"Not in the castle, Malum won't. It's the safest place on Earth."

The girl's tone lowered sharply. "You don't understand. I need that scroll."

Her lips firmly pressed, Revekka thought for a moment. "I assume you've been told about me, and the scroll." She faced the girl, tilting her head at different angles, trying to get a good read. "I know who you are, Vanessa. And I know Malum probably told you to kill me before I spoke a word, and yet here I still live."

Vanessa's unfriendly, frosty beauty, and undaunted appearance, settled flat, unmoved, but even-keeled, yet branded an unconcerned bother. "So, I do what I wanna do. I'm my own person, not some puppet like you, so don't try to psychoanalyze me." She narrowed her eyes. "You don't know me."

"You're not even your own person." Revekka smiled. "Malum's playing games with you...with all of you," she earnestly offered.

"I know what he is," indifferent, Vanessa said. "I know what I'm doing, so spare me your sanctimonious advice."

The two stationed at a distance from the other. Revekka in the middle of the field while Vanessa walked out from the edge of the woods.

Revekka remained composed and sure. "That high-sounding, pompous talk is Malum, not you."

"Blah, blah, blah. What do you know?"

"A few things."

"Like what?" Vanessa stayed gently disagreeable.

"Like, Vanessa, you're a talented girl, but dishonest."

"Whatever. Snooze." Vanessa fanned a yawn.

Revekka ignored her, and continued. "You're feisty. You're endowed with beautifully curved, ornate shapes. However...you are also full of schemes and trickery."

"Screw you!" Vanessa shouted, her forehead pulled tightly downward.

Revekka struck a nerve. "You beguile and mislead with charming delight."

"Yeah, so..." Vanessa smirked. "I'm good because I'm bad. That's why I'm every man's type." She narrowed her eyes again.

"You don't have to coax or cajole for people to like you. You have enough good inside you still. But on your present course, you won't live long enough to see it."

"Is that a threat!?"

"No." Revekka tipped her head. "It is truth."

"Tsk, tsk." Vanessa slowly wagged a single French manicured fingertip back and forth. "The Shroud offers me status, not just a bunch of outdated creeds and doctrines like the knighthood."

Revekka countered, "The Shroud is self-serving, with an agenda more terrible than you can imagine."

"Whatever."

"Vanessa, you can still help us bring everything into harmony. I sense the condition of your heart is still good."

"Ha-ha-ha." Vanessa laughed, with a tilting of her head backward. "You're so out there. Give it up."

"I'm a listener, so you don't have to do this."

"Do what?"

"This!" Revekka threw her hands out toward Vanessa. "Acting like you're too cool for everything and everyone."

"It's not an act." Vanessa's face developed its first ugliness. Though she tried to look away until it flamed out, she was irritated. "No more talk. Give me the scroll...NOW!" she screamed.

Ever peaceful, Revekka's words searched for a way into Vanessa's hardening heart. "Malum didn't tell you what this is, did he?"

"Errg." Vanessa growled. "Stop playing mind games. I should have killed you before you spoke, at least that would have saved my ears the aggravation of hearing your psychobabble." She started walking with clear, focalized intent toward Revekka.

Revekka remained where she stood. "This scroll is one part of the Sphere Atlas, and with any luck, the other half is inside the castle by now." Vanessa, some distance away, marched with a relentless stride, so Revekka kept speaking. "The Sphere Atlas, when combined, does the most wondrous thing."

"I don't care." Vanessa clinched her perfectly lined, white teeth hard.

"The Sphere Atlas is an instrument of peace and discovery."

"Fascinating," Vanessa blankly said, still intently honed in on her hostile approach.

"You're not every man's type. You've been hurt by someone. Betrayed maybe?"

"Shut up!" Vanessa shouted, her eyes shooting an obstinate glare. "Listen, here's something you don't know, we already have the other half of the scroll." She grinned.

"You're lying," Revekka accused.

Vanessa sneered. "Am I?"

Shaken, but not stirred, Revekka calmly spoke as Vanessa closed in. "Yes. I feel it clearly now. You loved him. He loved someone else. You hated her." Revekka looked away for a moment, then back up in puzzlement. "No, it's worse than that. What did you do?"

"God!" Vanessa yelled as she neared. "If you shut up now, I'll kill you painlessly."

Revekka disregarded her. "Let go of your anger."

Rizzz. Vanessa summoned a translucent pair of silver sai. The strikers discharged an initial, bright, rapid burst of flames, though they themselves were not on fire. They were not the typical weapons materialized by immortals, but the narrow, long daggers appeared devastating for an up-close assault. Her knuckles bent around the sai securely. Vanessa's hands blanched as she clutched the knife-edged batons. The short daggers extended out a foot, with U-shaped, shorter curved prongs on each side of the blade. Though not the preferred weapon of most immortals, in her skilled hands, they were instruments of pure destruction. "You really want me to let go of my anger? Huh? Do you?" Vanessa yelled.

"You really don't get it?" Revekka shook her head. "I'm trying to help."

Vanessa seethed. She stomped through the long grass, her boots crushing flowers, smashing a path over any delicate thing until it was broken, twisted in half, or crushed. "No, you don't get it. Give me that scroll. I don't wanna have to..." She left the rest to Revekka's imagination.

Her feet squarely upon the earth, Revekka kept enlightening Vanessa without surrendering a portion of her ground. "You don't need this scroll. The Shroud might. Malum might. But you don't." Still speaking with a steady pace, Revekka looked to the castle and discovered her ease, almost reasoning if in a classroom, as a threatening menace to her safety advanced ever closer. She continued trying to persuade. "Come with me. Leave this path. Start a new life. The past can't hurt you if you don't let it."

"Do I look like someone to be trifled with?" Vanessa's tone turned deep and low, with a wailing madness. In a show of power, she backhanded her sai against a small eight-inch thick tree sprouting from the field. *Swash!* The top half of the tree fell sideways onto the field. *Flap.* She carved through in one gash, and cut the tree in half without even breaking stride.

Unfazed, Revekka spoke louder. "Your spirit is in a state of flux." She waved her hands across the air. Using the ocean mist, she created a lovely, but brief image of familiar things she thought dear to Vanessa, much in the same way she did for Vincent, yet it seemed to have no effect on the girl. "Don't you want to know more?"

"When the time is right, Lord Malum will tell me what I need to know." Vanessa objected, with a gleam in her eye. Her brilliant white teeth compressed, her vivid pink lips plumping outward and up. "Information is sacred, and shouldn't be shared with just anyone. That's the problem with you and the knights, you want to expose all of our knowledge to the world. Well I won't allow it!" she heatedly said, now running in a straight line toward her mark.

Chapter Forty-Three

Revekka calmly held her grace. Acting helpless and unarmed, almost as if she intended to sacrifice herself, yet even with Vanessa upon her, she kept speaking as before, calm and confident. "You're not getting the scroll." Revekka closed her eyes and tilted her chin up toward the heavens.

Vanessa jumped at full speed, hurling herself some ten feet through the air. One leg was straight and the other bent upward as she flew. With the sai stretched over her head, the daggers pinpointed a goal, aiming in line with Revekka's heart.

Revekka leaned to the side, easily stepping away from the airborne landing. The two were now face-to-face.

With an assassin's discipline, Vanessa moved with deadly precision. Her assaults resembled a fluid poise of artistic jabs, kicks, swings, and yet, each time, she missed completely.

Revekka balanced on one foot, flipping backward, springing away. Her long maxi dress acted as flowing drapery, blinding Vanessa. Revekka appeared still, waiting it seemed to be gashed, yet every time she evaded Vanessa's attacks, and continued untouched.

Rizzz. Swoosh. Shmm. Over again Vanessa mounted violent blows, using every part of herself, weapons and all. Revekka did not deflect, repel, or engage in any form of combat. Rather, she dodged each aggressive action with an illusionist's flare.

The two bounded around the field.

Vanessa soon lost her breath, tiring from swiping at nothing except air. Revekka appeared at ease, becoming more comfortable, and as if practicing Yoga, she bent and flexed more easily than she had in the beginning.

Vanessa sucked her stomach inward and breathed out hard. "Stop moving. Fight me!" She leapt quickly as Revekka remained motionless just feet in front of her.

Full of ire, the internal reflected Vanessa's abstract heart. She was not misunderstood it seemed, yet rather, only malicious intent persisted inside the girl with the beautiful exterior.

"You really want to kill me. I can feel it." Revekka stared into Vanessa's undaunted eyes.

"Well duh, what gave you that impression?" Vanessa mocked. "Now be still..."

"No." Revekka reached out and gently touched Vanessa's forehead with a fingertip, while whispering the rest in her ear. "You be still."

Vanessa froze in place, after straightening and withdrawing her daggers. She was paralyzed. Her face lost all expression. She simply ogled the beautiful field, sea, trees, and sky, yet she appeared lost inside the peaceful thoughts of her own mind, blinking sporadically, speaking slowly, and resembling a ponderous amnesiac.

"I never...I never realized how amazing this place was." Vanessa's character mended passively. "How could I have not seen all of this before?" She began to cry. Her mascara lined off her face in swells.

Revekka formed a sad smile. She rested her hand on Vanessa's shoulder, walking past her, uttering only two words once more. "I know," she said, before continuing toward the castle.

Vanessa remained unmoving, even tranquil on the field, her back facing the departing Revekka, who only looked back with a moping glimmer. For she knew knowledge was the easy part. Anyone could be taught, but getting the heart to connect with the brain was sometimes an impossible task.

Not long after, Revekka discovered a winding dirt trail. The dusty road looped along two parallel worn lines up the hillside, with bands of fresh grass maturing between the clearly worn tire marks. Straight ahead, a solid, firmly fixed, medieval castle of large granite blocks, with a massive wooden gate, pointed spires, and hundreds of heavily armed archers dominated the highland with a balance of majesty and power.

Torches hung from the side and top walls, burning both day and night around the imperial structure.

Revekka heard the bell tower toll. She held a distant focus toward the steeply ascending castle. Deep, flat ravines and jagged rocks lined along duel vertical banks. The jagged rocks of the ravine were hundreds of feet wide and with a perilous depth. The deep quarry both entirely surrounded the fortification, and connected to the mainland with only a single lane, stone bridge, which by all accounts, seemed easy to cross.

Along the backdrop, the elongated gorge hollowed into what appeared a bottomless pit, making the single lane stone bridge the lone passageway for all would-be visitors to the castle.

The castle dominated the land. An immense forest was to the north and east just outside its walls, and the ocean protected the reinforced structure to the south and west. The castle was an imposing refuge, aloft on a flat plain along the mountainous region, and near, but not on, or overlooking the sea, yet it was protected by the ocean's rising slopes, bluffs, and booming waves. All of this, and the castle stood out for the world to see, but it did not attract attention, for it was completely hidden to the human realm, because only those with trained eyes were able to see its grandeur.

"Halt!" an archer called out. He aimed his crossbow from high atop the massive, front castle wall.

Several other archers strung back their bows, while lining next to each other's side. Some archers aimed arrows from bows, and other bolts from crossbows. Still, Revekka calmly walked upon the dusty road and neared the stone bridge, which converged to cover the jagged gully. She stopped and gazed up at the battalion of archers, yet without a single word, she continued toward the castle's main gate.

"I said halt!"

The commanding archers prepared to fire.

"No, wait!" a male voice shouted from inside the castle walls. "Put your arrows down." The rigid man wore a long, black trench coat over black pants and a black shirt. "Revekka, is that you?" he asked hesitantly. His shoulders squared broadly, he physically pushed the archer's weapons down and off to the side as he rushed along the thin, high wall causeway.

She nodded. "It is, Maximillian."

"I need proof," Maximillian shouted back.

"Here." Revekka reached into her shoulder bag and pulled out a scroll.

"Open it."

"What? Here?" Stunned, she asked, "Are you crazy?" Revekka looked back toward the murky woodlands.

"Yes!" Maximillian cupped his hands around his mouth. "These are strange times. If it's real, I'll know you're who you say you are."

Revekka untied and unraveled the scroll. Her eyes full of wonder, it glowed, lighting her face like the sun. She then flipped the scroll around for the dozens on the castle wall walkway to see. "It's amazing! Even like this, it's still amazing," she exclaimed. Revekka then pulled the amulet Acuumyn had given her at the ruins and held it up in the air as well. The amulet coin too changed, as did the Sphere Atlas moments earlier. Instead of strange markings etched along the coin, a picture of two equally balanced scales appeared. "The Reckoning is imminent," she yelled.

"Go ahead!" Maximillian waved the archers past him. "Quickly now!" He upturned his trench coat collar over his neck. Atop the castle walls, the archers ran past him along the inner walkway at his command. "Open the gate quickly and let her in!"

Chapter Forty-Four

Throughout the four corners of the globe, whether crowded cities, rural country towns, mountain top villages, or vacation island getaways, each night the Dwellers hunted with purpose.

The Dwellers slaughtered excitedly. Their derangement was without equal. They killed indiscriminately and were not bound by moral intellect. As hostile beasts of prey, the Dwellers murdered in sprees. Their blood thirst knew no bounds.

Like apparitions and phantoms, the Dwellers pulled people out of large, populated groups without so much as a sound.

Nocturnal creatures, they shuddered and renounced the light of day. They were the greatest, unknown harmful threat to the welfare of people everywhere. The rich, the poor, the famous, the infamous, it mattered not if it was man, woman, or child, the Dwellers took them all, but not all shared the same fate.

Through a single aperture along the coast of California, they were set upon an unsuspecting modern world, to eat, consume the appearance of, or gather new Dwellers from among the population of humanity.

No target was unobtainable.

The Dwellers snatched one walking on a city street as quickly as one sleeping comfortably in their bed. They took those fast asleep or wide-awake at all hours of the night, every night. Two things were sure, the Dwellers always hit their target, and the ones they marked, were never seen again.

Underground, in a maze of subterranean passageways bathed in darkness, Malum, with his bony, knuckle bent hands, held a lone wax candle, its flame wavering as the deep passageways seemed to inhale and exhale with a single breath.

A strong rush of air bellowed up and down the underground corridors. Farther, Malum walked through the restricted backend of his concealed kingdom, until he reached a large chamber with many random noises of gurgling, mumbles, and snorts.

A flash of the wick, and the candle revealed a sight of malformed, vile, decay, inspiring heaves in wretched intestinal pulls for the good and sane, yet it was a very pleasing thing of brilliance to Malum. Rotting flesh, putrid stench, with gruesome parts of mutilated bodies, culminated in monstrous, barbed profiles.

Huddled in clumsy groups, ambling in what appeared to be sleep, the Dwellers bumped off walls and into each other. They were slow-motion drifters without purpose, not rousing, not really sleeping, but unconsciously waiting for the sun to make its nightly retreat.

For as the sun set upon the world, the Dwellers rose from their state of inactivity. They hunted to kill, and to make many more in their image, longing lastly to take the image of humans, so that once again, for a short while, they could feel the warmth of the daystar upon stolen skin, which in their present form, the sun would liquefy the Dwellers in a matter of seconds.

Their dreams were a collection of confusing images. Too many to sort through evenly, they were more than just their own thoughts. Dwellers saw memories in random nightly terrors during their daytime drifting. The images collaged in a medley of bits and pieces from all whom they pilfered the souls of in times since past. No longer could they distinguish between who they were and what they are. However, they clung to a thousand thoughts, which overloaded and wiped their minds each day. This forged less of what was known before, causing the Dweller to accept a new reality. Subconsciously besieged and disturbed, Dwellers always desirous to morph with chaotic pleasure, lived for the hunt, joyously causing death to gain another life for themselves. They took solace that anyone else in their position would do the same thing to live.

What was a life worth after all? Humans slaughtered humans routinely. The Dwellers had a purpose for killing. It was nature. It was survival. Humans justified their murders, the Dwellers did not. Humans maintained the moral high ground when taking a life, and they also cornered the market on delusion. Dwellers knew what each human life was worth, and they were all worth the same.

A deep, crashing voice stirred from the tightly hollowed, murky passageways. "Rise, my children!" Malum waved his candle, the single flame whooshing through the air. "The day is over. The night is here, and so is your time to hunt." He extolled them. "Make yourselves many. Feast on all you choose, but grow your numbers and become a great army. Destroy those who dare stand against you." Malum's face red, his throat gurgled, his words pronounced bitterly in a strict manner. "I said RISE!"

The Dwellers halted their mindless, jarring movements. Their backs arched forward and curved frontward with spiny vertebra spiked down the middle of two inverted, dislodged scapula. Their necks hung, bobbling on a swivel. Closed eyelids abruptly jetted open, with instant pull as if by a string, they released their black, reflective saucers, which were departed and ravenous, with a distant, lifeless reflection of the living world.

The air was musty and foul. It permeated even into the dirt walls. The ground crammed with roaches, maggots, and every sort of crawling, slinking critter from the backend of spider legs, which rapidly hastened from the light, to things with tails, their tips disappearing into holes along the three boxed, room wall.

Fwip, fwip. Some of the Dwellers shook like wet dogs, and each time swarms of eight legged insects dropped off their bodies. As the Dwellers gradually roused, stiff jaws snapped from side to side and up and down. Necks twirled around, and joints bent in directions they should not.

With a hive mentality, what was once merely a dozen or so Dwellers, now filled a large burrow from end to end, and close to a hundred, it seemed, all connecting on a level only understood by others of their kind.

A Dweller urged the others. "It is time to hunt, time to hunt."

"Yes," Malum proudly said. "I am sending you in groups of threes to many different parts of the world."

The Dwellers' black eyes, now affixed on Malum, perfectly reflected his image, along with the rickety glow from his candle. Their oversized, black saucers were a gateway window of murky intent, yet zealously occupied in a hungry resolve.

"We are growing stronger." Another Dweller flipped his long talons outward and flexed his arms and shoulders.

The once emaciated Dwellers had become bulky in size and weight. Exposed ribs and skeletal joints were now covered with beefy mass and brawny, lean, hard cuts of mighty strength.

"Yes, Slash," an unconcerned Malum retorted. "That is why you..." He disregarded Slash, pointing at other Dwellers instead. "Recur, Killian, and Snare, you are my first generals." Malum shook his finger at each one of them. "You will appoint the packs of three, and in return, they will report to you, and you will report directly to me." He placed his finger to his chest.

Snare howled. "Then the hunt is on!"

"We will serve you...For now," Slash muttered.

"It is an honor, an honor," Recur added.

Killian just shook his head in slack agreement as he reached for M's hand. "Come, it is time to learn."

The Dwellers began to march from the large burrow, but Malum had not finished.

"Know this, Dwellers." Malum raised his nose and chin into the air. "Do not fail me. For the penalty of failure is not what is promised you, which is your humanity, but a fate worse than death, and then, I will let you die. And even then, it will not be a release, but it will be torturous with an agony that you, even in your debased state, cannot imagine." Malum straightened his arm and pointed to multiple small apertures, each swirling with haze, lightning, and churning colors. "Now go!" he shouted an imposing boom.

In packs of three, the Dwellers jogged on all fours. "Aroo!" They yowled like baboons and galloped as hyenas. Wearing only a loincloth, they had neither shoes, nor shirts, or clothing of any other kind, but their skin was dense and resilient. With a sort of supreme confidence, they traveled the apertures to their nightly hunting grounds.

Under cover of darkness, the unreasoning Dwellers prowled. Obsessively lurking about, their hunger grew harsh along with rumbling gastric pains to fill such needs.

The fear of daylight fueled a simple desire to be human again, and walking in the sun's warmth without threat of bursting into blisters, boils, and blazes, appeared an impossible dream. Yet of all these, the black tar, a sick blood that made them sicker, they longed for above all else. Its copious, dark, molasses like sludge, made decay feel like life at times. The black tar gave them superhuman speed, strength, and extra senses, yet cursed the Dwellers with a kind of rotting immortality.

The Dwellers were closer to death than life. With an undying appetite, night was their day. Insanely unpredictable, they consumed humans in order to temporarily morph, taking the shape of their victim as a reward.

Dwellers craved their portion of humanity once again, but it was forever aloof, just out of reach, close, yet distant. Each night they hunted and multiplied, eyeing those humans who already fit a mentally corruptible inclination for the black tar to take hold, thus becoming a Dweller without the chance of systemic, bodily rejection.

There was only one thing they wanted more than their humanity, and that was doses of black tar, which Malum provided from his apothecary in sealed, glass ampules.

The black tar tormented their souls, mutilated their spirits, and corroded everything else, leaving only an aberrant presence of what used to be. The intense pain caused by partaking of the oily goo, was well worth the short-lived spurts of euphoria, the next never as good as the last, but like the hunt, it was the only thing worthy of chase in an everlasting death without an apparent end.

In the dark corners of rooms, behind doors, and misshapen shadows inside closets, the Dwellers waited and watched. When the time was right, they pulled bodies from warm beds, creaking out windows with their captured prey. The Dwellers were bold, believing no one was beyond their reach.

The windows in an old farmhouse flared like signals in the rural, countryside night. Each light glowed brightly with life, but the barn was in the dark portion of the property, and at some distance away from the farmhouse.

The air murky and chilled, and as the wind swirled, it was a night neither fit for man nor beast. *Tlot-tlot.* The horses clipped and clopped their hooves inside the barn stalls. *Neigh!* The horses were spooked.

Hearing the ruckus, the farmer begrudgingly left his warm fireplace and loving wife, grabbing his shotgun. "It better not be those damn coyotes again," the farmer said to his wife.

Upset, the farmer made an unexpected, late night trip out to the barn. A gust of wind blew his hat from off his head. The large red door to the barn flew open on its own as he approached.

The farmer peeked inside.

Hay rustled in bunches above the stalls. The farmer scanned the commotion, shining his kerosene lantern, while hooking his shotgun in his elbow's crook. *Click, clack. Click, clack.* Animal paws ran around above. The farmer shooed the wild animal off. Uneasily he peered over at his horses. The farmer had never seen them startled like this before, so slowly he began loading his shotgun.

The farmer stepped inside the barn. "Go on. Get outta here!" he demanded in a loud manner, shaking his lantern hard, rattling the squeaky parts of rusted metal.

Swoosh. A large critter ran on the planks high above. A cyclone of exploding straw erupted, with hay floating down to the barn floor, and covering the tops of the farmer's boots. Suddenly, one critter broke into three directions, circling the farmer.

Haah-haah-haah. A panting came from all sides. *Gurrhr.* An animal growled. The farmer's face struck a nerve of terror. He dropped his gun and turned to run for the exit. *Erreekkk.* The large barn door slammed with a screech, banging against the frame two times before resting firmly shut, and trapping the farmer inside.

The farmer's hushed screams muffled in among the wind's cold, blustery wails. The horses jumped on their hind legs, blowing large puffs of air from their nostrils. *Neigh! Neigh!* The horses watched, they snorted and squealed, as three beasts pounced on the farmer. The horses' eyes reflected this new predator's ghastly form. *NEIGH!* The horses tried to jump from their stalls while the three beasts ripped and bashed the farmer's body. Blood spattered the stable as the beasts dragged what was left of the farmer off into the night.

One of the creatures turned toward the horses, and opened its fangs wide enough to fit a head inside. *Gshaaaa.* It spit a hiss, quieting them in shivers as the horses huddled against the stable walls.

The farmer's wife sat and crocheted, watching television loudly. She glanced toward the barn, but continued with the farmer's new sweater, humming while waiting for his return.

Chapter Forty-Five

Five friends waited for a cab at two in the morning in downtown Miami. Outside the Mynt Salon, two of the girls, despite objections from their friends, decided to walk toward the beach, hoping to sleep until the morning. Staggering with a broken high heel, one girl took her shoes off, following suit, so did the other. Giggling and laughing between the patches of orange streetlights, the boulevards were hectic with activity and events all around.

Boys whistled and stopped their cars to give them a ride, but the girls smartly avoided all potential danger, for as with Spanish moss on trees, in a place like Miami, at two in the morning, danger hung on every street corner, and spread as wildfire upon parched brush.

Nevertheless, some dangers are just unseen hazards waiting insidiously to destroy lives. These hazards are not to be spoken of, and through evil spirits, they plunder both body and soul.

Two normal young adult females, both just out having a good time, neither looking for any trouble while out with friends. Two pretty girls, with bright futures, talented, well employed, having street smarts, with the cusp of the world at their fingertips, were unknowingly stalked since they had left the Mynt Salon. Down one wrong street they accidently turned, only stopping and giggling long enough to realize their mistake and return from where they came.

The lights on this side street were lowly lit and dim. The main drag was up ahead, and teeming with activity, but the two pretty girls had veered slightly off course, just for a second, yet enough time to be caught off guard.

Laughing one moment, the girl turned toward her friend. Poof. She was no longer there. They had just been holding hands, but now her own hand was empty as if her friend had never held it at all.

She chuckled, and turned all around, calling out, "Liz, where are you?" Frustrated by silence, she called out again. "Come on, I wanna get goin'!"

Still, no answer, yet the silence had been broken, with a growl, and a few angry words. A gravelly, demonic voice spoke from the hidden places between the dim streetlights.

"Your friend is gone, is gone. Now there is only you, only you."

Her laughter instantly turned to tears. "Who said that?" Then she wised up, or so she thought. "Liz, stop it. I know you're just trying to scare me. Well, it's not working."

Silence resumed, and though she could see the people up at the dazzling end of the street, she felt so far away from them now.

"Oh, girly, girly," the voice in the shadows repeated.

"Listen creep, I'll scream unless you let me and my friend go," she looped around in a circle, yelling into the air.

Her weight tensed in her quads and calves. She suddenly ran, hurrying up the avenue. *Kata-kata.* The strides of a four-legged animal drummed on the pavement from behind.

A creature—a grisly, visceral monster—bounded from the air and down in front of her from high above. It planted itself, straightening its curled beastly appearance slowly upward, until it resembled a human. The beast blocked her path to the main boulevard. Moreover, with every inch of new flesh uncovered while straightening its curved spine, a hellish atrocity, the likes of which no one should ever see, exposed the true nature of life and death before the girl.

"AHH!" She screamed again, "AHH!"

The monstrous vision wrinkled and sagged, with a greasy, pale, grayish skin. Disfigured with skeletal sockets and distended points, its sharp, sickled claws were second in menace only when compared to its mouth full of fangs, and each fang had tiny serrated edges up and down along the sides of its teeth. The creature spoke, swelling to a size twice that of the girl. It puffed out its chest, and flung open its switchblade talons. "Go ahead...scream, scream."

The girl did, letting out several at the highest pitch her lungs and voice box could carry. "Help! Help! I'm being attacked! HELP!"

But not one person, even the ones that heard her, cared at all. No one came. No one called the police. No one even yelled back. The girl, now sober with grim reality, her eyes wide, backed away from the monster and its scheming grin.

Two other beasts stepped out from the dark and hemmed her inside a triangle. The scent of iron floated in the air. One of the three monsters was covered in blood, her friend's blood, yet still seemed hungry. The beast had clearly gorged itself, yet stared at her, reflecting only her dread in its large, black saucer eyes.

"I told you, told you." The creature gloated. "We are Dwellers, are Dwellers. And no one cares about you, about you."

She began to scream again. A cold hand raked against her neck, scraping abrasions and pulling her into the darker wedge of the street. Cars fifty feet up ahead on the main strip raced, their motors revving as tires burned smoke toward the crowds of hoots and hollers.

The girl fought as best she could, yet the Dweller inflicted steady pain. All three Dwellers pierced and bludgeoned her with talons and teeth. She stretched a hand upward as one Dweller carved her throat. Soon she quieted. Her blood oozed everywhere. The creature bit through muscle, cartilage, and arteries, severing her neck from her spine.

Chapter Forty-Six

A tropical island in South America has a reputation for the strongest men on Earth. In an illegal arena, these colossal gladiators battle each night in a secret club for entertainment, riches, and fame.

Two hundred and fifty to three hundred pounds of muscle brutishly bash skulls, tear ligaments, and even occasionally kill for a few extra dollars, and a host of callous cheers and chants of, "Kill! Kill! Kill!" The crowd begs and stirs for blood to be spilt, for pain to be inflicted, so money can be passed from one greedy, moist hand to another.

Long after the witching hour, three mammoth mounds of bulk, each tall as they were wide, carried their gym bags and left through the side door between the old airplane hangar at a deserted airfield.

After heavy rains, the air was muggy, with a humid oppression that only jungle downpours broiled upon a sweltering heat. The tropical rains brought sizzling temperatures, even at night. Temperatures so hot, they had been known to cause malaise, overwhelming reactions, and even sickening the mind, bending the firmest resolves into psychosis.

The musclebound gladiators, still dripping with beads of perspiration, both beaten and bruised, with eyes cut, lips swollen, and stitched and bandaged, were the victors of the evening. One of them grinned, flipping through his cash as he walked out the door. The jungle was oddly quiet, yet he did not notice as he shuffled his cash like a deck of cards, before tucking it gently back into his gym bag.

Their cars were up ahead, the last cars around in the lot, and only a few dark patches of wooded brush separated them from a well-deserved and air-conditioned trip home.

The leaves in the trees vibrated unnaturally, rustling from yanks and tugs. The three colossal men halted, one pulled a handgun from his gym bag. Hesitation immobilized them all. A long chain-link fence ran hundreds of yards to their left. The old airplane hangar ran a solid wall nearly as long as the fence to the right. Everything else was dark, save for a sporadically blinking light above a self-locking door the fighters exited.

The shadows trailed at the rear, in front, and all around the enormous jungle behind the fence. The strong man in the lead halted his two large companions. Their bravado was piqued, just like their abnormally high testosterone levels. Each of the strong men prepared to defend his hard-earned money to the death.

Confident, even to the point of cockiness, they challenged the invisible threat, certain no one was stronger than any one of them, and certainly not able to take on all three of them at once.

In a strained voice, one of the musclebound men yelled, "Come on out, esse, so I can break your little neck in half." He spun his head back toward his friends, and hid his anxiety with a grin and laugh.

The three shared a grunted laugh.

The trees had ceased rustling.

Bavuud. Bavuud. Bavuud. Multiple feet pounded the airplane hangar's metal roof, some sixty feet above the men's heads. *Clomp, clomp, clomp.* Faster and harder the steps pounded around in circles. The noises eerily taunted and teased the large, musclebound men.

The men ended their boasting. Their heads sunk in a valley between their massive shoulders. They resembled turtles shrinking into shells, and no longer brave goliaths, unafraid of anything the world had to offer. They had reverted to their childish, bedtime fears, no more in control. Wells of emotion spilled out in quick succession one after the other. And while they were still large and strong, they were now weak and flimsy, when matched with the unknown and unnerving.

One man stuttered, "Whaa...what's going on?" He raised his gun and erratically fired it several times into the air.

Sweat poured down another man's face. "I'm outta here." He bolted, running toward his car, his breath labored, his strides slow, he knew he would be faster if he released his gym bag of money, but he figured that he could make it, because dropping his money was not an option. "You're on your own." He scrambled away from his two friends.

"Wait for me!" One of the other men followed his friend to his car.

Still another man thumped his chest, while standing his ground. "You chickens!" He mocked his friends. "It's just a bunch of weakling kids messin' with you. Well I'm goin' to mess them up. I'm goin' to mess you up! You hear me!" he shouted at no one in particular.

The jungle, bustling with life earlier in the evening, was now unmoving and strangely quiet. The strong men had not previously noticed the unnatural lack of jungle noises, but a clamoring whisper, *sussurrah, sussurrah*, offensively lurid, dominated the night and approached from every direction.

Of the two men that fled, one was gone in a flash. *Whoosh!* He was pulled by something into the nearby thick brush. His massive body became that of a flimsy ragdoll. The strong man was swiftly hoisted from off his feet, pulled through a small opening in the chain-link fence, shaking the metal links and anchored poles up and down in a wave of clacking steel. "Aaah!" He quickly shrieked and then disappeared into the dark jungle with silence. All that remained were rustling leaves and his footprints in the gravel.

The largest of fighters stood his ground, dropping his gym bag as he watched one of his friends vanish into the rainforest, while his other friend continued running toward the car.

The planted, towering block of muscle doubted his unseen combatant had the strength to best him in a fight. He mashed his fist into his palm, cracking his knuckles. "Come out then, show yourself, and fight like a man." He was trained in mixed martial arts, and still loose from winning all his matches that evening. "Come on!" he screamed. "You coward! Show yourself! Fight me!" He banged against his chest, beating it numerous times.

From high above the airplane hangar, a hefty body jumped down. *Whaam!* A thud pulverized the ground in front of the strong man. A lesser sized, yet bizarrely grotesque creature, and not a man, looked up at the strong man in amongst the vast shadows.

"Ha-ha." The man laughed. "What is this, a costume?" The man became indignant. The man, over six-foot-five-inches tall, and weighing three hundred ten pounds, expanded his muscles, with a grinding of teeth.

The sinister figure puffed itself larger. It slowly rose, climbing from out the hole it created in the ground after diving from the sixty-foot high, airplane hangar roof.

The strong man and the creature stood toe to toe. The strong man gulped, yet a lump lodged in his throat. The sporadic light hummed on briefly, revealing an awful truth. He stepped back as the creature stepped forward. The man's brown skin shaded white, even in darkness. The man simply uttered in a hushed voice, "El diablo."

The creature spoke. "I'm not the devil, but I can arrange a meeting."

The man stammered. "Whaa...?"

"What am I?" *Gurrhr.* It growled. "I am Dweller." It extended long, thick, razor-tipped talons.

The man backed away, the gravel beneath his feet grating with each step. "Here, take the money!"

"Not interested in money."

"Why are you doing this?"

"Because I can." The Dweller grinned. *Cling!* It sprung open its black, sickle claws.

The strong man took a single step backward. He then refocused his battle plan. The strong man punched, elbowed, kicked, and attempted to grapple the Dweller, but the Dweller was faster and stronger than any other fighter the strongest man of the strong men had ever fought.

"Diablo, I'll kill you!" the strong man called out.

Unfazed by the strong man's onslaught of hits, the Dweller callously asked, "Are you the best this world has to offer?"

"I'll tear you up!" The strong man punched the Dweller repeatedly, landing blow after blow with devastating accuracy. The strong man dislocated the Dweller's jaw. Sideways the jaw hung, bent down and crooked. The strong man then punched the Dweller in the ribs and stomach, but the strong man tired out in a matter of seconds. The strong man's fists were bloodied. It was as if hitting a mound of stale gelatin. The Dweller's core body vibrated and shivered, but remained intact, untouched, and resilient to any possible damage.

"Hmm." The Dweller let out a relaxed grunt. "That felt good. But I think you missed a spot."

The two were not equal, and now the Dweller intended to show its might with an overwhelming, destructive attack. Five unkind, razor-tipped talons wrapped around the strong man's neck. The Dweller lifted him a foot from the ground. The strong man's eyes bulged. He desperately gripped at the Dweller's hand wrapped around his neck. The strong man tried to remove the Dweller's hold from him, but the creature's grasp was unmovable, cutting off the strong man's air supply as his eyes drifted backward, rolling up until only the whites remained.

The strong man's brutish arms flapped to the side, dangling limply. The Dweller's blunt muzzle issued a disappointed snort, while still holding the once strong man by the neck.

The Dweller suddenly flung back its sickle claws, and with a gash, black talons tore the strong man's chest into an open cavity. The Dweller went berserk. The beast split through the ribs and sternum, breaking bones, crushing them apart. It grabbed the man's aorta—the main artery carrying blood from the heart—and unplugged it. The aorta gushed with blood as if a geyser, shooting a solid stream into the air, falling red with showery droplets. The Dweller sucked on the aorta, drinking the crimson fluid as if through a straw. The strong man's body shriveled.

"The white cells are delicious." The Dweller wiped its blood-soaked mouth, and then tossed away the rest of the man as if he was a piece of crumpled, handheld rubbish.

Blam! The Dweller threw the man off the side of the aluminum airplane hangar. The aluminum dented inward, and the man's body flopped to the ground, face down in a sloshy puddle of muddy red.

"How utterly worthless," the Dweller lamented aloud. "Must leave no body." The Dweller wrapped its talons around the man's head, and sluggishly dragged his floppy carcass toward the jungle.

Not knowing what became of his two friends, the last of the strong men had reached his car, yet in his peripheral, a creature resembling a wolf on all fours raced toward him at speed. He fumbled with his keys. They jingled as he tried to find the right one. The man panicked, dropping his gym bag for a moment before picking up the bag along with falling money. He unlocked the door, revved the engine, and his tires twirled, kicking back pebble and asphalt chunks. His car blasted down the long, dark, empty parking lot.

The car's speedometer reached sixty miles an hour. Its headlights on, the car bounced up and down the uneven road. The man angled his rearview mirror, breathing easily at the sight of nothing in chase. He patted his bag, checking his money, and then ran his fingers through his hair, fixing his shirt collar after. With both hands on the wheel, he felt safe and in control. He even grinned to himself in the mirror.

Tup! Ba-boom! It felt as if a rocket hit the driver's side. The door to his car ripped away with a single tug. The creature hung from the side, holding the car door, its claws tearing into the metal frame. It then tossed the unhinged car door and reached for the man.

"Ugh!" the man yelled with a child's voice. The car zigged, kicking up waves of stony gravel in its wake.

"Ta-da!" The creature displayed rows of fangs. It swiped at the man, gashing him, ripping his flesh into stringy pieces. Plasma emptied out, the cold warmth flowed a river, coursing down, saturating his clothes.

The man winced, grabbing at his injury. The agony was visible, yet all the man said was, "You stained my seats!"

The creature chomped at him, missing several times. Its fangs hit a bicep, ripping a larger chunk of flesh from the man's body. The man cut the wheel, trying to shake the beast, but it was fastened tightly, so, with one hand on the wheel, and part of his other upper arm severed, he leaned over and snatched his handgun.

He aimed it at the creature's head and fired round after round into its head and chest. *Bang! Bang! Bang!* The gun popped, and fire flew with each bullet. His ears rang, deafened by the loud cracks of the gun.

The creature, filled with holes, squirted black tarry goo at first, then the tarry substance turned into slimy wads of swarming spiders, roaches, and wind scorpions, which climbed up onto the steering wheel and over the man's hands, biting and stinging him repeatedly.

The man clenched his teeth and quickly flung off the crawling swarms. The man hopped inside the car with nonstop, animated, freaked grumblings. The man turned pale. He acted even more disgusted by the bugs than the inexplicable creature itself.

A voice whispered in the man's ear, "We are Dwellers. And we can't be killed so easily."

The Dweller's head deliberately rose. Like a shark, the membrane above its eyes arched downward. The man's heart skipped a beat upon seeing the black, round death of his own image in the Dweller's lifeless pools of reflection.

The man shrieked. "Ahh! Ahh! Ahhhhhhhh!"

The Dweller pulled the steering wheel, and the car flipped out of control end over end. Parts and pieces of the vehicle tossed about in every direction, tires this way, glass that way, metal fragments everywhere else. *Kirik.* Metal twisted. *Sssshblamm!* The car exploded, bursting into flames, scorching out of control in the isolated parking lot.

The Dweller pulled the man from the car, dragging him away. Only the quiet, steamy jungle hid the remains of a terrible fever, a symptom of malcontented cruelty, which served to unleash the Dwellers' vengeance upon the rest of the world in need of their purging inclinations.

Chapter Forty-Seven

Vincent had heard the gossip, anecdotal stories, and whispers of sightings of hideous creatures in the night. Some in local Mediterranean towns swore their loved ones had been taken but were not runaways, as many investigators had concluded.

Ordinarily, Vincent would not have even inquired, or cared at all, but he worried, for it seemed a part of his past somehow had risen again. It vexed him most for Noemi's sake, his love, his only reason for living. His concern about what she would think if she heard the same stories, drove him to unwilling action.

Vincent discouraged Noemi from venturing too far past their pleasant cabin on top of the countryside wheat fields after dusk.

It had been many weeks since the immortal Revekka visited him. After a tense, introspective week or two, Vincent felt as if his relationship with Noemi had never been better.

It was a very hot day.

The sun parched all things with a profound heat. Vincent's shirt soaked, with an uncomfortable cling to his body. He unbuttoned his shirt. Bare-chested, his pectoral muscles hung parted, but symmetrically, not too large, but evenly toned with a six-pack of abdominal ripples down to the top of his pants. Together he was a collection of tan muscle fibers, appearing carved from solid rock, but soft and gentle to the eyes.

The sun branded enflamed prickles down upon his skin. He slid his suspenders off pronounced deltoids, and then removed his shirt, throwing it with a tossed, arched lob to the ground.

Vincent stretched his sculpted biceps and shoulders. He curved his back inward before letting go. The black, elastic suspenders dangled, looping near his knees. He casually stood there glistening in the sun, appearing as if on a photo shoot, accidently modeling the perfect front cover for any stylish men's magazine.

Vincent eyed the six-foot-tall, jumbled pile of wood nearby. Wiping his brow, he reached over, grabbing the unevenly weighted axe handle. He placed a block of wood on a large stump, and with two mighty hands, he raised the axe over top his head. His muscles expanded, heaving with lines of defined power. Vincent chopped down with a crack upon the block of wood, splitting it clear in half, and from the rubble, tossing the divided pieces airborne in opposite directions.

At first, he had been too distracted by the loss of his vigor, his power, and source of his strength to notice Noemi's sadness, but now he had restored a measure of balance within himself. Yet, he failed the first class of Boyfriend 101—not listening, while trying to solve. Not hearing, thinking he understood, and dismissing any problem as tiny and illogical, yet with every rationale, Vincent missed the hidden, parched well of despair deep inside Noemi's core.

And though she smiled, it killed her a little more each time he ignored, whether on purpose or by accident, the deprived, soft coal of her slow burning, resentful heart toward him.

Down in the swaying wheat fields, Noemi had plenty of time to think. Her face flushed, rosy red from the sun, she sauntered along, tending to the animals, while gathering a bouquet of aroma-filled flowers into her wicker basket. She plucked red clovers. An eruption of orange, black, and white spotted butterflies hovered circles around her. Their tiny, delicate wings fluttered up and down with gradual majesty. The butterflies slowly dispersed, their soft wings tickling her skin as they did. Yet one rested on Noemi's index finger. She carefully brought her finger to eye level, smiling while examining its fragile wings. The butterfly soon flew off into the vast, blue sky along with the others. Her smile straightened. Her eyes dimmed. She looked at her surroundings and sighed.

Noemi knew something was wrong, she just did not understand why Vincent refused to admit it. Not only was her heart exposed, it was breaking. She felt as if her soul were eroding, that a void widened an empty space in her chest, which filtered into regret. There were mitigating factors. She was still young, and Vincent was younger than she was by two years still. Noemi had been so many things in her young life already. She was a warrior, an immortal, a force for good, a tool for evil, but she was a woman, and most of all, a teen trying to play house.

She had been engaged to Vincent's older brother no less, but she tried to forget that tragic romance. Noemi felt treasured in Vincent's arms, though her own desire turned hostile, with a lessening of passion in recent weeks. She missed her parents, she missed her life, and she missed the world. She was isolated from her friends. She felt drained by her relationship with Vincent, and she wondered if he knew that everything she had sacrificed was for him.

At a considerable distance up on the hill, behind the cabin, Vincent looked back over each shoulder. His cut frame had a polished shine in the noonday sun. He wiped some sweat from his brow with his forearm. Discerning that Noemi was not around, he dropped the axe and placed the next block of wood on the stump.

Vincent recalled and repeated words lowly to himself over again. "Practice to reflex. Practice to reflex. Practice to reflex." He trained his breaths and closed his eyes. He fixated on the power within and summoned a knight's weapon, a sword of metaphysical valor.

A translucent sword, with a bluish hue of sheer energy, materialized. *Rizzz.* The striker droned as he cut through the free air. Vincent laughed, smiling at his restored ability. He watched the blade. It had changed in color from the last time he summoned a weapon. He wielded the striker at his command. It felt good. It was easy again. He moved, and the sword displayed its power. Though the sun was high and straight overhead, even its beams could not tarnish his striker's radiating protons of luminous bands encircling the blade. *Swoosh! Flap!* He delivered a quick blow down at the block of wood. *Voomp!* He sliced with a lone swipe from top to bottom.

The wood block remained intact.

Vincent sighed, shaking his head with a frown. Then the wood block split in two clean pieces, each gradually falling away from the other. Even the massive stump, used for splitting wood, cracked in half. Vincent grinned, bobbing his head. "I've still got it," he reassured in a whisper. With ease, he divided through the six-foot pile of wood, one block after another with little effort until the pile of single wood blocks were all split into pieces.

Through repetition, his diminishing skills had returned, but they had returned only because of weeks of meditation and from practice to reflex whenever Noemi was not around. He had honed his skills once again. He began to adhere to the ways of the immortal knighthood. He now wielded the greatest symbol of a knight, the striker, and he felt more empowered than ever. Yet, in the process, he had kept all of it from Noemi, including his recent, nightly escapades.

She had come up the hill early to the cabin from collecting flowers. Noemi heard a familiar, faint hum from behind the cabin where the woodpile was located. Her pretty face had hoped to surprise him with beckoning gestures of ecstasy. She twiddled her fingers along the ends of her white, floral, shapely sundress.

Noemi adjusted her twisted spaghetti straps back in place. She was covered in pollen from the freshly picked pink and green posies, which she planned to arrange center stage on the supper table. A deep breath and she decidedly avoided him. Instead, she took the flowers into the cabin for water and mixed up a drink for their thirst. There were no windows looking into the backyard woodpile, so Noemi quietly walked outside and toward Vincent with an icy glass of lemonade on such a scorching, sundrenched day.

Her waist was thin, her hips hugged the sundress with every move, and her legs were long and shapely as she strolled near. She put on her best smile, mostly for Vincent, but it thawed when she caught a preview of him from behind. She knew he was up to something, but he swore, he swore to her numerous times that he would never summon his powers again. Though here he was, stunningly agile in all majesty, yet holding the weapon he swore to her that he would never wield again. His abilities, it seemed, had grown in might. Vincent, never before, had the power to materialize a dual-sided, double-edged sword. He was able to cut a block of wood one way, twirl his striker like a baton, and then cut the same block of wood the other way. Before the block even had time to split from the first slice, all four pieces fell instantly apart at once.

Noemi hastily ducked behind the side of the cabin and wiped her moist lashes with the back of her wrist. She took a deep, nasal-filled breath, cleared her throat, and called out to him before turning the corner completely.

"Vincent," she said before circling the cabin again. "I brought you something cold to drink."

He immediately withdrew his striker, awkwardly averting his eyes away from hers. "Noemi, you didn't have to do that." He reached for the glass and tipped it up to his mouth. The condensation from the upturned glass rolled down his chin as he chugged the ice-cold lemonade. "I'm all done." He fumbled, "I mean...um...I was...uh...just about to come in. See, I'm done with the woodpile. That axe works better than I thought." Vincent had trouble looking her straight in the eyes, yet she made efforts for uncomfortable contact with his. "What?" He raised his palms upward with an irritated inflection.

"No, nothing." Noemi turned her neck and narrowed her eyes. "You finally shaved. I forgot how young you look."

Vincent rubbed his smooth chin and cheeks. "Well, it's gotta be more than that?"

"No," she replied, her tone hinted of agitation, her face long with bother. "Not like you'd care anyway." She crossed her arms.

"Whatever." He sulked and handed her the empty glass. "I don't have time for this stuff."

"Stuff?" Noemi squinted, tightened her lips, and shook her head. "What? I'm just stuff now?"

"No, you know what I mean."

"Do I? Because it seems like all we ever do is fight." She put her hands on her hips. "We didn't...at least we hadn't for a long time before..."

"Yo, I don't know what to tell ya." He shrugged his shoulders and left her there, walking away toward the direction of the cabin while the sun fell midway down the sky.

Noemi just stood and watched him pass right by her. She jetted her chin out. With arms crossed, looking to the side, she marched in after him.

Vincent walked into the cabin, slamming the door. She flung the door open and followed closely, grabbing his wrist and turning him toward her.

"Hey," she said with a soft intention. "I want you to know that I...I really love you. You know." Noemi always loved peering deep into Vincent's icy, blue eyes, and into his warm soul.

"I know," Vincent halfheartedly replied. "I know you love me."

"And I want you to know that you can tell me anything...anything."

"What's to tell?" Vincent shrugged.

Her dismay turned indignant.

He turned away from her again.

"Why won't you look at me when I'm talking to you," Noemi's soft voice became jarring.

Vincent said nothing.

The cabin was stuffy from the leftover, midday heat. Noemi stomped, her shoes clunked past him as she opened the windows. The draperies carried in an easterly wind, flapping the cloths about, folding the curtains over onto each other before straightening, only to take an erratic flight upon the next cool gust.

Without a word, Vincent left the stuffy cabin and sat on the front porch instead. He took a swig from the large container of lemonade. It was warm like everything else, so he spit it to the ground.

Noemi, though crying inside the cabin, wiped her tears and stomped out for a seat next to him on the edge of the porch. She placed her hand on his knee. He glanced down suspiciously, yet kept drinking the warm lemonade, tipping the large glass container up in the air as he guzzled the last drop.

"Hey," Vincent casually said, still refusing to look her in the eyes, "this lemonade tastes like crap."

"Well...it's been sitting in the sun. Besides, I'm not here to talk about lemonade." Noemi regarded his handsome side profile. "We've been through a lot over the past year."

"Yep." He looked straight ahead.

Feeling awkward, not wishing to say more, she did. "We survived the other immortals. We left our home forever to come here. We almost died. And you kil–" She abruptly ceased.

He flashed an evil, hateful glare. "What did you just say?" His tone bottomed out with an irate drop.

"Um...you lost your brother." Noemi winced. "We both lost Jak I mean."

Vincent shot upward and threw the glass container to the ground. It exploded into large spikes and tiny slivers everywhere in front of them. "That wasn't what you were gonna say!" he yelled.

A fiery urge kindled inside Noemi at the sight of his outburst turning violent against her only large glass container. She shot upward and stood face-to-face with him. She stared into his eyes, her thinly contoured brows crinkled together and down. "I know what you're up to." She blurted out. "I've seen you training. I know you go out each night when you think I'm asleep."

"So!" he shouted.

"So, I'm not stupid." She shouted back. "Ever since that day I saw you talking to someone down in the field, you've been different toward me. You've been lying to me, and you promised me, dammit!" She wiped the trickles at the outer corners of her eyes.

"Not this again." Vincent groaned.

"Don't you love me anymore?" Noemi placed her hand on his bare chest. With her other hand, she took and grabbed his hand, placing it over her own heart. "I don't want to be with someone that doesn't love me. Just say it if it's so."

He hemmed and hawed, frowned and pouted. "I still...I always..." He stopped short of saying the words she needed. "I just feel so trapped sometimes!" He ripped his hand from off her heart.

Noemi stepped backward. "Trapped?" She narrowed her eyes.

"Yeah, trapped," he said evenly.

Tears filled the lids near her bottom ducts, giving them an unintended, lovely, glossy finish. "By me?"

"Yeah." His face shared no emotion.

She held the middle of her chest. "ARAAH!" she screamed with pitiful anguish. She bawled and cried. Noemi removed her hands to cover her face. She started to smack her own head, rapidly and with heavy blows. He took her wrists and held them back, preventing her from hurting herself more.

"Oh, my god! Oh, my god! You don't love me anymore!" The words melded in a single, almost inaudible weep. "Don't touch me!" She reeled back and away from him with a thumping cry.

An overcasting guilt shuffled between anger and frustration, so Vincent tempered his immediate feelings for her sake. "I swear, it's not you, I'm just having a tough time right now."

She wiped her eyes and sniveled. "Oh, yeah, then tell me, what's going on?"

A long silent period, with unwavering glances replaced words, mellowing spaces between incited tensions. Vincent shrugged his shoulders. He knew how he felt, but he could not give her what she needed to hear, at least not at that moment. "This thing we have." He waved his hands between them. "It can't last. It won't last, unless..." Vincent abandoned his sentence.

"You don't care about me!" Noemi yelled.

His face softened. His frustrated appearance shifted to concern. "I do. No, no, I do!"

"Then tell me what's going on." Her voice sank to a lenient, yet bitterly crammed request.

"I told you...nothing's going on. I'm just tired of everything."

Noemi glared at him as he walked inside the cabin and lay sideways on the couch, his back facing her. She knew he had been sneaking out in the middle of the night, every night for the past few weeks. She had seen him using his immortal abilities again. The same abilities both of them swore they would never practice after they miraculously woke up on the beach together, both of them still alive, after their fight with Malum all those months ago. They had promised to live as mortals until time, as they knew it, ended.

She felt exposed by confronting him for love's sake. "I don't know what's going on, but with all the mistakes we've made, all the things we've overcome, we're here now, and we don't have to prove anything to anyone."

Vincent sat up and stewed an unwavering guise of displeasure. "I want to be your star. I want to be everything for you, always, but I have to see this to the finish, and then I'll quit, forever this time."

"You can't change anything, no one can," she pleaded, on knees in front of him, reaching for his hand. "What's really going on?"

"Really, nothing you need to know about."

For as boats are tossed about a stormy sea, and as water engulfs a vessel until it can no longer stay afloat, her love was drifting into a tempest. Noemi desperately wanted to ride out the storm, but she was tiring, and ready to abandon the sinking ship this time.

"Vincent, why won't you talk to me?"

"Just leave me alone!" he yelled.

"But I love..."

He stopped her words with a shout. "Go away! Leave me alone before I get pissed!"

She wept terribly, which was only hushed by her slamming the bedroom door. Moreover, unlike before whenever she was sad, this time, he did not go and check in on her, or hold her like he used to whenever she was scared or felt alone. Rather, he lay back down on the couch like a rock, fuming, justifying, and planning. He had to keep her safe from what was coming, but he would not share what he feared most with her. Instead, he listened to her muffled cries from the couch, refusing to comfort her until he had something tangible to offer in exchange.

Things could be settled and explained later. He figured she would forgive and love him as she had done after Jak died, but he needed to do what he had already set in motion. He could not deviate now, and would not make the same mistake of getting her involved as he did before.

Then an epiphany landed in amidst Vincent's racing thoughts. This was why the knighthood forbade marriage between two knights. If a loved one were in peril, a knight might very well neglect their duty for the greater loyalty to save the one, and let thousands die in their place. He shook his irate head. He almost got her killed the last time danger surrounded him, and he could not doubt himself now, for he would kill Malum before he had a chance to find either of them, and the future would be much safer for Noemi, he reasoned.

Noemi locked the bedroom door and fell onto the bed, her face sullen, the pillow wet with salty brine. She drifted off into a semi-sleep, a disturbed sleep, a nightmarish, riddled sleep. Liquid sadness drenched the pillow. Her face felt sore from the teary, saturated fabric. Since they had been living in among the wheat fields, she only had sweet dreams. She never worried much while in Vincent's arms. She never had reason to worry about his intentions or honesty. But doubt stuck its dirty little fingers into the cracks of her heart, and crept through fractures, filling her with suspicions and concerns, and most damaging of all, she now wondered if he had ever loved her to begin with.

Vincent pretended sleep. He watched the clock on the wall and listened for the squeaky mattress coils of Noemi tossing back and forth in the other room. At about two o'clock in the morning, Vincent quietly got up, dressed, left the cabin, and headed into town.

Chapter Forty-Eight

Unbeknownst to Vincent, one town over, at the same time he walked the dark, wooded trails to the nearest town, three Dwellers hunted in the night.

The creatures raced in the shadows, spying victims who had recently left a tavern. A man and woman exited, walking hand in hand. The man was handsome, with brown eyes, and appeared to be in his mid-twenties. The woman, also in her twenties, was pretty, slender, and blonde.

The couple walked as lovers down the empty, silent streets. Few lights lit their way, but it mattered not, for this was a safe area, with low crime and fewer worries. They caressed. She stopped, put her arms around his neck, and gave him a lingering kiss.

From out of the darkness, a startling voice threatened, "Give me your money." A grizzled, unshaven, top-heavy, nasty thug eyed the lovers and demanded with a polished knife that reflected its metallic, sharp edge.

The blonde woman anxiously handed her purse, and the handsome man, his wallet over to the grizzled thug. Nevertheless, the grizzled thug appeared to want more. He introduced a wily leer at the blonde woman, while raising his knife toward the handsome man.

The thug cocked his arm back over his shoulder. The blonde woman and the handsome man leaned away. Their eyes widened. Their faces struck a stony, fearful arrested look. Their hands up, they called out. "No! Please!" The blonde woman closed her eyes and covered her handsome man. The handsome man tried to cover her instead, and each looked up, puzzled by the thug's disappearance. Without a sound, the grizzled thug was nowhere to be seen. The two stood tall and gazed up and down the deserted street, but like a ghost, the grizzled thug was gone.

The man and the woman let out a sigh of relief, waving into the dark, thanking whoever had saved them from certain tragedy. The couple readied to go back the way they had come, but suddenly the handsome man was snatched from the street into the dark as if on a string. The blonde woman cried a half shout, before she was ripped away into the night as well.

Three monsters stood before them at the end of a sinister, crowded alley. The handsome man and the blonde woman bunched together, shivering in the wide shadows of three beasts approaching, blocking out any background streetlight as they did.

"Wha...what do you want? Money? He...that other guy..." The handsome man pointed out the alley. "He took it all."

"Please leave us alone," the blonde woman whimpered, her face buried in her mate's shoulder.

"Now we eat," one Dweller said.

Another Dweller chopped its arms down with its talons, barring any other Dweller from approaching the couple. "No! This is M's first. I will show how it is done."

With clasped and unclasped talons, the other Dweller lamented with a quiet rage. "What about me, Killian?"

"Go devour the man we pulled away from the two of them."

The Dweller looked over its shoulder. "He's already dead. Besides, he reeks of strong drink."

Killian became agitated. "Well go join Nytmar and his bunch the next town over!" He growled.

The other Dweller narrowed an eye. "What of you two?"

Killian, his voice a dry gully of well-kept intentions, replied, "We'll finish up here, and then M and I will meet up with you shortly. Now go hunt with Nytmar, and then we shall find each other at the fixed location for the aperture back to Malum before daybreak."

The other Dweller's black saucers shifted asquint back and forth from Killian to M. "Fine!" It reluctantly left Killian and M's company.

The couple was detained in their own terror. They were too afraid to call out. Their muscles stiffened, they quivered together against a short, back alley wall. They had neither fight nor flight left in them, but only a deathly freeze, which suffocated the handsome man and the blonde, slender woman in listless shock instead.

"Go on now." Killian pushed M toward the couple.

"I–I can't." M turned back.

Killian held M by the shoulders. "All of the pain will go away if you do this. All of your doubts, all of your weakness, all of the dead you feel inside, will become alive again."

M sighed a reviled yet impelled breath. "You mean it?"

"Yes."

"If I do this, all of the pain will go away?"

"Forever." Killian finished M's thought.

"But how do I..."

Killian reassured. "Deaden your mind. Make yourself numb."

Hesitant with mixed feelings, M turned toward the human couple. M's body wasting away from hunger, its eyes now full of boggy desire, found a new perspective. M stared at the blonde female, tilting its head before diving, fangs open, talons sprung.

M grabbed the blonde woman, opening her mouth and forcing in a waxy substance secreted from its own mouth. Killian joined after M made the first move.

A quick set of bloodcurdling screams rang and then died out in the silence of the dark. And whatever follows death emerged from the alley. Smiling, she was now a slender, pretty, blonde woman, and he, a handsome, brown-eyed man. They walked from the dark backstreet with hands entangled. She had a spattered, fresh red spot on the tip of her white high heels. Yet nothing else was out of sorts. The two looked perfect in youthful afterglow. They beamed with health, and bloomed as only young lovers could—fruitful in the prime years of early life.

She leaned in for a kiss. He pulled back in surprise, but indulged himself, accepting her offer. Their two lips collided. They embraced. M licked Killian's lips. He kissed her neck. Killian pulled her smooth hips closer, pressing his chest up against hers. They had bliss and cheerful happiness, for a short while anyway.

She unlocked from his embrace. "Do you remember our first date?" M blushed pale pink.

"Our first date?" Killian recited back in vague tone.

"Yes...our first date, silly."

"Um, uh."

"Ugh, men." M huffed, releasing her emotions, while loosely draping her arms around his neck. "You remember. Your friend Marko and my friend Jenna both had us over to their place. They both pretended it wasn't a set up blind date, but the joke was on them, because we were already secretly dating for weeks." M tipped her head up toward the stars in the black sky. "I knew I loved you when I saw you at Jenna's party earlier that month." She kissed him again.

Killian held M by the shoulders. "M, what are you talking about?"

"M, what's M?" She chuckled. "I know it's late, but you really expect me to think you forgot my name? It's Kristen, remember?" She laughed. "We've been together for over a year, ya know."

Killian cracked an uneasy, half upward, corner lip twist. He suddenly remembered how this had happened to a few Dwellers the first time they partook. He had a set of similar memories, but he knew they were not his own. Then Killian realized that M could not tell the difference. M believed she was Kristen.

Killian considered calling her by the name Emma to snap her to reality. But he just watched her instead.

She used his unwilling hand to twirl and turn, swaying in the street as if everything was anew. She was jubilant and smiling, euphoric even, and for the first time since the night in the catacombs, all those nights ago, she seemed herself again.

Killian pondered. He felt like all else was a descent from important to trivial. From the preceding rise in excitement, anything short of this fantasy for her would be a crushing letdown at this point. One that M might not recover from until her mind could accept it on its own.

It broke his shrunken, shriveled heart to tell her the truth, so he said, "Of course I remember our first date...Kristen." He submitted to her dream, though it would not endure past the stroke of the clock twenty-four hours from this moment. Yet he could not kill another thing this night, especially her dreams.

"Come on. Let's get you home before the sun comes up." She pulled his hand.

"I've got a better idea."

"Oh, yeah?"

"Yeah. Let's not go home."

She giggled. "Are you crazy?"

"No, I mean yeah. Let's just keep on going."

Bewildered, she rounded her chin up, tightening her lips. "You have work, and so do I."

"Who cares. Let's just keep going. Let's just follow the night and see where it takes us." Killian kissed her cheek, holding the small of her back, dipping her as he did, and then releasing for a reaction.

"What...we need money. Are we supposed to live off of love or something?"

"Something like that," he retorted.

She stood there, silently holding his hand, waiting to see if he would let slip a smile, or a grin. He did not. "You're really serious, aren't you?"

"Yep."

"But what about..."

He knifed into her sentence. "It doesn't matter. Nothing matters to me but you."

Her head bobbled up and down slowly. She reached out and firmly held his hand. "Let's go then."

The two of them walked up the street and out of sight, out of town, and kept happily walking from there onward.

Chapter Forty-Nine

Meanwhile, as the other Dweller who departed from Killian and M neared the next town where Nytmar and his pack hunted, another edible target on their indiscriminate killing spree had been spotted walking in and out of the gloomy, shaded places of the dark, peaceful hamlet.

Buildings of small and wide sizes bunched like a crooked cross, from four directions, until they converged in the main opening at the center of town. Monuments of men stood in place for lost soldiers in forgotten battles. Their cold eyes incapable of tears, their ears unable to hear, and though having mouths, they could not speak a word. They had wonderfully sculpted heads, yet these monument men lacked even the ability to understand simple words engraved in concise statements of truth, bolted on plaques, and framed under them: *'They will not learn war anymore.'*

These iron relics, a true vestige of glorified ideals, provided a short, entertaining account of events idolizing wars—wars that meant little at the time and nothing at all now.

The buildings all around were old, with chipped paint. Less than presentable, the dated, tiny shops remained open, with few customers all day long, while the pubs filled to the brim throughout the night.

Still, this tiny town was an ironic icon. A few houses remained glorious mansions on the distant hills. Wealth, though present in worthy spots, stood blatantly among the impoverished alcoves. The muddled streets lined like reckless dots speckled on canvas, sketching a portrait of pretense and denial. The run-down image forged a print of the destitute, with numbers uncountable as starry clusters in the night sky. However, the impoverished were ignored as the ugly things in an ugly world for those who wished to taste only the sweet portions in life.

With hands in trim, slack pockets, a slender, lone human figure appeared strolling toward the middle of town. It seemed a male at a distance, skinny, with height near six feet. The Dwellers, positioning themselves for another kill, bound silently from one staggered row of packed rooftops to another set of roofs forty to fifty feet across the same street.

The slender man looked over his shoulder a time or two, almost as if he could hear the quiet, impending ambush. Conversely, he buried his hands deeper into his pockets and continued walking ahead, toward the monument in the center of town.

Three Dwellers now formed a triangle of doom high above on the rooftops. Their human prey unknowingly ambled at a leisurely pace. He sauntered along the town streets, in the Dwellers' perfect kill-box below.

Nytmar held two talons in the air, signaling one of the Dwellers to go in and make the capture. With a nod, one of the Dwellers swung its arms down for a power jump from a rooftop. It leaned its body opposite the direction of the man, and vaulted down toward him with a blitzing thump of speed.

Flying through the air, the Dweller unleashed its ten razor-tipped talons, opening its fangs for a large bite.

The man suddenly disappeared, and the Dweller crashed, face first on the hard ground, breaking several of its fangs, leaving it dazed and stumbling about from side to side on the street below.

The two other Dwellers looked on, and for the first time since their nightly hunts, they were in full disbelief. Nytmar and the other Dweller jumped down to where the stumbling Dweller staggered about, confused and temporarily incoherent as if it had just left one of the local pubs.

Suddenly, a whistle from above, the three Dwellers braced and looked up. Their edible target balanced himself on top of the monument. On the monument's head, the man supported the entire weight of his body with a single hand. His arm straight, his body and toes vertical up in the air, his exploit of gymnastic display was more than human. He steadied himself, peering down at all three of the Dwellers.

With outward curved legs, the Dwellers moved crabwise. "You're not human." Nytmar gave a swift, enquiring look.

The man replied, "Neither are you, foul beast."

A gruff voice strained. "What are you?"

"I'm Vincent."

"I don't care *who* you are." Nytmar pointed. "I want to know *what* you are."

"Vulgar demon, you are bold for attacking me. I don't owe you any further information." Vincent remained indignant, with a certain swagger. He continued antagonizing. "You are the point of disgust. I knew of your dubious schemes before you even attacked me."

"How?" Nytmar barked. It ground its fangs at him, while indirectly looking for a way to get up to Vincent.

"I know what you're doing." Vincent smirked. It was apparent to him even in his compromised state. "I don't like it, so why don't you knock it off before I do you a favor by killing you."

Nytmar scoffed. "One Dweller can kill twenty men."

"But as you said, I am not just a man." Vincent winked.

The Dwellers continued to position themselves around Vincent as he nimbly balanced on the monument high above the ground.

Its blunt snout huffed with strong outburst. "Then what are you?" Nytmar demanded.

Vincent openly insulted them. "Far superior than a freak like you."

"You're an immortal," Nytmar shouted. It talked to itself. "Are you Shroud? No. Are you a knight? No." It kneaded its talons.

Vincent remained silent, yet stunned all the same.

"Yes," Nytmar repeated. "That's what you are. You are an immortal, but what kind?"

Another Dweller spoke up. "But master did not tell us immortals would be out here."

"Shut up!" Nytmar spit at the other Dweller before it turned its attention back toward Vincent on his high perch. "You'll have to excuse that one. He's a little stupid in the head. Not all of us freaks are created equal, if you know what I mean." Vincent appeared baffled, and Nytmar read with a glance. "No...no I suppose you don't know what I mean."

A more serious tone replaced Vincent's taunts. "I expected other immortals were stealing certain humans again, like during the Shadow Harvest..." He pulled back. He knew he had given the Dwellers what they wanted, more information.

Nytmar cracked a miserable smile. "So you are Shroud?" Nytmar talked aloud to himself again. "Or at least were. But no one leaves the Shroud alive."

"I'm not Shroud, but you're certainly from Malum." Vincent's words sucked the breath out of his own chest. He hated the taste of that name—Malum. He puckered as it rolled off his tongue. Always fearless, Vincent knew fear again, not for himself, but for his beloved Noemi.

Two Dwellers bowed when Vincent uttered Malum's name. Except Nytmar did not bend in reverence. He straightened his hunched spine, standing even taller than before.

"I serve what puts food in my belly." Nytmar's large, black saucers stared. It noticed Vincent's weight-bearing arm begin to tremble. "Losing your strength, immortal?"

Vincent's face turned red. "Not at all." His pulse increased.

"Humans are tasty, but I've always wanted to try immortal meat." Nytmar ushered the two other Dwellers inward and screamed, "He's weak. Get him!"

With unsurpassed speed, Vincent pushed his body off the monument's head, springing backward onto his feet in the middle of the town square. In reverse, Vincent landed with a backslide, and a distant focus.

Trying to catch Vincent, one of the Dwellers pounced on top of the monument, but it captured only the iron head of the statue. Its talons jammed deeply into the iron. The Dweller ripped the iron into shreds, eviscerating the pieces off its claws, while ripping the statue's head clean from its shoulders, before throwing the pieces of iron head clanging to the ground.

Vincent's chest heaved convulsively. He braced his legs wide apart, and with a dazed look, he hunched himself forward, though slightly winded, he slowed his breaths. Vincent had not fought in quite some time, and the last fight was a terrible loss. He attempted to hide his anxiety and doubt. His weaknesses were evident when he fought Malum. His self-taught, repetitive tendencies cost him last time. He closed his eyes and began mumbling, "From practice to reflex. From practice to reflex," he repeated.

The Dwellers were baffled, their necks angled up and down.

"GO!" Nytmar yelled again. "He's hallucinating."

A keen sense allowed Vincent to see even with his eyes closed. He balled his fist, summoning a double-edged, twin-bladed striker. *Rizzz.* The sword droned an incandescent, menacing, blue specter with rotating luminous bands around the striker among nightfall's blackish air.

Like beasts, savage and brutal, all three Dwellers attacked from different sides. In disordered chaos, they merged upon Vincent, aggressive, physical, and violent.

The Dwellers were a collection of jagged, bony points, leathery skin, fangs, sickle talons, and rounded, lumped backs. They rushed about in a fury, and in a total, vicious loss of control. Without restraint of moral sense, the Dwellers indulged in a deranged feeding frenzy of mad bloodlust.

They should have been afraid of this immortal and his striker, but they were too busy preparing to eat, and so the Dwellers considered nothing else.

His practice now in action, Vincent swung his blade with deadly accuracy. *Swash!* His sword struck the air, one slice right after another.

The Dwellers hurled themselves with speed and strength toward Vincent. A speed and strength that he began to respect.

Vincent's striker clashed against the Dweller's black, tar like talons. *Clang!* Blue sparks flew as each repelled the other.

"That's impossible!" Vincent, taken aback, shouted.

"What?" Nytmar retorted. "You didn't think we could defeat you, immortal?"

Vincent sneered. "Nothing is so strong as a knight's striker." He huffed and puffed. *Fash!* With agility, he dodged swipes, kicks, and grabs, still staying two steps ahead of the Dwellers. "Yet your claws, they...I can't break them. A striker breaks all things."

"Ha-ha-ha!" Nytmar chomped at Vincent. "You can't even chip them."

While fighting all three Dwellers at once, Vincent said with shocking surprise, "I can cut through steel and solid rock." His striker blazed. "What are you?"

Black, sickle talons clanged against Vincent's striker in reverberating sounds, loud and powerful. Hard hits jangled and clacked like metal blades, each hammering against the other with rough, harsh, and deflecting blows. Vincent, more nimble than the Dwellers, sidestepped their overeager stabs.

With a quick strike, Vincent's luminous blade severed one of the Dwellers' arms. It fell off and dissolved into gooey mixed splats of pus and scuttling bugs. Yet the Dweller's black, tar-like talons remained intact on the ground. Holding its shoulder, the Dweller howled in pain, soon swiping back and forth with its other arm, nearly piercing Vincent's skin.

Vincent recoiled a cartwheeled jump high into the air. He swung forward, springing over the injured Dweller, and while in midair, he landed a decisive blow, splitting the injured Dweller's skull in two, its body fell limply to the ground, and then dissolved into a larger pile of scattering bugs and juicy pus.

Vincent looked upon the mess with diverging wrinkles.

The remaining two Dwellers, along with Vincent, paused and gawked at the death scene for a brief moment. The Dwellers ceased their advance. Then Nytmar saw another Dweller arrive from far behind the immortal. Unlike the other Dwellers, Nytmar was patient for an opportunity. Vincent appeared unknowing of this fact, so Nytmar diverted the immortal's senses by plunging its black talons forward, thus renewing their fight.

"And here I thought you demons had no weakness." Vincent smirked. "I guess I was wrong," he taunted.

Gurrhr. Nytmar growled. "You are an arrogant immortal, just like the rest of your kind. No wonder humanity is so haughty."

"What can I say—I'm perfect." Vincent thrust out his open hand, his fingers spread. *Swoosh!* He moved air, sending it forth. He pushed one of the Dwellers with an invisible wave, hurling it backward many feet onto the ground. "Psst." He looked squarely at Nytmar. "Somebody's getting stronger." He winked with a grin. Training had enhanced his abilities. He now had the advantage.

The newly arrived Dweller dove from high above. While launching itself airborne, its ten razor talons protracted. The Dweller landed against Vincent's back, propelling him forward. Shocked, Vincent braced himself, digging his striker into the ground for balance and support. The Dweller pulled back its elbows and then drove all its talons deep into Vincent's muscles near his spine. Red, immortal fluid spilled onto the street as the Dweller clawed into Vincent. With fangs smiling with glee, it readied for a bite.

"Ahhhhhh!" Vincent's head and neck flung upward as he screamed. He flipped the Dweller off him, sending it tumbling end over end down the road.

The Dweller recovered to its feet and licked the immortal's blood from off its talons, eyeing him as it did. "That tastes good, better than human blood." The Dweller roared at Vincent.

Nytmar backed off and away. It watched with pleasure. The immortal seemed stunned and injured.

Vincent winced, hunching forward. He reached at his lower back, pulling in front of his face a palm full of wet, red liquid—his own immortal blood. He had only seen his own blood one other time, and that was a scant amount compared to this.

"So immortals do bleed," Nytmar delightfully said. "You!" He pointed to the other Dweller. "Get up and get him. And you..." he said to the newest arrival. "Where's Killian and M?"

"They will meet us at the aperture."

"No, they won't." Nytmar growled. "Let's take this immortal down." The three Dwellers converged. "He's injured. We can take him."

Stunned, Vincent blinked several times. He shook his head and refocused his eyes. "Don't be so sure. I've already begun healing, and now I'm pissed off." Beaded sweat formed at his hairline. His dual-bladed striker blitzed with lightning. The sword's ethereal light smoldered with a hazy mist. The striker buzzed and flowed with sporadic bolts of blue voltage.

Whirr. Nytmar threw his bola—a long cord with heavy spheres meant to entangle legs.

Vincent cut the cords in half. The bola dropped to the ground on each side of him.

The Dwellers flinched and shrunk back. Dwellers felt fear only when caused by danger, which was not often, and this was now one of those times.

Vincent's body trembled as his adrenaline surged. Like a skilled craftsman, and in a blur of charging speed, he wielded his striker, removing parts and pieces from the three remaining Dwellers. Hands and fingers came off like gloves and jackets on a warm day from each Dweller.

"You will not touch me again!" Vincent shouted indignantly. He was now in a position of control, and at the height of his power. His muscles flexed in aggressive defiance.

Empowered, he twisted and turned, and eluded all attacks thereafter with eager anticipation. He threw a Dweller airborne. With another slice of his blade, Vincent ran his sword through the intestines of one of the Dwellers, and again, it dissolved into maggots and pus.

"And then there were two." Vincent leered as the slimy liquid remains bubbled and hissed, while his sword burned off the last remnants of goo like water dispersing from a scalding saucepan. "The fight's over. Tell me what Malum's up to and I'll let you live, vile monsters." Vincent glared at them with hatred.

"Go now! I'll hold him off." Nytmar turned and pointed at the last Dweller. "Tell our master what you have seen here."

"Wrong answer!" With his blazing striker, Vincent decapitated Nytmar with a single, rapid removal of its head. "Come here, you." He waved the last Dweller toward him with his index finger.

But the Dweller leapt toward the rooftops. It shot from the ground like a cannon and ran along the roofs.

Vincent sighed, wincing again. His backside began a painful reaction to the Dweller's talons. He reached and grabbed at the aching in his lower back. He felt a swollen abrasion. It felt like an abscess. His skin was inflamed and burning. It stung at the site with ooze. He was having a reaction to whatever toxin was on the Dweller's sickle talons. Spasms contracted his back muscles. The nerves went numb. His legs grew tingly and prickled. He felt death pangs, similar to when he was bitten by a pit viper once, but this was much, much worse, because his body was not healing.

Dizzy and blurred, Vincent focused on Noemi. He discovered enough power in her love to give chase. He had to catch the Dweller before it reported to Malum.

Vincent braced himself and flew atop the roofs as well. He pursued the fast Dweller. He began to catch up, but the Dweller, looking back in fear, tossed objects, some heavy and small, some large and light, yet all were torn in half by Vincent's blazing striker.

Several blocks, the Dweller ran, and for blocks more, Vincent chased until the end of town opened into a great, dark forest.

The Dweller soared high through the air, swinging its arms as if in water. Into the woods it fled.

Vincent, his adrenaline flowing, readied for his own jump, but something held him back. It wasn't physical, it was mental. He slammed his feet to the rooftop surface, clutching the knee-high raised part of the building. He bit his lower lip and punched a hole in the cement rooftop wall. Vincent gazed despondently out into the dark woods and sighed deeply several times. He watched the Dweller until it disappeared into the thick, dark forest below. He shook his head. He did not know why he did not make the jump. It was not hard, and he could have easily made it, yet something did not feel right. Nevertheless, he regretted not trying. Flapping his arms to his side, he was removed and tired. Then an unusual smell for the time and season fanned through the air—smoke.

Vincent sniffed for a direction. It was coming from the wheat fields, where Noemi was toward the south, so he abandoned his chase and raced toward the cabin, many miles away from where he presently stood.

Through the woods, he sprinted at full speed, ignoring the unbearable pain, and gasping until he reached the edge of the wheat fields in mere minutes. With the sting in his back now growing and spreading to his side, he held his stomach, while dragging in a single, productive breath.

The cabin was a torched inferno.

It was marked with red and orange flames, which rapidly burned an intense shine in the darkness. The firestorm was high and hot. The cabin completely consumed like a furnace. Smoke rose up as flames reached into and seared the night sky.

Vincent reached the burning stack of wood he called home, screaming, wailing, and bawling a single name. He let out a thumping cry, "NOEMI! NOEMI!"

Vincent dug through the agonizing heat, which cooked the flesh from off his body. It melted away his skin in distress, which only losing Noemi could evoke a deeper woe. He looked everywhere and cried out. The roof began to creak and pop over his head, so he fled outside the cabin just as the roof collapsed, flattening their home into a pile of scorching regret.

"WHY!?" he exclaimed loudly. "Why did this happen!" He watched the flames devour what was left of their home. He placed his badly burnt hands under the hollow parts of his arms beneath his shoulders.

A dead trance of grief ensued. His blue eyes turned red-orange as the flames glowed. Sinking to his knees, his mind instantly recalled how unkind he had treated Noemi of late. He loved her, and that was all she ever wanted to hear from him, but he refused to give a lone kind word, or touch, or gesture of any reassurance to that fact in recent weeks. It seemed so simple to tell her everything now. He could not understand why he was not honest with her. He just was not.

Everything seemed so utterly pointless. He blamed himself for this burning pile of carnage as he stared blankly into the fire, and this time, he learned the hatred of being right. His pervading mood and spirit were low at best, and all other things turned very displeasing as shock set in from every front. Vincent hurt inside and out. His body could no more endure and his spirit could no longer go on without his immortal love, Noemi.

A rustling in the woods at the edge of the wheat fields broke the somber moment. Vincent brought his hands to his face. Bloody, charred, and blistered, he was unable to bend them, thus unable to summon his blade. His active endurance was gone. Tears distorted his vision as the noise from the woods grew louder. He could not fight more of anything right now. His strength, skill, and stamina were all gone, along with Noemi, and his life lacked purpose. However, if he died now, not knowing what had happened to her, that thought also haunted his eternal mind, and he could not allow such a thing for Noemi's sake. So, he fled the wheat fields and ran toward the east, averting his eyes away from the burning, bittersweet, loving abode that used to be theirs.

Chapter Fifty

Days and nights had passed. Xander hung upside down, with a rope tied around his ankles and attached to heavy pulleys along the room's back wall. His hands knotted tightly behind his back. Having been exposed to the elements from holes in the roof while deep inside the recesses of the Victorian Era insane asylum, he felt as worn as the building.

He continually drifted in and out of conscious hallucinations. Ever since he fought the immortal knight, Maximillian, and lost, he had discovered many new feelings and beliefs during the days of inactivity amid the hauntingly quiet asylum.

One such day, a crow flew in the room where he hung. The bird rested high above on one of the rotten wood beams. It appeared another delirium at first, yet the crow angrily cawed at him. *CAW! CAW!* It then began pecking at the rope that suspended him off the ground. A noisy trudging of heavy boots shook the floor from behind. This it appeared was not an illusion after all.

Xander's eyelids expanded. He tried to call out, but a piece of tape remained, covering his mouth, so he made many other terribly incoherent sounds.

The footsteps got closer and the crow cawed louder, frantically flapping its wings in unison with the pair of stomping boots, and then...silence. The crow flew away, and the trudging ceased. Another hallucination Xander figured, but he was wrong again.

"Hello, Xander," a single, gravelly voice spoke. A head dipped down sideways to look at him. "I'm not angry that you failed," the crow flew back and landed on his shoulder, "but Alcazar is."

The man walked in front of Xander. He was dressed in a monk's robe, with a hood drawn over his face. In unexpected swiftness, his bony, knuckled hand ripped the tape from Xander's mouth, and an unspoken sharpness of anger was felt by a stinging pull of adhesive from across his sore lips.

"Lord Malum, I tried my best, but he was too..."

A knifing reply cut into useless words. "Your best isn't good enough." Malum raised an index finger and Alcazar cawed, flapping and then after receiving a treat, tucking his wings up behind.

Xander tried again. "If you just let me..."

"No," Malum gave another quick reply. "It's time for the grown-ups to speak." Malum walked around the room, circling Xander, talking as he did. "Let's drop the pretenses, shall we?" He smiled. His hands cupped one inside the other behind his back as his body leaned forward, his knees sagged, and his chin jutted. "The humans, their mortal world, their governments, their armies, their politics, their commerce, they are all of no consequence to me."

Xander's eyes scrambled in confusion, they chattered worry. His mouth pallid, half-open, and quivering, he dared not speak.

Malum continued. "Because you failed to bring me what I asked for, you should die!" he barked. "You see, all humanity is in a process of disillusionment. They want peace, but pursue war. Ha!" He laughed. "The only thing that unites them defeats them—death unites humans in a never-ending struggle of futility."

Xander spoke despite his fear. "But aren't we here to free them from the knights' blinding lies?"

With a deep forceful breath, the desire for guise snuffed out of Malum's only good eye. He squatted down face to upside-down face with Xander and just looked at every perfect pore on the young immortal's skin. "Do you see how scarred and deformed I am?" Alcazar flew back up to the beam above, and began pecking at the rope that held Xander.

Malum's nose touched Xander's. Malum's breath was foul as dung. Xander closed his eyes and turned his head. Malum grabbed his face, a hand on both sides and twisted it back toward him, then he pried open his eyelid. "Look at me! LOOK-AT-ME!!!"

Xander opened both eyes and straightened his head. Malum released his grip.

"What! What do you want?" Xander snapped back. "Just kill me. Get it over with." He added in passing, "At least the knight didn't torture me before he left me here to die."

"I'm not going to kill you, but you will be punished for your errors. Severely I might add."

"What?" Xander's eyes shifted back and forth.

Raising himself from a squatting position with difficulty, Malum said, "Humans, they need to die, and lots of them."

"Why?"

"Oh, don't be so naïve."

Xander stuttered, "Um, how?"

"Control their collective mind. Make someone in your region start a war, commit terror, or shoot up a bunch of people, or use pestilence, et cetera and so on. You get the picture?" Irritated, Malum threw his hands in the air. "Use your imagination, I don't care," he hollered.

"But what about the innocent..."

Malum laughed. "No one's innocent." Partly in cunning, partly in disdain, he said, "This is how you will keep your life and your post, but more importantly, this is how the Shroud grows stronger."

Malum met Xander's wandering look as Xander blurted, "This isn't..."

"What? Isn't right?" Malum snorted. "Isn't true?" He wrinkled, furrowed, creased, crinkled, and puckered. "Quid pro quo, which means...you owe the Shroud something for something already provided to you."

Xander knit his black brows together. "Why?"

"Why, why, why. I'm sick of that word. Kimi said that a lot before she...how should I say...left us." Malum's short, curled smile, high, arched forehead, and long, scarred neck told the tale. "When you were a knight, you learned to want more, so I gave you more." He tented his fingers. "You and the other young knights that joined the Shroud were all haughty and full of pride, so sure you would save the world and make a difference. You arrogantly thought nothing would be asked in return for the fame and power that the Shroud has afforded you." With a stiff upper lip, Malum glared down at Xander. "But you were wrong! It's time to pay up now."

The room took on a life of its own. The ambience grew darker. Shadows multiplied along the distant walls. Malum lit a candle, and soon, his own shadow came alive on the wall in triplicate.

At first, his shadows resembled his shape, but then, he spread his fingers apart and controlled his shadows like puppets. The shadows changed shape into many different things, and began telling his story between the splotches of light and darkness in the room. Even Alcazar stopped pecking and cawing for a time, appearing to watch the shadows on the wall.

Xander was aghast. His heart palpitated with the images presented to him. Like a set of explanatory notes, Malum centered the world's view through his immortal eyes. Empires rose with bloody might, and fell with arcane friction. Each civilization thought they were the greatest, yet each fell by the waste side, forgotten in both written and unwritten accounts, in a cycle of nonstop contentious bouts, filled with arid, sterile, and thoughtless ideas up until today.

Malum dispersed the shadows and the room slowly mended its original light. "You see now." He regained his calm. "I have experimented with every form of government there is for the mortals, and none of them work. We had an agreement with the knights." Malum grew sullen. "If by the end of five thousand years the Shroud had failed to maintain order in this realm, then it would be handed back to the people. The humans would be set free from our direction. But I can't let them go, just like I can't let you go." Malum turned a hard stare at Xander. "I'd rather see it burn than let it go."

"What are you going to do with me?" Xander asked. His fear increased tenfold.

"Alcazar thinks you talk about yourself too much." Malum waved his hand and then covered his mouth as he cackled. "Seriously though, we're here to make sure the status quo remains intact. The only way this world works, is if it is unfair. The Shroud commands you to cause suffering, misery, pain, loss, for these are strong emotions, and while they power the Shroud, they help weaken our enemies, too."

Incredulous, Xander shook his head. "That's all I'm here for...to destroy for the Shroud?"

"Yes," Malum simply replied. "Let's drop the charade. I am a royalist. Therefore, I am here to put a king back on the throne for all immortals and humans alike. One king. One government."

"What about free will and choice?"

Malum flipped the back of his hand dismissively. "Mere illusions of the mind. The knights, with all their glorified ideals, would have you believe there is a Reckoning, where everyone will live in ultimate wisdom—an ideal system without any sort of government whatsoever." He winked, shaking his finger. "But while I know this is impossible, these thoughts are dangerous, and can spread like wildfire if not subdued. Ideas are the most dangerous things there are. For you can kill a person, but not an idea."

Xander forgot himself. "Dude, this is getting wack."

"Oh, yes." Malum rubbed the thin, greasy, gray hairy strands drooping from his head. "That's Lord Malum to you, BTW." He clicked back his thumb and shot his finger like a gun at Xander. "The knights would take everything from us. Our power, our position, they would all be gone...why they would even make humans our equals if they could!" Malum's face reddened. His cracked teeth ground from side to side.

Xander squinted time and again. He felt woozy and lightheaded being upside down for days on end. He had been in that same position for so long, his blood felt as heavy sand deposited by moving water, swishing about his brain in frequent headaches. "What I've seen out here, it's anarchy." His own thoughts became foreign to him.

Malum paced, his boots clumping around the room. His brows arched up and then down like caterpillars, inching slowly along, occasionally pausing to consider Xander. "Picture a theater with a central stage surrounded by seats, and in those seats are people, lots of them. Now picture a platform projecting from an upper story and enclosed by railing, which projects out over the main floor." His tone swelled with pride.

"Okay?" Xander narrowed a single eye.

"We immortals are in the upper platform and the humans are in the seats below, and I own the building, so I own you now." Malum's deep tone carried. "There are hundreds of immortals walking the earth who you do not know. They all serve the Shroud, as *you* serve the Shroud! I don't know what lies Maximillian told you, but," he said with a sparkle in his eye, "Vincent and Noemi should serve as a warning example to any who question the Shroud."

"I don't want to kill people," Xander cried out.

Malum snarled a long groan. "You are young, Xander." He highly embellished the word young. "In all of your sixteen years of immortality, you have figured out the universe. Have you not? I suppose my seven thousand years, by comparison...is what...nothing compared to your infinite wisdom at sixteen. Don't incur my wrath, boy."

"No..." Xander shrank back.

"The humans are unreasonable so as to be ridiculous."

"What?" Xander asked, followed by a wary glance.

"They are a trite nothing." Malum placed his hands on his hips and his elbows bent outward. "They are unthinking animals. Their entertainment, their leaders, their entire society is influenced by ME!" he screamed, pointing his finger at his own chest, foaming at the mouth, spitting gobs of salivating rage. "They only live because of my will! And I will that the humans serve as fuel for the Shroud!"

Alcazar flapped his wings, jumping up and down high above the wooden beam. *Caw! Caw!* The jet-black crow continued pecking at the rope, unwinding the individual fibers, pulling at them with his beak, and each time, Xander felt it slack off with a dropping sensation.

Malum stretched his arm out toward Xander. From ten feet away, he squeezed his palm shut. Xander began to suffocate. His face strained and lips turned a bluish purple.

"You did poorly, and for that, this is your punishment." Malum trotted over and with balled fists hit Xander in the face, punching him with blow after blow, again-and-again, while a bedlam of laughs surrounded them in the asylum. He struck Xander's face until his knuckles drenched with blood. Malum took an old rag and wiped Xander's blood from his hands. Then he pulled a bottle of Absinthe from his pocket. He held the murky, green drink over his head in the air, licking his lips as he inspected it. "What a waste of a fine drink." He abruptly smashed the bottle against Xander's chest, and then summoned his blazing striker. "Don't worry. You'll survive this, but..." Malum wagged his finger, "it might sting a little." He touched the blazing striker to Xander's saturated chest. Xander instantly burst into flames from the combination of heat and Absinthe.

The fire scorched from chest up.

"AAAAHH! NOOOO!" Xander spun and thrashed wildly. The smell of cooked flesh permeated the room as he screamed.

"Yes, Alcazar, you're right, we have other places to be." Malum held a treat above his head, and the crow swooped down, grabbing the crumb, then landing on his shoulder while gobbling it up. Stroking Alcazar's feathers, he casually offered one last nugget of advice while Xander screamed aloud. "It wouldn't be so cruel or offensive if you just didn't think about the humans as significant."

Malum and Alcazar meandered out of the room, leaving Xander still bound. The flames spread quickly, now engulfing him. He howled and gyrated, swinging himself with momentum, yet this seemed to fan the flames rather than help him escape their scorching agony.

"You can't leave me like this!" Xander screeched. He moved his head back and forth, shaking his entire body as if in a seized fit.

Without a reply, Malum walked out the way he came, and back down the dark hallways of the insane asylum. He ignored Xander's desperate cries, yet he opened his hand, snapped his fingers, and the rope split in half.

Xander plummeted to the floor with a crash. Landing head first, he was unmoving in a pool of water, and all his sounds of protest were hushed in deathly silence.

Chapter Fifty-One

Moments later, a half a world away, Malum walked along a grassy knoll near a heavily wooded and remote area.

Up ahead, a blonde figure remained posed, clueless, and gawking at the distant landscape. Her face, once etched with contention, now seemed gazed upon nothing at all.

Malum snaked a sidewinding motion and slowly crept around the light-haired beauty. She was of fine breed. Her perfect skin was smooth, and reflected a porcelain glass quality in direct sunlight. Malum imposed the back of his hand against her soft cheek. He closed his eyes as he touched her silky, straight hair, rubbing the last follicles between his fingertips, and smelling it before he released the blonde, frosted tips.

When Malum had quenched his longings, he lastly plundered her moist lips, debasing them with the cracked, dry heat of his puckered skin.

At once, he held his hands at face level and clapped twice. Vanessa awoke from her stupor. She stood dumbfounded, with distressed scowls spreading from the center out to the far reaches of her attractive face.

"What? Where'd she go?" Vanessa looked at the wildflower clusters and sea-blown, long grass on which she trampled. But Revekka was nowhere in view. "I had her! She was right here a second ago!" She whipped her head in all directions, her eyes at a salute, her hands cupping over her brow, serving as shade from the glaring sun.

Malum removed himself near the dark wooded area. His hands each crossed parallel inside his long, belled sleeves. "My dear girl, don't tell me that you let Revekka speak, especially when I told you not to?"

Vanessa instantly realized her mistake. She covered her mouth, her eyes anticipating the worst. "I—I don't know what happened." She began to ramble incoherently and cry. "I had the map, and then she was telling me about what the Sphere Atlas does. Then...I guess she was gone and you were here."

A single black crow hovered high in circles overhead. Malum gestured a slithering shrug. "Save the false tears for someone else. You are my third first-in-command. The first, Noemi, betrayed me for that bum Vincent. The second, Dominic, was powerful and cunning, but his ambitions got him marooned on an island in the middle of the Pacific Ocean." With a swift, enquiring look, he tapped his index finger to his lip. "I had much higher hopes for you."

Vanessa's eyes fell. "I'm sorry."

"I know."

"Then what now?" She kept touching her long, silky blonde hair, moving lost strands behind her ear, while batting her lashes.

An uncomfortable pause advanced before Malum's next words. "Vanessa... what do you want most in the world?"

She quickly answered, "To serve the Shroud."

"Why?"

"Because it has shown me the truth."

Malum was not convinced that a stunning, clever girl in her teen years, like Vanessa, could be interested in such trivial things like truth, yet he played along. "You are beautiful, do you know that?"

"No." She admired the comment as much as she admired herself.

"Aha." Malum smiled. "Tell me..." He looked askance. "Was it troubling when Vincent chose Noemi over you?"

Vanessa hesitated. "What?" She shook her head, pretending not to understand.

"No, never mind." Malum flipped his hand up and away, dismissing the question with a frown.

Vanessa switched the conversation. "What of the other half of the map? Did you get it?"

"I tried to stop the other half of the Sphere Atlas from getting out of Europe, but one of our agents, Xander, was tortured by those," he pointed at the tip of a castle spire, which extended above the tree line, "hideous knights. I fear they will again use this map to destroy and kill many humans, causing only more fear among the mortal population." His eyes covered with a glassy film like sorrow hiding anger. "I believe an attack around Glasgow is imminent as a warlike act of revenge by the knights."

"What about those disgusting creatures you've been collecting?" Vanessa stroked her silky hair, inspecting the ends. "Can't we unleash them upon the castle now?"

"Soon the Dwellers will be ready, but not yet." Malum walked toward the dark forest. "Come, my dear."

"Where are we going?"

"We are following Alcazar. He is leading us to the next phase."

Vanessa watched as the crow silently floated in circles over the dense wood. Her innocent glimmer faded. She eyed Malum, who stood at the edge of the forest with its tightly packed trees and thick brush.

There was more to Vanessa than she ever cared to show. Malum knew as much, and enjoyed the game. Vanessa knew, but thought she had everyone fooled. She was a master of the arts, a skilled warrior, a beautiful girl, discreet and detached, yet complicated and able. Once a young knight herself, one of her former friends was Aurielle—a knight now hidden away in the castle up on the hill. And the best friend Vanessa wished she could forget was Noemi. Who, to her knowledge, was dead after Malum flung her off the ocean cliff behind where she stood, along with Vincent—who was a traitor to Vanessa's own jaded heart.

Vanessa took in a last pondering glimpse at the castle spire before entering the dark glen. She had unfinished business with Aurielle, and when she was done, this time, the redhead in the castle would pay back the favor she owed.

Until then, Vanessa was content to be Malum's number one in command of the Shroud. She would let the old, unsightly man look, and think he knew her, that is, until she was ready to stick her dagger into his heart and cut off his head.

Malum glanced back. "I say, child, are you coming or not?" He slipped through the forest, slithering between trees and weaving in and out of the thick brush nimbly and with nary a sound.

Vanessa eyed the beautiful flowers in front of her feet, admiring them, yet she smashed her foot down on top the bushel of blooms, crushing their petals, grinning afterward. She sped her pace, skipping, while following both Malum and the crow before each had disappeared altogether from her sight.

Vanessa paused briefly with a contemplative sigh before she too entered the dark woods.

After several miles up uneven, harsh, mountainous, rocky terrain, Malum and Vanessa reached a tall cellphone tower. Alcazar had beaten them there, flapping his wings and cawing from above on one of the metal branches of the tower.

"Now what?" Vanessa scratched her head. "Where are we?"

"We are exactly where we need to be." Malum slowly neared the base of the cellphone tower. He reached his hand out, and Alcazar suddenly flew from off the metal branch, quietly disappearing back into the forest.

Malum touched the cellphone tower. His body jolted forward, and his eyes rolled back before they closed. His body jerked in a controlled manner, and he began uttering gibberish.

At that moment, around the earth, cellphones of all kinds rang unexpectedly. In many different countries, and many different languages, hundreds of surprised owners grabbed their phones out their pockets and purses, yet before they could even say hello, a stranger in each case walked up and took the phone from out their hand.

Male and female alike, stole the phone, held it to their ear, speaking a single word, "okay," and afterwards, destroyed the phone, smashing it on the ground, much to the protest of the phone's owners.

Back at the cellphone tower on the mountain, Malum removed his hand, and he returned to his baseline self. "They're on their way." His knees gave out. He braced himself against a tree, almost dropping face first.

Vanessa grabbed his arm. "Are you all right?"

"Fine." Malum hunched forward, rubbing his sparsely growing strands of white, stringy hair. "Quick, we must get ready for their arrival."

"Who?"

"Hundreds of immortals that have dedicated their lives to the Shroud, and they are ready to destroy the knights' castle." Malum hurried his speech, appearing confused and unfocused. "Come, we must get back to camp."

"You need to rest." Vanessa was flustered. "Besides, what's back at camp, and what did you just do with the tower?"

Malum straightened his crooked, bony hands in prayerful fashion, placing them sideways against his lips, and then pointed them at Vanessa. "If you stay loyal, I will teach you the things of the Shroud, but first, a guest is coming."

"A guest?" Vanessa's voice pitched high at the end. "But what about that thing you just did." She pointed at the cellphone tower. "Is that why you're so weak now?"

"Oh, that." Malum flipped his wrist limply. "I'll teach you how to control every piece of human technology in the world, and I'll recover in time, so come, for we have much to do." He ushered her down the mountain with him, and back into the dense forest from which they came.

Chapter Fifty-Two

In one of those places where Malum caused the cellphone to ring, a young, baby-faced, gorgeous man entered Vatican City.

His entire being wrapped in style, he had an aqua-green suit jacket, with only a single of the coat's buttons buttoned. Underneath, he wore a loose white dress shirt, undone halfway down his chest, and faded jeans, along with sporty loafers on his feet without socks. With large, dark aviator sunglasses covering his eyes, his hair was short, nearly shaved on the sides and back, but long and flowing in layers, with a dry, natural look on top.

He strutted with a sort of entitled conceit, yet appeared unnoticed by the thousands of tourists gawking about. He seemed to know where he was going as if he had been there many times before, and he had a confidence of posture, a sureness few of his tender years possessed in the abundance he did.

He walked up to one of the restricted sections and waited for a moment. He glanced up at the sign on the ancient church before ignoring the restricted part. He ducked under a rope, after, walking up the building's stairs.

A man dressed as a priest put his hand up, stopping the youth from entering the building.

"You cannot be here!" The priest shot an immovable glare and stood in front of the baby-faced, young man. "Where did you come from? Who are you? I'm calling security."

The baby-faced youth simply pressed his lips together, quirking an upward, easy grin. "Though you do not know me, this is my house." Then with a piercing look and drifting grin, he said, "Now go and make me a sacrifice for your sinssssss!" He carried the S sound for a long second after.

The priest's eyes emptied. He dropped all individual thoughts, and his face sank into a waking sleep. "Yes, I can see you now in all your wonder and glory," the priest said to the baby-faced youth before he ran from the building entrance and down the street.

The baby-faced youth entered the building. With a casual flip of his finger, the heavy double doors opened for him. He sighed, walking up the middle aisle, passing rows of pews, until he took one of the front pews of the enormous, decadent cathedral.

He browsed around at its stained glass windows full of saints. He peered at a golden chalice representing The Holy Grail, and gilded crosses to Christ in the front above the altar. Though the building's wooden pews had a worn appearance, they were shiny, with a polished finish that even reflected the brilliant colors of the stained glass on each side from where he sat.

Soon after, the heavy double doors behind him opened again. This time, two large, brutish men in black suits appeared. They immediately parted on two sides, remaining at the back of the church as a small, but aggressive older man in a black, ankle-length, shiny silk robe approached.

He had a high forehead, with a receding hairline, and a beak-like nose. He walked toward the baby-faced youth in the front row, while the two larger men remained near the double doors on each side, with their backs against the wall of the building. The man with the beak-like nose carried an agitated expression as he walked down the aisle. His hands folded one on top of the other in front of him. His hard soles clicked, reverberating off the far walls, growing louder the closer he got.

The man with the beak-like nose stopped at the front row where the baby-faced youth was seated. He turned his beaked nose and gazed at the baby-faced youth, who did not look at the older man, but rather, ordered him.

"Sit, my old friend."

The man with the beaked nose in the black robe sat next to him, bowing before he did. "Yes, your eminence."

"Please...call me Skylar," the baby-faced youth graciously said. "We've known each other too long, so do away with formalities, Corbrak."

Corbrak nodded his head once. "It is done."

"Tell me the details then."

"I have taken over the council and disbanded it by using the corruption of the knighthood as justifiable cause before the people. I alone sit as the ruling party now."

"And the knights' temple?"

"Locked up and forbidden, but..."

"But..."

"But before we could apprehend the temple master, Acuumyn, I'm afraid he delivered the Sphere Atlas to the last remaining knights."

Skylar shrugged his shoulders. "I'm not worried. The knights are a relic of the past...not unlike this church." He gestured around at the stained glass windows. "The knights cannot harm us anymore. However..."

"Yes?"

"I am concerned about Malum." Skylar tilted his aviator glasses downward. His mild eyes hinted worry.

"Oh?"

"Yes, Malum seeks too much power. He's too ambitious." Skylar played with the handkerchief in his front jacket pocket, and then adjusted his aviator glasses over the bridge of his nose. "See how his army is coming along. Will you, Corbrak?" He winked at him.

With another silent nod, Corbrak tucked his heels under the hard, wooden pew. "Do you want me to...?" A commotion of screams outside the building interrupted his thought. "What was that?" Corbrak quickly stood.

Skylar remained seated. He also heard a crowd of people faintly moaning, yelling, and asking why. Nevertheless, he brushed it aside and minimized the commotion. "One of the priests just jumped to his death. It is a great day for the Shroud when one of little worth has fallen. It thus gives extra meaning and strength to our cause."

Corbrak gradually sat back down. Their body language regulated the conversation. Corbrak knew the answer now, so he dared not repeat the question. "I will use Dominic to kill Malum once he has finished gathering those vile...ugh...Dwellers."

Skylar turned toward Corbrak. A sly smugness kinked his lips as he leaned forward and gripped the pew's railing with his free hand. "Is he up to it?"

"Absolutely!" Corbrak said with conviction. "I have been watching him. He's been stranded, exiled, and alone on a small coral island for months. It has driven him crazy with rage toward Malum, and he has done nothing except gain skill and power."

"What if we're just trading one problem for another," Skylar retorted.

"Dominic is controllable." Corbrak subconsciously rattled his head from side to side. "Dominic wants simple things like prestige, wealth, and women. He takes no heed of the larger picture at all."

"Hum." Skylar rubbed his strongly chiseled chin. "Then make it so."

"Since there are no leap zones for apertures where he is, I will have a fishing boat veer off course. They will see Dominic and bring him back to the mainland," Corbrak elaborated.

"Good, now that just leaves me with the problem of my little princess."

Corbrak inquired with an upward eyebrow. "Your little princess?" he asked.

Skylar moped. "Well, I have to show some legitimacy before the people. And since the council is no more, we cannot leave the people without a ruler. Therefore, Danielle James, the only daughter and half offspring of the only successful human immortal union, is the heiress to the throne." Skylar tapped his index and middle fingers to his chest. "I will rule as king with Danielle, whether she likes it or not, as my queen for all eternity." His mouth soured a little. "I myself believe species should keep to their own kind, but as no other union has ever produced a child, let alone royal offspring, half or full blooded, it matters not at this point." He then pointed squarely at Corbrak's beak-like nose. "Times have changed," he said in an annoyed tone.

Corbrak tensed his lower lip. "What of Danielle's brother, David? Is he not a threat to the throne?"

"Danielle will kill him, ergo, completing her purpose for the Shroud."

"She has a boyfriend, Seth I believe," Corbrak chimed in again.

Skylar breathed loudly through his nose, spitefully glaring at Corbrak. "Have Malum send one of those repugnant monsters, one of those...Dwellers to deal with this Seth." Skylar shrank and tightened his lips into an easy frown. "Now go. Get what you need done, for we have other matters that need tending." He seemed abruptly disquieted in spirit and agitated by Corbrak's questions.

With that, Corbrak bowed again. He walked up the long middle aisle, and the two large men in suits left with him out through the double doors of the building.

Skylar just sat there. He looked all around. He crossed his arms and legs, leaning an elbow back atop the pew, exhaling in reflection, and relishing the silence of the church.

Chapter Fifty-Three

Thousands of miles and yet minutes later, Corbrak and his two large, brutish men in black suits approached a disheveled campground in a densely, wooded glen.

Flies swarmed the area and dung covered the dirt. Corbrak held his nose, pinching it with his fingers, biting his lip when he realized it was all over his shoes and freshly pressed black robe.

"I hate this place," Corbrak lamented. "I hate this realm. The whole thing is disgusting." He put his free hand in the air, halting the two large, brutish men with him to stay put as he neared and entered a green tent to a subterranean world.

Steps led down toward the burrowed caverns in the dirt. There was a single passageway bore out as with pike and shovel. Corbrak's pupils contracted from the bright sun as he entered the tent. His eyes dilated blindly in the darkness with each step down into the cool, moist underground. He touched the wall, smearing damp soil against his palm. He wished to rub it away, and though he peered everywhere, only the clean, upper half of his black robe seemed an option, so he left his hand dirty, grinding his teeth, and holding his palm far from his water silk robe.

A gravelly, male voice from up ahead in the unseeable dark called out, "Council member, Corbrak, how nice it is to see you with my one eye again." He walked up with a candle and plucked out his glass eye, holding it up to Corbrak's face.

"Get that thing away from me." Corbrak slapped, missing as the man put the glass eye back into his left socket. "And that's Duke Corbrak to you, Malum."

"Well...since we're playing those kinds of games, then it's Lord Malum to you."

"Yes, very well then." Corbrak became overly preoccupied by his surroundings. "Is that little Vanessa?" He leered. "Why she has grown up nicely indeed." His tone turned firm. "But she's hardly a suitable first-in-command for such a one as powerful as you, Lord Malum."

Without a word, Vanessa moved with cat-like reflexes, summoning a translucent dagger, its tip held inches near the carotid artery of Corbrak's neck.

"What were you saying?" Vanessa asked, her red lips just inches away from Corbrak's ear. "Is this suitable enough for you, Duke Corbrak?"

Malum crossed his right arm over his stomach, and his other hand cupped his chin under a wide smile. Laughing, he said, "Vanessa, is that any way to treat our guest?"

Vanessa removed her dagger from his throat.

Corbrak's tense frame relaxed, though moisture glistened on his high forehead. "I guess she'll do then." He had nothing with which to wipe his wet brow.

"Here." Malum offered a cloth that had bloodstains on one side.

Corbrak glared at the cloth, then at Malum before snatching the rag, patting his brow with the tiny clean section, and then wiping his hand before dismissively tossing it to the ground.

Vanessa, now at Malum's side, held a half smirk, but no words. Vanessa used her radiant, silver dagger as light in the dark tunnels.

"Do you have news, Duke Corbrak?" Malum asked emphatically.

"I do." Corbrak regained his composure. "The first immortal is pleased, and he wants to know if you're ready for the next phase."

"The next phase," Malum repeated. "Well then, this way." Malum waved Corbrak to follow him and Vanessa. "Did he say anything else...perhaps about me?"

"He did. He said he admires your ambition, and he has a special reward for your loyalty after the knights and their castle are destroyed."

Malum opened his crooked fingers, spreading them apart, bringing his hands together, he bounced tips against tips with delight. "Finally, I'll be noticed for all my service to the Shroud."

"I'm sorry." Corbrak interrupted. "I can't understand how you've been able to tolerate it here for so long."

"How do you mean?" Malum replied with an upward inflection.

"I mean, I hate this place. I hate everything in it. I can't wait to get back home, so how do you stand this foul smell, this filth, this chaotic place!" Corbrak locked his hands bent inward as if he were strangling a neck.

"It's not so bad...once you're here for a few thousand years that is." Malum tilted his head. "Right, Vanessa?"

"Yeah, whatever." Vanessa simply replied, rolling her eyes at Corbrak.

The three had walked for some distance. Malum reached up and unhooked a long stick wrapped in cotton rope, with beeswax melted on the top end of the stick and rope. He then instructed Vanessa to hold her radiant sai dagger up to the cotton beeswax portion of the long stick. She did and the torch lit a bright flame. It soon died back and burned a slow, dim flare for them.

Malum's free index finger pressed against his lips for silence among the group. He then gestured with the torch for Corbrak to inspect a dark room to his left side. Corbrak peeked in and saw hundreds of tame Dwellers bumping off each other and the walls in a sort of sleep-like state.

"Huh," Corbrak scoffed. "Is that all?" He quickly pulled his head out of the stinking, putrid chamber for a slightly fresher breath of air.

Malum grinned. "By my count, there are only seven knights left, all of them inside the castle."

Corbrak raised his voice and corrected, "Well, by my count..."

Malum held his index finger to his lips again. "Shush. Don't wake them."

Corbrak lowered his voice. "By my count, there are five hundred archers guarding the castle, thirty human children with our gifts guarding this realm, and seven powerful immortal knights protecting them all."

Malum nonchalantly countered, "The archers are mere humans, easily defeated, so too the children they train as knights. Those kids are just insolent wastes of time, trust me on that one."

"You don't have enough of these things." Corbrak's whole body shook and face reddened even in the dimly lit tunnels. "A single knight can kill a hundred of your genetically enhanced creatures. And while a hundred of your Dwellers hunted and killed millions of humans centuries ago, it took only ten knights, during the human's Dark Age, to exterminate five thousand Dwellers in one battle." Corbrak smashed his fist into his palm. "To this day, the world is none the wiser, but it was a crushing blow for the Shroud, and tipped the scales in the knights' favor."

Without a word, Malum glanced over at Vanessa. He squatted down and tossed the torch along the hallway up ahead. The torch skidded many feet before it came to rest, exposing hundreds of rooms on both sides of the passageways, and they were all just like the room Corbrak peeked his head through.

"Is that enough Dwellers for you?" Malum's arrogant tone resounded.

With his mouth agape, Corbrak's eyes widened. "Yes. Yes, it is! There must be ten thousand of those things."

"As usual, Duke Corbrak, you think too small," Malum retorted. "There are many more Dwellers than that."

Vanessa rolled an upturned chin and a short, curled smile at Malum. "Yes, Lord Malum, you are magnificent." Her eyes darted quickly toward Corbrak.

Malum stood straight. He raised his palms upward over his head, and with trembling hands he thundered, "Behold! My legion of Dwellers!"

Chapter Fifty-Four

From the peaceful Mediterranean fields, Vincent fled. Hunched over, he winced, grabbing at his back. Ulcers filled with pus oozed from puncture wounds around his spine. His legs grew heavy, so he dragged them onward. Taking the road less traveled, he groaned with each step, and with each step, he felt weaker. Rags wrapped around his burnt hands. His cheeks sucked inward, his jaw and cheekbones protruding, and the rest of his gaunt face blackened in patches with charred dust.

The howling winds pushed him backward. The hot sun beat upon his head. The cold rains soaked, chilling him to the bone. The clear nights were icy, yet quiet and comforting. Gingerly lying on his back, examining the night sky, only among the stars could he see her now. The constellations outlined Noemi's curves. The intolerable solitude detached his physical pain. Regret and remorse bogged Vincent in a state of constant denial and despair.

The images appeared so real, he could reach out and interlock fingers along the golden wheat fields with her once more. He felt her soft skin. Her flowery aroma dallied on his clothes. Her laugh, her smile, her kindness, and love, forced him to smile while beholding a universe of glittery charms in the black expanse. A cold wind rustled leaves past his huddled place in the shadowy woodlands. His smile, like her spirit, suddenly vanished.

He got up and kept walking, though he knew not where or why. At least, he figured, walking felt like he was doing something to find her.

He shut off his thoughts, for they consumed and slowed him to nothing. He ignored the grumbling in his stomach. His tongue became dry and unbearable. He did not understand how the cabin, safe and secret, burned to the ground. He mumbled incoherently to himself. "What happened? Where are you? Who did this? By god, they'll pay!"

Vincent learned many things he never knew during those slowly rapid passing days and nights. The pain from his back grew worse. The Dwellers had wounded him badly. He vomited, and dry heaved many other times. His core felt uneasily warm. It was cold out, yet his heart restlessly fluttered and his brow dripped.

He avoided people, even hiding when he saw them.

He could not remember the last time he ate, so against his better judgement, Vincent diverted travel to the nearest town. His balance off, his eyesight dim, he experienced spurts of dizziness. The people's faces were distorted, they all seemed to stare at him, some talking, others pointing.

He bumped into various people. They pushed him to the ground, muttering "filthy bum," before continuing on their way.

He stole a woman's scarf from a vendor, ducked down an alley, and tied it over his head. He grabbed a discarded wooden crutch, and leaned most his weight on the Y-shaped divide before exiting town with a portion of donated bread and water.

Two large men had been following Vincent since he walked into town. One wore a black, wool, Greek fisherman's cap with a leather band around the crown and short visor. The other bunched rolls of extra skin under a double-breasted, dark gray, tattered navel coat. Both were large men with scowls and scheming eyes. Neither exchanged a word with the other. Rather, a series of head nods and looks guided the other to follow. They tailed at a distance, and then closed in on Vincent when he made his way out of town and onto a wooded trail.

"Hi there, mate." One of the men grabbed Vincent by the scruff of his collar.

"What da ya got there?" The other punched him in the back.

"Aaah!" Vincent screamed. His ulcers popped. More pus oozed from his back. The pain from the sores buckled his knees, dropping him without a fight.

The two men rummaged through Vincent's belongings, sparse as they were.

"This filthy bum don't got nottin'."

"Let's kill him."

"Why?"

"Why not?"

One of the men pulled a knife from inside his coat pocket. The other man kicked Vincent repeatedly in the stomach and head, grinning between kicks.

"This is for not having anything to steal," the man kicking Vincent said.

"Ohhh! Argh! Stoppp," Vincent faintly uttered. He reached toward them. "Noemi..." his words faded. His hand dropped. His head and neck lurched upward, but rolled to the cold ground after. Saliva and blood flowed out his mouth as words and movements ceased.

The man with the knife raised it back. "Yeah, and this is for bein' a filthy bum, you filthy bum."

Neigh! Neigh! A horse appeared suddenly. Its hooves high in the air, it clopped down in front of the men. Their eyes startled and spread wide, the man dropped his knife, and the two fled back toward the town.

The horse settled. It was hooked to an old, worn vardo—a Gypsy wagon. It had two small wheels in front and two much larger wheels in the back. It was green, though the paint blanched amid bare wood in missing chips and timeworn weather damage.

The wagon had four windows, one attached to a door where the horse reigns lay, and three tiny windows, two on the side with brown shutters, and one on the back end of the wagon without shutters.

The door swung open.

A pitchfork emerged. Jabbing out the door several times, then the pitchfork drew back inside. A frumpy, waddling older woman appeared. Her eyes pierced a weary haunt. Rows of beaded necklaces swayed back and forth, rubbing against each other as she moved. She covered her head with a long, purple bandana, yet her white hair flowed down her shoulders and back from under the bandana. Several heavy, gold earrings dangled, tugging at the skin on her earlobes. She wore a lengthy, not purposefully tight, Bohemian style, long-sleeved dress. She also wore outer layers of thinner fabric and a shawl covering over her dress.

Vincent, vision impaired and senses dulled, only saw the glimmer of a silver crescent moon necklace that hung low around her neck as she approached. She waddled slowly down the wagon's steps, and the wagon leaned from each side as she stepped. She narrowed her eyes and carefully glanced up and around through the woods.

She quickly walked over to where Vincent lay and kneeled next to him.

"After all this time, they still torture us." She wiped the blood from his mouth. "Oh, my!" she pulled up his shirt and put her hand over her mouth when she saw his skin. "You are in trouble, my friend."

His eyes rolled back. The light in the sky vanished. The trees and branches quieted. Everything went black for Vincent.

Sometime later, Vincent felt a jostling, his body ever so slightly swaying. He opened his eyes. There was a small window above him. The branches outside were moving. He was in a lumpy, but comfortable bed, wrapped in a heavy quilt. He pulled back the quilt and noticed his wounds were dressed. A white cloth wrapped firmly around his stomach, back, and hands. He tried to sit up, but grimaced and settled back down when his body could not move as he needed.

"Where am I? Who are you?" Vincent softly shouted. It hurt to even speak.

The wagon came to a stop. A large, round shadowy figure blocked the light as it neared the part of the wagon where he lay.

"You are hurt. You are too thin. What happened to you?" a low, dense female voice gently said.

Vincent moved away from her. "Those demons back there, the ones that attacked me in the woods..."

The large woman lit a lantern and held it to her kind, aged face. "My friend, that was days ago, and they were not demons, but just bad men." She moved closer and sat next to him on the bed. "I didn't know if you'd ever wake up."

"What? No, I have to...I have to...I don't know. I can't remember."

"It's a shame they won't leave us Gypsies alone." She reached out and touched another bandage wrapped around his head.

"Gypsies?"

"Yes, Gypsies." She raised an eyebrow. "How did you get such deep puncture wounds on your back?"

"I was fighting...I think." He winced, grabbing at his back. He sat up with her help. "I don't really know."

"My name is Mala."

"I'm..."

"It is all right." Mala placed her hand over his. "You will remember when your body heals."

Vincent vigorously rubbed his palm to his forehead. "The pain, why won't it stop?"

"I have medicine for you." She reached over, lifted a teakettle, and poured foul-smelling liquid into a cup. "Here. Drink."

Vincent inched the cup to his lips. He looked up at Mala and sipped. "Oh, that's worse than it smells."

"I know, but it is making you better."

"Are you sure?" Vincent puckered.

"You were septic, my friend." She touched the binding wraps covering his back and stomach. "If not for the silver dressings to the ulcers from those punctures, and this tea from an ancient tree extract, you would be dead by now."

Mala smiled. She got up and walked back toward the front of the wagon.

"Thank you." Vincent took a deep, painful breath.

Mala stopped and peered back at him. "Just get better, my friend."

"Mala."

"Yes?"

"I keep seeing the face of a beautiful woman in my mind. I think she's in trouble, or something bad happened to her. I need to go."

Mala turned around to face Vincent. "You can't move, so how can you help? You don't even remember your own name. Here." She untangled one of her many long, beaded necklaces and placed it in his hand.

"What's this?"

"A tool for deep thoughts." Mala turned around and went back to the front of the wagon, and it began to move again, gently swaying from side to side.

Vincent looked at the beaded necklace. He stared out the window above him.

The melancholy sky darkened with clusters of gray clouds, none of which had a silver lining. He unknowingly rubbed the beaded necklace together. The friction hummed in his hand. Quicker he rubbed the beads between his fingers and thumb. Other images danced around his mind, images too bizarre to explain. He remembered a man with a scarred face and glass eye, a strong young man in a trench coat, and a subway station. Then he saw three demonic creatures attacking him from all sides at nighttime. He saw a vivid castle on a mountaintop, with grand spires, flaming torches, high walls, and hundreds of archers. He saw a glowing sword in his hand, and then, he saw her—she was in amongst golden wheat fields. She smiled and beckoned him to follow her. She was beyond beautiful. She was beauty itself.

"Come on. Hurry up, come get me," her feminine voice echoed, and she playfully laughed.

"Who are you? WHO ARE YOU?" Vincent whispered with frustration. His eyes grew large. He gasped and dropped the beaded necklace. Reaching toward the window, he sat up and yelled aloud, "She needs me!" He slid back into bed and repeated, "She needs me. She needs me." An orange, black, and white spotted butterfly briefly rested on the glass before it flew off, and Vincent gently faded into sleep.

Glossary

THE PEOPLE, PLACES, AND THINGS

Once, immortals had a singular vision...until the Shroud appeared. Now thousands of years of human history have been shaped by something other than humankind. Two immortal factions have developed a long-standing and ever-growing divide. Unseen to human eyes, immortal knights are trying to protect our world from the Shroud's manipulations.

Yet as the pendulum of power fluctuates between the immortal knights and the Shroud, an ancient evil arises. Dwellers threaten to unveil the immortals' mystical, cloaked presence to the eyes of humanity.

Today, the most dangerous is that which is least likely, and the truly impossible lies in changing one's mind.

And so begins the epic journey...

Acerbus, age 6,483

The last immortal king, his reign was pure and true, yet then, Acerbus forgot his vows, and lost his purpose.

A magnificent king who brought peace to the immortals, yet when he was a small child, his grandmother had his siblings and parents killed by his father's own royal guard. Acerbus was hidden away, thought dead, but at a tender age, ripped the throne away from his grandmother. Nevertheless, as a young adult, his obsession with the prophecy of two children born of two worlds became his undoing. Jealousy crept into his soul. Acerbus permitted his own heart to harden against his people, his goodness melted away, and his rule over them became a harsh one.

Acuumyn, age 6,501

Acuumyn is only a title for the spiritual leader of the knighthood as their guiding compass in a desolate world.

The keeper of the temple where younglings are chosen to become knights, Acuumyn has never seen a bleaker time than now for his students. The temple has been locked from his access. Almost all of his former knights in training have turned to Malum and the Shroud, but still he hopes, for a person needs hope, even if all hope is lost. That is why he has broken every sacred command of the immortals to deliver the Sphere Atlas to Revekka and Maximillian. He needs them to transport the powerful device to the knights' last stronghold, a castle on the other side of the earth. To Revekka alone he gives a cryptic message—to bid his son inside the castle, a last goodbye.

Alcazar

Of all Malum's companions, Alcazar is his most trusted, even if he is just a crow.

With feathers so black they appear blue, Alcazar jealously defends his master every chance he gets. One of the smartest creatures on Earth, Alcazar fashions himself the smartest of his kind. Madly hopping about on his T-shaped perch, he caws for Malum's attention as well as the crumbs in his pocket.

Apertures

Portals and gateways for instantaneous travel around the world.

Not every immortal is powerful enough to summon an aperture. Not all locations have an aperture to summon, but if you can find one, it's the only way to travel.

Apollos, age 15

Undersized for his age, he is the only son of the keeper of the temple, Acuumyn. Even if no one else believes in him, he quietly embodies the greatest ideals of the knighthood, but not the fight.

A knight in training, Apollos hasn't the stomach for a fight, but he knows all the rules. He's found it hard to be the son of the knights' guiding overseer, but he is secretly watching David James and Danielle, protecting them without their knowing.

The Artifex

A skill, a craft, a power wielded by the Shroud and knights alike.

The Artifex can be used by more skilled immortals to summon metaphysical weapons. The striker is the weapon of choice. Immortals can summon swords/strikers of unique and great power. With this power, immortals can push objects, pull fates together, and bend the collective will of humanity.

Aurielle, age 14

A young, fiery knight with a strong sense of righteous indignation.

Aurielle wants to be the knight she was always meant to be. However, in order to do that, she needs to remember the story of Vincent and Noemi when matters of her own heart are at stake. Balanced and sensical, she is well aware that knights are forbidden to marry or have intimate love, for it pollutes dedication to the commitment made when facing the ultimate price.

Benoit, age 17

Big, strong, muscular, and fast, he has the bravery and power of a knight, but still there is something lacking.

Full of bravado, and second in command to castle master Caaron, Benoit is ready to lead the knights into the coming immortal war, even if he's the only one who thinks this. Fighting on behalf of humans, which he's certain are inherently flawed and unredeemable, Benoit quietly bides his time for something better.

The Bleary Guild

From father to son, and mother to daughter, the archers have served as mortal ambassadors along the castle walls for thousands of years.

An esoteric society, some humans have friended the immortal knights from the beginning. The Bleary Guild is such a group. These archers were trained by immortals, so their arrows soar with accuracy. One notable member of the Bleary Guild once called Sherwood Forest his home.

Blood Eclipse

A time when Malum will use all his powers to block out the sun.

In order for the Dwellers to attack the castle, the sun needs to disappear. Fortunately, for the Dwellers, Malum has that covered.

Caaron, age 6,595

He is the keeper of the castle in the mountains of southern California.

Elderly, Caaron has lived a long and rich life, but alas, he was mortally wounded by Malum during the Shadow Harvest. Caaron is now bed fast. His immortal powers have faded with his advanced age. His time is running out, and a new successor has not been chosen to lead in his place. Yet, he foresaw this, and back in the Dark Ages, he planted a seed in all the races of humanity to save them in our time.

Cascades of Nicodemus

Hidden in a cave along a vast desert, the pools of water reside, and it is here that every mortal life can be viewed in full.

Named for the philosopher that discovered the cascades, Nicodemus said that no one should take liberties of judgement by watching the cascades watery reflection upon gross imperfection. Acerbus knew the writings of Nicodemus well from youngling to adult, yet he kept looking, so as to desire things he ought not, thus twisting his thoughts unfavorably.

The Castle

The castle is the last safe place on Earth. The castle is a refuge for the knights, the Bleary Guild, and a few mortal children who have the gift.

Invisible to mortal eyes, the castle is immense, with hundreds of rooms, secret tunnels, hanging gardens, and hundred-foot walls. This is where the knights battle and train. The last flicker fruit tree resides within the castle's walls. The source of all life remains hidden beneath its cobblestone streets.

Celestial Pyre

A flame that lives and breathes life into all life.

Only a few knights know of its existence. The Celestial Pyre provides the mystic power harnessed by all immortals and a few mortal children. The flame has been dying for a thousand years, and not even its keeper, Ericson, knows what will happen when it finally burns out.

Corbrak, age unknown

A former member of the Doyen Council—a council of immortals who ensure that dealings between humans and immortals remain free from tampering—Duke Corbrak has dissolved the council in the midst of an uprising by the knighthood.

Corbrak loves his secrets, secrets he's kept from Malum, and even secrets he's kept from the Shroud itself. Corbrak is content to serve the one who leads the Shroud. He has locked the doors to the knights' temple, and as far as he's concerned, the knights are an outdated culture fit only for destruction.

Danielle James, age 15 and ¾

Twin sister of David James, though she tells everyone she's older, if only by a few seconds.

The only daughter of a hardworking, single mother, Danielle has always believed her father died in a car accident the day she was born. Recently, Danielle discovered the truth, that her father was an immortal, and that he died while protecting his two children from those that would take them away. Danielle wants nothing to do with her immortal half. She wants to go to prom, keep a boyfriend, and go to college...that is if she can see the point to anything in life anymore.

The Dark Arts and Sciences

The things in the darkness are not always evil, but rather gifts and powers that are poorly understood by the willfully ignorant.

How can a knife be used to both cut a tomato and yet kill a person? Many immortals have wondered how and why the power gifted them from an eternal source could be used for both good and bad deeds. Malum coined the phrase "dark arts and sciences" because he's the self-proclaimed professor of gray, and he believes gray has more to teach than the black and white imparted by the knights.

David James, age 15 and slightly less than ¾

Non-identical twin of Danielle James, he's a happy-go-lucky sort with a quick temper and a talent for being bullied.

In the history of history, no immortal human bond has ever produced offspring, but David and his sister are the first and only. Their birth remained a secret from even the wisest immortal, yet when the siblings grew, they garnered attention both good and bad for their unique gifts. Unlike his sister, when learning of the immortal's prophecy concerning them, David embraced the idea of destiny and freewill as not opposites, but equals in his life. School bores him, yet he always knew greater things called from afar.

Dominic, age 19

Once the first-in-command under Malum, he was banished to a desert island by the Shroud, yet he is plotting his revenge, and though there is no rescue in sight, his vengeance will not be late.

A former knight, Dominic hates Jak. Dominic hates Vincent. Dominic hates humans, especially half-breeds, but Dominic loved Noemi, that is, until she got with that loser Vincent. Now everything just plain sucks, so he'll have to settle for the next best thing...power, lots of it, and then maybe he'll get Noemi back, or kill her while trying.

Doyen Council

A council set up to prevent the misuse of power by any potential monarchy.

A group of eleven overseers who decide matters of right and wrong versus legal and illegal behaviors. Acuumyn and Corbrak are both members of the Doyen Council. To disobey a command from the Doyen Council means death, even for a king.

Dwellers, ages unknown

Dwellers do three things very well. They kill to eat, they kill to briefly take the shape of a human, and they kill to create more Dwellers.

History has been rewritten hundreds of times to protect the present. One of those times, the Dwellers had nearly wiped out all human life, and ever since then, the power of immortals over human society has shifted out of balance. Dwellers are not simply a mindless horde, but rather they are as unique as you and I, for they once were like you and I. Some have been so many people, like Killian, they can no longer remember who they were in the beginning anymore. The same substance that gives the immortals everlasting life, keeps the Dwellers in a state of everlasting death and decay. For the legend of mighty Dwellers now thought to be extinct, only a few lowly ones hunt the Parisian catacombs as specters for whatever the tunnels provide.

Echoes

A brief opening into an aperture after another immortal passes through.

Whenever an aperture is opened, there's a split second between when it closes and when it disappears, and these split seconds are called echoes. In theory, another could follow the one that opened the aperture through the echoes left. However, echoes can be unstable, unpredictable, and dangerous, and thus, unsuitable except as a last option of travel.

Emma Rose, age 14

She craves acceptance and love from her mother, but feels her mother is selfish, which lowers her own self-worth.

An only child of recently divorced parents, she is on her first trip to Paris with her mother. Resentful of her mother's constant texting and recent plastic surgery, she secretly laments her own drab appearance when compared to other girls around her. When Killian takes notice of her, Emma's entire view of life changes.

Emma's Mother, age 32

Recently divorced, she loves her only child Emma like a best friend.

When life gives you lemons, go to Paris with your daughter. Busy texting and looking good, life is short, so eat dessert first, besides, it's not like anything bad ever happened to anyone while on vacation, right?

Ericson, age unknown

A quiet and reserved man, he is the lone keeper of the sacred Celestial Pyre.

Ericson usually doesn't say much, but when he speaks, you can bet his words are well thought and holy. He communes with the mystic source of all life with profound respect, even though many immortals know not of its existence, he guards and cares for it both day and night.

Eruditus

A paradise. A place where all immortals originate.

Eruditus is a place of bliss, at least it used to be. It is not another planet, but rather a realm, a state of mind, a perfect place for all well-meaning immortal inhabitants.

The First Immortal

To some, the first immortal is the bogeyman, to others it is myth, yet a few worship the first immortal as a deity.

Someone has to be pulling the strings of the leaders and money in the system, yet almost no one knows who that person is. The knights scoff at the notion of a first immortal, for they argue no such thing exists. However, the Shroud claim to answer to said first immortal, vowing to fight the immortal war to rid the earth of those who doubt his presence.

Flicker Fruit

A fruit that flickers every color of the rainbow. It is the source both of everlasting life and everlasting death.

Flicker fruit used to grow in orchards, yet now there is but a single tree left. Its properties are life itself, but those who separate the colors in concentrated juices, bring forth a scourge upon the world.

Galinea / knights / knighthood — to be gallant

A Galinea is a knight who has taken the vow of knighthood: To have faith and to be noble.

The Galinea are knights that have fulfilled their training and experienced a mission. Knights are forbidden to partake of worldly pleasures, most of all, relations with another knight or mortal. Many Galinea have lost their lives protecting humanity. Many still have died trying to destroy the dark lord Malum. There are no more knights in training. The last knights are waiting for the final war–the immortal war.

Golden Glass Orbs

One of the items left over from the immortals' technological age.

The Golden Glass Orbs are golden orbs that radiate safe, cold fusion. They are everlasting sources of clean energy for immortals.

Immortals

A group of people not unlike their human counterparts.

Not supernatural creatures of any kind, immortals have manipulated human society invisibly for thousands of years. With the best of intentions, some have helped advance human knowledge, while others purposely steer humankind off into destruction as a sort of sadistic game.

Immortal War

A war in which the world will not end, but rather change forever.

The knights have dwindled to a handful, all of them holed up inside the castle. The Shroud has hundreds of immortals and thousands of Dwellers waiting to tear down the castle walls at the rising of the Blood Eclipse.

Jak, age 20

Vincent's older brother. A mighty knight secretly betrothed to Noemi. Jak pushes Vincent hard, only because he knows how strong his younger brother truly is.

Unlike his younger brother, Jak believes a person is defined by their actions. He studied under the greatest knights in the temple, and now he's ready for his mission. Jak was disheartened when Vincent left the temple, forsook the knighthood, and followed after Noemi. During a stormy night in a deserted New York subway station, Jak finally caught up to Vincent.

Joanne James, age 36

Mother to David and Danielle James, she is widowed by her husband Nathaniel.

Much debate remains whether Joanne knew any of her husband's immortal beginnings before they met. Yet, after she learned the truth, Joanne protected her children from what she knew of their father's secret life.

Killian, age unknown

A gorgeous, young, edgy man with eyes for Emma, who is much more than the stylish boy he appears to be.

There's a cool, yet desperate quality about him. His cold eyes can look upon Emma as she has always wished to be viewed, or gloss over with instant contempt. He's full of questions, not least of all remembering who he used to be. Now a Dweller, he has never fully committed to their ways, and so harkens toward Emma—a hint of what he desires from his present life, to live again.

Kimi, age 12

A young Native American girl from the Lakota tribe, Malum has promised to protect her from the evil world.

A human, she has the gift. There are several humans around the world endowed with a rare ability only immortals were thought to have had. At a certain age, if not released, these young ones will simply grow up as humans, never knowing what power lies inside. During the Shadow Harvest, the knights and the Shroud raced around the world to collect or destroy these gifted individuals before they could be turned to the other side. Kimi is one such human, but her tender years may very well be her undoing.

Knights' Temple

A place of mystic, spiritual energy and enlightenment where younglings learn the way.

It is hoped that just a few of the younglings chosen by the temple turn into balanced, wise knights. However, no one foresaw the destruction of the temple and loss of the entire class of youngling knights in one fell swoop.

Leap Zones

Cars, trains, and airplanes are fine in a pinch, but for immortals, nothing beats a leap zone.

The transit system for immortals, leap zones are hotbeds where aperture travel is most viable. Leap zones can be miles in diameter, or a few feet. Leap zones are plentiful, but vast areas of Earth have no leap zones, making normal travel necessary in the forms of boats, cars, planes, as well as other commonplace travel until an immortal reaches the nearest leap zone.

M, age 14

The newest Dweller, M has Killian's eye, and protection.

A reluctant sort, M never wanted this so-called life of everlasting death, but choices can be ironic like that. M can't remember what she, he, or it, was or is. However, nothing feels right, everything seems wrong, even if Killian says those feelings will disappear once a first life is consumed.

Mala, age unknown

A Gypsy, she's an elderly woman traveling across Europe in her weathered, horse-drawn wagon.

She doesn't have many possessions, but she's willing to give those in need what is needed. Little is known about Mala, but she knows who she is, and that's really all that matters.

Malum, age 7,326

An immortal endowed and practiced in the dark arts and sciences, and leader of the Shroud.

He is one of the most powerful immortals that roam the earth. Malum has shaped human society from fledgling tribe to empire, and finally to civilization's ruin countless times, all in the name of experimentation. A fickle and pedantic man, he loves power, and manipulates people and outcomes just for the sport of it. He single-handedly destroyed the source of the immortals' immortality, all to gain a resource he deems fit only for himself. Malum, in a failed experiment, both created the Dwellers and lost his left eye, scarring his face terribly for time indefinite.

Maurice, age 18

A true geek who pursues the supernatural down in the catacombs.

Not nearly as clever as he thinks he is, and after stealing a 12th century book from Notre Dame Cathedral, he is on the trail of the legendary, urban myth of Dwellers. A self-proclaimed cataphile—one who tags the deepest sections of the catacombs for sport—Maurice has recently acquired a videotape of a competitor, another cataphile that was dragged off by Dwellers just months before, never to be seen again. Sophie and Maurice argue and fight about its validity, but soon the two kiss wildly, making up, while plotting their next crime.

Maximillian, age 5,593

One of the old guard, knighted in a more civilized time, he is much stronger than even his blade.

Full of self-denial and individual restraint, nothing is ever personal, but it is the duty of obligation that drives Maximillian to judge the worth of those around him. Knighted long ago, he knew Malum as a force for good. He had a chance to stop the self-proclaimed dark lord Malum once, but Maximillian hesitated, for he loved peace and despised killing. However, that was then, this is now, and the darkness has grown too powerful to be stopped even by his mystic blade.

Mortals

Humans.

Humans are subject to sickness, death, accidents, and many other non-immortal occurrences. Some immortals hate humans, some immortals feel pity upon humans, but all immortals are forbidden by the Doyen Council to directly interfere with their civilization, though this command has gone widely ignored. The Shroud and knights are nearing the end of five thousand years to prove whether humanity has the right to rule itself.

Nathaniel James, age unknown

An immortal with more than just the secret of immortality in his blood.

Nathaniel is the father of David and Danielle James. He died while protecting their presence. An unknown person, with enough power to kill an immortal, hunted him to the ends of the earth. Nathaniel, a royal, is the last heir to the throne of Eruditus. As heir, his kingship is above that of any who has ever ruled on Earth.

Noemi, age 19

The onetime knight, the onetime first-in-command for the Shroud, she gave it all up for Vincent, but would she do it again?

To know her is to love her, yet can one ever really know someone? An ambitious romantic, Noemi has forsaken the ways of the sword. She has turned her back on everything except the only one she has in this world. She loved Vincent's older brother Jak, yet she was in love with Vincent from the start, which eventually led to Jak's destruction at the hands of the Shroud. For too long, she played both sides, never knowing which side she really favored until the day Vincent jumped to his certain death while trying to save her life. They embraced once more as the jagged rocks from the fierce ocean below reached up for them in thirsty revenge for the life they had taken.

Nytmar, age 666

Appropriately named for its skill of snatching bodies from warm beds without so much as a scream.

Nytmar is the thing that goes "bump in the night." Under cover of darkness, recessed in the shadows of closets, and underneath beds, Nytmar has quietly marked its prey. Once a target has been marked, a final splash of red is the only color that lingers amidst rows of serrated fangs.

The Prophecy

In the knights' temple, there are many scrolls that say a great many things, and those things are all open to interpretation.

One of those prophecies alludes to a half-immortal, half-human child, or children. Though even among the knights and holy men of the temple and Doyen Council, there is disagreement. It is believed by Acuumyn that David and his sister Danielle James are the ones the prophecy is talking about, for they are the only offspring of an immortal-human conception. Many prophecies speak in general terms. Some prophecies speak of one sibling killing the other, while another prophecy speaks nothing of this, but rather, of a future free from uncertainty due to the siblings. Whatever the prophecies say or do not say, the knights and the Shroud seek the same thing, to control the future.

The Reckoning

Little is known about the Reckoning, but according to the knights' prophecies, it is coming for us all.

Those with money, influence, and power, know their real strength resides in knowledge. The Reckoning, like the Big Bang, will instantly disseminate the esoteric knowledge of a few, to everyone, thus restoring balance to the world. During the Reckoning, individuals will be faced with their true selves. Some will try to escape, but no escape from themselves will they find. Others, those crushed by the system, will rise up with the ability to both know, and the gift of reestablishing a world meant for so much more, a world of delight, a world of their making. For as the prophecy says: Whatever they do, they will accomplish, and whatever they accomplish, they will have happiness in doing. Never again will monarchs rise, subjecting their citizens to harsh rule and devious manipulations.

Recur, age 753

Recur is twice as good as any other Dweller, other Dweller.

Once a cult follower of the Shroud, Recur willfully traded the precious gift of human life for the meager existence bestowed upon him. When many Dwellers were killed by immortal knights in 1534, Recur was injured badly. His head nearly crushed, yet somehow he survived, but at a cost. Recur repeats the words of everything he says twice, and even when he consciously tries, he still can't stop, can't stop.

Revekka, age 6,042

The last empath, she is an envoy attempting to bridge the gap between humans and immortals before time runs out for both.

She truly has her finger on the pulse of the world. Revekka has served on Earth in the capacity as watcher for five thousand years. She has sworn an oath, like most knights, to never unduly interfere with human history. Recently though, the world has turned bleak with an invisible darkness, and after being contacted by the mysterious source of all life, she is called into action. Nonetheless, Revekka has the directive to transport the Sphere Atlas to the knights before the Shroud attains the living map.

Royalist

There will always be rulers, and if there are always rulers, someone needs to be ruled over.

For thousands of years, the royalists have waited for a time when people could be subdued without war, and that time is now. Malum, a proud member of the royalist party, knows humans need a strong hand to govern them. In the past, Malum has waged wars, but he underestimated the people's will for freedom, so now, he has lulled them into a passively stagnant state of existence. Royalists seek to bring about a one world government to Earth. They desire an immortal king upon a throne rather than human presidents and leaders. Malum knows that before you establish a permanent world government, you need to divide the population, break its will, and though trust is not important, many have to rely only upon the system for their needs.

The Shadow Harvest

A race by the Shroud and knights to gather the mortal children with the immortal gift.

For a short period of time, human children were discovered to possess a certain power and ability on a subconscious level. Immortals sought to either destroy or adopt these children. Some now reside in the castle, while others joined the Shroud.

The Shroud

A group of former knights, former aristocrats, and former politicians.

The Shroud believes ideas are the most dangerous things in the world, and hope, more dangerous still. Humans need a strong, one world government, and now, religion, the Shroud's tool for distraction, has served its purpose and needs to be abolished. The Shroud has blamed the knights for the destruction of all immortality with the death of the flicker fruit trees. The case of humanity vs the Shroud is now considered null and void, and only the immortal war can subdue the earth in the eyes of the Shroud.

Skylar Blackwell, age unknown

Always thinking ten steps ahead, he's the last person anyone would expect to be the first immortal.

To him, the Shroud is just a ploy, the knights are a nuisance, but religion is his greatest device to divide and conquer humanity, why even Evolution is a religion. Everyone on Earth believes in something, even if their something is nothing at all, it's still something to believe in. Skylar seeks to control all facets of human and immortal society, and to rule over them without end. For this to happen, many must die at his hands, those most dangerous first. He believes in the prophetic writings in the temple, for if he did not, he wouldn't be stalking the last royal female on Earth. For Skylar knows to win the immortals' support, he must marry the hybrid human and immortal teen, Danielle James. However, her younger brother David has claim to the throne, which is a problem for them, because neither sibling is aware of this as they live out their quiet life going to school and doing whatever else human teens do these days.

Slash, age 921

Some say Slash is the first Dweller. Others say he's the first of Malum's mistakes.

With exceedingly long, razor sharp talons, Slash has earned his name by eviscerating whatever's in his way. Slash, the self-appointed leader of the Dwellers, a chief rival to Killian, has forgotten an important detail—why Malum looks so familiar to him, yet Malum looks forward to reminding Slash of their shared history.

Snare, age 723

They taste better when they run.

Snare lives for the chase. According to him, the increased adrenaline tastes so much better than frozen fear. Snare is on the hunt, and the hunt is always on. He's been known to play with his food by allowing it to escape several times before hunger and boredom rips all flesh apart.

Sophie, age 15

Worldly beyond her years, she's cunning in all the wrong ways.

The streets are the only home she's known. Sophie controls every situation, especially those that seem out of her control. She's the brains behind her grab and ditch plots, and Maurice, her on-again, off-again boyfriend, is the muscle. She doesn't share any of her boyfriend's superstitious ideas, but she's in it for the loot while trudging through the catacombs.

The Sphere Atlas

A vestige from the immortals' technological age.

The Sphere Atlas is two scrolls that when combined, becomes a living map to every aperture in the world. It is a most rare and sought after device.

Striker

There is no weapon so powerful as a striker.

It takes an immortal years to master the art of summoning a striker. The striker becomes part of the one who wields it. Each striker is unique to its user, absorbing the personality of the one exerting its ability. Strikers glow with translucent shades of blue, green, red, black, purple, and many other colors, each color revealing the heart's intentions of its master. Strikers manifest with electrical currents, subdued flames, and even ashy smoke, yet like immortals, though strikers are durable, they are not indestructible.

The System

Like the Easter Bunny, Santa Claus, and the Tooth Fairy, the system needs its subjects to put faith in it, or otherwise, it will crumble.

The system is the embodiment of everything the world offers in exchange for the most precious gifts a person truly possesses, their time and their mind. Immortals are not subject to the system, but all humans are. Rich or poor, famous or infamous, king or peasant, the system owns them all. The system is powered by belief in its processes. The system thrives on ignorance. The system takes from many, and always takes back what it gives the few. The system lies to everyone, because everyone is a slave to the system and its architect.

Vanessa, age 17

An assassin, and Malum's number one in command, she uses her physical gifts of beauty to get what she wants in this world, with eyes set on loftier things.

The ultimate thespian, Vanessa plays along until she gets what she wants, and then she'll slit your throat. Another immortal and former knight now turned Shroud, yet she is fully aware of what is going on almost all of the time. She loved someone once, but he betrayed her, so she turned her heart cold to everything else until she sees him again.

Vincent, age 17

Cocky, arrogant, brash, and those are his good qualities.

Never lacking confidence, Vincent is a person of action. Nevertheless, he was tricked into killing his older brother Jak by the dark lord Malum, so when he realized what the Shroud truly was, Vincent went underground. Having one weakness, well, the only one he would ever admit—his love for Noemi, he resurfaced for her and her alone. Of many females who adored him, she was the lone girl who happened to be betrothed to his older brother in marriage. However, she too loved Vincent, and their passion for each other ruined many lives around them, least of all their own. The two were banished by the knighthood, and both thought killed by Malum as traitors to the Shroud, but Revekka knows differently. Vincent is the only immortal that nearly defeated Malum in over a hundred years, but he stopped just short of killing the dark lord to jump from a cliff to save his immortal paramour, Noemi.

Xander, age 16

A teenage agent of the Shroud, he was once on the path to enlightenment, but Malum influenced him otherwise.

One of several hundred young, immortal, former knights, he is, whether he believes it or not, a tool of destruction for the Shroud. Having great, unrestricted power and abilities without direction, Xander truly thinks he is fighting the fine fight. He thinks the knights are evil. He learned, just recently, how they have kept secrets from other immortals, so now he is convinced the knighthood should be eradicated.

Younglings

Hope is strongest with the young, and younglings are those belonging to a group where hope rests as the cure to a sickness growing inside immortalkind.

In five thousand years, there has not been a birth among the immortals, and then many children were born as their parents suddenly aged. Their once immortal parents gave the children as a living sacrifice to the temple for the knighthood, but darkness entered into the hearts of many younglings, and so many of them were led astray.